THE
BOAR
STONE

A BOOK OF DALRIADA

Jules Watson

THE OVERLOOK PRESS
New York, NY

This edition first in published in paperback in the United States in 2014 by
The Overlook Press, Peter Mayer Publishers, Inc.

141 Wooster Street
New York, NY 10012
www.overlookpress.com

For bulk and special sales, please contact sales@overlookny.com,
or write us at the address above.

Cataloging-in-Publication Data is available from the Library of Congress

Manufactured in the United States of America

ISBN 978-1-59020-149-7
2 4 6 8 10 9 7 5 3 1

To Alistair, for Scotland.

Acknowledgements

I would like to thank some wonderful people for the generous support they have given me during the writing of this book. To Catherine Vann and Cathy Caitlin, for reading an early draft and giving me just the right feedback. To Jan and Ray Stocker, for lending me your beautiful home and its sweeping view of the Indian Ocean. To Amber Trewenack, Lisa Holland-McNair and Lara Tinley, for listening to me, believing in me and offering unfailing support. To my mother Barbara Fletcher-Brewin, who stepped in with the most fundamental and critical support when I needed it most. To Claire Swinney, who, as always, gave such loving encouragement when I was faltering. And to my husband Alistair, who has gone far, far beyond the call of duty many times with the writing of this book: I thank you for not throwing me in the loch outside. Your patience and generosity staggers me. I love you.

·ALBA· (SCOTLAND)

← ATTACOTTI

SAXONS →

▲ DUN OF BRIGHT WATER
(BURGHEAD)

P I C T S

THE GREAT GLEN

DALRIADA

HIDDEN
VALLEY

TAY INLET

FORTH INLET

▲ DUNADD

ERIN
(IRELAND)

(FIRTH OF CLYDE) CLUTHA INLET

HADRIAN'S WALL

▲ LUGUVALIUM
(CARLISLE)

Names and Pronunciation

Irish and Scots Gaelic sounds much more beautiful pronounced than written (if you are a non-Gaelic speaker). So I have chosen names that – with anglicised spellings – are easy for English speakers to read as well. The personal names of the inhabitants of Dunadd are old Irish, as in this book the fort is the seat of an Irish kingdom located in Scotland. At the Dun of Bright Water, Gede, Garnat and Taran are Pictish names, without known meanings, inspired by records of ancient Pict kings.

Eboracum

Mamo	'grandmotherí
Broc	'badger'
Cian (KEE-arn)	'ancient one'

Dunadd

Cahir (KA-heer)	'battle-lord'
Maeve (MAY-ve)	'she who intoxicates'
Oran (UR-awn)	'sallow'
Garvan	'little rough one'
Orla	'golden princess'
Finola (Fyun-OO-la)	'fair-shouldered'
Brónach (BRON-ack)	'sorrow'
Ruarc (ROO-ark)	'hero'
Donal	'world ruler'
Finbar	'fair hair'

Gobán	'smith'
Fergal	'brave man'
Tiernan	'lord'
Mellan	'lightning'
Ardal	'high valour'
Brogan	'little shoe'
Clíona (Clee-UN-a)	'shapely'
Keeva	'beautiful'
Lonán	'blackbird'
Darach (DA-rack)	'oak tree'
Davin (DA-veen)	'fawn'
Riona	'queen'

Pronunciation of other words

Lennan (LAN-awn)	'sweetheart / lover'
A stór (AH STOAR)	'beloved'
Mo chridhe (MO CREE)	'my heart'

Author's Note

The Romans invaded Britain in AD 43 and established a province of their Empire. But Scotland – Alba in this book – always remained nominally separate. The Roman army tried to subdue it many times, but brief successes were followed by counter-raids and rebellions by Scottish tribes. In AD 122 the Emperor Hadrian began to build a wall stretching from coast to coast, dividing Alba from the Roman province of Britannia.

By AD 366, the lines between native and Roman had blurred. The ancient tribal way of life had in certain areas blended with the Roman world. The Wall was no longer guarded by crack legions but by soldiers of mixed Roman and native blood. The Empire was officially Christian, but people continued to revere pagan gods, both Roman and Celtic.

Although the Wall divided the island, it was not a fixed border. The supposedly 'free' tribal lands to its north were roamed by Roman scouts and garrisoned by Roman outpost forts demanding tribute. In return, the tribes raided across the wall, pillaging Roman farms, as treaties were made and broken.

Alba itself was also split. The kingdom of Dalriada from Ireland – Erin – gained a foothold on the west coast in the early part of the first millennium, with the king's seat at Dunadd. In the east, the original Alban tribes drew together into one fierce people that the Romans knew as the Picts: the Painted Men.

In such turbulent times, in such a restless land, it must have been difficult to know friend from foe.

BOOK ONE

LEAF-FALL, AD 366

Chapter 1

'**M**ay the Christos be with you in love,' the old priest wheezed, gripping the sandstone altar.

Minna snorted under her breath. It might be the Sabbath, a sacred day for the Christians, but as she stood in the chapel of the Villa Aurelius she knew there wasn't much love coming her way today.

We have to make a decision, her brother Broc had said. *About you, Minna.* Now his words flew dizzily around inside her head, like moths. *About you. About you. About you.*

She caught the gaze of Severus, overseer of the Aurelius estate. He was a plain, solid man with pepper and salt hair. His face was florid with ale and sun-creased from being in the fields with the slaves, his palms callused from the whip handle, and his brown eyes speculative as they rested on her now. Next to him stood Broc. He watched Severus watching Minna, but there was no softening in his sour expression.

She flicked her black braid off her clammy neck, squaring her shoulders. Let them look.

'Minna!' little Marcus whispered, pressing his face into her arm. 'Is it over yet?' He was only three, and his voice echoed in the austere surroundings.

Master Publius Aurelius and Mistress Flavia turned as one, frowning not at their son but at his nurse. Minna gave Marcus a smile, pressing a finger to her lips. His brother Lucius, all of ten, rolled his eyes, and she shook her head. Master Publius was too free with the leather strap on his sons, and she had just sat up all night nursing Marcus through a fever. Thankfully, he seemed better this morning.

The heat of sunseason had bled into leaf-fall, and although the chapel was cool and dark, with plaster walls and a new mosaic floor, it was tiny and everyone was crushed in together. Although the Master and

Mistress were Christians, most of the native estate workers still clung to the old gods, to the Mother Goddess, and attended this ceremony only because they had to. The air was a miasma of sour sweat and the Mistress's cloying Egyptian perfume.

The boys settled into mutinous silence as the priest continued. Minna sighed, peeling her scratchy dress away from her hot skin. The only time she could stay still like this was when Nikomedes, the Greek tutor, told the boys tales of Trojan and Roman wars, of the capricious gods and jealous goddesses. The walls of the chapel were painted with red and white diamonds and she counted them three times, until she caught the cook's two daughters glaring at her. Ah, yes, she'd forgotten *them*. She could read their thoughts on their plump faces. What right did she have to stand before the Christos, with her unnatural eyes and strange ways? The girls whispered behind their fingers, and she turned her flaming face away. Severus was the only worker on the estate who didn't think her one of the fey, the touched, the half-human. How ironic!

'Amen,' the priest coughed at last.

'Amen,' everyone murmured with relief. Minna forgot to say the word, gazing longingly out the door instead. She could just smell the tang of smoke from the burning harvest stubble, and the scent of ripe apples floated from the orchards as the slaves piled them into barrels. Mistress Flavia had told her to take the boys away from the house for the day. She could hardly wait.

At last, Master Publius, all severe brows and clipped hair, pinned his cloak and bustled out. As one of the rich villa owners on the fertile vales east of the city of Eboracum, he was a councillor and had important meetings to attend in the nearby town of Derventio.

After he had gone his sons burst outside with relief. Minna followed them, squinting in the sun that bounced off the white walls and red-tiled roofs of the villa. The main house and its two wings enclosed a courtyard splashed with light. Beyond, the green hills beckoned.

But before she could call to the boys, Minna was caught by Broc's fingers around her wrist, pulling her back. 'I meant what I said, little sister,' her brother muttered. 'I'll have no more arguments about it.'

He glanced over his shoulder as Severus left the chapel. The overseer tipped the whip handle to his forehead, and his eyes never left Minna as he loitered by the wall for Mistress Flavia.

Breathless, she wrenched herself from Broc's grip. 'I told you—'

'And I told *you*!' Sweat and chaff clumped Broc's red hair. Though she was two years younger she often brushed his heavy fringe back with a maternal swipe. But not today. As the servants poured out into the courtyard, Broc dropped his voice. 'You can't be a nursemaid for ever, Minna.'

'I don't see why not.'

'You are already eighteen!' he hissed. Anger sharpened his freckled face. 'We have lost too much time as it is, because I've indulged you. But no more.'

Their ancestors were once slaves, freed by Master Publius's grandfather as servants. But Broc and Minna's parents had died young – their mother from a fever, their father after a fall from a horse – both so long ago that Minna had no memory of them. They had lived with their grandmother ever since. Now there were just the three of them, safe in their little house by the stream. How could Broc say these things?

Her shoulders stiffened. 'I am happy with you and Mamo.'

'Mamo won't always be here.'

'Then there's you.' She held Broc's gaze, her chin up.

Just then they became aware of people staring at them as they whispered furiously together. With a scowl, Broc dragged her around the corner of the building, where a yard opened through a gate to fields.

'You didn't need to do that!' Minna cried, rubbing her wrist. But something in her brother's face silenced her.

'I will tell you why we've no more time.' The tendons stood out in Broc's wrists, and Minna realized he hadn't only changed in mood lately. His shoulders had thickened: he was a boy no longer. Her belly flipped over as Broc took a deep breath, bracing himself. 'I've joined the army. I'll be leaving for the Wall in three days.'

All the blood drained from her face.

'The Master has already let me go,' Broc hurried on.

She watched his lips move, but could not take in his words. At last she croaked, 'But you're going to be manager one day and ... you have us, Mamo and I, to look after ...'

'I will not moulder away here until I'm old and fat!' Minna gaped at his outburst, and he grabbed her hand. 'Ah, sister, it's a great honour, see? I've been accepted into the *areani*, the scouts, and they only take the best riders.' His eyes were alight with a flame that passed straight through her, as if she and it were of such different substance it couldn't touch her.

'And what are we supposed to do?' she demanded, but her voice quavered. 'You'd leave Mamo and I alone?'

'I cannot stay just for you: you're my sister, not my child. It's time for some other man to have the keeping of you, under the law.'

She slowly withdrew her hand. She had been clinging to dreams of this life going on for ever: Mamo's stories around the fire; afternoons roaming with Marcus and Lucius. And look at her! Her sandals were caked with mud, her dress streaked with grass stains. She had been running about like a fool, lost in fantasy. 'But there's no one, is there, brother, because of my – what do they say? – my *strange ways*.'

5

'And when you have these awake-dreams, as you call them, and flail about with glazed eyes, talking nonsense, what do you expect? People hear of it. You never heed me about acting more modestly.'

She gasped, clenching her fists, but Broc rushed on. 'As it happens, one man has at last offered to wed you and keep you – and only one. It's got to be done.'

'No.' She struggled for breath. '*No.*'

Broc folded his arms. '*Yes.* Severus has the best job on the estate. He is respected. And he hasn't been put off by all this talk, so he must be a sensible man.'

Sensible. Severus breathed hard when he was near Minna, through his nose. Why, oh why, did *he* not find her repulsive like all the farm boys did? Then she knew, like a lamp flaring to life in her mind. Severus considered himself on the way up, salvaging chipped pottery, tarnished dishes and broken tiles from rich houses to furnish his own. It would have been amusing if it didn't now mean this: he liked odd, exotic things no one else had. Unusual things.

'Not this way,' she ground out. 'Not him. I won't do it.'

Broc tried to argue again but Minna tore free and stalked away, shutting her ears. Her throat ached and she swallowed it down impatiently.

The boys were swinging on the gate to the fields. Seeing her stricken face, Lucius grinned a smile chopped in half by missing teeth. 'Just think, Minna, a day away from *all* of them!'

'All of them!' chubby Marcus repeated.

Minna sighed, lifting her face to the sun. The trees, grass and birds didn't judge her. 'Then let us go,' she said hoarsely. 'Now.'

Up on the moors, her anger cooled and a sense of reality began to set in. Beneath a windswept expanse of heather lay the remains of an abandoned Roman fort, its ditches and banks mere humps in the turf. She sank into a ditch and left the boys to play, gazing blankly down at the patchwork of fields and pastures. A bumble bee blundered into her cheek. The shouts of the workers floated up from the orchards. Up here was peace, but down there the white Villa Aurelius stood out starkly in the green land. Severus belonged to that world. Minna's heart plunged; her eyes closed.

As a woman she had no rights of her own. Her family was of mixed native and Roman blood, but Roman laws held sway in this land now. And the law said she had to be under the rule of a man: father, brother or husband. There was no middle way, no other choice.

Half the girls on the estate were after Severus; that much she knew. He was a widower with a secure job, and was trusted by Master Publius. He was weather-beaten, but not grossly ugly. *He was a catch.* That was the whisper from the spinsters and maidens. A catch, like a whiskery fish that gave good eating.

Her thoughts shifted to the mating part. She had been reviled by every man on this farm since she was a child so it was easy to bury the stirrings that came when her blood was first called by the moon. Now, the thought of a man grunting over her like a pig elicited no feeling at all – and that was the worse thing. Minna wanted to *feel*, to live.

The fear rose, choking her. She struggled with it until, all in a rush, dread turned to resolve and she opened her eyes.

No matter what she said to herself, or what Broc bellowed, something in Minna absolutely refused this path. She could not accept it and remain alive, she realized with a surge of passion, sitting bolt upright. She could not go back and say yes, for it would not be *her* blood in her veins, her heart beating.

'Ho!' Lucius screamed from the bank above. 'I am a soldier and I come to kill you, barbarian!' He hefted a bent hazel sapling as a spear, his face contorted.

She forced a smile. 'Oh, don't hurt me, brave soldier.'

'Hurt you? You are a savage, my enemy, so here I come!'

'Here I come, here I come!' Marcus also screeched, and both boys crashed on top of Minna with shrieks and whoops. She wrestled and fought, until they were all lying in a breathless, tangled heap among the bracken.

She pushed her braids back, pulling down her dress. 'Why do I always have to be the enemy?' she wheezed, wincing.

'Because you're so pale and funny-looking,' Lucius replied, with a quizzical frown.

'Why, thank you, Lucius.'

Marcus collapsed over her legs, his plump tummy exposed under his tunic. 'People say your eyes are odd but *I* think they look like water.'

Lucius rocked on all fours. 'And they say your face is too bony and your eyes too large, and your skin too white with that black hair, and you look *unearthly*,' he recited faithfully.

Minna's smile faded. These were Broc's thoughts, too. She could have her pick of men, he said, if she stopped scraping her hair back, making her features so stark, and began belting her tunics to give her body some curves. But she knew there was no solution for her reviled, mistrusted eyes, which were a pale, icy green surrounded by a dark ring that made them glow.

'But ...' Lucius ran on desperately, his grin faltering, '*we* think you are pretty, just like the painting of Minerva on Mama's wall! *And* the statue by Papa's study of that lady in Rome.'

Marcus linked hands around her neck. 'Don't be sad,' he lisped. 'We'll let you play battles with us.'

She cleared her throat, heaving Marcus off her lap. 'But I can't be a soldier, because I'm a girl.'

'No, you can't be a soldier because you've got *barbarian* blood,' Lucius teased, relieved.

'The blood of the Parisii tribe, who came from these very hills,' she corrected. She was proud to claim that, for it was Mamo's blood – even if Broc hated every drop, thinking it muddied his pure Roman aspirations with that shameful taint: the blood of the vanquished and dispossessed. He despised anything that looked back, not forward. The nights she and Mamo murmured the old stories to each other drove him mad.

'I'm no kin to the wild men over the Wall in Alba," she added firmly to the boys. 'If you blurt that to your parents, they will have a fit.' Everyone saw the Alba tribes as vile, savage beasts, and even when Mamo protested the Parisii came from the same bloodlines long ago, Broc scorned her foolishness. Well, now he would get to face the northerners himself, across the braced shaft of a spear.

Lucius had begun tearing around the bracken. 'Minna's a barbarian,' he chanted.

'Barbarian, barbarian,' Marcus mimicked, jumping up and down.

'Baby eater, baby eater!'

'Lucius!' Minna choked. 'Wherever did you hear that?'

Lucius looked guiltily at his feet. 'I heard a soldier say it in the city. About the men over the Wall.'

'Hmm, well, don't repeat that around your mother.' Minna peered at Marcus, whose cheeks were scarlet. 'Come and climb on my back. You've had enough sun.'

In the hazel woods along the stream it was cool. Minna rubbed her cheek on her shoulder and dug in the pockets of her dress for the remains of lunch – an apple and a broken piece of bread.

In honour of Mamo and that old blood, she would leave a harvest offering at the little shrine to the goddess of the stream. And she had something to beg for now.

Among the trees the stream formed a pool bedded with brown pebbles, and on its banks sat a small cairn. Wedged into the stones was the barley-doll from last year's harvest, decorated with faded red ribbon, and dying flowers were tucked into the crevices.

The boys ran around as Minna cleared the dead flowers and picked daisies from a sunny clearing. 'Lady,' she murmured with bowed head, as Mamo had taught her, 'take my offering in gratitude for your blessings, and may your eye continue to favour us all.'

Please. Especially favour me. Just this once. And I'll never ask again. Severus's knowing smile was there before her, and she desperately squeezed her fingers over her eyes.

Mamo said she heard the Goddess speak in this place, yet nothing like that had ever happened to Minna. As a child she sat here for hours straining to hear, as if the Goddess might at any moment step out of the trees to whisper in her ear. In Mamo's stories the old gods spoke: Minna was still waiting.

Instead, only the awake-dreams came to her. They took her when she stared for too long into fire, water or clouds. They interrupted her sleep, set apart from real dreams by the sense they came from outside her, and because of their terrible, vivid power. Minna could never remember them clearly, though. All they left was an echo of darkness and fear. And death – always the foreboding of death.

That night, the air in the house by the stream crackled with resentment. Sewing in her bed-box against the wall, Mamo frowned at Minna and Broc.

'What is wrong?' she asked.

But as Broc's mouth opened, Minna glared him into silence. 'Nothing,' she said curtly. 'Nothing that need trouble you, Mamo.'

Broc glanced at Mamo's shrunken face, the trembling hands that pushed the bone needle through the wool shirt, and he visibly swallowed his words. Neither of them must upset Mamo. After the fevers she had suffered all summer she wasn't strong enough.

Mamo coughed, one gnarled hand reaching for a pile of Broc's socks to darn, and Minna was on her feet, pressing her back. 'Leave that now, Mamo, and rest.'

Mamo clucked at the fussing, but Minna had a right to worry. Though she had given Minna her almond-shaped eyes, high cheekbones and pointed chin, her grandmother's features were blurred by sagging, sallow skin now, and her fingers were as twisted and swollen as knots in an oak tree. She still sat upright against the pillow, though, and wore her white hair in six long Parisii braids, her frail carriage imbued with pride.

Minna turned away with a tight chest, her head brushing the bunches of dried leaves and roots tied to the roofbeams. She had been taught herb-lore by Mamo herself, and had been dosing her grandmother with strengthening tonics for months. She couldn't face the fact they weren't working.

Broc slugged his ale and pulled a face at her frown, and Minna turned her back to stir the pot of lentils and mutton over the fire-grate. Let him think her acquiescent; let him go off on his boy's adventure, and then Mamo would surely come up with a way out of this. She would rally, she would plan and think and smile with Minna, as she always did.

And as for Minna, Mamo always said her mind was sharp as a thorn, swift as a river. But she had let that mind dull, drifting in summer dreams. Well, no more. As she stirred the stew, she vowed that never again would she be caught out like this.

Minna blinked as a dark shape passed across the stars.

Her bed was in a little room on the back of the house, looking over the hills, and she realized she was sitting cross-legged on it with the door open to the night. She had been awake-dreaming.

She cradled the familiar pain in her belly and peered up, recognizing Broc. 'What ... what did I say?'

Broc leaned against the door-jamb, looking out. 'How, by the Christos, would I know?'

Her heart was tripping erratically. Sweat prickled her temples. 'Did I scream?'

'Once. That's what brought me in here. Then you babbled some complete nonsense; I couldn't even understand you.' Disgust thickened his voice. 'Honestly, Mamo has ruined you with these old stories. She fills your head with foolishness, and then you wonder why you get nightmares.'

She wrapped her arms about her knees. 'I can't help the visions. And Mamo gets them, too.'

Her grandmother, however, honoured the gift – the *sight,* as she called it – and her dreams were never violent. *Surrender to them*, Mamo said. *There must be some reason the Goddess speaks to you this way. You resist them, so they bring pain.* But Minna resisted because the dreams made people hate and fear her. Because she could not control them, no matter how she tried. She didn't think any goddess would send such pain, anyway, and so sometimes, in her darkest hours, she wondered if the Christians had it right when they said such things were pagan and the work of devils.

'Mamo has never used her *sight* in front of others,' Broc pointed out. 'And anyway, she's old, and she is the herb-woman. People make allowances for her. But they're afraid of you. Severus is the only one—'

'Don't say it!' She hunched one shoulder away.

Broc squatted before her, a finger raising her chin. 'It's done, sister.' He sighed. 'I must do my duty and give you a dowry, however small, to make it legal, though that will have to wait until next month for my first pay. But I've agreed now in principle, and Master Publius has given his assent. I will tell Mamo tomorrow.'

Minna stared into the darkness.

'I will give you one last piece of advice. Apply yourself to learning from Mistress Flavia: start dressing like a lady, acting like a lady, speaking like a lady. Stop racing around the fields with your skirt hitched up. You're a woman, not a child. Forget Mamo's tales and strive to control these bizarre ... turns. Then people might start to accept you.'

Minna gazed into her brother's face. She thought of how they played together in the heather as children, how he had defended her from the worst taunts. But now she realized with a sinking feeling that after all those years, Broc did not know her soul at all, not if he honestly thought she could ever be that woman.

'Don't waste this chance!' he urged. 'At least try, Minna, to change. Just try.'

Heavy as stone, her heart followed her belly down. She turned her face towards the star glitter, beckoning beyond this house. 'Yes, brother,' she agreed. For she understood now he would not know that she lied.

Two days later Broc left for the Wall.

Chapter 2

'It looks as though there will be a storm, Mamo,' Minna observed from the doorway. She leaned her head against the cool stone wall.

Across the stubbled fields the sky was bruised. The air lay in a damp blanket over the dusky hollows, exuding the scents of turned soil and crushed grain. No wind stirred the turning leaves or the brown grass that grew so high on the pasture – ripe for running through. Four weeks ago, Minna may have done just that. Before Broc leaving, and the daily war she had been waging to avoid Severus. Before Mamo's crackling cough had deepened into this stubborn fever.

And nothing had been heard from Broc at all – as if he had forgotten about them already, Minna thought bitterly – and no dowry had been forthcoming as yet, though that at least was a relief.

'Is the fruit in?' Mamo spoke weakly from the bed.

'Nearly. Tomorrow is the last day of picking.'

'The Mother gave us a fine summer, a good harvest.' Abruptly, Mamo broke into a terrible fit of coughing, her chest as clogged as the weedy stream outside.

Minna propped her against the pillows, grabbing the wooden cup from the stool. 'Have some more coltsfoot, Mamo.'

'I'm going to turn green and sprout roots if I have any more.' Despite the spark of humour, bones ran in a ladder across Mamo's shrunken chest.

'Well, coltsfoot flowers *are* pretty.' She held the cup to Mamo's lips, biting down on her own.

Minna had tried every concoction she could think of to treat Mamo's illness. Long into the night, as her grandmother's breath rasped, she turned over all the scraps of herb-lore in her mind. Now she had a linseed poultice warming by the fire. She had begged one of the carters to trade her only bead necklace in Eboracum for dried starwort roots, imported from Greece. Some were brewing to drink, and some would go in a bowl so Mamo could inhale the steam.

When she had fulfilled her duties with the boys each day, Minna immersed herself in kneading and baking bread, gathering eggs and chopping firewood, but even the unwilling parts of her could see Mamo was growing weaker. Something in her eyes was struggling, when they had always shone with life, with wisdom.

She dabbed Mamo's chin where tea had spilled. The old woman's gaze was piercing, despite the fever sheen. 'Child, you know I will not be able to lead the harvest rite.'

Minna took the steaming kettle off the flame. 'The starwort will help. You'll be up and around by tomorrow night—'

'No.' Stray white hairs drifted from Mamo's braids, feathering the bones that seemed to push through her translucent skin. 'I am not well enough.'

Minna stared down at the curling vapour over the kettle, her throat tight.

'You've grown so much,' Mamo said suddenly.

She rallied a wry smile. 'What do you mean?' She poked her bony hip. 'It is sideways I need to grow.'

Those birdlike eyes didn't waver. 'I do not mean you have grown in body.'

'I'm not you,' she said quietly. 'I'll never be you.'

'Nor do you need to be. It's you the world needs.'

Minna blinked and looked at the wall.

'I can't manage the walk to the fields.'

'We can take you in the cart!' She dropped on her knees by the bed. The room was stifling from the pressure of the coming storm, and Mamo's papery skin was clammy. 'I will hold you.' Her throat closed. 'I'll never let go.'

Mamo's swollen fingers tightened into claws. 'No, you must do it for me. You know the words.'

Goddess of Light. Lady of the Forests. Giver of Life. Bringer of Death. Yes, she knew.

Mamo pressed one hand to her bony breast, as it struggled to rise and fall. 'If we don't speak to our Lady, then how will She know how much we need Her? How will She know to send us the sun and rain? If we are silent, She may forget us ... ' Exhausted by her fervour, she fell back on the pillows, coughing.

'Rest now, Mamo, and don't be upset. I'll do it. I'll do it.'

When finally the old woman slept, Minna rubbed beeswax with mustard into Mamo's feet to warm her blood and break the fever. She sprinkled cleansing herbs in the smoke. The healer in her – well-taught, detached – paused as every hour passed, stopping to reassess the timbre of Mamo's wheezing. But each time Minna's own chin sunk lower, and her eyes became fixed on the fraying edge of the blanket.

The fire dimmed; she got up to feed it with hazel twigs. When she came back, Mamo's eyes had flickered open, but they were glazed by the veil of the awake-dreams, the *sight*. 'Who are you?' her grandmother whispered, plucking restlessly at the sheets.

'It's me, Mamo, me.' The two of them were suspended in the glow of the lamp; the blackened hearth, pots, pans, baskets and work tools hidden in shadow on hooks around the walls.

Mamo's eyes wandered to the lamp-flame. 'Ah, you are a jewel,' she crooned, sing-song. 'A jewel hidden among men, long-buried, long-forgotten. But not for ever; not for ever, my love.'

Minna fervently kissed her grandmother's brow – the true eye, or spirit-eye, as Mamo called the sacred place in the middle of the forehead. When Minna was a child she would make her shut her eyes and try to feel things through this opening, see with her mind. *Your eyes can fool you*, Mamo would instruct, tapping Minna's brow. *Your spirit-eye never will.*

Now she rested her cheek against Mamo's forehead and took a breath, unwilling to break the touch. What was Mamo seeing at this moment? Minna didn't dare ask her. Just as she would not open her own spirit-eye this night, for fear of what it might show.

Then Mamo stirred under her hands. 'Minna, you must take all the honey.'

She sat back, wiped her face. 'What, Mamo?'

Mamo's gaze flickered back and forth across the wall, as if observing some invisible scene. 'Take the last of the honey to the city, and see if that wily old Craccus will buy it. We need cloth for Broc's tunics – he grows so fast! But don't take less than five *numii* a jar, child: no one else can sing flavour like *that* from their bees. Tell Craccus!'

Minna clutched her grandmother's cold hand. 'Yes, Mamo. I will take the honey.' Blankly, she stared into the shadows.

The Boar! The Boar! Men struggled in a haze of smoke that was rancid with blood and the stench of loosed bowels ... swords glinted, raised high to stab down ...
Minna lurched upright by Mamo's cot, those unintelligible cries spilling from her lips. It hurt ... the pain ...Terror clawed at her, until Mamo was there, her soothing voice calming her. *It is all right, my little one. All will be well. Hush. All will be well.*

Minna slumped back. Mamo always woke her from nightmares and held her. Her grandmother's special caress came then, a warm hand cradling one cheek and then the other. Minna felt tears falling on her own skin. She smelled Mamo's scent, wild thyme from the moors. She glimpsed a light behind her eyelids, like a spark of a bonfire, spiralling up into a darkened sky ...

The Light ... Goddess of Light. Giver of Life.

Bringer of Death.

With a second cry Minna was fully awake and staggering to her feet, knocking the lamp over. The tiny pool of oil spilled on the earth floor and guttered out. For a moment, she was blinded by the after-flare, blue across her eyes. The words she had shouted were already fading, her mind a jumble of images that left only a taste of blood.

But the house was silent. The house held nothing.

She swayed, and her legs buckled so she fell by the bed, staring down. The fire was burned to coals, the glow soft on Mamo's cheeks and eyelids, smoothing the age from her, the beauty of her youth shining through. She was gone. The light was gone.

For an endless moment Minna reeled over a yawning, dark hole, before numbness descended, cutting off the pain. She must not feel. She must not think. She grasped for Mamo's hand, held on, though it was already cold.

Her soul still caught in the awake-dream, Minna could sense the roof beams alive with flutterings and whisperings, the air shimmering with the insubstantial presence of the *others,* the sprites, the *fey* to whom Mamo spoke under her breath as she kneaded dough.

They cried to Minna, reaching to her pain with soft fingers and silvery voices. But she batted them away, staring dry-eyed into the growing dark as the coals died.

For a night and day she did not leave Mamo's side. The voices continued whispering among the rafters, but she resolutely ignored them.

The news spread. Mistress Flavia came and tried to get Minna to release the body for burial. When she would not answer, the Mistress threw up her hands and left her there. Everyone else stayed away.

She only found out why when Marcus and Lucius disobeyed their mother and crept into the silent house. Marcus slid into her lap while Lucius crouched by her stool, dark eyes fixed on her face.

'Minna,' Marcus ventured at last. 'Why do they say these things about you? I'm scared.'

She did not answer, only turned her face to meet Lucius's intent gaze. 'They say you are a *banshee*, a devil,' he whispered. 'They say you called down the death on your Mamo, that you fed it to her in draughts with your own hand.' His voice faltered. 'They say ... that you made your Mamo die.'

She turned back to her grandmother's still face, her fingers stroking through Marcus's fine hair.

At the second dusk, Minna stood beside a hole dug in the cemetery. Shrivelled oak leaves drifted down around her in the cold wind. She was wrapped in aloneness just as the shroud wrapped Mamo's frail body.

Everyone was staring at her while the priest muttered a few hasty words, their expressions suspicious, hostile. But Minna saw only one man, for the others left a space of deference around him and his gaze burned her like a furnace. Beside him stood Master Publius, his brows seeming heavier and his mouth more severe than usual. She could plead, but that expression would never soften. And her only shield – Mamo – was gone.

They were like an arrangement of statues from the forum: Minna at the end, Severus in the middle with the Master, and at the other end a host of squat, hard-faced people who would hiss at her every day of her life. She could see that life clearly, a straight path going on and on. And she knew that step by step along that road she would gradually shrink and fade, until she was nothing.

Withered by contempt. Shrivelled by hostility. A dried husk at last, finally pressed into crumbling dust by the weight of Severus's body upon her own.

Chapter 3

L it by the sputtering lamp, Minna watched with an odd detachment as her hands appeared to move without her will.

A leather pack was spread open on the oak table; she had no idea who had taken it from beside her bed. Cheese was set by, bread, cold chicken. A spare pair of boots. Her fingers, red and chafed, were folding a pair of wool trousers. They reached for her cloak.

From the edges of the room came a faint keening, just below hearing. It might be grief. It made the air shiver, the lamp-flame waver. It set her teeth on edge. 'I won't listen,' she said.

A meat knife was in her hand, then stuffed down inside the pack. Stiffly, her legs took her to the loose stone by the hearth; she levered it up to expose the hole and the nestled bag of coins. *Mamo's coins.* Something in her chest jerked, like a fish on a line.

The honey. Minna had to take the honey. Five jars – one, two, three, four, five – down inside the pack so the clay would not break. Then numb arms came through the straps and dragged the pack onto her back. She paused beneath the lintel.

The grief flung itself about the room like a crazed moth, hurtling into the rafters with broken wings. *Mamo by the hearth. Mamo cooking barley cakes. Mamo's cool hand on the back of little Minna's neck as she ran around the table.*

Minna turned away. Outside, the moon was as lop-sided as a squashed plum, and a pale mist gathered over the stream. The cold pricked her throat. The scents of home, of hay fields and muddy banks, rose around her. She closed her nose and her mind.

But one tender feeling she could not, in the end, ignore. Despite the danger of discovery, she crept to the schoolroom, a little shed in the villa's yard. Inside the musty room, she felt around for a wax slate and took it to the moonlit doorway. '*I must go,*' she wrote to her boys with a stylus, pressing the Latin characters into the soft wax. '*But it's not you. Look after each other. Your barbarian.*'

Then she slipped into the darkness along the field edges until she was out of sight of the houses, and stepped onto the moonlit road, which led in a silver trail over the hills. Her breath misted the air in white gusts. At the estate gate she stopped and stared down at the ruts made by carts in the mud.

What was she doing? Why was she here?

Ah, the honey. She must take the honey to Eboracum, as Mamo asked her to do.

At daylight, shivering, Minna hitched a ride on a farmer's cart of tethered chickens which by afternoon was swaying along the humped track that crawled west from the coastal hills into the city. When the cart crested the last hill, she slid silently down and stood blankly in the mud of the road, her pack held to her chest.

Eboracum was spread before her. The foremost northern city of the Roman Province of Britannia, it was the seat of Fullofaudes, the great Dux Britanniarum, commander of the forces on the Wall. The title was as grand as the white buildings that reared in tall columns and the sailing ships crowding the river. *Dux Fullofaudes. Eboracum. Britannia.* She repeated the words silently, though they fell down through the echoing vault of her mind and meant nothing.

Then the wind turned, and the city's stink hit her like a slap on the face. The stench of briny wharves and sewage battling with the scents of baking bread and roasting meat. The reek of lime furnaces and tanning yards set against the floating cloud of spices from over the sea. Urine and peat smoke; mule dung and raw timber. It was a heady mixture that hinted at bustle and trade, the ports of Gaul, Rome and Egypt. It threatened to wake her, to drag her back to a world of merchants and shopkeepers. *Thieves, cut-throats and whores.* A world of grief.

But she had nowhere else to go.

Minna stumbled down the road to the city walls, tall and grim beneath a cloud of blue smoke, and was drawn into the mass of people flowing through the towering timber gates. Once in the narrow streets, chaos swallowed her.

On the north side of the Abus river stood the stone fort of the soldiers, its walls pealing with trumpets. On the south was the civilian town. Here merchants shouted, children shrieked and hammers thunked on wood until Minna's ears ached. The white-washed townhouses of the rich loomed over the cobbled streets and shut out the pallid autumn sun. Shops lined the pavements, their shutters thrown open. Stalls were spread with fruit, bread, meat, skinned chickens, bronze pots, incense and clay bowls, and were crowded by people of all colours babbling in exotic tongues.

Vacantly, Minna wandered, tossed this way and that by the eddies of the crowd. She bumped into a butcher's stall, a sheep's head leering up with glassy eyes. 'Ho, mistress!' the butcher called. 'Knock that over and you'll have to pay.'

She stumbled from his sharp gaze into the road. 'Out the way,' a slave hissed, pulling a handcart with a perfumed lady in the back, veil held across her nose. Minna spun as a man shouldered past, his arms stacked with trays of fresh bread. Panting, she pressed herself against the wall of a nearby shop. A pair of soldiers sauntered by, their hard eyes raking over her beneath their helmets. Minna crept away down an alley, but was too slow to side-step a stream of putrid water thrown from a window, splashing her feet.

She stood blankly before Craccus's shop for a long time before she realized where she was. The alleyway was now steeped in shadow. Her head ached from the noise and pounding sun. Craccus, fat and florid, flung the door open. 'Ah, the little villa girl. Come, come. More honey from your grandmother, eh?' Distantly, she saw herself pull the jars out one by one and put them on the counter, breathing the musty air that was redolent with pepper and wild garlic, *passum*, coriander, and the tang of fish sauce. Without her opening her mouth, Craccus gave her six *numii* a jar.

Look, Mamo, she thought, back outside in the darkening alleyway. *I got more than five.* The thirty coins were so cold they burned her palm.

It was growing late, and her belly ached, so she exchanged three *numii* for a patty of mutton and herbs frying on a griddle at the back of a butcher's stall. Then she was sucked back into the river of people before being deposited at the forum, the marketplace.

A crowd was gathered in a rough circle, shouting and clapping, showering the entertainment in the centre with bronze coins. Minna wandered around the edge of the mob until she saw an empty space on the forum steps, warm from the pale sun. She curled up there, absently breaking off pieces of the patty and pushing them into her dry mouth.

Through the legs of the crowd she glimpsed brown bodies tumbling: acrobats. The young men were naked but for leather loincloths, skin oiled so their lithe bodies gleamed. Whooping, they flung themselves about, leaping to each other's shoulders, then flying into spectacular tumbles. Sweat sprayed from their hair and skin.

Minna brushed her hands clean, crawling down the steps to see better. They must be good, she thought. This was what cities were for; it must be why she came. *Why had she come, again?*

The acrobats were juggling now, flipping into somersaults then stopping to pluck fruit from their palms and flinging them up. The crowd yelled encouragement.

A black-haired youth danced over to juggle directly in front of Minna, and she stiffened as she felt the eyes of the crowd upon her. She glanced up at the grinning boy, with his tanned skin and fierce blue eyes. Though his comrades had chosen apples, he clutched a handful of figs – harder to juggle and very expensive. Her mind caught on something she would say to tease Lucius. *Show-off!* An hysterical giggle rose in her, an ache that wanted to become tears.

The acrobat flashed white teeth at her and sent the figs flying, tossing sweat from his black curls as he neatly executed a backwards somersault and caught them. The people laughed.

But Minna was suddenly blinded by the sun, and the crowd's laughter was like a dozen gnats buzzing around her head. She had to get away. She clambered up, but just then the boy darted forward and, with a wink and flick of the wrist, sent a fig flying straight at her.

She could not think, let alone move. Her joints jammed as she instinctively ducked to catch the fig, but it tumbled through her fingers. She clutched for it, her senses narrowing to that expensive fruit lying on the dirty stones. *Mamo liked figs. Didn't someone in a tale get better from eating a fig? Mamo might get better.*

Laughter rumbled through the crowd once more, and above it all soared the peal of the acrobat's own mirth. Minna's awareness snapped back, and slowly she straightened.

'You need some practice, young mistress,' the youth called, hands on lean hips, blue eyes glittering above a mocking grin that made her chest burn. She welcomed it, that feeling. Anger, yes, anger was safe.

'Come.' The acrobat extended one hand. 'Throw me my fruit ... or perhaps bring it closer yourself, and I'll give you all the juggling lessons you'll ever need!' The men in the crowd snickered.

She stood for only a moment, swaying, then she dropped the fig and, with a dazed deliberation, stepped on it. Purple juice and pips spurted over the dirty marble.

The youth's grin faltered, and the whoops of laughter then were louder than any before, as Minna turned away.

Dusk came and with it a bitter wind, the crowds thinning as shop-keepers swept out their stalls. Shutters were pulled closed, and, as Minna wandered by, she saw the glow of lamps being lit inside the houses. The remaining people hastened along, their heads down, the wind blowing scraps of rubbish and fallen leaves around their feet. Soldiers marched past in hob-nailed boots, their quick eyes scanning the darkening alleys.

As the streets emptied, Minna's heart began to beat faster. But it was only when horns blared from the walls that she realized she had forgotten the curfew. The soldiers shouted as they marched: 'The gates will shortly be closing! Conclude your business. The gates are closing!'

She could not stay here in the city. The urgent thought tapped on the blankness in her mind. It wasn't safe. She raised her chin to the dying sun. That glimmer of dusk would be soft on the river outside the gates. There were copses of alder and hazel there, and bushes lining the banks.

Her feet were already turning, her head down.

The shadows of the trees along the riverbanks were still and cool after the chaos of the city. Beneath a lavender sky, the last sliver of sun edged the dying grass with gold. Other people had come through the gates with Minna, following the road home. One by one they disappeared until she was alone.

She stopped to touch her cheeks, grimed with sweat. She thought of the river running clear from the eastern hills above the city. Her hills, her stream. Before she realized it, her feet were thudding down the bank, her pack bouncing on her back, until at last she collapsed by the river. Chest heaving, she flung her pack aside and plunged her hands in.

Frantically Minna splashed her face, pouring the icy water over her head so it trickled down her neck. She scooped more, drinking to drown the ache in her chest. Then she sat there dripping and trembling, gazing out over the darkening water.

'Trying to drown yourself?' someone drawled.

Chapter 4

Minna grew very still.

'That's not how you do it, sweetness. Just jump in, clothes and all.'

Slowly, she turned. The speaker was lying in the river grass, a long, lean shape in a faded red tunic. She summoned up a dim echo of anger. 'What did you say?'

'Drowning. Better to do it with style. Off the bridge, say.' The youth leaned up on his elbows, and she could see he was tall and slim with a crop of black curls. She stared at him as water dripped down her cheeks.

He squinted, cocking his head, then suddenly sat upright. 'Why, if it isn't the little tiger! No wonder you growled at me just now.'

Minna struggled to her feet. A spark of life, of indignation, ran along her nerves. '*You!*'

The young acrobat grinned. 'Yes, me.'

'You made a fool of me.'

With fluid grace the youth was instantly on his feet. He bowed theatrically. 'I'm an acrobat, an actor, an *entertainer*. That's what I do.' She could see now that there was an odd dislocation between his smiling mouth and his eyes, which remained intense, watchful. 'And you ruined my fig.'

She peeled wet hair from her cheeks. 'That's the least I could do after you made them all laugh at me.'

'Well, you *are* a shockingly bad catcher.' He cocked his head the other way, glancing at the water. 'And swimmer, I'll bet.'

Minna plucked at her tunic, realizing it was stuck to her skin. Her face burned, the anger and embarrassment slicing through her daze. 'I wasn't going to drown myself.'

'Could have fooled me.'

She edged towards the yellowing alder trees, her mind scrambling. 'Thank you for your assistance,' she said coolly, 'but I don't need it.'

'Oh, *really*?' Those intense blue eyes flitted over her dusty boy's clothes, taking in the pack with its winter cloak and rolled sleeping hide. 'Surely you know that nice young ladies don't venture to this part of the riverbank when the troupe is in town?' He waved a hand over his shoulder. 'Our camp is just over there. It's not a place for pretty girls. Unless,' he raised one brow, 'you're a boy after all, a street urchin running from the watch – or a runaway slave.'

'I won't dignify that with an answer.' She turned on her heel.

A whistle pierced her ear, and suddenly the youth was loping along-side. 'Jupiter and Mars! There goes that tiger again.'

Minna halted. 'Why do you keep calling me that word?' she demanded. 'Are you insulting me?'

The boy was puzzled, then amused. He spread his hands. 'A tiger,' he explained with exaggerated patience, 'is a creature the gladiators kill in Rome. It is a huge, *ferocious* cat with stripes.'

'And how am I ... *that*?'

'Well.' The youth stepped around a birch tree, leaning one elbow on it. 'It has sharp teeth, wicked claws and fierce eyes – just like yours when I threw the fig.'

She turned as he circled her. 'How do you know of such a beast? You're making it up, I know you are.'

'I'm not.'

'Are you telling me you've been to Rome?'

'Once. And I saw a white tiger there in the arena, with silver stripes, its eyes pale and icy instead of yellow. Just like yours.'

She couldn't think past a sweet rush of fury. 'I don't believe there's any such creature. You're just ... a gangly boy with no brains and no manners!'

This explosion delighted the acrobat, and, as Minna resumed trudging through the river grass, he loped beside her again. 'So, do you want to know my name, then?'

She violently shook her head.

'It's Cian.'

He stepped in front of her, and she had to look properly at him for the first time.

His hair was so dark and his skin so tanned that at first glance he could have been Egyptian or Greek. But his eyes were a clear blue, and his features not swarthy like eastern men. Instead, the contours of his face all angled upwards: a narrow chin, slanted cheekbones, a cynical mouth, and tilted eyes. Despite his height he was still lean like a boy, and there was something insubstantial about him, as if he were barely chained to the earth. In contrast to his slightly exotic air, his hair was severely cropped into Roman lines.

'So where are you from?' she asked sullenly, interest prodded despite herself.

Cian bowed again. 'Everywhere,' he intoned grandly. 'Our troupe is on the road most of the year and travels to all the towns. We've stayed too long in Eboracum, but the people were showering us with coin, so it was hard to leave.' He snorted. 'Farm clods must have had a good harvest.'

'It was.' Her lips moved softly. 'It was a good harvest.'

'So, we're leaving for the north before it gets too cold. The forts along the Wall provide good pickings – all those bored soldiers.'

Minna turned to stone. In the stillness, a realization dropped into the blank pool of her mind. 'North?' she heard herself asking. 'The Wall?'

Of course. Broc didn't know about Mamo, and so she must tell him. Broc would change his mind when he heard, when he saw that Minna had the courage to travel all the way to him, to the Wall. She would go down on her knees and kiss the hem of his tunic, tell him she would be good from now on, quiet and compliant, if he would only let her stay near him and not make her marry Severus. 'When do you leave?'

Cian's brows went up. 'Tomorrow. That's why I was here trying to have a rest before ... well, before you appeared.'

She leaned back to look up at him. Somewhere she knew she had to return from the shadowed realms in which she'd been wandering, pick up the broken pieces of her wits and use them. 'Cian,' she said slowly. 'My name is Minna and I have business in the north, too.'

Amused, Cian folded his arms and stared down at this unexpected apparition.

She didn't fit any of the slots in his mind labelled 'women': dried-up old hags like the troupe's herb-woman; painted whores; or the young ladies who looked down their long, refined noses at him. That left a plucky girl fallen on hard times, who'd already learned to open her legs and grow a tough hide. *Perhaps, but ... no.*

Standing in her shapeless tunic, arms braced, head up, she was trying her best to look tough, but her features were almost elfin, and there was no slyness or guile in those extraordinary pale green eyes. 'You can't just attach yourself to us and expect us to feed you,' he said. 'It doesn't work like that.'

Those eyes flashed. 'How *does* it work?'

He grinned at the change in her, for the vulnerability she showed by the stream had suddenly been checked. This set mouth and firm chin were familiar to her, comfortable. Cian also knew how to don a mask, after all. He understood that.

'You have to pay your way, earn us something.' He raised his fingers, one by one. 'We have actors, who put on plays. Acrobats like me, who juggle and tumble.' He paused. 'The girls who sell their bodies, of course, though that's pretty easy.' Her eyes flickered, pained. 'Some people trade in ribbon and embroidery, leatherwork, belts, shoes. And there's the herb-woman—'

Desperation leaped in the girl's face, startling him. 'I can do that!' she cried. 'I am well versed in herb-simples and remedies, bone-setting and wounds.'

By the gods, an innocent. Cian squashed an unnerving spike of pity. 'Well, then. Sounds like you could at least give the old dear a hand. Her eyes aren't so good any more.'

'I could, I could!' the strange creature agreed and, forgetting herself, she reached unconsciously towards him, to convince him. Instinct pushed him smoothly back a step, and her hands dropped to her sides.

She tucked her fists under her arms instead. 'Do you really think the troupe will take me?'

Cian scratched his ear. 'There won't be any big council: just come with me and join in. If you pull your weight you won't get thrown back out.' Her eyes widened. 'It's not that bad,' he added gruffly, turning away. 'Come on, camp is quiet at the moment. It will be busier tonight.'

The girl called Minna walked along the riverbank behind him, and though her footsteps were light on the damp earth, her fear was a weight at his back.

Downstream, around a campfire sprawled an untidy scatter of wool and leather lean-tos, moth-eaten tents and painted carts. Colourful items of clothing, harness and costume hung from trees, ropes and poles. The tents were guarded by scrappy dogs that barked as they passed, and on the outskirts, mules were tethered in lines.

There was no leader of the troupe; everyone just mucked in together, Cian said. So it was all easily arranged. The old green-woman, Letitia, who sold the herb-simples, blinked blearily at Minna, her breath reeking of sour ale, and shrugged her acceptance.

As dusk deepened, the actors and jugglers came back from town, arms slung about women with painted faces. Cian had disappeared, so Minna huddled on a log at the edge of the firelight, overlooked in her boy's clothes and scraped-back hair.

Barrels of ale were opened, and the atmosphere grew more raucous. Men attempted to swallow burning torches as women shrieked with laughter. A group of actors quarrelled, while some of the acrobats practised their tumbles on the damp grass.

Cian came back, shoved a cup of ale in Minna's hand and carelessly introduced her to a dozen people, none of whose names she afterwards remembered. She was rolling the musty ale on her tongue when a drunken man with his arm about a whore lunged into the opening of the woman's dress. The gaudy cloth gave with a loud rip, and Minna was confronted by the sight of painted nipples being jiggled boldly in the firelight.

The whore screamed, while Minna tried desperately to gulp her ale rather than gag on it. But when the man flung himself to his knees and buried his face between those ample breasts, she ducked her burning face away.

Her eye fell on Cian. He wasn't drinking anything, and his watchful gaze shifted from the antics of the half-naked whore to Minna with a sardonic smile.

'Welcome to the real world, Tiger.'

Minna had no trouble falling asleep in Letitia's stuffy tent that night, as the men continued to shout and laugh outside. She had barely slept for days, had walked far in the sun, and was wrung out by the effort of holding her feelings at bay.

But when she woke suddenly before dawn it was to find herself lying rigid among the damp hides, her nails clenched into her palms.

Even in sleep she had guarded herself against the keening grief, which had, after all, flown with her all the way to Eboracum.

Chapter 5

They rode away from the city two days later, and Cian left Minna to make her own way among the wolves.

Wising up fast, she grimly threw herself into work, picking herbs and bottling remedies, standing for hours in rain and shine to urge the people in each steading and village to exchange cures for coin. When the old woman Letitia saw her persistence she left her to it, happily losing herself in drink. Minna didn't mind. The exotic smells and sounds, the chaos of the camp, and its frightening and amusing people, became a blessed blur through which she walked, untouched by feeling.

After a week, she learned to parry rude quips from the men and hostile glares from the women. But, one night, as she was wending her way to the fire from her tent, a young actor grabbed her in the dark, pushing her up against the stinking leather and thrusting his tongue in her mouth as a hand groped for her breast. Her cry was muffled by his lips, until something that Broc taught her kicked in and she brought her knee up sharply between the boy's legs.

'Ow!' he howled, releasing her and grabbing for his groin.

Minna shrank back against the tent, panting.

A cool voice sliced through the night air. 'The little tiger has a bite; you should have known that, Bren.'

Minna's assailant squinted at the tall figure standing in the open, shoulders outlined by moonlight. 'Off with you, Cian,' he growled. 'She's fair game.'

Cian took a step forward, stretching his frame by leaning one arm on the tent-pole. 'There are plenty of slack-eyed whores around for you to take your pick,' he said evenly. 'Leave her alone.'

Bren was still panting, cradling his crotch. 'And what's it to you?' he slurred. But he was already backing away, for though Cian was slim, he was by far the tallest of the men, and Minna had already seen him easily win at least three fist-fights.

Cian shrugged, but his eyes did not waver. 'You don't need to know my mind now, do you, Bren?'

The young actor glanced belligerently between them, but he was swaying with drunkenness and contented himself with spitting on the ground and staggering away.

Minna's tension rushed out of her. 'I ... thank you.'

Cian shrugged again, then tilted his head, the moonlight catching his one-sided smile. 'Not a bad little move you have there, Tiger.'

'My brother showed me,' she said faintly. She should be relieved, but it was hard to feel so before those glittering eyes, shifting with indecipherable thoughts.

'Then you'd better keep in practice, just in case,' he said, and was gone.

That night, she appeared to pass some unspoken test. For the very next day Cian began riding the acrobats' pony up behind Letitia's cart, regaling Minna with tales of his travels, most of which she only half-believed.

'Wherever did you become so good with horses?' she ventured once, seeing how carefully he brushed his pony at the end of each day.

He paused imperceptibly, his fingers easing knots from the horse's black tail. 'Where we all did, Tiger: on the road.' He cast a mocking glance at her. 'Don't you know you aren't supposed to ask travelling people about their past?'

Minna bit her lip, watching him. 'Sorry.'

'Anyway,' he went on, tossing his head, 'I have better taste than to get stuck with a grouchy old mule.' His eyes glinted at her, and she smiled.

'Oh, I don't know,' she returned, encouraged. 'You and mules seem a good match to me.' That was another thing he'd taught her: banter provided a refuge. Never stop to think or be quiet and still; talk fast, jest about everything.

He snorted, rubbing vigorously at the pony's flank. 'You're right about that.'

He was certainly unlike anyone else in the troupe. While juggling he was fluid and graceful, but outside the ring his movements were contained, his habits rigid. The other men had wild hair they never combed, dirty skin and stained clothes. But Cian carefully washed his worn tunics, and though threadbare they were of good wool, the hems stitched. Each morning he sat down with a blade and scraped his jaw and cheeks clear of stubble, and every week took shears and cropped his hair into short, Roman lines.

And he kept himself aloof. The other men brought whores back to camp, when he did not. The girls in the troupe tried hard to get his attention, scowling when he spoke to Minna, but he never indulged them, merely overwhelming them with merciless teasing until they gave up and backed away.

But his eyes missed nothing, Minna saw. They were always darting about the camp, never at rest.

They travelled further north, into the realm of the Brigantes, the last people conquered by Rome below the Wall. They still wore skins and checked cloaks, and sported long, braided hair. Cian scoffed at their gaudy brooches and neck-rings, their raucous speech and songs.

Roman soldiers also became more numerous in every town, and at last Minna remarked nervously on it.

'The Dux Britanniarum has his frontier army, the *limitanei,* spread all over these lands,' Cian informed her. 'He has to guard the Wall against the barbarians on the other side.' He glanced north as he said this, to where the hills rose higher along the knobbed spine of the land, dark and clouded.

Minna followed his gaze. Those gloomy hills led to the Wall, and the Wall meant safety – and so many other things. *Memories starting up again.*

She picked bark off an alder tree as Cian filled a leather bucket with water from a stream. 'Listen to you,' she said, falling back into the comforting speech that had grown between them. 'You're just like a tutor I knew once: facts, facts and more facts.'

His eyes narrowed and he flicked water at her. It just missed as she ducked aside, and when he went to do it again she dashed away, sliding on the muddy bank. By the time he caught up she was ready, scooping a handful from the icy stream and tossing it over him.

As he stood there with his hair plastered to his face and water dripping down his cheeks, she pressed her knuckles to her mouth to stop a laugh.

His eyes sparked, his mouth twitched. 'That was not very polite.'

The laugh burbled out of her, for it was the first time she'd seen him anything but immaculate. He looked like a little boy, like Lucius. Like Broc a long time ago. Without thinking, she reached out as if to flick the dripping hair from his brow.

With an imperceptible movement he was out of range and she touched nothing but cold air. She froze as the shutters came down over his eyes, then, embarrassed, she spun on her heel. 'Come on, the cooks are waiting for the water.'

He was silent as they walked up the bank, toting a bucket each, but then took her by surprise, elbowing her in the side. She stumbled and spilled water over her feet, and he grinned, tossing his wet hair. '*That's* for soaking me when night is coming on.'

She stamped her boots, relieved by his smile. 'I'll dry your tunic at the fire.'

'And give me your share of meat.'

She elbowed him back, and he shoved her again, and there was less water in the buckets when they got back to camp.

Cian was grooming the pony one chill dusk, scrubbing its flank with buckhide, while Minna sat in a patch of withered blackberries, tossing them at him every now and then.

'Letitia said we're going to cross the mountains now,' she said.

Around them spread a rough plateau of heath and wind-blown birches, some still dressed with their last tatters of gold.

'Mountains!' Cian scoffed. He flung a berry up and caught it in his mouth, as Minna looked deliberately away. She hated him showing off. He stifled a smile, chewing. 'They aren't mountains, they're hills. If you want mountains, go to Gaul.'

Her mouth tightened. 'They're the biggest hills I've ever seen.'

Grinning, he threw himself down beside her. 'Aw, Tiger, don't grimace at me like that. It squeezes your pretty face up.'

She whacked his arm. 'And *don't* call me pretty!'

While she dug about in her lap for more berries, Cian faintly shook his head. It was a mystery to him why she thought herself so ugly. He found her appearance – her ebony hair, crystal eyes and marble skin – both startling and unnerving. What was more, a certain untouchable air about her, a sense of being lost in her own world, somehow kept all the men away. To his surprise, he found himself hoping she kept that knack. Too many things had been spoiled by associating with him.

Uncomfortably rubbing the back of his neck, Cian pointed past the bare, hunched trees along the river to the northern hills, their crags already dusted with snow, slopes red with dying bracken. 'We can't go dead north any more because we'd have to climb those *hills*. The road to the Wall forks left and west over the pass, or right and east. We are going up the west side, which is better, as on the east we'd be closer to the Painted Men.' He scrubbed his stained fingers on the grass.

'Painted Men?' she repeated. The edge of her mouth was stained with blackberry juice, like a child's.

'You haven't been listening, have you, Tiger?' He held up one purple finger. 'First history lesson: the Emperor Hadrian built the Wall across Britannia to keep out the tribes of Alba in—'

'Two hundred and fifty years ago,' she interrupted crisply. 'I looked after my master's boys, and they had a Greek tutor.'

He saluted her with a finger to his brow. 'Then you'll also know that some of the men up there in Alba – only in the east – are tattooed all over with blue markings.'

'Blueskins?'

'Yes, but the Roman nobility, the learned types, call them Picts. Painted Men, see?'

Minna hooked her arms around her legs, the trousers grubby at the knees. 'And you're Roman nobility, I suppose?'

Her words stabbed right through him. 'Oh, yes, of course,' he shot back. 'It is the greatest empire in the world, after all: wine, wine and more wine.'

She snorted, because she must have seen he didn't drink wine. 'Have *you* gone north of the Wall, then?'

He shrugged nonchalantly. 'Of course. There are outpost forts there for the *areani*. They are the scouts that patrol the borderlands and keep the tribes under the thumb of Rome.'

She went still at that. 'But aren't you afraid to go among the barbarians? They attack the Wall, don't they?'

'The western tribes of Dalriada have treaties with Rome.' His lip lifted ever so slightly. 'The Picts don't, but you just take your chances with them.'

'But they go about naked, my brother said, covered in bloody furs with hair grown to the ground, and they spawn children together, all the men with all the women, and they eat raw meat—'

'Gods, Tiger! You've been listening to too many stories from people who have never set a toenail north of that Wall.' Her words triggered a surprising bleakness in him. He gazed over the river, where wisps of mist were curling up from the dark water, winding about the bare alder branches. The lonely cry of geese floated over the marsh beyond, wings black against the pink sky. 'Everyone is the same everywhere, and none of it any good,' he muttered. 'I've seen more of life than you. There's only one person you can rely on, and that's yourself. I have no loyalty to anyone. I look after me, and me alone.'

There was a pause. 'That's a foolish thing to say,' she whispered.

The murmur of pain was there between them again: from him, her or both of them, who knew? He often glimpsed it bared in her face, because she hadn't learned to hide it yet. But now, when she turned those unearthly eyes on him, he could swear she saw right into *him*, too, stripping away all the masks. His throat closed over with fear.

'It's not,' he returned harshly, 'it's reality.' He leaped up, brushing himself down briskly. She was staring at him, and so he deliberately breathed out and veiled his eyes with a smile. 'That's why this life suits me, see?' He took a few steps and flipped over into a handstand, balancing there on his palms in the damp grass. 'I drift around on the wind, wherever it takes me. And if I trip, I look down ...' He righted

31

himself, landing neatly on his feet, 'and there *I* am to catch me. Just me.'

Minna was regarding him warily now. He threw himself back down. 'Oh, come on,' he prodded. 'You are a girl who relies on her own wits, aren't you? You were running away, after all.'

She stiffened, turning away to the streambank. 'I am running *to* something, not away.'

Cian stared at the curve of her cheek. She'd never offered anything of herself, and he didn't know why she did now.

'My brother joined the army on the Wall. And my grandmother ...' She pressed her hands into the cleft between her knees. 'My grandmother got sick and she's ... not here any more. Broc, my brother, doesn't know she's gone, so I have to go to him now.'

'*Live* with him?' Cian determinedly shut out the weight of her grief. 'But he's in the army.'

'The families of the soldiers live in the *vicus* at each fort, you told me.'

His brows drew together. She *was* running away from something, whatever she said. 'And you have some plan of what to do when you get there, assuming you can find him?'

She braced herself and turned, defiantly lifting her chin. 'I'm going to become a shopkeeper or learn a trade. I can make honey and herb-simples, even teach children grammar. I'll get a little stall, and sit out the front like the butchers' wives and make *my own money*.' Though she spoke as if she'd rehearsed this, her face was wan and lost.

This was too much for Cian. 'Good luck to you, then,' was all he could think to say.

He got up and held out his hand for her to take. After a moment of looking, she did. Cian was tall for twenty-one but Minna almost came up to his collar-bone – no fragile child, but a woman with braced chin and stiff shoulders, whose luminous eyes held secrets like his own.

His breath stirred the black hair at her brow, and he reached for the horse's bridle, clinging to the reins.

That night, after the voicing of her desperate plan, Minna heard a voice in her dreams.

Who are you, Minna-girl? it crooned. *Who are you?* Stirring, she felt fingers caress her face just like Mamo did: along one cheek with her palm, then the other with the soft back of her hand.

She woke abruptly in the darkness of Letitia's tent. There was no one there, apart from the old woman snoring and snuffling in her smelly hides. Shivering, Minna got on hands and knees and crawled to the tent flap, huddling there. Outside, the sky was growing lighter grey over the black northern hills. Frost sheened the ground with white.

North.

Away from the villa with its moonlit fields of barley and hooting owls, the stream with the singing frogs, and the little house beneath the ash tree. She wrapped her arms tight around her thighs and pressed her face into her knees, grinding her eye sockets into flesh and bone.

Forcing her ribs hard against her heart.

Chapter 6

By the time they neared the Wall, Minna kept her feelings contained to an even more narrow place inside, allowing out only impatience. But the pressure was there beneath the surface, strangling her. She could not keep it at bay much longer.

They reached Luguvalium, the old Roman fortress and town, three weeks after leaving Eboracum. From a meadow to the south, Minna gazed at the ruins of its now disused stone fort, the twin forks of shining river and the mossy town walls. But then her attention was arrested by something far more exciting.

She could see the Wall.

An enormous, dark snake of stone, it wound across her field of vision as if uncurling from her dreams, driving in from the east and crossing the river, marching relentlessly for the coast. It was taller and grimmer than even she could have imagined, a stern slash dividing the green land – a line gouged by an Emperor's pen on a map. An edifice that said, *'This side, in here: that side, out there.'*

Barbarian lands. Wild lands. Outlands. Minna had heard Alba called all these things. Mamo had called them simply the old lands, but even that conjured up a scent, a shiver, of something ancient and untamed. Her mouth dropped open and her heart began to race.

She was so taken away she did not at first recognize the shouts being passed back along the line of carts. The troupe would stay at Luguvalium for two weeks. As soon as the wheels rumbled to a halt, she jumped down and ran to Cian. 'I can't wait here for that long!' she cried. 'The weather is getting worse and I have to get to Broc. Don't you know where the *areani* are posted?'

Cian pulled up the pony's head from its feed-bucket, as all around them mules were unhitched to be watered, and people bustled about

34

stretching their legs and unpacking. 'Probably in the Cocidii outpost fort north of the Wall. You'd need to send a message, then cross over at Banna.'

'Cross ... the Wall?' Minna was aghast. Her entire life she'd been told that the Wall repelled the murderous, barbarian hordes. And now he was talking about crossing into those wild lands as easily as walking out of the villa gate. *The other side.* But she had no choice. She had to get to Broc. He was all she knew, all she had left.

'I have to go right now.' Her voice quavered.

'Not so fast, Tiger!' Cian raised one hand. 'You can't travel on your own – you'd get eaten alive. Just send a message to your brother. I'm sure he can come for you.'

She tucked her cold fingers under her arms, stricken. Now she was so close, she had begun to remember the hard expression on Broc's face when they argued.

Cian was looking at her shrewdly. 'You never told him you were coming, did you?'

She turned her head to avoid those vivid blue eyes. What was the point of lying now? 'No,' she answered in a low voice.

Silence fell. When she dared to glance at Cian again his face bore an unfamiliar expression as he slowly rubbed the back of his neck. At last he put his hands on his narrow hips with a casual shrug. 'I ... ah, I suppose I could take you. It's not that far.'

Minna blinked. '*You?*'

He smiled wryly. 'Look, I'll take you only because I need to go there anyway. I left some money at the Cocidii fort with an old friend, and I was going to pick it up before winter. And it's not so bad. The tribes on this western coast are trussed up by treaties. Traders and whores go back and forth across the Wall here all the time.'

She hardly heard any of that, insensible with relief. Impulsively she clutched at his arm, holding it as if she were drowning. 'Gods, thank you! That's ... so *kind.*'

At her touch he went still, then the muscle under her fingers moved as he slowly disentangled himself. 'All right, come on,' he said gently. 'Don't embarrass me now.'

She released him, flustered and annoyed at herself. There was no soft Mamo now with whom to lay down her head and weep.

As she walked back to the cart she slowly exhaled. All that mattered was that the last thread of her family would soon be there to cling to. Perhaps then all this darkness would dissolve, like a dream upon waking.

'If yer brother kicks ye out on yer bony rump, come back!' Letitia cried, as Minna donned her pack the next day, leaving the troupe camped on the town meadow.

'She's made more money from you in two weeks than in her last two years,' Cian muttered, striding along the path away from the river. 'You should have taken it, stupid.'

Minna already felt lighter. 'I didn't want the money. The shelter was enough kindness for me.'

'You won't make much of a living if you go around thinking that.'

She glanced at him, wrinkling up her nose. 'And don't call me stupid.'

Cian stifled a grin and cuffed her on the shoulder as if she were a puppy.

A road ran parallel to the Wall, and they took this as it unrolled eastwards over the hills, sharing the trail with traders and wagons, families trudging on foot and riders trotting briskly past. To their left the Wall snaked away, unbroken across the bare northlands, the grasses burnished by the morning sun. Minna could not stop gazing at it. As high as two men, its grey stone had been levered from the same crags that thrust up through the ridges of heath, making it look as if it were cunningly built by gods, not man. Watchtowers and small forts were set at intervals all along. If she narrowed her eyes she could glimpse the figures of men pacing on top, watching the north.

It soon rained, veiling the land in curtains of grey. Water trickled down Minna's cheeks and under her cloak, beading her eyelashes, soaking her boots. But the next day the clouds cleared and she stopped watching the road, her attention caught by something else that made her raise her head from her feet. It was the air.

In the wake of the rain the wind blew from the north in a lonely song, lifting the hawks high in a pale sky. It gusted through the emptiness inside her, filling up her hollow chest. She could not remain unmoved by such a wild, haunting breeze, and her soul began to stir with a primal feeling that made her heart skip.

Cian saw her breathing it in. 'Pretty grim, isn't it?' he remarked, shifting his pack. He looked strained. 'Cold, wet, muddy, windy and barren.' He shook his head. 'Hellish place.'

Minna had wrapped a woollen scarf around her mouth and chin, and from behind this she directed a sidelong glance at Cian. She found the cold pricking the back of her nose exhilarating, not grim, like a draught of clear water. He obviously didn't feel the same, judging by the sour twist of his mouth.

For two days she wandered along with her eyes on the sky, until on the third Cian suddenly called her name. She stopped, shaking herself awake. Away to their left an escarpment reared above a river, and cresting it was a large fort with many gatetowers, the sky above smeared with smoke. Carts and people were peeling off the road towards it. Banna.

'Come on,' Cian said, frowning. 'We have to cross the river further along and head to the milecastle with the gate that opens north: that's where everyone crosses, barbarians and Romans alike.'

The north gate of the milecastle was set into the Wall, which stretched west to Banna and east across the hills. Atop the exposed tower over the gate, Vabrius of the First Cohort of Dacians squinted into the driving wind. That wind could scour flesh from bone and eyeballs from sockets – he still hadn't got used to it since his posting from Lindum in the south.

'Eyes down,' his comrade Aelius grunted, holding the edge of the wall to peer over. Tufts of grass sprouted from the stone between his hands, nursed by the constant rain. That rain beat at the soldiers on the frontier like blows from an invisible enemy: freezing into stinging hail, driven into eyes beneath helmet guards. Even when the blueskins weren't in sight, still Alba attacked, with sleet, creeping fog and biting wind.

'What?' Vabrius snapped, stamping his feet.

'That.' Aelius pointed down at the band of hairy men picking their way up the northern slope to gain admittance through the Wall into the Province. Their shaggy sheepskin cloaks and wind-blown hair obscured their outlines. 'Those packages on their horses; are they spears? Or those barbaric longswords? I don't like it.' Fear was a keen edge in his voice.

The Wall soldiers never lost those nerves, held constantly taut as bowstrings. There had been enough ambushes by screaming Picts over the years to tighten the neck muscles of every man who ventured forth on patrol. The land seemed empty but it wasn't, for Vabrius always felt the eyes on his back, as if the hills themselves watched him.

The unpainted Dalriadan tribe in the west had signed treaties; the Picts in the east had signed none. This should have made Vabrius feel better, posted to a western fort. However, he had seen the faces of the Dalriadan warriors who came to deliver their taxes of grain. Stripped of swords and pride they should look less dangerous, but they did not. They might take a cup of wine with the commander, bow and smile, but the sullen hatred was still there in their eyes.

'I don't like it,' Aelius muttered. He took up the bronze trumpet on his belt and blew one blast into it. A row of white faces looked up from the winding path below, pinched and bony.

'You! Halt right there!' Aelius turned to Vabrius. 'Come on. We'd better search them before they get to the gate. I can smell their stink from here.'

The milecastle was small and cramped, just four walls with two opposing gates and twin barrack blocks. Minna and Cian crowded in through the south gate and joined a motley line of people waiting to be admitted through the Wall to the north.

Guards pacing the walkway looked down on the crowd, faces cut into tense lines by the helmets with their cheek and brow-guards. The civilians kept being forced back as soldiers marched in and out, and once a band of cavalry trotted through, their horses tossing their heads, swords and spears clattering against iron mail. Minna stared up at each horseman, but none was Broc.

Some traders in the line looked like those at Eboracum, with their different skin hues, hair and clothing. Others were obviously barbarians, with white skin and ruddy hair, and pale blue eyes that did not change expression when they moved over Minna.

The soldiers were also mixed; some fair and grey-eyed, others swarthy and dark. Minna had imagined the Wall soldiers in polished, gilded armour and scarlet wool, just as the old tales said. Like those in Eboracum, however, these men wore sturdy mailshirts, unadorned helmets and plain tunics – though here the mail was battered and the hide trousers stained. She felt oddly disappointed, until she noticed that every iron ring of the mail was oiled, the straps and buckles of helmets, boots and weapons triple-sewn. Swords were fast-bound to sides, leather hilts shiny with the imprints of fingers. The men looked infinitely worn and desperately wary, and every face bore the same drawn cheeks and hard mouth.

All of a sudden, a trumpet pealed and soldiers poured down from the walkway and streamed through the north gate to challenge a party on the barbarian side. Roman swords were unsheathed, spears braced. The queue of people at the south gate crowded forward, necks craning.

Minna could just see a group of ragged men with pack ponies. They put their hands up, babbling something she couldn't hear. Beside her, Cian's eyes narrowed. The soldiers prodded the voluminous cloaks of the Albans and swarmed around the ponies, tugging packages off saddles and tearing them open. Inside there were only bundles of wool, rolled hides and furs, and one which held tines of deer antler. Trade goods, that was all.

The tension flowed out of the soldiers. With sharp words they thundered back up the stairs to their posts, leaving the scowling Albans with their belongings scattered in the trampled mud.

Minna's shoulders lowered, and she swayed back as the line re-formed.

'Watch it!' a voice growled behind her. She turned to stammer an apology and saw a stocky, broad-shouldered man with skin like cured leather. His dark hair was pulled back in a tail, his short beard threaded with silver. In one ear he sported a gold ring, though his tunic and cloak were plain.

But before her curiosity could take any more in, someone barked, 'Next!' and it was their turn.

Annius rocked on his stool by the gate, hawking a gob of spit into the mud. *Stinking Alban scum.* He wished they had found forbidden goods on the bastards, for it would give him something to report to the Dux, and then the garrison might get an increased measure of ale. The Christos knew they needed it. Or better yet, cloaks that actually kept the rain out, though the fat little administrators in the south seemed more interested in cutting costs.

The next in line were a young woman and man of close age. Annius tapped his pen on the table before him, as his guards patted them down for weapons with grimy hands and searched their packs. One guard looked at him and shook his head. Annius's tax tally this month wouldn't look too healthy to the commander. Sourly, he swung the stool back, leaning against the wall. 'Business?'

The youth melted into the shadows, whistling, so he fixed his eyes on the girl. She gulped. 'I'm going to join my brother,' she faltered. 'He's a scout, just been posted up here.' She spoke better Latin than most of them.

'Name?'

'Broc ... of the Aurelius family ... at Derventio. Near Eboracum.'

'Last detachment of new scouts from Eboracum went to Fanum Codicii. You're on the right road.'

The young woman glanced at the youth with relief in her curious, light eyes. Annius rapped his pen on the table, making her jump. 'But he should have notified us of any such visitors. You are aware the road to the Codicii fort is a restricted area?'

The girl ran her palms down muddy trousers. 'Well, I'm a surprise, actually.'

'A surprise.' So here were the trade goods. *Her brother, my balls.* Annius glanced over to the tall youth. 'Plenty of whores up there already, boy. Every barbarian girl within ten miles of here gives it up for a bit of bread and a warm bed.'

There was a muffled exclamation from the girl as the young man stepped forward. 'We'll take our chances.'

Annius cocked his head. This youngster was brimming with an oily confidence that irritated him. All three legs of the stool thudded into the grass as he sat forward. 'Your name?'

The cocky youth grinned, though his eyes were hard. 'Cian the acrobat. We'll pay you a tax on the way back. We've got nothing right now.'

With a grim purse of his lips, Annius scribbled on a wooden tag. 'There's a watchpost on the road. Try to impress them a bit more than me, boy, or they might not let you through.'

Shoved through the arch of the north gate by Cian's firm hand, Minna stumbled from shadow into light. She was about to turn and rebuke him when the words died in her throat. Behind them, the ramparts of the Wall loomed up sternly, but in front a path wound down a slope to a pale track that led north.

Rust-red moorland. Bleached gold heath. Bent, wind-scoured trees.

Alba. She was suddenly speechless, her legs almost nerveless.

Cian ran into the back of her. 'Come *on!*' he grumbled, ducking around and stomping down the path.

Minna, however, was held there. She should have been daunted by the bare plain, which swung low to marsh and then rose again to hills; by the shreds of mist which hung in that scoop of moorland like an Otherworld veil through which she must pass.

But she was not at all afraid. Instead, the further she and Cian travelled from the safety of the Wall, the more her heart soared, like a great bird lifted higher with each beat of its wings. Swifter her blood ran, until she tore her wrap away and stretched her chin to the wind. She felt suddenly as if she could fly free of all fetters here, under the upturned bowl of this endless sky.

Cian turned and barked something, but she could not hear his words. She could only stumble along behind him, quivering, the land under her feet drawing her in with its song.

Chapter 7

By the end of the day, Minna's sore feet and runny nose had drained some of the poetry from her soul.

The land rose to a plateau of heath, the grasses bleached by cold, gold-tipped in the lowering sun. It seemed uninhabited. *And why would people live here?* she wondered, with one of the odd insights that had been entering her mind ever since she crossed the Wall. This land, pounded by the hooves of Roman horses, raided by Picts, was no safe place for a little hut, a wife and babe.

The road was not deserted, though. The rough-looking man behind them at the fort had passed them earlier with a party of men leading mules and a few carts, their sharp eyes scanning the land ahead and then pausing to study Cian and Minna. Cian stared boldly back, but Minna dropped her eyes. It was not only the air that had changed. She was no longer in the Roman Province, part of the Empire. She was beyond all law now.

They had started out late, and at length Cian decided not to push on in the dark. The sky glowed with the embers of sunset as they left the road to seek camp. The heath was now a misty, purple sea, broken by clumps of ghostly white birches.

'Do we have to go so far? I'll break my ankle.'

Cian stopped and turned. 'Tiger, the watch doesn't like people skulking about after dark. They would shoot first and ask questions later.'

She blinked. 'I thought you said there were treaties, that everything was safe in the west.'

Cian gazed down at her, though she could not see his eyes for shadows. 'Did I?' he said softly. 'But the night is always full of enemies.'

Minna was silenced, and they resumed walking. 'What about tomorrow?' she eventually whispered. The sounds were making her jumpy:

the trickle of a stream, something cracking twigs in the underbrush. 'Will they let us through then?'

'Oh, aye.' Cian's voice turned dry. 'Then they'll see we're just a girl and a swordless boy.'

Dark had fallen in a damp veil all about them when Cian grunted, 'Over there is a likely place, out of the mist.'

Minna stumbled along behind him in the blackness as they trudged up a slight rise. But just as he was about to speak again the ground fell away and they saw the glow of a campfire that had been hidden by the hill.

Cian swiftly shoved Minna behind him as two men stepped out of the dark trees on the edge of the hollow. 'Who goes?' one growled.

'No one,' Cian returned. 'Just travellers on the road, forgive us. We'll be leaving now.'

After a cough from the other man, the first voice softened into gruffness. 'You are a long way from the road, friend, so you may as well join our fire. There are many of us, only two of you. Or are there more?'

Before Cian could answer, another man came from the fire, striding up to the lip of the dell and peering at them in the ruddy glow. 'Well, well,' he drawled, in a gravelled voice. 'If it isn't the little whore and her boy.'

Tucked behind Cian's shoulder, Minna squinted at the man. 'You were behind us at the fort. And you passed us on the road.'

The man with the gold earring unveiled a startling white smile in his swarthy face. 'Why, yes we were, and yes we did, little lady. What a good memory you have.' Minna could not place his accent. He spoke Latin, but with an exotic lilt.

Cian eyed him warily. 'You have misjudged us. She's no whore. We're just on our way to see one of the soldiers – family.'

The man shrugged. 'As you say.'

'Well.' Cian nudged Minna backwards again. 'Sorry to startle you like that.'

'But wait!' The man stepped forward, hands spread. 'Do not be so hasty! I am Jared, leader of our little band of travellers. There are wolves around these hills, marauding blueskins and Roman soldiers. Surely you would be safer staying here this night, with us?'

Wolves, Minna thought, every nerve tingling. That was new.

Cian's breathing was heavy in her ear. 'No disrespect, friend, but I think not.' He glanced at the others, who had left their fireside seats to gather close by. There were around fifteen, with patched clothes and sun-burned faces, though each sported pleasant expressions.

'Please, I insist.' Jared took Minna's arm and drew her firmly from behind Cian, his eyes twinkling. 'You know, lady, in these parts it is considered a grave discourtesy to refuse hospitality.'

The ranks of men parted like gates opening, and she threw a look of confusion at Cian as she was gently marched between them. His face was set in grim lines.

They were seated on bundles of hides beside the fire, and given bowls of steaming mutton stew with hunks of dark, nutty bread that Cian did not touch until their hosts had been eating for a time, Minna copying him. His knee was squashed against hers, so she could feel the tension in him.

'What's your business away up here, anyway?' Cian asked boldly, after a long silence.

Jared swallowed ale from a horn cup. 'We bring the soldiers valuable goods, boy. Better wine than they can get from Eboracum; finer flour for bread; trinkets for their sweethearts.'

Cian frowned, his ale untouched. 'How can you afford to bring grain this far north, and still do a better deal for the soldiers than the local tribes?'

'Ah!' Jared grinned at his men. 'Hark to the boy! He's got a sharp business mind, eh? Should we invite him to join us?'

Laughter rumbled, and Minna glanced over her shoulder at the camp. She couldn't see their carts or mules any more.

'Let us say,' Jared went on, 'that after a lot of hard work and travel, we've forged some very *favourable* relationships.' He caught her eye and winked. 'Bribing, cajoling, charming – with perhaps a *little* threat here and there – we have used every advantage open to us, as honest traders.' He laughed.

Minna stared into his black eyes, thinking this Jared might be lots of things, but honest wasn't one. The gold earring winked and her imagination ran riot, seeing him on a ship, squinting into the bright eastern sun as it glided into some perfumed port of painted women and dark-eyed men.

Cian was briskly brushing crumbs from his lap. 'I must thank you, friend, for your hospitality.' He got up, hauling Minna with him. 'But we have an early start and will seek our beds. We can make our own camp—'

'No, you must sleep here!' Jared frowned as if offended.

'We've abused your goodwill quite enough.' Cian polished his meat dagger down his trousers before sticking it back in his belt, unsheathed.

'Nonsense! I insist, for your own good.'

Cian's jaw tensed. 'All right,' he said evenly. 'Then we'll just spread our bed rolls on the edge of your camp.'

Jared hesitated. 'As you wish.'

After some hearty farewells they took themselves off to the north side of camp, near a copse of birch trees. As they rolled out their sleeping hides Cian muttered, 'When they are asleep, we go.'

Minna nodded, and, as they stretched out side by side, she was surprised at the comfort she felt from his nearness and his familiar scent, the wool-fat that greased the pony harness and oiled his body when he juggled. The brittle smiles of those men had unsettled her. But then, there were the wolves.

Cian put his hands behind his head, letting his tension out in a snort. 'Honest traders! Thieves, more like. They're up to something, and we're in enough trouble without getting wrapped up in theirs.'

Cian's fingers pressed on Minna's lips, waking her. 'Hush,' he breathed. 'I think I heard something.'

She rubbed her eyes, annoyed she had fallen asleep. The moon was higher now, silver not bronze as it wove in and out of the clouds.

'I can hear snoring,' Cian whispered. 'But not the dogs. I think—'

There he was abruptly cut off as the black shapes of men swarmed about them, spidery shadows in the moonlight.

Cian was hauled away, scrabbling and swearing before he grunted as if he'd been thumped. Minna got out one scream, struggling up on all fours, before a hand clamped over her ankle. Then it gripped her thigh before others came down on both arms, wrists and neck. Men were shouting at each other in Latin.

Cian cursed and cried out to her again, as feet thudded in the turf all around her head. Her ear was ground into the soil and someone stood on her wrist, pinning her there.

'Get the damn cub down!' There were more muffled yells.

'Thump him, Ori, in the head!'

Cian bellowed again as Minna was roughly flipped over, and then someone was kneeling on her arms. 'Get it in, then, Jared!'

She choked on a horrified cry, squirming with all her strength, arching her back.

'Little wildcat, she is! *Hurry up!*'

Fingers pinched her nose and her mouth gaped to breathe, and then something cold was pressed to her lips. A stream of foul-tasting stuff poured down her open throat. Spluttering, Minna tried to tear her face away, to spit, but the hands were implacable. They held her jaw closed, her head still.

'Enough! Don't kill her,' Jared barked, 'and get it down him before he kills *us!*'

Minna kept trying to struggle, but something was happening. Her thrashing limbs were losing their strength and a mist was closing in around her. Everything grew blurred and slow-moving. Her soul was shrinking, disappearing down into a pinprick. And that pinprick was receding along a dark tunnel, away from everything that was sharp and loud and clear.

At last the tunnel ended in darkness, and she fell away from the solid earth into nothing.

She must have been dreaming, though it was unlike any dream she had ever had.

Awake-dreams were sharp and vivid, but now she was heavy and trapped, forced down into a dark, viscous soup that bound her limbs and flooded her throat, silencing her screams. She was drowning.

Every now and then, she gained a sense that she was struggling up to the light, fighting free of the dragging weight. At those times, other snatches of sense would filter through.

A rumble of wheels. The stink of urine. The close reek of bodies. Cold metal around her neck.

And then the hands would grip her again, and bitterness flood her tongue, and she would find herself sinking back into the sticky mire. *No!* she cried, inside where they could not silence her.

But then, as the black despair claimed her, she would hear a voice singing close in her ear. She would feel warm lips breathing into the side of her own. *Safe you will be,* the voice sang, *when you come to me. Come. Come.*

Chapter 8

Minna woke at last to a stench that clawed its way up her nostrils and down her throat, and she immediately gagged it back up again.

Her cheek was pressed into a slimy floor, while the world lurched underneath her. Pain lanced her temples and aching limbs. Far away a man shouted, answered by another. She dragged her eyes open. She was in a dark place, lit by a dull glow spilling down a narrow ladder from above. Thirst curled her tongue up like a shrivelled leaf.

The world tilted again, and Minna slid across the slippery floor and slammed into a wall, her arms brought up short by a chain locked to an iron ring in the floor. Whimpering, she gritted her teeth against the darts of fire in her head. She was enveloped in a musty fug of tar, salt and fish, urine and vomit. It was the reek of the docks at Eboracum, the stench of a ship.

'By tomorrow you'll be used to the smell.'

She turned her head, blinking. In the dimness she made out Cian. He was hunched against the other wall, his tunic stained with vomit. A line of blood curved from one eye to cheek, sickle-shaped.

She tried to croak his name, but was stopped by a cloying wave from her belly and she could only turn her face and retch weakly down one arm.

'Good, good,' someone rumbled cheerily, and Jared swung himself down the ladder with a lamp he set on the bottom rung. He crouched by Minna and lifted a cup to her lips. Seized by thirst, she forgot all else as she gulped greedily at the water.

'That's a girl,' Jared cooed. 'Keep purging the red flower from your belly. Its caress takes you to some fine places, but it's not so good for your looks, eh?' His voice was still hoarse, but the ingratiating tone had gone, replaced with a note of satisfaction. One callused hand turned her chin to the lamplight. 'Well worth it indeed,' he muttered. 'A fine jewel from the moors of the north.'

Minna had heard that before. *A rare jewel.* Her mind stumbled, groping for the familiar. *Mamo. Mamo.*

'Now.' Jared turned to the ladder and came back with an iron pot. 'Seeing as you're awake, my lovely, I want you to piss in this now, and not all over your clothes.' He smiled as he thunked down the pot. 'No sense getting sores on that smooth white skin, eh?' It was only then she realized she was no longer wearing her wool trousers, just her long tunic. Her legs were bare.

Jared spared a glance for Cian. 'And you too, boy – your flesh is almost as sweet as hers. Kick it back and forth between the two of you, as you will.'

Minna's head thumped back on the wall, some sense restored by the water. Jared glanced down. 'You'll need some fingers, though.' Stepping over, he unlocked the chain with a key at his belt, freeing one hand, then re-locked the other. Fury flooded her, rousing anger, and she spat at Jared, spraying saliva over his fingers.

His smile did not falter. 'Good,' he chuckled. 'Keep fighting free of it.' He neatly dodged a feeble spasm of her heel, then freed Cian's arm. 'The weather will be smoother soon, my lovelies. Sweet dreams!' He thudded back up the ladder.

Panting, Minna flexed her tingling fingers. Then she understood it all. For those fingers crept up to a metal ring encasing her neck. The thin shackle was in two neat halves joined by a hinge, with a forged ring at the other end. The ring could be attached to a rope – or a chain.

'It's a slave shackle.' Cian's voice was as thin and pale as his face.

'I know.' Her heart plummeted. 'I know.'

'They are slave traders ... I should have known ...' Cian rolled his head on the wall, then thumped it back. 'They ply their filthy trade in Alba, and the Roman soldiers turn a blind eye to it – fewer barbarians to kill, after all.'

'But we aren't barbarians.'

'No.' Cian's eyes, she could see now, were shadowed underneath. 'Just in the wrong place at the wrong time.'

They were in that place and time because of her.

'Gods! Don't look at me like that, Tiger.' His voice was sullen with suppressed fury. 'I was beyond stupid. I knew we should have walked away.'

'But I made you come with me in the first place!'

Cian mustered a tight smile. 'Made me? I'm not a pony to be led about by a girl – and a clumsy one at that.' She clenched her fingers, her eyes stinging, as he shifted to ease his back. 'Think on this,' he said. 'Slaves are like any other goods. To get the best price you must look after them. If they were thieves they could have killed us there and then, but now they won't.'

It was a bleak assessment either way. She closed her eyes, sick with guilt. 'Do you know where we are?'

'I woke up yesterday. We stopped in some port where they were still speaking Latin. But whether we are for Erin or Gaul or Rome, I don't know.'

Minna turned her cheek on the wall. She would never see Broc, or breathe the air of home again. She was a slave, after her family fought so hard to be free. She slowly curled on her side, her bound wrist caught by the chain. The drug that Jared had called the red flower still pulsed in her blood and she gave herself up to it now, tightening into a miserable ball.

An argument, raging above her head on deck, roused her many hours later.

'But Jared,' one of the men was whining, 'she's pretty flesh, what does it matter?'

'You damn well know where we're going, and it does matter,' came Jared's voice. 'Those savages at Dunadd pay good money, but only for *unmarked* flesh, and if she's a maid I want her to stay that way.'

'Gods, Jared!' another protested. 'The barbarians don't give a bear's ball about women's holes, open or shut!' His tone turned wheedling. 'So let's have her, then, all of us. Finest flesh we've had aboard for years. Better than those poxed whores worn out by dirty Romans.'

There was a silence as Minna lay in the blackness, her skin crawling. 'Few care for such things, aye. But some do, and they pay for it.' There was a stomp of feet up and down. 'So she stays untouched, or I'll have your balls off with my knife here, and your cock not far behind.' A few dared to grumble, and Jared raised his voice. 'I have your whole year's wages hidden ashore, you bunch of mangy mutts, and only I know where it is, and it *ain't* on this ship. So obey me, or you'll lose more than your cocks!'

The men dispersed, muttering, while Minna stared into the empty darkness, shame a burning trail from belly to throat. When she at last heard Cian stir she turned her head. Dawn had crept over the world outside and beneath the hatch she could see his face was grey, bleached of feeling.

'We are going to Dunadd,' she whispered fearfully. 'Where is that?'

Cian's eyes were suddenly blank. 'Alba,' he said. 'It is a fort in Alba.'

★

On the fourth day the sickening yaw of the boat calmed. The blows of the waves echoing around the hold turned to slaps, and they glided on more sheltered waters.

For Minna and Cian, the taint of the red flower had lifted only gradually, dulling their minds and tongues. By the time Minna felt the ship nudge against something solid, however, a yearning for land had shaken off her malaise. She strained her chin up, longing for air.

Ropes rasped across wood; feet thudded on decks. 'We'll be ashore soon,' she murmured, through cracked lips.

Cian's eyes flickered towards her. 'Yes,' he said, and then laughed, a shocking, bitter sound.

'Come on, then!' Two sailors slid down the ladder, unchained them and bound their hands in front with rope. When she was hauled on to the deck, Minna's eyes squeezed almost shut against the dull, grey light. Someone tossed them, stumbling, onto a wooden jetty.

Through slitted eyes, she glimpsed a silty beach and a humped rock outcrop scattered with little, round houses, smoke leaking from their thatched roofs. To the south were shining mudflats at a rivermouth, and all around, looming hills. The jetty was crawling with people unloading ships, the grey beach beyond scattered with hide boats and canoes. The air was split by shouts and laughter, the thump of barrels and crates. A cold mist hung over the black water of the bay, and a freezing wind cut to her bones.

Jared stood before them, scrutinizing Minna's grimy legs and stained tunic. She wanted to spit at him again, but her mouth was too dry and she was weak after little food but stale bread.

'This won't do,' Jared muttered, taking her rope. She noticed dizzily that the dark water beside the jetty was growing paler as they neared the beach. Jared halted. 'Into the drink, then, both of them.'

Minna was shoved from behind, her breath extinguished by freezing water. She scrabbled ineffectually with tied hands, struggling upwards, until someone grabbed her by the hair and hauled her head free. Above, Jared's sailors laughed as she spluttered and gagged, curious faces peering over their shoulders. Alongside, another sailor was dunking Cian in the thigh-deep sea. Before Minna could speak, her head was shoved under again and shaken around.

Hands rubbed roughly at her legs, arms and hair, and at last she and Cian were dragged from the water onto the pebbly beach, where Jared sawed away their bindings as they crouched there shivering. He prodded Cian, tossing him a tunic and trousers. 'Here.' He dragged Minna to her feet. 'Strip down and put this on,' he directed, holding out a folded column of red wool.

Rubbing her wrists, she looked behind him to his men. Most had gone to unload the rest of their cargo, but four remained, eyes greedily fixed on her wet, clinging tunic. It was too much; it would be her undoing. She looked Jared in the eye, though she trembled all over. 'No.'

He considered her for a moment, gaze roaming over her fair skin. Then – utterly exhausted, shocked out of her old self – Minna's mind made a surprising leap. She saw into Jared like a gull diving into the sea; sensed his thoughts, felt his emotions. *She heard his mind.* It had never happened before.

Jared was wondering how much she would bruise if they forced her, and how it would affect his price.

Her wrists were already chafed from the chain, and the slave-ring, though thin, was wearing welts on her neck. She clenched her fists, bracing her arms. If Jared forced her, she would bruise badly. She showed that with her face, her body.

'Right!' Jared snapped, and pointed behind her with his dagger to a tumble of boulders at the base of the outcrop. Weak with relief, Minna wedged herself in and tugged off her wet tunic. Still shivering, she held its stinking folds for a moment, thumbs moving over the embroidery sewn by Mamo. She touched it to her lips, slowly, and then drew the barbarian dress over her head. It fell to her ankles, a shapeless tube sewn on each shoulder with long sleeves attached. Slowly, she emerged from the rocks, trailing her old tunic.

Cian had pulled on his trousers to the sound of jeering laughter from the sailors. A tremor ran across his lean muscles as Jared studied his naked torso with a keen eye. 'Well, well, I had no idea you were as sweet and hairless as the girl.' The trader's teeth flashed. 'Could get more money for him, lads. Might sell him to one of the warriors as a body slave, ha!'

The sailors yelped, and Minna stood defiantly by Cian's side as he tugged the tunic over his black curls. 'I am the finest horseman you'll ever see,' Cian announced suddenly.

Jared's face hardened. 'You keep your mouth shut and do what I tell you.'

Cian took a deep breath. 'They can have me for the horses. They value their horses above all things.'

Jared's eyes went blank as he moved closer, then, without warning, he sunk a fist into Cian's gut. Cian grunted, doubling over, and Minna dropped her tunic and sank by his side, holding his shoulders. They were crusted with sand, quivering between her fingers.

Jared ignored her, flexing his fist. When he spoke he was perfectly pleasant. 'I think it's time you learned your place, boy. No one cares what you think. If they say carry, you'll do it; if they ask you to lick their feet, you'll do that, too. Got it?'

Cian was winded, his chin tucked into his chest. It was Minna who answered. 'You are an abomination to all the gods.' Her voice was strained with fury. 'I bring all their curses down on you, trader Jared.'

Jared grinned. 'I've been called worse things than that, sweetness, and cursed better in a dozen languages. But don't worry, you'll have a new master shortly and if you're lucky you won't need to see my puking face again.' He threw a bone comb in the sand at her feet. 'Comb your hair and his while we unload.' He yelled some instructions at his men and made his way back to his ship.

Cian knelt in the sand with Minna's arms around him until he could breathe again. Then he pushed her away and staggered to his feet. He turned his back on land, faced the water, and wouldn't meet her eyes.

When they were finally dragged away, Minna's embroidered tunic was stamped into the sand by marching feet. She never saw it again.

As she was prodded inland along a road that hugged the river, Minna kept her eyes lowered, her breath swift and shallow. But she could not blot out this land that somehow still forced itself inside her.

Instead of pastures and tame fields, Alba was the hue of rusted iron and blood, with ruffled grasses bronzed by cold and wind. Yellow trees lined the brown, foaming river, and the marsh beside the path was a copper sea, carpeted with moss. The wind had a blade's edge as it sliced down from the mountains, flinging spatters of rain into her face.

From downcast eyes, she caught glimpses of muddy boots as people passed. Voices babbled unintelligible words. Cart wheels rattled and the spindly feet of bleating sheep being driven along the track pock-marked the mud. Then her gaze came to rest on the painted hooves of what must be a warrior's horse.

She saw the tip of a scabbard and the gaudy check of the warrior's trousers. She saw his broad fist, curled around his spear. But she could not bring herself to raise her face and see his eyes, his wildness.

However, after nearly an hour of trudging along the riverbank, Cian silent behind her, something did at last draw Minna's head up, and she stopped then and could not go on.

Ahead rose a crag. It loomed up alone from the marsh, circled by an arm of the river. The teeth of rocks showed between houses clustered on its slopes, and on the crest sat an enormous roundhouse swathed in cooksmoke, its roof sweeping the ground. A village sprawled around the base of the crag, on the river meadow.

Minna's eyes desperately darted back and forth, as if the shapes might make sense to her. But there were no great town walls here, only rough palisades of timber stakes, one around the village and one circling the crag. There were no straight roofs, marble temples or colonnades, just squat round walls and thatch. It seemed squalid, awash with mud and smoke.

One of Jared's men cursed her, prodding her forward, and her legs wobbled back into life.

As they came closer, the stink of dung and smoke enveloped them. People milled about the gates chattering, saddling horses, hefting barrels into carts. Warriors with shining spears paced the timber walls above.

At that point, Minna ducked her head and squeezed her eyes almost shut. And so, as she entered the fort of Dunadd in Alba, she beheld only one thing: her own shoes, splashed with mud, the bare skin above crusted with salt.

The gates were flanked by two timber towers. Inside, she was jostled in a crowd, and startled by a dog thrusting its wet nose under her skirt. Houses, barns and stables were jumbled close together, the wood running with damp. The babbling voices beat on her temples.

The path curved higher to climb the crag, and the crowds thinned. Soon Jared was dragging them up tumbled stone steps so steep that Minna had to clamber on hands and knees. She glanced up, then wished she had not. Rocks reared up from the higher slopes like fangs, forming buttresses above the narrow path.

Through a gap in the wall of rock, capped by another immense gate, they emerged on to the upper tier of the fort. Here the houses were larger, decorated with lurid banners, painted walls and carved doors, their colours glowing through the drizzle.

Catching her breath, Minna plucked at the slave-ring and stumbled backwards into the path of two Alban warriors. Their long, ruddy hair was braided with gold thread, and moustaches drooped over shaven chins. Bronze rings and brooches adorned shoulders, forearms and fingers. But it was their fearless, bold eyes that struck Minna like a blow. One said something about her and they both laughed as they went through the gate, leaving her reeling.

'Oi! You two, get over here!'

She pulled Cian towards Jared, as the trader suddenly stiffened and bowed to someone behind them. Minna and Cian both turned, dazed.

A woman was gliding down the rocky path in a hooded cloak. A wisp of grey hair showed from the hood, but she was unbowed by age, her stride proud. Jared greeted her deferentially with the name 'Brónach' and some other address.

The imposing woman put back her hood. Beneath coiled braids her flesh was pared back over prominent bones, and slate-grey eyes gazed down an eagle nose. Her bony fingers shone with rings of jet and amber.

Until this moment, Minna had been too stricken to take note of the language spoken around her. Jared and his men used Latin, but she realized now that the flow had entirely changed to a musical cascade of barbarian speech – and she had not noticed.

Stunned, Minna was caught by the old woman's commanding voice. Somehow, she sensed a meaning: the boat was late. She tensed. The woman spoke a little like Mamo, that must be it. Her grandmother used the Parisii dialect when they were alone, and here the rhythms were similar. *Surely she could not* ... But she did. It was like a tune she had been taught as a child and now dimly remembered.

The old lady turned to inspect them. Her keen eyes swiftly dismissed Cian before resting on Minna. As the woman's nostrils flared, Minna had the strangest sensation of her belly being turned inside out. She thought she might be sick again and her hand went to her mouth.

At the point it became unbearable, someone else cried out, and Brónach swung around, releasing her.

Coughing, Minna squinted up from watering eyes. A blonde woman of middling age was prancing down the path, accompanied by a gaggle of younger ladies, all brightly dressed. The noblewoman halted in a flutter of silks, exclaiming in accented Latin, 'You are late, trader Jared. So have you brought me some fine jewels this time, hmm? Falemian wine? Iberian olives?'

At the shock of the Roman speech in this barbarian land Minna glanced at Cian, but he was staring straight ahead, his face white as bone.

Jared bowed. 'No, my queen. But I have something better – two fine, young slaves from the Wall.' He unfurled one arm.

A queen? Minna thought, struggling to take it in. The woman's small mouth pursed, disappointed.

It was then that Cian did something unexpected. Raising his chin, he blurted in Latin, 'The girl is from Eboracum, mistress. She tutored the children of noble Romans. She is highly educated.'

Jared frowned, but the queen's attention had already focused on Minna.

'The sons of a councillor,' Cian continued desperately.

The queen stepped up. One of her hairpins was hung with tiny golden balls, and they chimed as she tilted her head. A heavy perfume wafted around her.

Minna saw in a glance that cosmetics and jewels gave her an aura of beauty at a distance that faded somewhat up close. Those buttery curls were bleached with urine, the plump cheeks stained with berry juice. Her skin had been whitened with flour, but the powder had caught in the petulant wrinkle between her brows. 'Is this true?' she demanded. 'Can you teach Roman writing and history and poetry?'

The image of Nikomedes was there before Minna, gazing sternly at her, and she felt compelled to reply that she knew nothing about teaching. But Cian's eyes were boring into her, twisting her tongue back on itself. In that pause a messenger that Jared had sent scurrying off returned. With him was a young warrior, more gilded than all the rest.

The warrior was clean-shaven but almost as bejewelled as the queen, his golden hair stiffened into a spiked mane that fell down his back. Rings shone on every limb as he sauntered up, crossed his arms and surveyed Minna and Cian.

The queen glanced at him and snapped, and it came to Minna as a tantalizing flash: she had said his name – Ruarc – and told him to go away.

The warrior answered smoothly with a little bow, and the queen said, 'Tsk,' and began preening. But this Ruarc's eyes, a darker shade of his green tunic, slid languidly over Minna now and it was that look which jolted her instincts back to life. Jared had dispatched a message to *this* man particularly, as soon as they entered the gate, a warrior who reeked of boredom and vanity. She remembered the argument on the ship: *Those savages at Dunadd pay good money, but only for unmarked flesh, and if she's a maid I want her to stay that way.* Jared intended to sell her for his bed.

Instantly she straightened, and her eyes swept up to the queen with a deference honed over years with Mistress Flavia. 'I did teach, *domina*,' she agreed humbly.

The queen's eyes flared with pleasure at the noble address.

'I had charge of my master's two boys at a great villa in the south. I taught them grammar, poetry and history.' The lie tainted her tongue, but Minna made herself swallow it.

'Ah,' the queen breathed, clasping her plump hands together, eyes bright with a mysterious triumph. 'Quite a find then, aren't you? Such a fine surprise, and just what Garvan needs. All right, you will be mine, then – how dreadfully amusing.'

With that cryptic comment she waved over the lady called Brónach, murmured instructions and then continued on down towards the carved gate, her attendants fluttering behind her.

Brónach glanced at Minna with more interest now, her gaze sharp as a stone barb, and drew Jared aside to negotiate. In the meantime the young warrior stepped up. Minna stiffened as he gripped her chin and tilted her face, turning it so the gusts of fitful drizzle spattered her cheeks and eyelids. The glare of the clouds blinded her, but she forced herself to remain still, refusing to meet his eyes. A lifeline had been thrown and she must hold tight to it.

With a regretful sigh, the warrior turned to Cian and hammered out a few terse words in the barbarian speech. Cian replied in kind. Minna stared at him.

When the warrior went to join Jared's negotiations, Cian ran his fingers through his black hair, mumbling, 'I am to be the golden god's new horse-boy. So you'll be in the hall up here, and I'll be down in that stinking village – though at least I'll sleep in the stables, with the horses.'

She was still reeling. 'But how could you talk to them?'

He shrugged, his lashes sweeping down. 'I've travelled north of the Wall many times, you know that.'

She wondered about it, went to touch his slumped shoulder and then pulled back. 'Thank you for speaking up for me.'

His head whipped up, the line of his mouth white with strain. 'Stop it, Minna! Stop trying to make this better when it's all my ... ' At her stricken expression he struggled to soften his voice. 'I wanted the money I was owed as much as you wanted your brother, and I should have been smarter, quicker.' His eyes burned into her. 'Look, Tiger, we've been tossed into the ocean now, and all we can do is swim. Swim as hard as you can until I can get us out of here.'

Though it sat loosely, the slave-ring still strangled her. 'Swim,' she agreed hoarsely.

The bright warrior came and led his new horse-boy away.

Chapter 9

'Come,' the Lady Brónach said, mustering up that distasteful Latin she had to use with the traders. She turned on her heel, the slave-girl hurrying to keep up.

She strode past the houses of the nobles to her own dwelling on the cliff-edge, where the crag fell away to the marsh. Her home was so much more restful on the eye, with plain walls devoid of those boastful carvings and paintings. With the unimpeded view to the southern hills, Brónach could easily pretend she lived entirely alone.

Inside, she drew her robes out and sank into her rush chair by the hearth. Around the walls of the roundhouse, bed-boxes were neatly separated by carved screens, and the piles of baskets, pots and clay crocks on her workbench were orderly. All was calm on the eye, as she liked it. And now this.

She stared at the girl, tapping her fingers on the chair. Trust Maeve to take her on a whim and then leave her to Brónach to manage. *But then, to her, what else have I to do?* A Roman-born queen could never know what secrets ran in the female royal blood of Dalriada.

In the sputtering glow of a seal-oil lamp, the startling hue of the girl's eyes blended into her dark hair. 'Sit.' Brónach pointed an imperious finger at a bench. The girl hesitated, peering up at the bunches of dried herbs, twigs and bark that covered Brónach's rafters before gingerly perching on the edge. She was afraid, which was expected, but Brónach had sensed something more sinewy in her spirit when she probed her heart outside. She needed to know more about *that;* to be sure of someone who, slave or not, was to tutor royal children.

Brónach reached for a box behind her chair, clutched leaves and sprinkled them in a pot over the fire. Steam rose in an acrid cloud. The slave coughed, glancing at Brónach. She tried to block the vapour, then choked and drew it all the way in. Brónach watched her from hooded eyes, stirring the pot one way and then the other, humming under her breath. After a time the heavy air made the girl's eyes flicker.

Brónach abruptly sat back. 'You are of the old blood,' she said in Dalriadan.

At first the girl did not realize she'd spoken. Then she blinked and coughed. 'Lady?' she replied in Latin. 'My ... blood?'

Ah. She didn't realize that Brónach had spoken the local language, and she had answered the question. Odd. Suspicious, perhaps. Could she be a Pict spy, sent here in some treachery? She certainly had the dark hair. Pict women were only tattooed on belly and breasts, so unless she stripped her off right here, Brónach couldn't know for sure. There were, however, other ways.

Brónach reverted to Latin. 'Your Roman blood, it runs less strong than the other.' She had smelled it at once. The queen had the mingling, too – she was a princess of the Carvetii tribe near the Wall – but in Maeve the traces of old blood had been stamped out by her family's avarice and aping of Roman ways.

'Yes,' the girl whispered, eyes wide. 'My Mamo was part Parisii. From Eboracum.'

Ha! Brónach smiled. Her senses weren't completely dulled by age, then. She exhaled and closed her eyes, opened the spirit-eye on her brow. She felt the fear churning inside the girl and tried to probe beyond it, though it took all her effort. She wanted pictures, memories, thoughts. Sweat was beading her lip when she opened her eyes at last, frustrated. All that came was a vague feeling. 'I do not think you would harm a child,' she said heavily.

'Harm a child!' the girl repeated indignantly.

'Not even the son of a barbarian king?'

The girl's face was flushed by steam. 'No ... I would never ...'

Brónach nodded, covered the pot and got up to pull back the thick door-hide over its peg. A salty breeze rushed in, blowing the herbs away. She sighed as she sat. Every year the meagre glimpses of sight were harder to gain, when they should be easier. With age. With wisdom. She crushed that sharp pain. 'And the Latin teaching? Is that true also?'

The slave nodded, shivering. Then the girl surprised her, pointing at the rafters. 'My Mamo also taught me much of herb-lore,' she said, visibly firming her mouth. 'I looked after the children when they took sick. I nursed my Mamo ...' She trailed off.

Brónach's brows arched. This odd one got more interesting by the moment. Her face wasn't sly or stupid like most slaves, but strongly drawn and intelligent. Brónach folded her hands in her sleeves, resting her head back. 'Then we share something. There are many healers in my royal line. My ancestress lived here in another house long ago, and she was a queen and healer both.'

Silence fell. After a moment, something alert in Brónach wondered why this girl, as a stranger, a foreigner, did not grate against the harmony of the room. Instead, she was staring at the niche beside Brónach's door that held the goddess figurines. There were a clutch of them: Rhiannon the Great Mother; Brigid the healer; Ceridwen the crone, birth and death goddess; Andraste of war; Flidhais of the woods. Each was different, the pale clay yellowed with age, their feet stained with ochre and the residues of milk and split grain.

There was a light in the girl's eyes as she gazed at them that discomfited Brónach. Abruptly she rose. 'Come. You will not sleep here, but in the king's hall. I will show you.' She watched grimly as the slave's face fell.

King Cahir and Queen Maeve of Dalriada – the Alban kingdom of which Dunadd was the seat – had a son of thirteen and two daughters, one seven and one five, Brónach explained. Minna would teach Latin grammar, writing and history to them all – they already spoke the basic language because of their mother. The girls would be Minna's charge at all other times.

As Brónach strode along dispensing these scraps of information, Minna kept her eyes down, trying not to slip in the mud. The wind blew across the exposed crag, passing through her thin dress.

The old woman glanced at her. 'You are very lucky, slave-girl. The children had a nurse, but she died. Only the queen and a few Roman-loving nobles keep slaves here, let alone learned ones. It seems your timing was providential.'

'Died?'

'Died with child.' She stopped for a moment. 'It would not do for that to happen again,' she said pointedly. 'It is expensive for the queen and inconvenient for me.'

Mouth dry, Minna clambered up an even steeper set of steps, under the shadow of another arched gate, watching her feet, before she and Brónach emerged on the wind-blown crest of the crag.

The view of the marsh and hills spread in every direction, but Minna's attention was claimed by the enormous roundhouse which crowned the entire fort and which she had seen as she trudged along the riverbank. This timber hall of rough wattle-and-daub could not be compared to the elegant, columned forum at Eboracum, but its vast size and girth bellowed its majesty and power as it towered over the houses and the village below. The wind buffeted it on all sides, plucking at the weighted thatch roof, and still it stood there, immovable, impassive. A red and white banner streamed from its peak in the high wind.

Minna's new-found courage quailed.

A crescent of spears were planted before the double oak doors, each capped by a streamer of bristly hair. 'Boar crests,' Brónach remarked briskly. 'The king's totem.' Dropping her eyes, Minna hurried after her, past grotesquely leering heads carved into the door-posts.

On the threshold, they crossed from daylight into an immense smoky cavern. Two circles of oak posts held up the soaring roof, and a roaring fire sat in the centre. Brónach strode past servants stirring cauldrons, chopping roots and kneading bread. All paused to bow their heads to her.

Minna gained an impression of luxurious wall hangings and floor cushions, and shields and spears lining the walls, before Brónach led her up a set of wooden stairs.

A gallery ran around inside the thatch roof and tucked under the eaves were beds separated by wicker screens. The hole in the upper floor opened to the hall below, flooding the eaves with light and the heat of the hearthfire.

'The king's bed,' Brónach directed as she walked, waving a hand. Minna was rushed past, unable to see clearly. 'The queen's bed-place is down there at the end.' Meanwhile, Brónach had stopped at another bed, which was almost as wide as the gallery and was covered with blankets and pelts, flanked by chests strewn with dresses and shoes. The woollen face of a little doll peeped out from the pillows.

'You will sleep here with the princesses,' Brónach announced, the drowsy air of her house dispelled by this stream of orders. 'You are the queen's property. You will not speak to her unless she speaks to you. You will remain with the girls at all times, and teach them every morning after breaking the fast. Can you sew?'

Biting her lip, Minna sifted through her skills. 'I can sew basic things, but I cannot embroider,' she confessed. Mamo had done that for her. She briefly closed her eyes. 'I can teach the girls about herbs and healing, though.'

Brónach pondered. 'That is not a bad thing for a princess to learn, and the Mother knows I do not have the time for such indulgences.' She nodded sharply. 'As future queens, the girls will run their husbands' households, and some healing lore is useful for mothers.'

Minna held her breath, staring in mute entreaty at the little doll.

'You cannot take the girls out of the dun, the fort, for some time,' Brónach continued. 'Later perhaps, although you will always have to be accompanied by a guard. The Picts are our enemies, and we must be careful about raids even this close to the dun.'

Minna swallowed an exclamation. This was worse than any physical punishment. She needed to be outside, to walk in the woods, or she would wither away. The marsh and hills had felt threatening, cold and wind-swept, but she still remembered how the air of Alba had sung to her.

Brónach turned, her stern face caught by firelight. 'For now, stay close to the houses on the crag. You can no longer go where you wish.'

These words were like a douse of icy water. 'No,' Minna forced out. 'No longer.'

Brónach stared at her. 'You have not long been a slave.'

'I was stolen.' Bitterness loosened her tongue. 'A week ago I was as free as you.'

Brónach's gaze was fathomless. 'Life does not always give you what you yearn for, girl, though you sacrifice everything for it and strive with your very bones and blood.' A tense edge had crept into her voice as she grasped Minna's face with cold fingers. 'Now, I will give you a warning. We are not a cruel people and the queen does want your learning. You will find things only go hard with you the next time you use that bold tone or flash those eyes like that.'

Minna swallowed a lump in her throat and, when she was released, dropped her eyes. 'Of course, *domina*.'

'And don't use that Latin on me.' A hint of grim humour lightened Brónach's mouth. 'The queen is a princess of Luguvalium and that's why it pleases her. I, however, am the king's aunt, a Dalriadan of pure blood. You may call me lady.'

'Yes, lady.'

'If you have any questions, ask the maidservant Clíona. Don't bother me or the queen – she likes her children tidy and out of sight. Report to me every full moon, no more, no less.'

'Yes, lady.'

'Come. We will find the girls.' With an austere nod, Brónach sailed back down the stairs.

In a burst of inspiration, Minna grabbed the doll and tucked it under her arm.

Chapter 10

Brónach led her back down the first steps from the crag's crest and stopped halfway. A small platform was scooped out of the turf and Minna thought she must be dreaming, for this was surely a Roman building: a square hut with a pitched roof, albeit thatch, not tiles.

'The queen's hall,' Brónach said drily. 'She spends her days here.' Queen's hall and king's hall, side by side but a world apart.

They entered a miniature haven of Roman taste, with couches, walls painted with trailing vines and braziers of burning coals. A tiny window set with bubbled glass brought the light across the stone floor. Two children were running circles around the hearth, trailing wool for an unkempt grey puppy that leaped and snapped.

'Girls!' Brónach commanded in Latin. The children skidded to a halt, one scooping up the puppy. 'This is your new nurse and tutor, by order of your mother. Be polite to her.'

Minna was surprised by the look of disdain on Brónach's face, before the older woman turned back to her with a brusque flick of skirts. 'What is your name, girl?'

She told her, and Brónach grunted with approval. 'Something easy to say, at least.' She spoke sternly to the girls in their own language. With wide eyes they bobbed awkwardly. 'I will arrange the materials you need,' Brónach said to Minna on her way out, the grey light harsh in her slate eyes. 'For now, I've told the princesses they must assist you to settle in, and speak Latin. At dusk, seek out Clíona in the hall and she will see to food.'

'Yes, lady,' she murmured.

Gathering her cloak about her like wings, Brónach strode away.

Minna's shoulders lowered, as she regarded her new charges. The taller girl put the puppy down and it ran off around a couch, gripping the ball of wool and shaking it, growling.

As the children continued to stare at her, panic assailed Minna. What she needed was a small space to crawl into and rest her forehead on her knees. But here she had only one chance to secure a relationship with these barbarian children, and if she didn't, she would find herself in that warrior's bed. She ground words out. 'Well, then.'

The elder girl was gawky, with auburn braids framing a square jaw, her green eyes suspicious. The younger took after her mother, with creamy hair and a round face.

The elder crooked her hands on her hips, her little chest pushed out. 'I am Orla,' she said in Latin. 'It means golden princess. And I *am* the first princess, only *she* got the golden hair.' She pointed at her younger sister.

Minna wavered, but she must conquer this. 'Hail, Orla,' she murmured, then crouched down to eye level before the younger girl. She pulled the doll from under her arm. 'And who is this, then? She said hello when we met.'

The little girl's face lit up. 'Anya,' she whispered.

Orla was scandalized. 'Finola cannot bring Anya *outside*! Mama said she looks *stupid* with her. She is too old for dolls now.'

Minna gazed impassively into Orla's sharp face. 'Well, I have been given charge of you and Finola now, so I might change things a little.' As Orla's mouth dropped open, she rolled on. 'And for now I need Anya to tell me everything about the … dun. I don't speak your other language, so you will have to teach me.' She laid the doll in Finola's outstretched hands.

Orla's green eyes narrowed. 'I thought you were supposed to teach *us* things.'

'I am. But before I can do that I need to speak as you do. So you have the first job of being teacher, see.'

Finola beamed excitedly, while Orla scowled. 'We teach you,' she repeated.

'Yes.' Minna pointed to a spindle on a side table, and a basket of unspun wool. 'You can tell me the names of that and that and that in your language.' She indicated a pot of water on a tripod in the coals. 'And that and that.'

Finola clapped her hands together and pointed. 'Wool!' she cried. 'Fire!'

'This is stupid!' Orla pronounced, stamping her foot. 'I'll tell Mama.'

'If you like.' Minna kept her voice pleasant. Stupid was obviously a favourite word of this child. 'But we'll make it a game. Let's see who can give me the most names. Whoever wins will be shown how to write their name in Roman letters.'

'So what?'

'*So* when you know how to write your name, you can sign letters and orders, And ...' she leaned in close and whispered, 'you can write your name on things *so no one else can take them.*'

Both girls glanced accusingly at each other. Then Finola sidled to her knee, Anya cradled in one elbow. 'Spoon!' she cried. 'Bench! Rug! Wine!'

'That's six now, Finola. You're in front.'

From the corner of her eye, Minna saw Orla's mouth snap shut. She shoved herself in front of her sister. 'Let me do it. She doesn't know *anything*.'

Minna was lulled into a sense of safety by the familiar surroundings of the Roman room, but then she had to brave the dun itself, as Orla dragged her outside.

'Look!' the girl cried, pointing west. 'There's the marsh, where the birds live, and there's the sea.' Far across the plain, the bay where the boat had arrived was silver in the smoky dusk, speckled with black islands. Orla dashed up a small rise below the king's hall, to a rock slab exposed in the turf. 'See here, this is the royal footprint where the kings stand when they're crowned.' She put her small foot in the carving. With her shoulders back, she gazed gravely around.

Before Minna could do more than glance at the carving, Orla had clambered down the steep steps, crossed the green between the nobles' houses and raced up on top of the timber palisade that ran around the high crag. Minna followed more slowly. 'And there's the river,' Orla yelled, pointing to the north where the river curved around Dunadd in a wide arc, edged with russet trees.

Finola joined her. 'And *there's* the meadow, where the warriors train their horses.'

Grinning, Orla ran to the east, past two burly warriors pacing the palisade. They stopped speaking and stared at Minna. She hunched away. 'They are my father's men,' Orla declared proudly. 'Though he is *much* taller and his hair is the same colour as mine, and when he walks, they bow to him, and when he looks at them like this ...' her brows drew into an intent frown, 'then everyone goes quiet.' She pointed down at the village on the north-east corner, sheltered by the crag. 'There are the stables, and the storehouses for meat, and the granaries, and the smithy.' She dashed down the stairs and around the arched gate to tear up the palisade on the south.

Minna noted the stables and wondered desperately if Cian was all right. Taking a breath, she followed the girls. As she did so, a dog in a yard broke into frenzied barking, jumping up at her with snapping jaws, making her leap back. Disturbed by the noise, someone burst out of the house, and she came face to face with a native girl of around her own age.

The young woman waved a spindle threateningly at the dog, cursing, then her glower dissolved into curiosity as her eyes fell on Minna. She had never received such a bold, frank look before. The girl's fair hair was braided around a proud head, and rings flashed at her ears. She carried herself upright, but not stiff like Roman women, nor were her eyes cast down. Striding forward to cuff the barking dog, this girl walked freely, her arms and legs strong and loose.

'Minna!' Orla cried, and she hurried away, the woman's gaze resting on her back.

'The druids live there,' Orla declared, pointing south.

Minna squinted through the greyness at the ridge outside the dun scattered with thatched huts. On the flat of the marsh sat a circle of tall posts. *Druids*. She knew that word well, for the barbarian priests featured heavily in Mamo's tales, with their incantations, prophecies and divinations – and the Roman whispers of human sacrifice and lewd rites.

'Come,' Orla cried. 'There is more!'

Night fell early in the north. As darkness gathered, Minna hovered on the threshold of the king's hall, her heart pounding.

The great fire roared and torches stuck into the earth floor spilled light over the chaos. Servants rushed past with armloads of firewood, and maids plucked chickens as they gossiped, rubbing them with fat. Others stirred cauldrons, disappearing into clouds of steam when they lifted the lids. People bellowed to each other, kicking squabbling dogs aside as pots and pans crashed.

Minna shrunk back, then forced herself after Orla and Finola. They were hopping around a plump woman of middle age. Her feet were planted at the hearth as if rooted there, and her fair hair was damp from steam. Her finger jabbed about, ordering people, weaving the pattern of dashing servants like a squat, red-faced spider.

The woman paused to grab bowls from a stack and ladle in stew, shoving them at the princesses, who ran off. One gimlet eye swivelled towards Minna, and there was another bowl in those rough, red hands. 'Here.' The woman's voice was hoarse from yelling.

'Minna,' she stammered, pointing at herself.

The woman's eyes were set close together, like matrons gossiping in a doorway, missing nothing. 'Clíona.' She mimed eating, as if Minna were an imbecile, before her attention was claimed elsewhere and she turned away.

Minna found the girls on a bench set apart from the bustle. Behind them, the rugs and cushions gave way to alcoves piled with pots and baskets, and pallets of rough hides for beds. She sniffed the stew, relieved to smell fresh beef and thyme.

'Mama doesn't eat this.' Orla's chin went up, superior. Minna knew she wasn't a bad-tempered child, for she recognized hurt – as well as the defiance a girl cultivated to cover it. 'Mama has wine and … and …' Orla fumbled for the Latin words, '*chicken* and *oil* and *walnuts* off the ships, and that smelly fish sauce on everything.'

'*Garum*,' Minna supplied, trying to hear through the din. Logs rumbled into wood baskets, and the servants shouted at each other, everyone large and ruddy – even the women. Eventually one voice rose above the others: Clíona. Orla and Finola's faces fell.

Orla's voice changed, her lisp deepening into an uncanny imitation of the older maid. 'Mama has bathed in her hall and she is coming, so the servants must simmer down now or Clíona will box their ears with a spoon.' She looked at Minna. 'And we must be up the stairs and out of sight now. We bathe our faces in bed.'

'Bed,' Minna repeated slowly. Somewhere that did not shift on the waves, or stink of vomit. Exhaustion suddenly swamped her, down to her bones. 'How do you say it?'

Orla told her, and Minna placed the word carefully in her mind.

At first Minna found it hard to rest among the unfamiliar smokiness of tanned hides. The bracken mattress crackled, wafting up a pungent herb that she fervently hoped was to keep fleas away. The thatch was oppressively low over her head; she could see each piece of straw gilded by firelight. The girls wheezed and, at the foot of the bed, the grey puppy, solemnly introduced as Lia, whuffled in sleep.

At least the hall was quiet. Orla had explained that her father and brother Garvan were away touring the northern forts, taking oaths of allegiance from the chieftains. When they were gone, her mother banished her father's bard and warriors and sat with her own advisers, eating on a dining couch.

With only darkness for company, Minna's chest ached like a festering tooth, but she kept a stony face on the pillow.

Instinct said she must show courage in this place, whatever it cost. If she displayed weakness she felt she might be torn apart, like the bones Clíona had tossed to the floor, which were ripped into pieces by the snarling hounds.

The murmuring voices downstairs had long fallen silent when exhaustion at last overruled fear, and Minna tumbled into a dark sleep. Her weary soul wandered in blackness … blankness … nothingness. She sighed and surrendered the knots in her body …

… but suddenly men are struggling all around her in battle. The air is

rancid, the sun glowing red through a haze.

Minna-in-the-dream gulps for breath, as a horse shifts beneath her. Her thighs grip its flanks, and sweat runs along bare, muscled arms on the reins and down her face from her brows, flooding her mouth, washing away blood. She is lost in a sea of screaming men jostling and falling, leaping in, staggering back. Swords twist in bellies. Spears run slippery with blood, staking throats to the ground. Arms are hacked off, the sinews split.

'Lord!' someone cries. 'My prince, look to the east. More Romans have come!'

Minna-in-the-dream doesn't know the words ... she can't know... but she understands. And as she starts to turn in her saddle, shock crushes her chest, extinguishing the blood and stink and screams in one cry of despair ...

Orla was tugging on her shoulders. Minna swallowed the cry, scrabbling at the mattress. Everything smelled unfamiliar, and a roof was pressing down on her head ... *No. No.* In the way she had learned, her consciousness fought free of the vision, instantly flinging itself up and out into awareness. The images were cut off, and she grabbed the panic and shoved it down, stilling her flailing legs.

Only when she was rigid did she breathe out, unclenching her fists from the sheets. She turned to see Finola staring at her with enormous eyes, the puppy clutched to her chest. Orla sat back, her head nearly touching the sloping roof. 'You were thrashing and moaning,' she announced matter-of-factly. 'It woke us up.'

Minna pulled herself up, dragging fingers through her unbound hair. The sheets were damp with sweat. 'When you sleep somewhere new,' she stammered, 'sometimes it makes you restless.'

Orla shrugged and pointed at her sister. '*She* gets those dreams, too, and she cries really *stupid* things I don't understand.' Her teeth shone in the dim firelight from below. 'I see things when I'm awake, which is much cleverer.'

'I do, too!' Finola whispered, outraged.

Minna stiffened with astonishment. 'Awake?'

Orla plucked at the wool blanket. 'Mama says the dreams are the work of devils because that's what the Christian priests say. She wants a priest here, but Fa said the minute a priest came he would slit his throat.'

Finola pushed the puppy down as it tried to lick her. 'The Lady Brónach says it is a gift and not the work of devils, and Fa says listen to her this one time but don't tell Mama.' She raised her chin, lip trembling. 'But we don't talk about it, so none of them can get angry at us.' She glanced at Orla. 'We don't talk about it.'

Minna rested her chin on her knees. 'Your mother is Christian?' she ventured.

Orla nodded. 'Of course. The Emperor is Christian, and she says,' her voice slipped eerily into the shrill tones of the queen, 'by the tearing of her womb to give Fa his mewling children, she will have this family Christian one day, too.'

Minna swayed, light-headed. She still tasted blood. 'Do you want a priest?'

'*No!*' Orla hissed with childish passion. 'Last year our brother Garvan went with Fa to a council on the Wall and a boy there had a priest tutor and he had to study all sorts of nasty things.' She paused, breathing hard. 'I was *glad* when Fa said we could have no priest. He said to Mama if one comes here then ...' She made a cutting motion across her neck and now imitated a gruff man's voice. 'No head, no priest.'

When Minna stifled an exclamation, Orla hastily clarified, 'But Fa doesn't shout at us.'

'No?'

'We only make him smile, don't we, Finola, because when we grow up we're going to fight by his side with swords – he would love us for ever then. And *that's* why,' she finished, returning to her theme, 'we don't want any old priest, because Fa hates them.' She folded her arms. 'And we don't want to learn any nasty priest things from *you*.'

'Orla!' Finola squeaked, kicking her sister beneath the covers.

With a cry, Orla flung them back and delivered a pinch to her sister's arm. The younger girl burst into sobs; the puppy ran around the bed madly.

At long last Minna calmed the girls and got them to sleep. But she could not easily join them, for the tremors running through her.

She could still feel the dread that slammed into her belly in the vision, like a fist doubling her over. But she had never seen so much; never remembered it so vividly, felt it, tasted it, smelled it. What could it mean? That something had cracked open in her – perhaps she was going mad.

Minna lay down and cradled her cheek, eyes wide to the darkness.

Chapter 11

The next morning Minna ate a bread roll with gritty eyes, the hard dough forming a knot in her belly. 'Bannock,' Orla instructed through the crumbs. 'That's what we call them.'

She turned to run off with Finola, but Clíona's hands held both girls there as she turned to inspect Minna. Clíona was deceiving, that plump body, gold hair and milky skin suggesting softness. But there was nothing soft about this woman: her square hands were reddened, her brows lowered.

Through Orla, Clíona told her she must care for the girls' clothes and baths once a week, learn to cook bannocks on the hearth-stone and porridge in the pot, and when she wasn't busy with them, bring firewood and grind grain and any other things she saw fit.

Minna had never been ordered this way. Ashamed, her fingers brushed the welt on her neck, stinging after her restless night. Clíona saw and pointed at a small clay pot. This time Minna caught one in five of her words. The woman mimed rubbing something between her hands. 'Sheep fat. Skin.' She pointed at the slave-ring. 'Help skin.'

'She said—' Orla began, but Minna cut her off.

'I heard what she said.' She didn't know what to make of this unexpected kindness, until Clíona shrugged and said something else before turning away.

'She says if that chafing turns into a wound you'll be no use to anyone.'

Minna halted the sinking of her belly. She was just the same now as the pigs that gave meat, the cows that gave milk and the geese that gave feathers. Just the same, and no more.

Two weeks slid by with Minna confined to the king's hall, the tiny shed she had taken over for the lessons, and the waste-pit on the cliff edge. At first she only spoke to the girls. The queen was still asleep when they all crept down in the morning, and they were abed when she came into the king's hall at night.

Clíona barked only brief orders at her, but now and again she caught the maid watching her, as did all the servants. Wondering, Minna supposed, whether she would sink or swim. She thought of Cian's last words to her: *Swim as hard as you can, until I can get us out of here.* He was her only – albeit tenuous – link to home. And he had risked himself to save her, despite his brittle sarcasm and scorn of loyalty. She clung to those words and the last sight of his pale face.

After a few days, Clíona sent one of the servants to teach Minna her tasks. Keeva was around her age, but small, with a wiry build, black hair and dark eyes. She wore her hair in a side-braid threaded with gull feathers, which, according to Orla, denoted her as Attacotti, a tribe allied to the Dalriadans who lived on islands in the western sea. She was quick-witted and sharp-tongued, and studied Minna with great suspicion.

Beneath those beady eyes, Minna threw herself into working hard, pride prodding her to prove all the servants wrong. After a week, her dress was stained with a mix of salt, meat blood, flour and mud, the old wool already wearing through into holes.

Sniffing disdainfully, Clíona dug out a pile of old clothes from the storage baskets, indicating that Minna should pick what she wanted. After a wary moment she pounced on two pairs of worn deer-hide trousers – for to her surprise women wore them here – tunics in a dull brown check, a flax belt and a hooded cloak of rough, undyed wool. Avoiding her eyes, Clíona also threw in some sheepskin boots. Minna gratefully peeled off her muddy sandals and dug her toes into the warm wool. The wind was growing more bitter up on the crag, blowing in blustery sheets of rain.

Minna's attempts to speak Dalriadan were clearly frustrating Keeva and she seemed to assign herself to setting that right first, instructing her as they worked side by side. Between Keeva, Finola and Orla it wasn't long therefore before she was swiftly picking up the barbarian speech. Uncannily swiftly.

Minna told herself it must be because of Mamo, shrugging away the unease at how familiar it felt. Mamo's tales had many words from Erin, and Erin is where the Dalriadans came from, Orla said.

As the days passed, she gradually sank into the sea of language around her, snatching at meanings until words resolved into sentences and then sense. Fluency came easily, as if floating up from inside her. She spent her days asking and listening, leaving no time for anything else to make its way in.

She did it to exhaust her mind, so the only time she was alone, in bed, she prayed to the Mother Goddess for Cian and then curled into a ball, fleeing grief. Hiding in sleep.

The sky clouded over from the sea, and when storm rain began to pour down one day Minna thought she might at last be able to slip unnoticed to the village to seek out Cian. After all, she wasn't leaving the dun, as Brónach had expressly forbidden, just the crag, and since everyone was inside for once there was no one to see her go. The drops pounded the earth so hard the air was a curtain of needles, echoing her frightened, thudding heart. The few who braved the sodden paths were buried in cloaks, heads down. The guards at the rock arch were huddled in their tower, no longer pacing the walls.

The land all around the crag was obscured by rain, the thatched roofs streaming. Minna leaped over muddy rivulets and edged under dripping eaves. She kept pausing to listen and found the stables by the whinnies of the horses – and the smell.

The doors at each end of the long building were propped open for air. Avoiding the end where the horse-boys diced and cleaned tack, Minna went to the other side of the stables and discovered Cian in an empty stall on his own.

He was sitting in the straw against the wall, eyes closed, head back. The first thing she saw was the vivid purple bruise along one cheek and other, fading marks over his neck and jaw. She sank on her knees beside him. His eyes opened quickly, flashing with an instinctive, wild defiance. 'Oh ...' she breathed, and went to touch the bruise, as if she might soothe it.

He jerked his head away, avoiding her eyes. 'Don't.'

She sat back, crooking her arms about her knees. His tunic was smeared with blood and manure, and he had no knife or shears so his jaw was shadowed with stubble, his black hair longer and matted with straw. 'How did this happen? This wasn't ... your master?'

'Not yet.' His smile was bitter as he tilted his head towards the horse-boys. 'Little bastards down the other end don't take kindly to being bettered by a Roman, that's all.'

'Bettered?'

'I'm the best rider by far. And I curse them in words they can't understand.' He shrugged. 'I can hold my own against two or three, but ten ...' The others were boys of thirteen and fourteen, scrappy and bold.

Her eyes fell to the scabs across his knuckles, and a pang of fear for him loosened her tongue. 'You told me we had to swim.' His head came around, his eyes sparking dangerously, but she ploughed on. 'I thought you meant ... well ... keeping our eyes down and our mouths shut, biding our time.'

A desperate anger flared in his face. 'Don't tell me what to do, Tiger. You don't know ... anything.' He bit off his words.

'Then tell me what I don't know,' she whispered. All this time she had been struggling to make her way here, trying to keep her mind blank, and he had been suffering like this.

He merely turned away, his chin jutting out. 'Surely it's better not to provoke them,' she said softly. 'Or they might hurt you worse.'

He stared out of the open door. 'You have to show these people that you have no fear, or they will be on you like a pack of wild dogs. You don't know what they can do: they're animals.' The loathing in his voice turned her stomach, and she searched what she could see of his face, confused by this change in him.

His humour had often been self-deprecating, his smiles sardonic. But now a mask had been torn away and it was raw anger that beat upon her senses. Her belly twisted with a frightening, instinctive revulsion. How could she feel that for Cian, who had saved her, who had teased her? Only now he wasn't teasing, and there was darkness in his face beyond the bruises, a pressure in the air about him that thrust her back.

After a moment the tension went out of him and he sighed, pressing his head back against the wall. 'I'm sorry, Tiger. I just ... hate ...' He stopped himself, forced a bleak smile that went nowhere near his eyes. 'I hate this.' He touched the slave-ring around his neck.

Gingerly she curled up beside him, relieved by the hint of smile. 'Me, too.' They both gazed out into the rain, their combined frustration so heavy it was almost tangible.

'They are bloodthirsty savages,' Cian hissed after a while, 'and we are going to get out of here and find our way back home to civilized lands, and never see another filthy, stinking barbarian in all our lives.'

She understood the words, but all that came to Minna in that moment was that she had no real home to go to. As the rain hammered the earth outside, they sat and watched without speaking again.

Chapter 12

'**F**inola,' Minna prodded. 'Answer me.'

The dreary rain had trapped them inside for days at their lessons. This meant that both girls could now write their names, and that Minna had grown more fluent in their own language. However, though Orla galloped swiftly along with her astonishing memory for language and letters, Finola struggled, often slipping into a dreamy state, staring into space.

Now it was late afternoon and needles of rain pattered on the tiny window in a drowsy rhythm. The heat of the small fire in the corner had thickened the air; the puppy Lia dozed in a basket. Finola was gazing at the window, eyes glassy, small white hands spread over the sheet of birch bark on the table.

Minna put aside her charcoal and brushed her dusty fingers. 'Finola,' she repeated sharply, pressing a hand against the girl's cheek. It was burning. She waved her fingers before Finola's vacant eyes.

'She's seeing.' Orla squirmed under Minna's elbow and poked her sister's shoulder. 'Finola, wake up!'

Finola blinked, and her body went rigid from feet to head. 'Sails ...' she whispered, her soft mouth quivering. 'There are sails and boats and red men and ... the swords hurt, they hurt!' Then her eyes rolled back and she shrieked, 'No, *no!*' and tossed herself over before Minna could stop her, striking her head on the bench.

'Finola!' Minna cried, taking the child in her arms. At her touch Finola shuddered and broke into sobs, her eyelids fluttering. *Goddess ...* She raised Finola's chin, brushing back her wispy hair. Just above the child's temple the skin was marred by a trickle of blood and a bruise. 'There, little one,' she soothed. The child wailed, her arms hanging onto her neck. Slowly, Minna dragged herself up, the puppy jumping up her legs, yipping excitedly.

'She hurt her head,' Orla observed.

'I know,' she replied unsteadily. 'We will have to get it seen to. Here, take her cloak and help me wrap it around her. And put that dog back in its basket.'

Minna's knees shook as she staggered under Finola's weight, the whimpering girl clinging to her like a limpet as Orla trotted beside her. She had to brave Brónach's house. The refrain ran through her mind. She had only seen the old lady from afar – a full moon not having passed yet. And now she must come to her with *this*. A royal princess injured in her care.

She paused at the healer's door, moistening her dry lips. Orla put her head beneath the door-hide, then leaned back and shook it. Inside, the room smelled only of herbs and peat: Brónach was away.

Minna tipped Finola onto the sick bed, surveying the room. The pulse of energy she had felt in this house was here again, raising goosebumps on her arms. 'Orla, take that pan and fill it with water, then set it on the coals.' With one look at her face, Orla ran to do her bidding. Minna pressed her hair against her temples, staring down at Finola. The bruise had spread and sweat dampened the little girl's dress. *Think!* she berated herself. *Act!*

Her heart hammering, she stood before Brónach's workbench. The herb bunches were curled and dry from the fire, their leaves shrivelled. Tentatively, she reached to bowls on the bench and jars on the shelves, peeling back lids to smell, dust powder on her fingertips, slick unguent on her wrists. The answer was here, somewhere, but so many plants were unfamiliar to her, the way they were prepared unusual.

Then, gradually, a kind of trance crept over Minna, and her panic began to dissolve into the swirl of musky scents. Her spinning mind slowed, then paused, suspended. Her eyelids closed as if pressed by an invisible hand, and it was her fingers and nose and some other sense that reached for what she needed. A jar here: she pushed it to one side. And here, a glass vial, and there, a bark packet that crackled as she unrolled it. Then her fingers sought of their own accord a bundle of leaves and stalks tied to a post with twine.

In this haze, time moved peculiarly. As she ordered Orla to stir the pot, Minna pressed raw leaves into a mortar. When the scent was released, a song came to hover on her lips, rising and falling in the back of her throat. Distantly, she knew that the song was meant to call to the life in the plants, the … the *source* of it all … and draw it up so it would give that same life to a child's blood. She knew the song as she had known the language; she unconsciously understood how the bubbling water and rhythmic grinding of pulp in the mortar went perfectly together.

73

The song was spun thread, knitting everything into a shimmering weave. A pattern that would heal.

At some stage – how much later? – she slowly became aware of Brónach standing before her. The old woman brought the smell of night mist with her, clinging about her cloak and hair. Her cold, grey eyes were boring into Minna.

Minna stirred and sat up. She had been slumped on the sickbed beside Finola, and Orla was curled asleep on the hearth cushions.

'What are you doing here?' Brónach's voice tore the remnants of the veil, the song, from her heart.

She rubbed her eyes, her gaze straying to Finola. The girl was asleep, breathing deeply. 'The princess had a fever, and then she fell and hit her head . . .' She trailed off.

Above Finola's brow a lumpy compress trickled dark green liquid down her cheek. Beside the bed, an empty bronze pan with speckled dregs stood on a three-legged table. Minna didn't remember doing any of these things clearly, but in the hours since, the heat had faded from Finola's face.

Brónach picked up the pan and sniffed it, then leaned over the bandage on Finola's brow-bone. She dabbed at the liquid and touched it to her tongue before finally sitting down on the bed and regarding Minna with a set face. 'What did you use for the fever?' They had both slipped into Dalriadan.

'I . . .' Minna bit her lip, then took up the pan herself and sniffed it. 'The one with the little white flowers, that grows tall . . . I think.'

'There is more than that,' Brónach snapped. 'Why use the sun stalk? Why that? I keep it for stomach troubles and the flux.'

Minna was pinned there by the intensity of her stony gaze. 'I don't know. I don't even know the plant of which you speak.'

Brónach flung out a bony finger. 'Show it to me!' she demanded. 'You must know it if you plucked it.'

Her eyes followed that finger to the roof-posts. 'I don't know,' she confessed, just as confounded as Brónach. Now, all the bunches looked the same, a mass of dull green twigs and leaves. 'It . . . it called to me to take it. It wanted me to.' Her voice subsided in embarrassment.

Brónach's breathing had quickened. 'And the poultice? You've used noon-flower and long-hood together. Why together?'

'I don't know,' she repeated helplessly.

'I would not have thought that,' Brónach murmured to herself, studying Finola's face. 'It keeps the fleas away, but that is all.' She pulled up the edge of the bandage, peering at the skin. 'How bad was the fall?'

'Bad. She had some kind of dream, a fit. She fell to the ground

74

before I could catch her, and her head cracked the bench. It bled and there was a dark bruise.'

'There is no bruise now.'

Chewing her lip, Minna craned to see. Beneath the pulped herb, the angry colour had been leached from the cut. The only bruise was a sliver of purple around its edges. Abruptly, Brónach replaced the bandage and peeled off her cloak. The sleeves of her blue dress were rolled up, exposing her wrists. In the glow of the coals Minna could see dark stains on her palms and nails.

'So,' Brónach murmured, 'you know not only the plants, but how to use them.'

Minna stared down at the floor rushes. What she had done for the boys, treating their scrapes and sniffles with the same herbs everyone used, bore no relation to *this,* the blossoming of knowing inside her, the way her hands had moved without her conscious direction. A tremor ran over her. 'I truly did not know what I was doing.'

'And yet the fever and bruise you say she had is gone. This is not someone who knows nothing.'

Minna rubbed her face again, exhausted.

'Do not fear me, child,' Brónach said softly.

She lowered her hands slowly, so she did not have to look up. This unexpected thing was too tender to be exposed to this woman's hard gaze, but she could not escape.

Suddenly, Brónach strode to the workbench and searching among the clay jars peeled off a waxen lid, waving it at Minna. 'Smell that and tell me what it is.'

Resentment pierced her weariness. 'At home ...' she said slowly in the barbarian speech, 'it is the tongue of the ... the dog. Dog's tongue.'

'What about that?' The old woman pointed a bony finger at a scattering of leaves to one side. Minna knew the plant, but not the barbarian name. Anger flared again. 'I don't know.'

'That, then.'

'I don't know.'

'Oh, come, girl!' Brónach snapped. 'Are you as witless as a slave?'

That was enough; Minna was on her feet, her cheeks flaming. 'That is thyme, then. We have it on the moors at home. That we call knit-bone, and that golden head. That we use for wounds and broken bones, and that for fever.' The words spilled from her, hot and proud. Let Brónach see what was there, then; that she had not always been a slave.

The older woman stared. She had said once never to speak so boldly. Suddenly deflated, Minna swallowed her words.

But Brónach did not seem angry. 'So you did not lie.' She walked stiffly around and sank into her chair. 'About the herb-lore.'

'No.'

Brónach tented her fingers under her chin. 'I would say,' she observed, 'that you are a girl who does not like to be confined.'

'I have no choice about that.'

'True.' Brónach pursed her lips and abruptly changed tack. 'You may wonder why I have no one to assist me.'

Minna had barely thought of this lady at all, too consumed by her own survival.

'It is simple. No one has shown any interest or aptitude, but more than that, I couldn't stand having some simpering maid around who did not know how to hold her tongue. A slave, though,' Brónach mused to herself. 'I never thought of that. A learned slave.'

Understanding flooded Minna's mind, as if she could hear the old woman's thoughts. *A slave has no rights. A slave will not speak unless spoken to. A slave is a pair of hands, not a mind or a heart.*

Brónach moistened her lips. 'If you know that many of the more uncommon plants, do you also know the mushrooms?' At Minna's blank look, she added impatiently, 'The pale cups that grow on logs? And berries ... the little things like this, red, orange or black? It is late in the year, but there is still much to gather. Do you know these things, the ones that heal?'

'Some of them,' she replied warily.

'Good. Then you will gather what is left before the frosts come, when I do not care to face the woods and moors.'

Her anger was eclipsed by hope. She needed fresh air, the outside world, as she needed food. 'I would be honoured,' she replied breathlessly. 'Though it may be hard to find time. I am with the girls teaching, and then I have other tasks.'

Brónach's eyes were like two wet pebbles. 'And was it not you arguing with me that the princesses will benefit from the herb-lore? The queen is much occupied – as long as they are alive and being Romanized she will be content. As for your chores, this is more important than the others.' She glanced towards the door, where cold night crept under the hide. 'The snows will come soon, and of course I move ... less swiftly than I did.' That admission seemed to cost her; she looked as if she had swallowed something bitter. Without another word she briskly emptied a net bag and gave it to Minna, along with a digging stick and a pair of iron shears, the points blunted.

Looped over her shoulders, the net bag with the heavy shears swung against Minna's thigh. The digging stick settled into her hand as if her palm had worn its shape smooth for years.

As if it knew who she was.

The next day was cloudy but dry. Finola was still resting, and Brónach said she would watch her so Minna could go gathering plants. Orla was darting fearful glances at her grim great-aunt, so Minna wrapped her up and took her as well. She clutched her digging stick to give her strength: this was the first time she was venturing off the crag.

They were nearly at the arched gate in the rock wall when the queen appeared on the path below, accompanied by an older man. For a moment Minna thought he might be the king returned from his travels, but the girls spoke of their father as some awe-inspiring, splendid god, and when Orla spotted this man she froze. Minna remembered then she had glimpsed him in the hall with the queen.

Maeve waved an indolent hand as she walked, so deep in conversation she did not at first see them. 'The timing would not be good,' she murmured in Latin. 'There is a council soon; we should wait and see what transpires.'

'The king will only dance along that thin line again,' the man replied silkily. 'He chooses neither one way nor the other. His hand may need to be forced.' The man was as polished as his accent, with trimmed, greying hair and a neat, pointed beard. He wore a white Roman tunic and sober cloak, with one subtle bronze pin. Like the queen he smelled of oils and unguents.

The two saw Minna with Orla and stopped. 'Daughter.' Orla pressed into Minna's side as the queen's kohl-rimmed eyes fluttered over her like restless butterflies, searching for something more interesting on which to alight. It was Minna. 'By the sacred Christos, girl, you look like one of my husband's scouts!' She frowned. 'Can you not dress more fittingly?'

Minna's face remained still; she was learning. 'I need to be so dressed to keep up with your daughters, *domina*,' she improvised swiftly. Nikomedes' words rolled off her tongue. 'The Greeks teach that young people must be active in the outdoors for their good health, and the discharge of excess energy keeps them obedient.'

The queen snorted, eyes already fluttering away, bored. The man's gaze, however, sharpened. '*Domina*: how nice to hear such an address,' he murmured. 'It reminds one of home.' Beneath a domed forehead his grey brows were two extravagant sweeps, but his dark eyes were small and cold.

'Yes, Lord Oran, the traders bought me a new slave – a Roman girl of some education, if you would believe.' The queen flashed a sly smile at him. 'How amusing when Cahir finds out what has dropped in my lap, with no effort on my part! We needed a new nurse, after all.'

Minna's attention was caught by the reference to herself as a 'what' rather than 'who.' Her hand tightened around the digging stick.

'And how are your lessons coming?' Maeve addressed her daughter.

'Well, Mama,' Orla answered in a tiny voice. Her grip on Minna's hand was numbing.

'It has not been long, *domina*,' Minna interrupted hastily. 'But we have started learning some letters already. The girls are very well-behaved.'

And they were, even the headstrong Orla, trying already to please Minna and make her smile with approval. She had supposed it was because they were starved of attention, like neglected plants in a garden. Seeing Orla with her mother, she knew she was right.

'Writing?' Maeve repeated distractedly. 'Ah, good, though it is when Garvan returns that your real work begins, of course.'

The Lord Oran's eyes remained on Minna. 'And where are you going with the princess, girl?'

Minna dropped her chin, belatedly remembering the demeanour of slaves. 'For her exercise, as well as learning, we are going into the woods after herbs, at the request of the Lady Brónach.'

'Then you must be well-guarded.' The Lord Oran hooked one hand in his belt. 'Your charges are valuable to us. Do take care.'

Maeve waved them on, falling back into conversation with Oran, their two heads close together. 'So when?' Minna heard behind her, in a whisper.

Chapter 13

Minna's shoulders drew up as she and Orla approached the village gates. People flowed back and forth under the towers, leading stamping horses to stable, loading sacks of seed into carts, chasing after children.

She imagined all those eyes on her, but when she raised her head they weren't paying her any attention, of course. A pallid sun had cleared the clouds, and women were hurriedly boiling sheets and hanging them between the houses, beating rugs and cushions, raking up the tiny yards to gather turnips and the last beans. The smith's hammer clanged as they passed the forge, hoes lined against the wall for repair, for it was sowing time, Orla said.

'Hurry up!' she cried, dashing for the stairs that led on to the timber palisade. 'Come and see.'

Minna reluctantly followed, but at the top she stopped, paralysed. The walls were awash with warriors, their polished swords, spears and shields flashing in the sun. A group of young ones lounged about playing dice and, despite the early hour, slugging ale. Older men paced the gate-towers, leaning on their spears to gaze sternly over the shining river.

Orla dashed between them all, unafraid, but Minna's legs would not move as the men stopped talking and stared boldly at her. One caught Orla's cloak as she flew by. 'Ho, little princess, what are you doing up here this fine day?'

Minna could just follow what he said. He was very young, with flaming red hair that reminded her of Broc. Orla grinned broadly. 'I am showing Minna the walls, because she doesn't know anything, and then we are going to pick plants.'

This gained the attention of a guard at the gatetower. 'I have orders that you must not go anywhere without an escort, princess.'

After a pause, a young voice cried, 'I'll go!'

A burst of laughter followed. 'And a fine protector you'll make, boy,' someone taunted. 'You have to be able to *lift* that sword of yours if the Picts come!'

The laughter swelled. Out of the corner of her lowered eyes Minna saw a fist come flying and a kick being returned. She shrank back against the palisade.

'Though it seems that's all we're good for,' another young warrior muttered, leaning in and dropping his voice. 'So our king gives us naught to do now but babysit little girls and pretty slaves.'

The murmured responses were grim, and the older warrior at the gate frowned, the lines across his sun-burned forehead deepening. Then the clack of dice was cut by a ringing voice, as fair as struck glass. 'You squabble like wolf-pups, my friends. Enough!'

Orla's face lit up, and she stood on tip-toe to see over the palisade. Minna joined her, clenching one of the oak stakes. Sitting tall on a black horse before the gates was Cian's new master. Her fingers curled up, pricking her palm on the rough wood. Not him.

'Ruarc,' the older guard greeted him, his voice carefully even. 'I am surprised you can pull yourself away from that beast at all. If its coat was any shinier, you could curl your hair in it.'

This elicited a great shout of laughter, and the young men downed their dice and draped themselves over the palisade. 'He's right, Ruarc,' one called. 'You wash that horse more than you wash your own balls!'

'That may be because he gets so *personal* with it. Have to make it smell pretty as a maid, eh, Ruarc?'

'Prettier than a maid, I reckon.'

Ruarc bared his teeth in a mocking smile. Again he was resplendent in a yellow tunic that matched his hair, his posture nonchalant, supremely confident. The horse side-stepped nervously at the laughter, until someone stepped from behind to catch the bridle. Cian.

There was a new cut under his other eye, and his bruises were now a sickly, mottled green. He saw Minna, and answered her stricken stare with a thin half-smile. He hadn't listened.

Ruarc's green eyes flicked between them, and he turned to Cian. 'Stop loitering, boy, and making moon eyes at the girl, or it'll be my fist blushing your other cheek.'

Cian's face suffused with blood as the warriors guffawed. Minna's nails bit into her palms; she grabbed Orla's hand and nudged her down the stairs, then braced herself as they walked out under the gate arch.

Ruarc's eyes followed her. With one graceful movement he dismounted and tossed the reins at Cian, who led the horse away with a last, unreadable glance at Minna.

'Ruarc,' Orla demanded, 'can't we take him? Can't I ride him?'

Ruarc patted her head, his other hand resting on the ornate hilt of his sword. 'Not now, little one. He's a stallion, and you'd need to be a trifle taller first.'

Eyes on her feet, Minna flicked her gaze to the side. Ruarc's hair was gilded, his skin burnished, but up close she saw he was only a few years older than her, which made the awe in which he was held by the men more surprising. He looked like Apollo, the sun-god, though whereas Apollo was a healer, a law-giver, this golden snake could strike at any time.

'Ardal!' he bellowed, beckoning to someone on the walls. 'And you, Mellan, and Lorcan: you are the lucky fellows to play escort today.'

'What about you, Ruarc?' someone taunted.

Ruarc traced a heated gaze over Minna's body, his fingertip lightly touching her chin. He smiled as she went rigid, then carelessly dropped his hand. 'Oh, I have better things to do than play nursemaid for our king.' Then he winked at Orla and turned away, his interest cooling as swiftly as it came.

Minna was swamped by relief, though it swiftly died when the other warriors came bounding out, brash and loud, eying her up and down.

At first, it seemed she would be left alone.

They crossed the river on a crude wooden bridge. The three warriors crouched beside the rushing water, muttering to each other, as Orla played in the wet autumn leaves. Minna hunted for mushrooms and any interesting plants, trailing stalks indicating roots below ground. She picked scarlet rowan-berries, juniper and hawthorn. She kept one eye on the warriors and one on the ground, but after a while she forget the men altogether, for the feel of the plants and the fresh, cold air soon took her mind away.

Fields spread north of the river, the furrows dotted with people sowing seed and raking cartloads of stinking seaweed into the fallow soil. Woods of red and gold edged them, and to these Minna was drawn, winding between the alders and feathery birches to copses of oak.

She knelt, the earth staining her fingers, absorbed in the scents of damp leaf-mould and wet wood. In the silence, with only the wind in the trees, it was then she heard the call.

Like a note plucked on a ghostly lyre string, a fine, high chord quivered in the air. It came from everywhere around her ... and nowhere. *The land sang.*

She straightened, her pulse quickening. She slowly rose, holding to the bole of a hazel tree. The snatch of airy music came again, and in the next silence she was tugged onwards, pushing her way through the trees, nudging branches aside more urgently until they began to thin.

Out to the north the woods gave way again to pasture, and at last she stepped into the open.

Minna's very breath, voice and thoughts were simply taken from her. The land that had been clouded by rain for weeks was suddenly revealed to her in all its sunlit glory, and above it reared the majesty of the mountains, unveiled for the first time. Every colour was ablaze as if Alba were on fire, from the flame of the red bracken to the golden crowns of birches. The hills curved up from gilded woods to vast expanses of russet slopes and bare scree, and finally to soaring peaks crusted with snow.

She could do nothing but sink to her knees. That blaze spoke to her own soul: her vivid heart was reflected in those colours, her strength echoed in the hills. And the wind-song was no longer ethereal now but demanding, insisting that she listen. It said, *don't forget ... remember who ...*

The warrior called Lorcan stepped in front of her.

Minna flinched back, but he swiftly crouched down, bracing himself against a tree trunk as he groped her arm. 'Come, girl,' he murmured, with a knowing grin and intent eyes. 'You look pale – perhaps you should come back into the trees.'

His hand brushed her breast. Brónach's words arrowed into her mind: *The nurse died with child.* Her nerves leaped, and she didn't pause to think as the shears flashed up then down, one blade catching the edge of the youth's hand as it buried itself in the bark.

For a moment they both stared at the welling blood, equally astonished. As the youth's eyes widened, his face contorting, she staggered to her feet, holding the shears before her like a sword. Their blades glistened with blood.

'You little ... *bitch!*'

He stepped towards her with his other hand raised to strike, but instantly Minna felt words rise to her lips from a well-spring inside. 'Ná déan é, a mhic.' *Don't do it, my son.* 'Onóróidh tú an mháthair.' *You will honour the Mother.*

The shears wavered between them. 'By Rhiannon,' she muttered desperately, not knowing what she said. 'By Hawen, by Manannán.'

Shock clouded Lorcan's eyes, followed by fear. He edged back, muttered something to himself. Then, his cheeks mottled with embarrassment, he stalked away.

'Minna!' Orla shouted from the distant riverside.

When she emerged on the river meadow, the young warrior was already striding angrily ahead, his friends laughing and pummelling his arm as he cradled his hand to his chest. Orla's eyes were large as platters, but after one look at Minna's face she swallowed her chatter, hurrying alongside.

Minna walked fast, her eyes blurred, the net bag banging on her thigh. When she reached the bridge she stopped. 'Orla.' Her voice quavered. 'Who is Rhiannon? Who are Hawen and Manannán?'

Orla smiled, relieved. 'In Alba Rhiannon is the great goddess, the Mother Goddess,' she explained. *Honour the Mother.* 'Manannán is the sea-god, her husband, and Hawen is the boar god of the warriors. They revere him and take his name as an oath.'

A loud shout from the gates interrupted Minna's wonder. As Orla raced ahead, she drifted along behind. When they got to the gatetowers, people were talking excitedly.

'Fa is coming home!' Orla shrieked, and hurried inside to tell Finola.

The warriors that had accompanied Minna leaped up the stairs with no glance for her, their faces grim.

Minna's feet, however, were rooted to the spot. For above the gates a banner hung, scarlet and red. She knew it must have been there before, but the only time she had entered these gates she was staring at her feet.

Now the wind was blowing straight from those fiery mountains, and the banner spread over her head against the sky, unfurled. A red boar was caught racing furiously across a white field, crest raised in attack. It drove every other thought from Minna's head.

The Boar! The Boar! The cry she had uttered by Mamo's deathbed.

Chapter 14

It was a freezing dawn, the grasses white-tipped on the meadow.

Up in the gallery of his hall, Cahir, King of Dalriada, unbuckled his sword-belt and flung it wearily to the chair. This small space for two seats and a brazier was his only retreat from the sharp eyes that were always following him: servants, warriors, druids, nobles. Everyone watching him, all the time.

At least he didn't have to face his wife yet, he thought with a grim smile, listening to Maeve's faint snores further along the gallery. Judging by the volume, she had guzzled her usual bucket of Roman wine last night.

Cahir massaged the knee which played up when he rode, then caught himself doing it and frowned. When tired he often slipped into thinking himself old, even though he was barely past thirty. He briskly stirred up the coals instead and left the poker in to heat the mead. There. He sat back. One moment with no one staring at him. One moment with no one trying to look inside him while masking their own thoughts. He leaned his head back and closed his eyes. Five heartbeats. Nothing.

'Fa!' Orla squealed, dashing over in her night-shift and throwing herself across his lap. His little Finola followed, padding up on baby feet.

Cahir mustered a tired smile. 'Hush, lass. You don't want to wake your mother, do you?'

That always quieted them.

'Did you just come back?' Orla asked, in a loud whisper.

Tenderly, he nodded and smoothed her braids. She was the only child with hair like his, dark with an auburn tinge. Finola, clutching her doll, gazed up as if his size and sword and smell of horse scared her, but that wouldn't last. Though she resembled Maeve, his younger daughter had a heart as courageous as the elder. If only it was his son who looked up so adoringly, desperate to wield a sword for him like these foolish, brave daughters of his.

Cahir drew Finola close with one arm, and, after a moment, she melted into his side. 'Did you see the Wall?' she whispered.

'Not this time, but I've seen it many times before.' Cahir tried to hide the roughening of his voice. 'The Wall is tall and grey, I told you, and long like an eel.'

'Taller than you, Fa?'

Cahir's heart stopped. Those trusting eyes only made the rest of his life seem so barren, full of treachery, compromises and betrayals. 'No, not taller than me,' he said, as if a simple lie could make the Wall shrink, the Roman soldiers on it fade away. As if he could shield his children from the swords that one day must come for them, along with Roman ships massing in the bay and fires blooming like scarlet flowers on the thatch.

For Cahir had already seen with his own eyes Alban land laid waste by Rome, and Alban bodies hung from trees with Roman rope.

Minna heard the girls gasp, 'Fa!' and bound from bed.

She roused herself, pulling a wrap around her shoulders and going to follow them. Then a deep voice sounded like a bell, and she slowed her steps. The voice rumbled again, answered by the girls in tones of affection she had never heard them use, except when they spoke of . . . their father.

Holding her breath, she crept to the wicker screen that shielded the alcove and pressed her eye to a gap.

The brazier was small, the coals dim, so it was hard to see him. His face tilted as he spoke and dark hair fell over his shadowed cheeks. She could only make out a glimpse of clean-angled jaw and nose. Why, he wasn't old at all. Then he moved back, the firelight gilding his outline, and Minna's thoughts stopped altogether.

Everything she had ever heard of barbarians and Albans, even men, collided with each other in her mind.

She could see how powerfully built he was, clad in polished mail, with muddy boots laced up long, sprawling legs. Next to him leaned a daunting sword in a battered scabbard – blood-stained, she was sure. But in the midst of all that his hands moved gently, tenderly stroking through Finola's hair, then cradling Orla's chin. The clash was so unexpected that for a long moment Minna's eyes simply followed those rhythmic fingers back and forth, mesmerized.

And he was entirely still apart from his hands, though she could sense the force that would be unleashed by those arms and shoulders, built up far beyond those of the men she knew who worked the villa fields. She must be scared, for her stomach lurched in a sickening way. This man was the leader of the tribe which had enslaved her. He was a bloodthirsty savage. She had anticipated being repulsed. Minna turned her cheek to the darkness, unable to keep her eyes on that gentle stroking.

After a moment, the king said he was filthy and the water downstairs would be boiling so he must wash. He wanted his daughters back in bed until it was light.

Minna crept away before he saw her. When the girls crawled into bed, even though they were whispering with excitement they soon dutifully returned to slumber. *So he can even order sleep*, Minna thought to herself, and tensed with a shameful excitement. Here was a king straight from Mamo's tales.

The next night a welcome feast was to be held for the returning warriors.

In the afternoon, Minna worked by Keeva's side, rubbing butter and salt into a skinned pig and setting a pit with wood to bake it. Later, unable to stand without having her toes crushed by harried servants, Minna slipped upstairs and readied the girls for bed.

She had been afraid she would get into trouble for injuring the warrior, though no one had said anything, and in fact the young men downstairs were avoiding looking at her, which suited well. As for the boar banner, the boar god ... her thoughts could not venture there.

'Ow!' Finola cried, when Minna caught her tangled hair in the comb.

'I'm sorry, little one,' she whispered, but her mind was far away.

Soon the hall was resounding with talk and laughter, and the chiming of bronze cups. The din grew, edged with harsh male voices, jests and shouts. In their bed-shifts, Orla and Finola wriggled to the edge of the gallery to look down, and Minna joined them.

The entire fire-pit was filled with burning wood, and thick smoke clouded the air and stung Minna's eyes so she couldn't see. But just when she thought she might give up, the twang of an instrument pierced the chatter. Notes wandered up and down as strings were tuned, there was a pause – and then a rich chord chimed throughout the hall, filling it to the roof. Instantly, the room grew hushed.

And so the music began, a pure, voiceless song that swelled into powerful life. Minna had never heard anything like it, and after a moment she sank onto her back, listening. The music wove a shimmering web, one moment suggesting laughter, the next a lament. It was wind lifting her hair, then the cool of the hills, then the scent of salt spray. When a voice at last joined the music, wound about the notes like woodbine, she turned over and peered down.

'It is Davin the bard,' Orla whispered, her eyes shining. 'He sings like the birds.'

Mamo had told her about the tribal bards. Minna cradled a pained smile in her fingers, swallowing her fierce grief. *Look, Mamo!*

Someone opened the doors for a moment and a gust of air blew in. As the smoke lifted, she glimpsed the bard himself in the centre of the hall. Davin was ageing, thin and fair-haired, stooped from crouching over his harp. But his dignified bearing and the gold rings on his arms said this man was greatly honoured. With closed eyes, he lifted a transcendent face and opened his throat.

The longing in his voice gripped Minna, an ache for something almost outside the bounds of this world. Her hand crept to her throat. She knew this music in her soul, like a voice long missed. For a moment guilt fought in her, for she must be a traitor to feel these things. But the rapture was stronger.

Then, one by one, the words Davin sang began to gain sense in her mind, pictures forming then fading. It was a song of the ancestors of King Cahir, and a famous battle hundreds of years ago. The people below became hushed, the air expectant.

Rhiann, princess of Dunadd, Davin sang, *she of the russet hair and heart of courage, drawn by love to Eremon, valiant prince from over sea, the green jewel of Erin on his brow.*

Minna sat up and stared into the shadows. The names reverberated through her body. *Rhiann. Eremon.* She could not move.

Orla and Finola, their faces rapt, did not notice her discomfort.

The song told of the warrior Eremon, a prince of the province of Dalriada in Erin, who was exiled to Alba. There he wed Rhiann, a princess and priestess of the Epidii people at Dunadd, and hundreds of years ago they resisted the Romans when no one else would. Again and again the grim General Agricola tried to invade Alba with an army, and each time he was outwitted by Eremon and Conaire, his foster-brother, as they ambushed Roman patrols and burned down forts. Conaire was wed to Rhiann's sister Caitlin, and they had a royal son, Gabran.

Eremon. Rhiann. Conaire. Caitlin. The four of them loved each other, they were family. Faces swam before Minna's eyes, pale, unformed shapes in the darkness. Wisps of memory darted around her rigid body.

At last, Davin recited, Eremon and the warriors of Dunadd faced the Romans in a great battle at a place called the Hill of a Thousand Spears. No one knew where it was. There the steadfast Conaire died, and the Albans suffered a terrible defeat at the hands of the Romans.

Surprisingly, Davin sang of the defeat with immense pride. The bravery shown by Eremon and his warriors was all-encompassing, as if that was all that truly mattered to these people. The music rose, rousing and proud even as death claimed them, afire with a sense of courage, honour and glorious deeds done, outshining all thoughts of defeat.

> Lightning in his arm
> a storm in his eyes
> Eremon looked to the hills,
> defeat a cloud gathering.
> But against the red-crest sea
> Undaunted he stood
> Bright in truth's light
> Even as his enemy
> broke over the rocks of the land ...

Afterwards, Eremon and Rhiann were forced to flee the battlefield and sailed to Erin for their own safety. They birthed a family there, a dun where many found protection and justice, and strengthened the kingdom of Dalriada.

'Gabran became king here in Alba,' Orla whispered, reciting faithfully, her eyes bright with the war-light though she was but a child. 'And later the kin of Eremon and Conaire joined when Eremon's granddaughter wed Gabran's son, and their children founded Dalriada in Alba. So Fa is descended from Eremon *and* Conaire, the greatest warriors *ever*! Isn't that wonderful? And we are, too!'

Minna's breath whistled out, her eyes wide open as if she could see in the shadows the pictures Davin was painting. *A strong man on a horse beneath a banner, turning as the Romans poured down a slope.*

She did not want to face it, admit it, even to acknowledge the inevitable shock as the song ended with the same war cry: *The Boar!*

The chant was taken up by the drunken warriors downstairs, overflowing into a great roar that shook the hall. 'The Boar! The Boar!'

Gradually, the music slowed until Davin dropped his head for the last flourish of strings, a haunting refrain that spoke of a yearning farewell. As the final note faded, the smoke took the bard from view. Silence fell.

After a moment a great sigh was released, and rustlings broke out once more as people stirred. Murmurs began, growing louder, breaking into laughter. 'Open the doors!' someone cried drunkenly then. 'The firewood must be wet – I can't breathe in here.'

'Too cold,' someone answered.

'Bah! Open them, I say.'

Servants dutifully scurried, the doors creaked open and the air finally cleared. 'Look now, Minna!' Orla cried. Her eyes stinging, Minna did.

She had grown used to a quiet hall with Queen Maeve on her couch, her advisers and dull lyre player. Now it was as if one room had been replaced with another. A tide of colour and movement eddied around the fire: the sheen of furs, the bright dyes of tunics and cloaks, the lustre of swords and jewellery. Ruddy warriors with wild hair gesticulated while servants ducked under their arms with ale jugs. The firelight glinted on their arm-rings, and the torcs at their necks. Tall women in colourful dresses laughed and caught the eyes of passing men, bracelets looped up their wrists, jewel-drops at their ears, gold threaded through their long braids. The scents of roast meat, ale and sweat floated upwards.

'There's Fa.' Finola pointed.

Minna couldn't see much more than the top of his head. His long, dark hair was braided back at the sides, and an immense, twisted gold ring sat about his neck: not a slave-ring, but a royal torc. He strode confidently among his people, pausing to speak to a warrior here, a merchant there, clapping shoulders. But there remained something tense about him, which Minna could feel even from her place in the gallery.

'Ooh, and there's Darach,' Orla said. An old man in a pale robe sat on a stool, and the people had left a space around him. The forelock of his white hair was twisted into tiny plaits, each tipped with a gold bead. *The chief druid.* Darach was sitting where Oran usually positioned himself, beside Maeve's couch. Next to Darach the queen was frowning with a disdain she did not trouble to hide. Behind, half in the shadows, was Brónach, her face impassive, showing nothing.

King Cahir was speaking to that warrior Ruarc now, their stances betraying unease, hackles raised despite their smiles. But just as Minna was about to draw back, as if he felt her eyes, the golden king glanced up and looked directly at her.

She couldn't register any features beyond a glimpse of black brows, leanness and steady eyes, because a falling sensation nearly sucked her over the edge of the gallery. And all he would see, she thought, were the whites of her eyes and her knuckles in the firelight, like some crazed spirit gazing down from the rafters.

Minna rolled to her back, breathless, the words of the bard's song still ringing in her heart.

Chapter 15

The wax tablet slipped through Minna's fingers again and thudded on the earth floor. She cursed under her breath and squatted to retrieve it, praying it wasn't broken. Lia yipped, bounding about as Minna impatiently pushed her snout away.

On their benches, Orla and Finola were apprehensive as they watched her. She had been nervy and irritable all morning, Davin's song going around her head, the echo of the war cry ringing in her ears. She couldn't steady her hands.

The doorway darkened and Minna glanced up, then blushed and leaped to her feet, brushing herself down. 'Domina.'

Queen Maeve's hand rested on the shoulder of a sturdy, blond boy. 'This is the Prince Garvan,' she announced, her face still puffy from the wine the night before.

Minna hailed the child, but the scowl given in answer made her heart sink. Garvan was in body like his mother, round-faced and freckled, though with green eyes instead of blue.

'He is very intelligent,' Maeve continued, with a fond glance at her offspring. 'You will find his mind to be exceptional.'

'Mother—' the boy began.

'There, now.' Maeve, who never touched her daughters, pressed her lips to his brow, and he flinched, screwing up his nose at her stifling cloud of perfume. 'You will be good and learn all you can, as I asked you to do.'

At the door the queen glanced at the girls. 'Do not hold him back for the younger ones,' she instructed, blue eyes resting on Minna. 'He will be king; they will be married. Have I made myself clear?'

Minna felt the girls' eyes on her. 'Yes, domina. Perfectly.'

Garvan threw himself to an empty bench, barely glancing at his sisters, and folded his arms. There followed a most difficult hour. The prince spoke Latin well and wrote a small amount, taught by his mother, but sneered when Minna asked him to copy out the one line of Virgil she remembered, which she wrote on his wax tablet. 'Poetry is for girls,' he taunted. 'Not warriors.'

She breathed through her nose. 'And yet this is what your mother has ordered.'

'I don't care,' Garvan snapped, and dashed the tablet to the ground. Again.

With gritted teeth, Minna bent down for it. 'Then I suppose you know history better,' she said with narrowed eyes. A headache had started banging on her temples. 'Livy, pray tell? Tacitus? Plutarch? Polybius?'

Garvan merely scowled again, and Minna regretted her flash of temper. This sulky boy was to be king some day, though she couldn't reconcile that with her glimpses of his father. She decided to continue with the girls, hoping he might join in out of boredom, or even to boast. But Garvan turned his attentions to the puppy's tail instead, and when Minna admonished him mildly, he gave a sly smile and yanked Lia into the air by her back legs. Orla screamed and tried to reach her dog, while the puppy yelped and Finola burst into tears.

At thirteen Garvan was just shorter than Minna, and at last she managed to furiously wrestle the whimpering pup off him and hand her to Orla. 'That is not becoming behaviour for a prince!'

Garvan's plump cheeks mottled. 'You're a slave: I'll have you whipped for that.'

'I think your mother would be more concerned about your disobedience of her.'

'Oh, really?' he cried. Without further ado, he stalked out of the door.

Minna stared after him, winded. Then she slowly placed the stylus back on the table, struggling to keep her voice calm, as Finola sniffled and Orla, who looked stricken, stroked Lia. 'Stay here, and don't move.' Then she hurried to find Maeve.

The queen's women told Minna she was having her hair dressed at her bed-place in the king's hall. Minna took the ladder to the gallery, sick with dread, but when she approached the lamplight at Maeve's dressing-table, far from the stairs, she found herself ducking into her own bed-place first to summon courage.

Through the gaps in the bedscreens, Minna saw the queen wince as one of her maids caught an earring in her hair. She batted the girl's fingers away with her hand-mirror. 'That's enough of your clumsiness,' she growled. 'Go.' Gathering the pins, the maid bowed and fled.

This was the time. But just as Minna drew another breath, bracing herself, feet came pounding up the stairs. She shrank into the shadows behind Orla's clothes chest as the king strode past with Garvan at his heels. Neither saw her.

'Husband,' the queen said coldly.

'What is this foolery of my children learning the Roman tongue?' the king snapped. Minna stared at the back of his head as he ran a hand through his loose, rumpled hair.

Maeve placed the mirror down. 'A Roman slave fell into my hands by chance. She is the girl's nurse, that's all.'

The two of them had squared off as if taking up a long-running argument, ignoring their son. 'Don't play with me, Maeve.' The king's voice was ice. 'You know I do not want Garvan to have any more Latin. He speaks enough as it is.'

'I know what you want, and it is foolish.' Minna had a full view of the queen's face, her blue eyes hard, her thin mouth contemptuous. 'You know as I do who holds the power in this land, Cahir. Your son must take his place among those favoured by the Romans.'

Garvan was darting eager glances between his parents.

'I will *not* breed a Latin prince of Dalriada,' the king growled. 'There is precious little left of our blood, and I won't have you leaching the rest away.'

'Your *blood?*' Maeve snorted. 'Other tribes have been Roman friends for generations, and *their* wealth and power is unparalleled—'

'Wealth? Power? Is that all you think about? Roman wine and jewels and silk and ... and *figs,* by all the gods!'

Maeve's head snapped back, cheeks mottled beneath the powder. 'No, I think for *you!* I think about a proper Roman garrison that will keep us safe from those bloodthirsty Picts, about equipping your *son,*' she jabbed a finger at Garvan, 'with everything that will help him survive in this world!' Maeve leaned forward, eyes glittering. 'You owe it to him to give him *all* the weapons he needs – not just that sword and a spear. The world is shifting: he needs knowledge, he needs teaching. Would you deny him the right to lead his people under his own terms?'

Cahir's breath grated on the low roof. 'We all have to carry our fathers' yokes. I have had to.'

'It is not a yoke, it is wisdom,' she retorted. 'And you're a fool to think otherwise.'

Cahir took a step towards her. 'I would think twice about bandying that word *fool* around any more, my lady,' he said very quietly, and at his tone Maeve at last showed fear, swiftly veiled. 'Now, let me make myself clear. *My heir* is not to be schooled as a Latin prince. I absolutely forbid it. Do not gainsay me on this. Ever.'

Maeve's defiance quailed, before her face set into a mask. 'Of course.' She shrugged. 'I think you are wrong, but of course. They are your people, it is your dun. If it is burned to the ground around you, I can always go home to my father.'

'You can do that at any time,' Cahir murmured. 'But seeing as you were the gift that sealed our treaty, you might find him displeased to see you break it out of petulance.'

The queen's lips pursed sourly. Satisfied with her silence, the king turned to pound back down the stairs. Minna shrank into the shadows, her head down, and did not see his face. For a moment nothing happened, as Maeve stared into the mirror in her lap.

'Mother,' Garvan whined then. 'The sword and spear are what I should be learning. Not silly words!'

'Hush!' Maeve said sharply. She glanced around. 'You will learn the Latin because I command it. I do not care what your father says. I had underestimated how pig-headed he gets after visiting the uncivilized north, that is all.'

'But Mother, *not from a girl*.'

Maeve grabbed his wrist. 'I can make you a greater king than any other, but for this you need the word. You need learning, wisdom and cunning to see into the hearts of men, in Rome and beyond.'

'But Father took me south with him, Father—'

'Your *father* is not the king you will be!'

'He is ... he looks ...' Garvan faltered. 'I've seen him fight, Mother, and there is no one like him. Do not ...' His voice trailed away, a boy unable to speak with the conviction of a man.

Maeve glared him into silence. 'Since my brothers died you are the obvious heir to my father's hall as well as this. You could be king of both tribes.' She pulled him closer, shaking him. 'So tell me you do not want to be the greatest king in Alba; that you do not want gold to fill your coffers and men to bear a forest of spears for you. That you do not want to make Dunadd the flame of the west, the greatest trading port on the seas. That you do not want a fine hall of stone, and heated floors and proper baths – *tell me you do not!*'

A long pause, before Garvan answered, head down, 'I want this.'

Maeve's breath hissed out. 'Good. Then you *will* learn the Latin. We will just have to be more circumspect about it. I would rather have avoided the risk outside the dun, but there are people in the port who can be more prudent, and secretive.'

'What would you have me do then?' There was sullen defeat in Garvan's voice.

'You will do as I and the Lord Oran say, with no complaint. You must be ready, when the time comes.'

'Time?'

'For your accession you must always be ready. Life is so ... uncertain.'

In the great fort of Cilurnum on the Wall, Fullofaudes, the Dux Britanniarum, strode across the courtyard of the headquarters building, mud splashing up his riding boots. His junior officer dashed along behind him, trying to dodge puddles. He had just dragged the lad from his bed, and he was not yet uniformed, but that was the way it was.

There was never any time to waste on the northern frontier. It was a substantial responsibility, and Fullofaudes was the most active dux for years, forever in the saddle. This life had made him lean and wiry, the deprivations stripping any portliness from his slight frame. Now, only a thatch of iron-grey hair and weather-worn face spoke his age.

Fullofaudes tugged on leather riding gloves, squinting as the first rays of dawn penetrated the gloomy rows of barracks, storehouses, stables, yards and granaries. Around him the streets were dark, but in the bakehouse the ovens were glowing, smoke curling into the still air. A cockerel crowed in the *vicus*, where the civilians and camp followers stirred. 'Make it brief and blunt,' he said to his officer, acting as his scribe. 'There is no point vacillating with savages.'

The younger man was awkwardly balancing a wax tablet on his forearm, clutching a stylus. Fullofaudes could have done this in the warmth of the command headquarters, but he'd ridden in late at night and now it was dawn and already time to go.

'Write this: "Greetings to Cahir, son of Conor, King of Dalriada, so on and so forth. The office of the Dux Britanniarum demands your presence at a council of the Wall tribes to take place at the fort of Fanum Codicii at the next full moon. The council is for the purpose of discussing the situation of taxes, in order to continue providing protection to your trade routes. We look forward to your attendance." You know how to sign off.'

'Demands, sir?' His officer tucked the stylus in his mouth as he negotiated a pile of horse manure outside the stables. 'Is that not a little ... strong?'

Fullofaudes sneered. 'Our friend Cahir looks dangerous, but his father toed the line for so many years his tribe is used to compliance. He's merely a sheep in wolf's clothing, not the other way around – another petty little ruler playing at war.' He snorted, his breath steaming on the dawn air. 'They put a foot wrong and I'll give them war.' He resumed striding. 'I want the message in Luguvalium today and on a boat to Dunadd tonight.'

His scribe's eyes lit up as he hurried on. 'Sir, if I understand correctly, because the tribes north of the Wall in the lowlands have been so thoroughly subdued, we could have an army at Dunadd in days, couldn't we? Does this mean ... is it possible I will get to see ... Dalriada?'

Fullofaudes smiled grimly, glancing at him. These young pups, still scrubbed and shiny from the baths in Eboracum, had not yet faced down a tide of screaming blueskins, or felt the sting of their daggers. Once he had, this one would stop looking for glory and become like all the others: hard, resigned, bitter. Bitter at the endless wind, the sheets of rain, the bleak land. Bitter at the expectant silence of the moors that ate into the bones so a man could never sleep another restful night. Sometimes, when he was wearied, he found himself longing for the flat, soft greenness of Belgica, his homeland, as if he could almost taste it, scent it. 'You might see Dunadd, though I hope you'll escape that dubious honour.'

Fullofaudes strode out through the arches of the southern gate, to where his guard milled about, already mounted. Their horses stamped the white grasses while streaks of dawn gilded helmets and lit up the clouds of warm breath. The northern hills rolled away like endless breakers on a sea, crested with hoarfrost.

The Dux turned with one hand on his bridle as his guard came forward to help him mount. Let this fresh boy hold his illusions for as long as he could. 'Know this. The barbarians don't have the same wits we do. This King Cahir doesn't even realize how close we have crept to his borders. He's benefited from our alliance through increased trade, and we've managed to install the Carvetii princess as his wife – in short, we've got him trussed tight as a chicken, for blood ties are vital to these people, oaths are everything.' Fullofaudes laughed, though his throat was dry from the cold. 'It's a good thing we don't have the same scruples.' He leaned his foot on his guard's cupped hands, swung into the saddle.

The young officer tucked the tablet under his arm. 'Will *we* be attending this council in the west, sir?'

So he was also excited at the idea of sharing sour ale with hairy barbarians. 'Of course. I wouldn't deprive you of that.' The Dux took his helmet from his saddle and settled it on his head. Encased in cold strips of iron across cheekbones and brow, he felt himself again.

He was made of iron, too, and would never give in. Where once Rome marched into Alba with enormous armies, only to be beaten by rain and mountains, now he played a slower game.

But he would still win.

Chapter 16

Cahir watched the Roman messenger eat by his hearth-fire, though he himself could not touch food. He had listened to the man's news in private, and now anger sat thick as any gruel in his gut.

He could have tried to hide this from his nobles, but that would be disastrous. Too many wolves in Dunadd were waiting for him to stumble. They must hear this from the messenger himself at a public feast in the hall.

Maeve, of course, was beside herself, fluttering her fingers for more wine, tilting her head. Cahir eyed her. Fifteen years ago he had found her plump creaminess appealing enough, although she came as a treaty bride, and he took her to his bed unwillingly, surly at being forced by his father. Mutual anger had furnished fleeting passion between them, and at first she had responded to the frustration he worked out between her soft thighs. For even then her body had seemed the image of Rome to him, treacherous with luxury, growing fat on the toil of his own people.

Maeve didn't know what tenderness was, so she'd never understood what was missing between them. By order of both fathers Dalriada needed an heir, which she dutifully produced. Soon afterwards, she began to change. She did not grow more used to life here, but less. After every visit home to Luguvalium she came back plumper, scented by the luxuries of her father's house, her eyes sharpened by gossip. She grew more bitter at life in rainy, barbaric Alba. When Garvan turned out so much like her, in pain Cahir tried for another son and, after Orla, another. After Finola's birth he could not face Maeve's bed again.

So be it. His father sold him into Roman slavery. His own son ran to it with open arms. Only Cahir struggled between the dictates of reality and his own heart.

He glanced down at the untouched ale-cup in his tight fingers. Perhaps if he allowed himself the release of drink for once his headache would go away. He drank.

When the Roman messenger put his platter aside, Davin's music faded and Cahir got to his feet. He waited until the voices of his nobles and their wives died down. 'The Dux Britanniarum has sent us an important request that I must attend to before the long dark. It has gone out to the Carvetii, my wife's people, as well as the remnant chiefs of the Maetae.'

He nodded at the messenger, who wiped grease from his mouth while Cahir sat back down, holding tight to the arms of his chair. The man's Dalriadan speech was stilted as he read out the summons. Afterwards, silence fell. It was so quiet Cahir heard the logs in the hearth settle and the growl of a hound.

'More taxes,' one of the older nobles repeated in a harsh voice. 'Another increase, when we have had such terrible harvests for three years now? When even the grain stores are being emptied?' In the ensuing pause, the tension in the room rose.

The messenger glanced at Cahir. 'My commander decrees this for your own good. You enjoy our army's protection, and the Dux has determined that more ships are needed to guard your sea-coast from Pictish raiders sailing around from the north-east, and your mountains from their riders. Hence, taxes need to be raised to build and equip them.'

As the silence stretched out, Maeve swiped up her wine goblet. 'Of course we will pay this. Why, with safer sea-lanes we'll be able to increase our trading wealth tenfold.'

'More so, I would say,' Oran cut in smoothly.

Cahir's anger was building, though he could not afford to give it life. He had to walk a narrow path to keep his people safe. He knew only too well that the power of the Maetae and Novantae kingdoms near the Wall had been crushed by Rome long ago, one reason his father signed the treaty to protect Dalriada. But in Cahir's boyhood a dispossessed Maetae prince had mounted a final rebellion against Roman rule – and Cahir was there when his father's men cut the Maetae warriors down from the trees and gave them a fiery funeral. The southern Alban tribes were broken people now, shadows among the hills.

Harsh words were threatening to break out now, judging by the scowls. Swiftly Cahir said the messenger had suffered a long journey and must be tired; there was a guest bed waiting for him in one of the noble houses. The man bowed, glowering, and left.

As soon as he disappeared, Oran jumped in again. 'With more

southern forts and more Roman soldiers we can stop the Picts cutting us off from the Province,' he wittered. 'Ships will more easily be able to sail all the way from Gaul with tin and gold, and from the Saxon lands with amber.'

Cahir's head whipped around. 'And do you advise us to build a Roman fort in *our* lands, my Lord Oran?'

As Oran's thin lips chewed on a reply, someone cried, 'Hawen's balls, we will *not!*' Cahir glanced up. Ruarc was on his feet, blazing with a fury as bright as the gold torc around his neck. 'They are traitorous words, beneath anyone of true Dalriadan blood!'

Oran regarded Ruarc with irritation, like a whining fly. 'Which is why those of a different blood have more sense! We're talking trade and money, boy, not bard's tales of mindless battles.'

This remark inflamed all of the blustering youths, the mutterers who diced and lounged on the walls. They jumped up and began yelling that there would be no forts, no towns, and that the Roman army could shove their tithes back down their gullets. Cahir struck the arm of his chair. 'Sit down!' he bellowed. No one listened.

Maeve's mouth dropped open. 'This is the only sensible course, you fools,' she screeched. 'These things must be left to those who *rule,* not their witless bloodhounds!'

The uproar grew. Cahir looked over at his own guard, the only ones he trusted. Steady Finbar, Donal and Gobán were older than him, his father's men. Tiernan and Fergal were Cahir's age, his own swordmates who had sparred with him as children. They were all men with years on their brow and fights on their belt.

Responding to his glance, Donal strode to Ruarc's flame-haired friend Mellan, who, after another taunt by Oran, was stabbing the air with a finger, shouting. Despite Donal's bald pate, lumpen nose and ruddy hair sprouting from brows and ears, he was respected by the young ones for his sword prowess. He put a steady hand across Mellan's chest. 'Hold your tongue for the king, lad,' he said quietly.

A shudder went through Mellan, and he looked down at that calm hand before drawing a breath. 'Aye, all right, Donal.' When the older man just stared meaningfully at him, Mellan shrugged him off. 'It is well, man, leave me be.'

In the silence, Cahir propelled himself from his chair and turned first to Maeve. 'My lady,' he ground out, 'it should be no foregone conclusion of *yours* that we will come to the Roman heel when called, like a mangy cur. Conn is right: the harvests have been bad and we are low on the grain the Romans desire for their armies.'

He stared at the wrathful Ruarc, for a moment regretful. *Ruarc, bright flame.* Cahir was often angry at this boy, and yet he understood him. For Ruarc was an image of his own younger self, the prince before he became a king. The unfettered warrior living in a simple world of fighting, riding, raiding and bedding. 'You and your sword-mates must understand something: this is no simple duel, no game of war. I ask you to keep your sword honed for such things and your temper for diplomacy.' He spoke firmly, but not to shame. These youths were fine fighters, and as yet Cahir did not have a rebellion on his hands, a challenge to his kingship. Not yet. Cahir and Ruarc's gazes locked, but Cahir would not let his eyes fall. At last Ruarc shrugged angrily and turned away.

Straightening his shoulders, Cahir looked into the shadows behind his chair. 'And you, chief druid, what do you say to this news?'

Darach stepped forward slowly, his staff marking the floor rushes with each scrape. He bowed stiffly. 'My lord, ours is a difficult position.' He extended his swollen fingers. 'On the one hand, the treaty has increased our trade and wealth. On the other,' his fingers clenched into a fist, 'the Romans have ever been the enemy of the druid brotherhood, for they yearn to exterminate those beliefs that threaten theirs. To remain Dalriadan, with all we hold dear, we do not want to become like the Carvetii, with Roman towns and teachings and language and ways obliterating their own. Rome has killed our Maetae and Novantae brothers: if we allow them any more of a foothold in this land they will use it to wipe us out.' He looked at his king. 'Plainly you must attend this council and weigh up what comes out of it. All I can tell you is what is in the stars: they foretell a great shifting of the power in this land. That is all I know.'

I could have told him that, Cahir thought bleakly. *The Romans will conquer and all will be lost.* He raised his face. 'Thank you,' he said, the weariness in his voice overriding all emotion. 'I thank all of you for your succinct analysis of our position.'

And with that, to everyone's evident surprise, Cahir took up his cloak and left his hall.

Chapter 17

As Minna was passing the hearth-fire the next day, Clíona caught her. 'We start the salting of the beef today and we need all hands, girl, even yours.' She rarely used Minna's name.

'But … I don't know what to do.'

That elicited a triumphant smile. 'You soon will.' Clíona's deceptively soft, blue eyes gleamed with satisfaction. 'Slave or no, you might think you're something different with that *learning* of yours. But if we don't salt, we starve when the long dark comes. No one's exempt from that.' Her gaze flicked up and down. 'Not even you.'

Later, hands crusted with salt, Minna thought Clíona's explanation had left out some details. In an open-sided shed and with a biting wind off the sea, she had to grit her teeth as she plunged her icy hands into water and then took up more strips of frozen beef, pressing them into saltpans and barrels of brine. The shed steamed with the women's breath, and hummed with their chatter. Outside, the yards were a sea of bawling bulls and tossing horns, the air split by the shouts of the cattlemen.

Minna's hands were soon stinging, her eyes smarting. Keeva was tossing jests back and forth, and the women laughed at her quips, faces bright, noses streaming.

In the afternoon, a bronze horn brayed from the direction of the village gatetower. Excitedly, the women clustered in the yard around a small fire, warming their hands. Soon streams of warriors came hurrying past, belting on weapons as they made for the gate. The horn bellowed again.

Keeva caught Minna's puzzled look as she stood on the edge of the yard, shivering. 'The king and his warband are going south to the council on the Wall,' she said, casually offering Minna a cloth to clean her bloody hands.

Startled, Minna took it. 'I know.'

When Keeva raised one brow, she steadily met her gaze. 'I heard about it from the gallery.' As the maid's eyes began to twinkle, she added, 'When I was in bed.'

For a moment Keeva didn't react, then she laughed, her black braid bouncing on her shoulders. 'I was listening from my pallet, too. They think we have no ears when they speak of important things.' She cocked her head. 'I heard something else, too, about a certain cut one of the cubs is sporting on his hand.'

As Minna's face flamed, Keeva grinned. 'I did something similar when I got here, though it was a meat-knife, or boiling water, I can't remember. Now they know only to grope when I want them to. Ha!'

The horn sounded a third time. Keeva glanced at Minna and seemed to arrive at a decision. 'Come with me up on the walls. It's fun to see the men ride out.'

Surprised, Minna could only nod, and followed Keeva up to the ramparts. They were pushed aside by warriors clutching spears, thundering down the stairs to the ground. Below, others were leading horses out of the gates. The river meadow was in chaos. Women were stamping their feet in the cold, scolding their men, while the riders checked saddle packs and fastened cloaks. Children ran around under the stallions' legs, unafraid.

Far away across the teeming crowds, Minna saw Cian standing with Ruarc's black horse. She gripped the points of the stakes.

Last night she had found him in the alley behind the stables, nursing a black eye with a cold cloth. The more she tried to convince him to ignore the taunts, the angrier he became, as if he would be betraying himself not to fight. Foolish male pride!

'I have already been allowed out of the dun many times,' she argued. 'If you don't react, eventually they will ignore you, and you can move around unnoticed. *Then* perhaps we have a chance.' She didn't dare say the word *escape* aloud.

His face had been hidden from the starlight by the shadow of the ramparts. 'I won't bow to anyone.' His voice quavered with suppressed fury. 'So make an end of it there, Tiger. There will be winter feasts soon, when they drink all night and sleep all day. I'll figure out something for us then.'

Confused by his coldness, she clutched his arms. 'Cian,' she whispered. 'Why won't you listen to me? Or tell me why ...' She trailed away. *Tell me why you've changed*, she wanted to say. But then, she realized, perhaps she had never really known him anyway. A veil had fallen over his face. He hadn't even told her he was leaving with Ruarc today.

Was that because ... Her eyes bored into him from afar. Would he try to escape? Surely he would! He would run, as soon as he was close enough to the Wall to attempt it. Her heart beat slowly in her throat. He would, he must – but he couldn't! She wanted him to be safe, freed from this imprisonment *she* had wrought with her impulsiveness, even though he had insisted it was his doing. But if he left, she was alone.

All the while Keeva chattered, but Minna stood as still as a statue, her hands gripping the stakes until her knuckles were white.

Desperately, she stared over the clusters of spears until her eyes were caught by a flash of sun from the king's helmet where he sat on his horse, gazing out over the river. Above his head, the red and white boar banner cracked in the wind, as if taunting her. She resolutely moved her attention from that, too, pushing all thoughts of it down.

I have no loyalty to anyone. I look after me, and me alone. Cian had told her this right from the start, and she hadn't listened, because she was searching so hard for her own belonging. She thought about the desperation in his voice when they last spoke ...

'And that's why I won't tilt my head at a warrior!' Keeva was pointing scornfully at all the gilded youths strutting around in their armour, prancing their horses in skittish circles so people had to race out of the way. 'They ride off to war, and you don't know when you'll get them back. Now, a blacksmith's lad is another thing altogether. Hardworking, brawny.' She grinned wickedly, swinging back on her heels, clinging to the palisade.

'*Could* you marry a warrior?' Minna asked faintly, trying to concentrate on Keeva, though her voice wavered.

'Could, but wouldn't. They'd have a mirror stuck to their face all the time! They're so full of themselves. They think a flashy sword will make a girl open her legs and there's no need to *woo* her.' Keeva's smile turned sly. 'Nothing to stop you bedding them, though, no laws about that either way. Dunadd's full of men; even you can take your pick. Farmers, herders, potters, smiths, slaves, *kings*. Aye, some of the girls have even had *him*, though a queer time they have of it, I hear. All fire and no warmth.'

Now she had Minna's attention and laughed at her shocked face. 'You have that Roman thing, don't you? You get so embarrassed about any mention of the bed-furs. I saw a Roman priest speak in the port once. He had a fit when I asked him how much sex Christians were allowed to have, and on what days.'

Minna drew a breath, wanting to strengthen this fragile thing. Knowledge was safety to her, anticipation and defence. And Keeva knew everything. She kept her eyes on the crowd. 'I heard the king would allow no priests. I'm surprised he let the man get away alive.'

The maid's black eyes slid sideways with a new respect. 'He barely did. The king came down to the port and the man fled like his own devil was after him.'

The trumpets now all skirled at once, and the whole mass of men began to flow away to the south, hooves clattering, horses snorting, warriors shouting at each other as the horseboys and shield and spear-bearers trotted alongside.

Cian's black head merged into all the rest, and though Minna stared hard after him, everything blurred in her eyes.

Keeva had cut her hand during the salting and the wound grew inflamed. Minna saw her wincing as she ground grain and tentatively offered to salve it with yarrow.

That morning she had seen Brónach ride out with her pack, disappearing again, as the old woman often did for days at a time. She thought it would be safe to duck into the healer's house, grab what she needed and slip out. After all, Brónach was even letting her prepare some of the plants now, grinding, infusing and steeping herbs beneath the chill of that grey gaze. And the cut did look serious.

Keeva's eyes gleamed at the thought of sneaking into that lady's mysterious house. As they strode through the cold afternoon along shadowed paths, she murmured to Minna, 'She's the king's aunt, you know.'

Minna nodded, head down into the wind, and Keeva leaned even closer. 'She was a princess, would have been married off to some foreign king. But then,' her voice dropped, 'it was clear she was barren. Never got her moon bleeding *at all*. She's been the healer ever since, though, as you've seen, children aren't her favourite thing. The women have to force themselves to go to her with their bairns, and their own womb troubles.'

They both listened for a moment at Brónach's door to be sure she was not there, then pushed up the hide. Only when they straightened did they realize the house was not empty after all.

The young noblewoman Minna saw the first day over the fence, who gazed at her so boldly, was tucked up in the sickbed, her golden hair fanning over the pillow. 'I beg your pardon, lady,' Minna said hastily. 'I just came to get a salve.' She turned to Keeva. 'Wait outside and I'll bring it,' she murmured. The maid nodded and, with a glance at the lady in the bed, slipped back out.

As Minna turned, the young woman sighed and hauled herself up the pillow. She had a broad face, her freckles standing out like gobs of butterfat in whey. 'I was awake anyway, despite the Lady Brónach's potions. Do what you need to do.'

Nervously, Minna moved to the workbench and began sorting the jars.

'What happened?' the woman suddenly asked, watching her with that same bold curiosity.

'Keeva cut her hand salting the meat, lady.' She sniffed one of the pots and put it aside.

'You know green-craft? You, a slave?'

The woman was blunt, but the frankness in her eyes drew an answering pride from Minna before she could stop her tongue. 'I was captured by slave-traders, I was not born so.' She raised her chin. 'My grandmother taught me.'

'Ah, Roman healing.'

Minna couldn't explain that the song of the plants she heard in this room bore no relation to her upbringing at all.

The young woman was looking down now at her fingers, twisting the sheets. 'And what you will put on it, it helps the pain?'

'Yes.' Minna glanced at her from the corner of her eye. As she drew in the scent of the plants by Brónach's workbench, they whispered to her again, as a murmur in her heart. *She has trouble with her womb.* Minna lifted the lid on a basket of bandages and said evenly, 'Are *you* in pain, my lady?'

She thought the woman would put her in her place, and for a moment those proud eyes did flash. But then the girl blew out her cheeks and folded her arms. 'I am in pain every full moon. I come here but the Lady Brónach says there is not much to be done. She rubs my belly with something that smells awful; sometimes it helps a little, that is all.'

Minna glanced apprehensively at the door, as if Brónach might arrive back at any moment. But she was torn, for she had glimpsed in this girl's face not only pain, but fear. This was about children – or the lack of them. 'The difficulty is with your ... woman courses?' she ventured at last.

The patient rested her head on the pillow, closed her eyes. 'Everyone thinks I'm weak.' She bit her pale lips. 'But I am only just married, and my man's mother and his sister watch me. They all expect ... well, they sneer at me behind my back, I'm sure of it.' This admission seemed to cost her in pride.

Minna darted another glance at the door, the scents of the herbs clouding her nose. Then her eye fell on the niche that usually held the statues of Brónach's goddesses. Only the healing goddess was there, her small face lifted with compassion.

She wavered, holding the pot tight in her fingers. 'Lady,' she said at last, with a sigh, 'I might be able to find something to help.'

When she came back out soon after, Keeva leaped up from the bench outside the door. She said nothing until they climbed the steps to the king's hall. 'You can really heal?' she asked then, curious. 'How do you do it?'

Minna hesitated. 'My Mamo was a green-woman, a wise-woman.'

Keeva stared at her. 'Then you are interesting altogether, Minna the slave.' Her teeth flashed white in the dim light. 'I like that. Most people are interminably boring. That's why I've caught the eye of the blacksmith's lad, Lonán. I'm the only girl who argues with him and happily walks away. The others simper and flutter around him, and he hates it!'

For the first time, Minna expelled her breath in a light-headed laugh. The sense of the plants was tingling in her blood again.

'You often seem afraid, too,' Keeva said more gravely, 'but I don't think you lack courage.'

Now Minna's head went up. 'I'm a slave – how brave can I be?'

The maid shrugged and cocked her head, birdlike. 'Life is not always a straight path. I loved my island, but my father fell so ill he could not feed all of us, and so I came here seeking a different future than fish, fish and more fish. If you take any opportunity to make yourself useful to the nobles, then you never know what could happen. Even to you.' She turned and gazed down at the darkened village. 'You just don't know.'

Brónach was searching ... seeking ... fingers of her spirit reaching through the murky veils, endeavouring to part them ... to see ...

But all remained dark, the ether around her a thick, impenetrable fog. Wait ... there ... through the veils, was that a glimpse of something? Men fighting, struggling against each other with swords drawn ... or ... a horse galloping ... no, a huge bird, winging its way over mountains? *Ah ...*

Then the veils fell back, cutting her off, and Brónach could see nothing but darkness again. *She knew nothing.*

With an inner wail, she felt the edges of her spirit dissolving back into her body, becoming heavier, losing the lightness of soul. The walls of the mountain hut were forming around her once more, and she had a sense of herself spreadeagled naked before the fire. No! She would not come back yet, until she had *seen!* Desperately, Brónach grappled with the Otherworld mists, using her will, her rage, to try to tear them aside. *She had to see; she had to know.*

Would Cahir stand up to the Romans? Would he fall? What would happen to Dalriada? Great, important questions, and Brónach was from a royal line of seers, the descendant of Rhiann herself – it was *she* who must receive the answers! It was she who in her secret dreams stood before the king and spoke the gods' will. Not those wittering druids, who kept their feeble eyes on the stars and scorned the female power of the earth. That power had been lost over the centuries, the power of the Sisterhood, but she would find it again. *She alone.*

And instead of wariness, she would see respect in Cahir's eyes. No longer would she be the useless princess, condemned by a barren womb to a life of duty, sniffling fevers and festering wounds. She would be the beating heart of his people, and noblemen would bow as she passed!

Brónach flexed her clawed fingers and rolled on her side. She was shivering violently, but ignored it as she must ignore all privations – cold, hunger, pain. Her tongue stuck to the roof of her mouth with thirst, but she could still taste the self-hatred. *Weak, weak!* she railed at herself.

Beside her, a clay pot spilled the dregs of the potion over the earthen floor. Breathing through despair, she thought: *It was not strong enough. I must try something different . . . something more potent.* But she had already made herself sick twice this moon, and was now sallow-faced and exhausted.

Slowly, she dragged herself upright, pausing to hold her forehead as a surge of dizziness hit. The wind on the mountain scoured the hut, a draught gusting under the eaves into the fire. Brónach stared hungrily into the shifting flames. Was it there, then, in the flames, not the flight, that she would find her answers? Or in the sacred pool outside amid the old birches? She shuddered at the memory of the hours spent by that freezing water, in frustration plunging her hands in to grope for visions as if they were fish.

Her eye fell on the circle of goddess figurines propped around her. Their faces were stony, eyes blank and uncaring. Without thinking, Brónach dashed them all to the floor. Then she sat there panting, gazing down.

Chapter 18

At the outpost fort of Fanum Cocidii the Roman scouts lined up outside their headquarters in the rain, eyes fixed coldly on the barbarian fighters lounging about the courtyard. The barbarians stared back, teeth bared in feral smiles.

Broc felt the hatred burn in him. These men were not the dreaded blueskins whose raids he'd been repelling for months, but they were still Alban – Dalriadans. They were all the same to him: bloodthirsty murderers, beasts who could not appreciate the benefits of Empire. As a green boy, Broc had sneered at them like all of his blood, but now, riding this windy land, the hatred had sunk deep into his bowels. He was green no more.

A man couldn't be when hordes of tattooed men kept bursting from the trees, hacking with vicious blades, their eyes white; when his friend, a man he had diced with, and laughed with, crashed to the ground with a spear quivering in his guts.

Broc glared at the Dalriadan warriors jesting with each other in the drizzle. Though the Dux had deigned to meet with their so-called kings, these savages must be under no illusions about what the Roman *areani* really thought of them.

The door to the command quarters opened and men spilled out. Broc and his unit stood to attention as the Dux, a short, lean man, stalked past to the gate, his weathered face grim. Behind came the King of Dalriada, his chieftains, the King of the Carvetii at Luguvalium, and the cowed chiefs of the Maetae.

Kings. Chiefs. Broc's lip curled. How they clung to their petty titles, their foolish notions of power. When he thought about the thousands of soldiers just like him patrolling the Wall, gazing out across the bare plains, Broc felt the vast power of the Roman army behind him, and knew these minor kings were doomed.

'Looks like something got stuck in their gullets,' the scout next to him muttered, rain dripping down his chin. 'No smiles, no handshakes, no back-slaps.'

Broc glanced at him. 'I heard the Dux say he didn't expect them to take these new taxes lying down, anyway. You know he has something on his mind: we will be ordered into the saddle before dusk.'

'Keep it down,' an officer growled further along. 'Some of these bastards speak our tongue.'

Cian waited on the road with the other grooms and shield- and spear-bearers, holding the black stallion's bridle. Like them, he stared across the hills that rolled away from the Codicii fort, but unlike them, facing nervously north, he stood apart. Looking south.

From long practice his mouth formed a tight, contained line, revealing nothing. But his heart beat like a bird in a snare, and the more it struggled, the more he held it down. The muscles in his legs and arms all strained towards that road, urging him to break and run, to disappear into the hills, swift as a deer, racing for the Wall. He could feel every fibre tightening, yearning to be set free.

Then darkness washed over him. When he thought of running, his mind was filled with an image of Minna's face the first time he saw her, her eyes swimming with unshed tears by Eboracum's river. Another lost one, hurt and vulnerable. That's all he could remember about her now through the red fog of his endless rage. And the barbarians had caused her pain, too, those bastards who stalked his own dreams. So he couldn't *abandon* her – he had to protect her, or lay down his own life for being no man at all. He had to make it all turn out right this time. He could not fail, not again …

Then the other part spoke up, hard and gleaming as a sliver of bone in his heart. *Run, you fool. There will never be another chance.* Cian scowled and hunched into the wind, cursing himself with a passion. *Weak and stupid, useless beyond all measure.*

But he didn't run. Instead he turned his back on the south, burying his nose in the horse's neck, smelling the old, comforting scent of the animal, the lanolin and leather. And for once, he shut his ears to the hisses and taunts around him.

Outside the fort, Cahir mounted his stallion and said nothing to the man gazing anxiously from his own saddle: one of his southern chieftains from the Clutha river. The chief tried to speak, but Cahir held up his hand. 'Not here, Finn. Wait until we are on the road.'

Around them the hundred or so Dalriadan and Carvetii warriors were mounting up, talking and laughing in a release of tension. But up on the walls the Dux and his officers remained still and watchful, their eyes hidden by the shadows of their helmets.

As the large party trotted away from the fort, Maeve's father, Eldon, King of the Carvetii, spurred his horse to Cahir's side. He was heavy-set and clean-shaven, with clipped, dark hair. Hunched in a hooded cloak away from the rain, he regarded his son-in-law with disapproval.

Cahir stared back with raised chin, ignoring the cold drops trickling in his eyes. Eldon's nostrils flared, as if he smelled something unpleasant. *He did not consider my wealth so when he handed his daughter over.* Gold from Erin, amber from the north sea, tin from Kernow – that's all Eldon had ever cared for.

'Do not expect me,' Cahir hissed under his breath, 'to bow my head to any stray demand of the Dux Britanniarum without due consideration. I am not some dog, to curl up at his feet and lick them.'

Eldon's plucked eyebrows rose. 'It is not a stray demand,' he replied evenly. 'If we enjoy the army's protection then we must pay for it, son-in-law. They need the grain to feed the extra troops. After the recent Pictish attacks in the east, surely you can see the sense in what he asked?'

'Protection,' Cahir repeated, with a snort. He gazed over the rolling heath to the north, obscured by veils of drifting drizzle and mist. He longed to get back to his own lands, to leave these hills so scarred by blood and pain. 'I do not think,' he continued, meeting Eldon's eye, 'that you could class my relationship with the Roman administration as one of protection. After all, the Picts have not attacked us for at least a year now – they have been kept quite busy with their own raids on the Roman army.' He smiled stiffly. 'So what indeed am I paying for, Eldon? Perhaps to ward the Roman-kind away, rather than the Picts; to keep the Roman eagle from my door, not the Pictish wolf.'

Eldon's clenched reins made his horse skittish. 'Indeed you are, Cahir, and don't you forget it.' He glanced back at the disappearing Roman fort, its timber walls a dark blot on the rain-washed hills. Unconsciously, Cahir looked back, too, and fancied he could still see the outline of the Dux's helmet.

Fullofaudes had been unfailingly polite when he told Cahir he was raising the grain tithe and tax on trade goods by an enormous percentage. His narrow face had remained pleasant, but scrape that thin patina away and the man had iron inside him, iron and ambition. Cahir understood him better than he knew.

'Do not be foolish,' Eldon went on darkly. 'Resist and they will crush you. Instead, join us properly. Allow a Roman garrison at Dunadd, a Roman port, and you will enjoy the same privileges as we do. We can merge our two kingdoms,' he lowered his voice to a whisper, 'swallow the Maetae, the Attacotti, make us one block of power from the Wall all the way to the northern sea.'

The same privileges. Cahir scanned King Eldon's clipped hair, his manicured hands, the soft, pouched belly.

But he knew it wasn't differences on the outside that made them Alban or Roman any more, not with the mixed bloods. It was on the inside, the soul. It was Cahir's pride in his lineage that made him Alban; his passion for the land, the old tales and old ways, a passion he kept hidden from all but his most trusted men, because if he spoke of it he would be opening himself to ridicule from some quarters and outright rebellion from others.

He nodded coolly. 'I have heard you, father-in-law, but must make up my own mind. I am a king, after all, and have my people to answer to.'

Eldon frowned. 'Think of my grandson Garvan; what he could inherit if you do it my way. And what you will bring to ruin, Cahir, if you follow some foolish path of your own out of misplaced pride.'

'I *am* thinking. And I will take my own counsel.'

Eldon and his men peeled away to the west soon after, for Luguvalium. That afternoon, the Maetae turned off as well. Only then, as they crossed the wooded lands to the Clutha did his chieftain Finn come cantering back to Cahir's side. The rain had cleared, bathing them in pale sunshine.

'I won't do it!' he declared furiously. 'I cannot!' He glared at Cahir, though there was fear behind his grey eyes. 'No trade comes through our hills any more, for people are too afraid to travel when the Roman scouts scour the plains. Three sunseasons we have had too little sun and too much rain. The crop is pitiful, Cahir. We cannot do it. We will have hunger in the dun even without paying this.'

Cahir faced him in the saddle. 'I know there is hardship,' he said quietly. 'But I will make sure you have enough grain. We have stores in Dunadd.' *Stores that are fast emptying*, he amended silently. 'I need some time to think of other options.'

'And what about next year?' Finn said harshly. 'And the year after? Gods, Cahir, they are bleeding us dry!' Anger was bright in his weathered face. 'You can think, but I'm going to refuse. I'm not giving in any more.'

Cahir drew a deep breath. 'I understand your anger and, by Hawen, Finn, I share it. *But I need to buy time.* There is no easy way out here, no clear path, and I cannot have your people's blood on my hands.'

'Perhaps nothing is ever clear.' Finn wrapped his reins around his meaty wrists. 'But when our ancestors fought against the Romans at the Hill of a Thousand Spears, was that an easy way out, Cahir? They did it against all odds – in fact, they didn't care about the odds. They fought because they had to, for their own pride, their own blood!'

For a moment Cahir was silent, trying to steady his heart. 'I have listened to the bard tales more times than I can count. Eremon was wise as well as brave. He *did* care about the odds. He thought, mistakenly, that they were in his favour, which is the only reason he agreed to fight the Romans. He *thought*, Finn, he did not act rashly.'

Finn looked as though he'd been slapped. 'He acted boldly, with honour, and all I care is that he acted.' Abruptly, he wheeled his horse. 'I'm going to ride with my own men, and get as far away as I can from these Roman scum before I vomit up their damn wine.'

He rode back to the rear, avoiding Cahir's eyes.

The riders split as they approached the Clutha inlet, Finn and his men turning for their dun. He saluted grimly to Cahir, and Cahir nodded and turned away, smouldering with shame.

He was ashamed he had not taken a lance and driven it through the Dux as he sat there at the council table with that smug smile. *And if I had, I would already be dead, and my people led to Roman slavery.* Cahir stretched his throat to the sea air coming up the valley from the west. Sometimes the royal torc sat heavy around his neck, an honour and a burden both.

Donal and Finbar were, as always, only a few steps behind. 'You did the right thing, lad,' Donal said softly. These two – ruddy, balding Donal and greying Finbar – were still warriors to respect. They did, however, retain the disconcerting habit of seeing the young man in Cahir; the boy who had been idealistic and excited about life.

'Did I?' Cahir glanced at them. 'My heart is with Finn, but we don't have the forces for battle against the Romans. There it is.'

Finbar scratched his stubbled chin. 'There are no easy answers, lad. But we are all here alive and hale, so we've played it well so far.' His grey eyes were opaque, though, and he adjusted his sword-belt with a grim hitch.

Behind, the proud warband was a mass of sodden men, their flashing jewellery and arm-rings dulled, their hair dripping and clothes muddied. Ruarc, Mellan and their friends had subsided into glowering silence. Cahir wondered what action they thought he could take in a fort of hundreds of Roman soldiers, with thousands more on the Wall a few miles away.

What would Eremon have done? He set his face to the north, where the highlands rose in a dark line over the Clutha. Would he have found a way out?

Whenever Cahir asked that question, however, and yearned for an answer, it never came. Nearly three hundred years had passed since Eremon and Conaire lived. Cahir had no doubt they would be enjoying a blessed life in the Otherworld now, leaving behind only the pressure of questions unanswered and the gnawing shame of failure.

In the dark inside him, he wondered if he simply was not worthy of Eremon's counsel, or whether it was just that Eremon was too far now, too distant in time to give any aid to the man who had ascended his throne.

A young man who needed that wisdom, that comfort, and instead was alone.

One of Finn's warriors caught up with Cahir and his men two days later, in a narrow valley in the highland mountains.

They were watering their stallions in a rushing stream when the slopes of the glen reverberated with the sound of a horse being whipped madly along the path behind them. Cahir's heart stopped when he recognized the rider, and even as the man threw himself to the churned mud at his feet, he was bracing himself for the blow.

The warrior stammered out his story as his tears fell on his shaking hands.

Finn had only just arrived home when Roman soldiers came from the Dux demanding the tax from the harvest on the spot. There was no room for compromise. The soldiers formed a ring around the gates of the dun, their javelins readied. Finn went up on the walls and threw their demand back in their faces, saying his people would starve.

Without warning, a Roman javelin skewered one of Finn's men to the palisade. Roaring, the chieftain leaped to his horse, exhorted his warriors to follow, tore open the gates and charged the Roman line.

Cahir's eyes glazed over as the tale spilled out. He saw nothing before him but Finn's proud face, his defiant expression. The warriors threw themselves on those lances with their chief, the messenger finished huskily, and there they all died. The Romans took the grain and rode away without a backwards look.

A deathly hush fell over the Dalriadan warriors, as the stream thundered between its rocks. The hill-slopes pressed down on them, the wet bracken red as blood, the peaks glowering far above, shrouded in cloud. *They followed him home*, was all Cahir could think. *They knew from his face at the council table that he was resistant, and so they followed him and forced his hand. They gave him no way out.*

Nausea roiled in his belly. Finn had lived fifty years – years of fighting, loving and loyalty – but this man mattered less to the Dux than a swatted gnat. For Fullofaudes did this solely to send a warning to Cahir himself. He knew it in his heart, where this outrage, this sorrow, was lodged now like a barb.

'Then we will ride back!' Ruarc pushed the others aside, his face contorted with fury. 'We will hunt down every one of the Roman dogs and stake them to the ground with our spears!' He brandished his lance, the fox-tails tied to its haft swinging. A cheer went up, and, in an instant, seething anger turned to anticipation and excitement.

Cahir pulled his shattered mind together. Gods, yes, that was exactly what he longed to do: bury his sword in a Roman belly and twist it on its hilt. It was so compelling, so compulsive. But no, no. He shook his head to clear it. Too dangerous, too soon. His best warriors were here with him, the defenders of Dunadd. 'No!' he bellowed. 'That is not my order!'

The war-shouts died. Ruarc turned to him with a feral smile. Cahir knew then that he wanted this confrontation. 'You call yourself our king?' Ruarc screeched. 'Your own chief gets slaughtered by the Roman-kind and you will do *nothing*? You will turn your back and let them kill us without fear of reprisals?'

Fury coursed through Cahir's body: at the Romans, at Ruarc, at himself. 'That is what they want! We go back there and attack the fort and the Dux's army will be upon us, riding us down to Dunadd. *Dunadd. Think*, for one moment in your life! Of course they are watching us; of course he will have hundreds of soldiers at the ready, outnumbering us by many times! We would be walking into a death-trap; he wants the provocation.'

Ruarc barely heard him, his temper set free. '*No!* We whine and bow our heads enough. It's time to fight back, time to show we are Dalriadans, Albans, warriors of the gods Lugh and Manannán and Hawen!' He pointed at Cahir. 'And I say we have been led by a coward long enough!'

The warriors gasped and murmured, drawing back, catching the reins of the nervous horses. Ruarc and Cahir were left alone on the edge of the rocky defile that fell to the foaming stream.

Cahir's body had tensed from crown to feet: this cub needed swatting back into place. At least now he could release his rage, not to kill but to disarm, to subdue. With a roar that bounced off the valley sides, he snatched his sword from its scabbard, the pain over Finn flooding him. '*On, then, come on!* You challenge me enough with your words, now do it with your blade!'

Uncertainty flickered over Ruarc's face. *Yes, come on*, Cahir thought, crouching low. Slowly, Ruarc unsheathed his own blade. As a boy he had watched Cahir duel many times, and once witnessed him repel a Pictish ambush. In his cocky pride, though, perhaps he had forgotten. Or he might think Cahir was getting old. If so, he was a fool, for the king's sword-arm was strengthened by years of suppressed frustration, enough to override an eleven-year age gap: Ruarc was only twenty-one, Cahir thirty-two. He wasn't creaking and stiff yet, he wasn't grey, he wasn't beaten. But he was furious and ashamed.

Snarling, Ruarc and Cahir circled each other. But Cahir gave Ruarc no time to think, leaping in so suddenly with a bellow that Ruarc was taken completely by surprise. Forced on the defence he stumbled back, desperately blocking his king's sword, until Cahir tripped on a loose rock and Ruarc plunged into the breach.

Back they staggered, forward they lunged, sliding down the muddy slopes and skidding on pebbles. The warriors were entirely silent but their eyes followed every move, the tide changing between Ruarc on the attack and then Cahir.

Cahir was in a towering rage, but after many years of practice could hold his mind clear and cold. Ruarc, however, was all passion and fury, and that made him sloppy. Suddenly, he tried to get under Cahir's defences with a risky and hopeless leap that the king merely side-stepped. The sodden earth gave way at the side of the path and Ruarc stumbled to one knee. Cahir was on him in the next breath, flicking the younger man's sword away so it tumbled through the air, its point digging into the soil.

That should have been the end of it. However, with a scream of fury that startled all the horses, Ruarc immediately leaped on top of Cahir, bearing him down with his fists.

The two men rolled to the bottom of the slope by the stream, their grunts drowned out by the roar of water. With the danger of blades removed Cahir could at last let himself go, and like boys they threw themselves desperately at each other, rolling one way and then the other, hands scrambling for purchase in the mud. Fists came flying, as first Ruarc and then Cahir was pummelled.

After a while, Cahir's greater height and bulk began to win out, and eventually he managed to toss Ruarc over and clamber on his back, pinning him in a headlock. They were stuck like that, dripping sweat and spatters of blood from cut lips, covered in mud so only their white eyes showed in brown faces.

'Will you yield?' Cahir demanded, gulping air.

Ruarc said nothing, spitting out bloody saliva.

'*Will you?*'

'Aye,' Ruarc muttered at last. 'I yield.'

Cahir knelt by his prone body, panting. 'Now you will at least concede I am no coward.' He scrubbed mud from his face with his sleeve. 'I will do what is best for my people, and you must surrender to that.'

Ruarc's shoulders were heaving, but he still lay face down. 'We can no longer sit on our hands,' he hissed. 'This is not what we were made for – we need our glory!'

As I need mine. Cahir looked down at Ruarc's bright hair, matted now with muck and twigs, and saw a boy who only spoke what his own soul cried. Here they were with blades and fists when in truth their hearts beat the same.

He straightened and rose. Gods, his arms ached! 'I know what you feel, what you want,' he said quietly. 'But until you walk in my footsteps, you cannot know my burdens.'

Ruarc staggered to his feet, and the eyes he turned on Cahir were hurt more than wrathful. 'The people should live free or not live at all!' he declared passionately. 'If we become like the Romans then we have truly died anyway. Why can't you see this? Why do you bind us so?'

'Because you cling to an impossible dream.' The words were sawdust in Cahir's mouth; old, dry and leached of life. With slow dignity, he sheathed his fallen sword and, turning away, climbed the slope. Forcing himself not to stagger, he passed through the silent men to his horse, and there despatched ten warriors to go with Finn's man to guard their dun and carry promises of food and aid. The man kissed his hand, hollow-eyed.

Then Cahir rode away up the trail without looking back, Donal and Finbar scrambling to their horses after him. He did not look to see if Ruarc was following.

Chapter 19

Minna and the girls were collecting roots in the hills above Dunadd on a cold, clear day when a distant horn signalled the return of the king.

Two crusty old warriors had escorted them, but they ignored Minna, avoiding her eyes. They thought she could curse them, Keeva had confided with sly amusement, poison them with her herbs and, for good measure, even see inside them. Minna smiled grimly, easing the last bulbous root from the wet soil. For once, she did not mind such fancies.

At the second horn, Orla and Finola were running down the path, and by the time Minna got to the village gate there was no sign of them in the teeming mass of warriors and horses. She pushed between people clapping each other's backs, hugging and laughing, and struggled to the schoolroom with her heavy bag of roots.

Tucked inside was one specimen that Minna knew, when her fingers first touched it in the soil, was powerful enough to help the young noblewoman Riona. It whispered to her as a potent womb-heal, its pleated leaves not yet shrivelled by frost this close to the sea.

She pushed the door of the schoolroom open and caught herself, nearly dropping everything. For Orla and Finola were there – and with them was their father. Minna merely stared, paralysed.

He was dressed in a rough tunic, hide trousers and filthy boots, everything smeared with dirt and sweat. A bronze torc was his only decoration, but there was no mistaking his presence. The light from the window played over his dark braids, showing up the same copper glints as in Orla's hair. Beneath the stubble his face was finely drawn, with a wide mouth and taut jaw blurred now by a cut lip and bruises. But Minna could not look away, for his features were almost deliberately arranged to increase the power of his gaze. The lines bracketing his mouth led to sharp cheekbones, which angled to straight, dark brows that framed gold-sheened eyes as a doorway did a blaze of daylight. There was a wildness, an intense hunger in his gaze that did not match any kings in Mamo's tales. Or Minna's imagination.

He regarded her discomfort with grim amusement. 'My daughters find this place a haven, somewhere they feel safe. Somewhere to escape ... everything.' His mouth tightened as he gazed out the window. 'I see why they like it. From outside it is unnoticeable. No one would know you were even in here.'

She at last found her wits. 'It is small and basic, lord,' she murmured, placing the net bag on the nearest bench. 'But also warm, because the fire heats it easily.'

He turned and looked at her. 'And since you are Roman-born, I suppose you also think my land barbarically cold and wet?'

She heard the undercurrent of anger, and edged against the wall. 'I am from Eboracum, lord, not Rome.' Words rushed unbidden to her tongue. 'And I can assure you the moors of my home are every bit as cold and wet.'

The king blinked, as surprised as she was at herself. Finola threw her arms about his knees. 'Fa, Fa! Did you see the Wall again? Did you see wolves? Did you see Romans?'

Cahir smiled and brushed her head. 'All those things, beside the wolves, lass. They live in the mountains between us and the Picts, not the south, as I am sure you know.'

'Of course she does,' Orla scorned. 'Davin told us *that*!' She sat on Minna's desk, swinging her legs. 'Look, Minna! We grabbed Fa and dragged him here, and he came.' She giggled. 'We told him we spent all our time here with you and learned Roman things.'

Minna winced, thinking of the conversation she had witnessed between the king, the queen and Garvan. Cahir warmed his hands over the fire. 'Roman things,' he muttered. She held her breath. The coals were dying, since they had been out all day, and now he bent to toss on more wood, poking at the fire with a stick until the flames caught. By the time he glanced up, his voice was level again, the anger under control. 'I was not pleased to hear my girls were being schooled in Latin. However,' he raised one of those dark brows, 'they tell me they only enjoy *certain* parts, such as drawing, gathering plants and writing their names. That doesn't seem so dangerous.'

The glint in his eye flooded her with relief. 'They are very bright, lord,' she offered, placing a hand on Orla's shoulder. 'And very dedicated ... to their people. You can have no cause for doubt.' Every word seemed loaded, and she picked them carefully.

Cahir's stern face softened for a moment. 'Yes, they are Dalriadans through and through. Aren't you, girls?'

'Yes, Fa,' they chorused, glancing between Minna and their father, disconcerted by the prickle of unease in the room.

The king scratched his stubble, his eye on Minna's hand placed so naturally on his daughter's shoulder. 'They tell me that you care for them, too, that you heal them when they are sick.' Her heart skipped at his sudden change. His eyes were lucent, golden as those of a fox, and she didn't know if he was amused or angry. 'And all this, when I had made up my mind to be so unhappy about this Roman nursemaid ... of my wife's.'

She didn't miss the pause. Disconcerted, she blurted, 'But I am not all Roman! My grandmother was of the tribes, so I am quarter-blood, and I know all the old tales.' Her teeth trapped her tongue too late.

The king's expression lightened. 'Indeed? *All?*' As her face grew hot, a smile played about his mouth. 'Well, you make my daughters happy, and the gods know, give them more care in one day than my ... than they enjoy in a year.' He glanced down at his children. 'And they do get into scrapes, my little cubs. If only they were princes, what warriors they would make.'

Orla's grave little face lit up. 'We *can* be warriors, Fa. I'm nearly big enough to hold Garvan's old sword, and when we are even bigger we'll beat back the Romans with you!' A thought occurred to her. 'Just don't kill them all until we're big enough, Fa. *Please.*'

Cahir's bark of laughter was entirely bitter. 'No, I won't kill them all.' From the side, Minna saw his mouth crease, holding in emotion. 'There will be enough Romans, little one, even for you.'

A comb hit Cian on the back of the neck. He gritted his teeth but did not flinch, burying his head against the grey stallion's scented neck – Ruarc's other steed, since the bastard took the black when he disappeared in the mountains.

A brush followed the comb with a thump. Cian picked up both tools, tucking them with the horse blanket on a stool. '*Grates,*' he said in Latin, then in Dalriadan, 'I could do with an extra comb. Funny how they fall from the sky.'

His hatred beat in his blood, and all he could see behind his eyes was the man kneeling in the mud stammering out the story of his chief's death, the sorry tale falling on deaf, cold ears. He cursed the king under his breath, rubbing hard at the horse's coat.

'Roman scum.' The hiss came from the next stall. 'Gelded bastard.'

'At least *I* have something to piss with,' Cian retorted.

There was a pause, a guttural laugh. '*Did your whore of a mother couple with pigs?*'

Cian's hand stilled. He should ignore it; he had heard it all. But his mother ... Mamaí ... *named in their evil tongue* ... Taking a deep,

118

shuddering breath, Cian threw down the brush and leaped over the stall as easily as he had once jumped on Bren's shoulders.

Though he was stiff and bruised, his speed caught the little whelps by surprise. With a yell, Cian drove his worst tormentor to the ground and started pummelling him. Screeching, six other boys leaped on Cian and dragged him off, two sitting on his legs, two on his arms. The first boy, nose running blood, leaned over and, with great deliberation, began thumping Cian about the ears.

He reeled, lights sparking behind his eyes, but a noise from outside interrupted them and the boys melted away, guffawing. Cian crawled back to his own stall and staggered up against the stallion, which nervously twitched its ears, sensing his distress. Footsteps came to the end of the stable, and he scrubbed at his face with the cloth, hoping he did not bleed. The nobles beat them if they fought around their precious horses.

'Cian?' came a soft voice. His eyes briefly closed before he turned to Minna. 'You came back,' she said. Gods, he had forgotten, in the horror of the past week, how intense her gaze was.

His swollen mouth moved. 'So it seems.'

'But ... why?'

He swallowed hard, shifting his gaze to the grey horse and studiously thumping its shoulder, feeling over its legs with sensitive fingers. 'I wouldn't leave you here alone, if that's what you are suggesting.' His hurt blocked his throat. Even she thought that of him.

When he straightened, her eyes were luminous and open, and he felt the change in her. Something had happened while he was away; his acrobat's senses were attuned to such things. She was holding herself differently, more upright and contained, as if cradling a secret. Her hair was wound around her crown, the back falling in tendrils threaded with white gull feathers. The style softened her bony face. She looked ... she looked like *them*. Cian's pulse began to hammer.

'I did not think you would come back for me.' She hesitated, turning him inside out with her many-layered gaze. 'You should have saved yourself.'

The hammering became a lurch, and he stepped back in anticipation of her coming near, for he didn't think he could bear any hint of tenderness. But she didn't move.

Did he think she would have begged him back, or fall on him now, weeping? Instead, she simply stroked the horse's nose, absorbed in some internal world of her own.

'We got into this together,' he said hoarsely. 'We should get out of it so.'

She glanced at him. 'So this means that you will listen to me? That you will hold your tongue so we can bide our time?'

Scenes rushed through his mind: the Roman soldiers at the fort; the chieftain's glorious, hopeless death; the way the king did nothing. And then the clash of swords in the duel, the twisting of their faces into bestial snarls. After five weeks, he felt sick at the idea of holding on here for any more time at all. Death would be better than that, he thought wildly – a spear in the back as he ran over the bridge.

Minna frowned. 'What happened?'

His hands were tense as he untied the stallion's head and threw down some hay for it. But the tale was pushing its way out of him like rising bile, and in the end it spilled out.

'The bastard did nothing,' he spat when he finished. 'Even when his own chief was slaughtered. They are all craven cowards.'

She was calm, searching his face. 'I did hear them say there was a reason ...'

'Minna!' He cut her off, the fury overcoming him, utterly blinding. Yes, she had changed ... *she was going out of his reach* ... 'How can you argue with me over *them*?'

Her cheeks reddened. 'It's not like you to be reckless with your own skin; it's not like you at all.'

'Well, perhaps you don't know everything. And it's my skin, and my choice what to do with it.' A hole had opened beneath his feet, a gulf he hadn't seen coming, and so was helpless to cross.

Instinctively, he turned away from its blackness, stumbling sightlessly out into the village. Anywhere away from her.

'Ruarc and the other lads have not come back, Cahir.'

Minna was sitting awake by her bed, her chin in her hands, her mind gnawing over Cian. Now she leaned down and pressed her eye to a gap in the timbers above the hall, which looked down upon the hearth-benches and the few men lingering there.

'They will be the death of us.' Cahir's voice was infinitely weary.

'They are frustrated, that is all,' said the one with tufts of red hair in his ears. 'Too much energy and nothing to do with it. You remember how it was Finbar, aye? You remember too, lad,' he added quietly.

To Minna's astonishment he had just addressed Cahir, for the king answered, somewhat testily, 'I'm only eleven summers older than Ruarc, Donal. My bones don't creak quite yet.'

'At that age,' one of the others put in mildly, 'we fought the Picts in that battle for the Black Island, remember?'

'Aye, Finbar, I remember,' Donal chuckled, 'and how that blue bastard's sword nearly separated Fergal from the comfort of his wife's thighs!'

There was a rumble of laughter, out of which Cahir's voice rose.

'My father fought then, too, I believe. Right before he signed the treaty with Rome.'

There was a pregnant silence no one seemed willing to break, until Cahir got up with agitation. 'I am going out, and I don't want anyone to follow me.'

'You need your rest, lad. We all do.'

'I believe,' Cahir said stiffly, 'that despite all said to the contrary, I am king here and my decisions are my own.'

It was Keeva who volunteered to come when Minna slipped away the next day to find more of the Lady Riona's plant. The maid was bemused by all the secrecy, but Riona had ordered them to say nothing to Brónach, declaring she would come herself to the schoolroom, and Minna had complied, although somewhat uneasily.

She and Keeva left the dun with baskets, alone but for one surly old guard. 'I don't think this plant would grow near the fields or where people disturb it,' she explained.

Keeva squinted into the cold winter sun, thinking. 'There's the ancestor valley,' she suggested, pointing to the north.

But Minna had already seen that eerie place, the valley floor dotted down its length with old burial cairns, and stones and circles mysteriously raised by the ancestors to worship the sky. 'People till the fields up the valley sides,' she said, shaking her head. 'I don't think it will be there.'

Keeva swivelled the other way. 'There are hills that way, too,' she said, pointing south. 'And sacred places no one goes.' She sent Minna a challenging look. 'They don't scare me, though – do they scare you?'

She smiled. 'No.' But she had no idea what Keeva was talking about.

They climbed far up into the forest, and she found three of the womb-plants with their pleated leaves, along with enough roots and mushrooms to allay Brónach's suspicions. Her palms were soon stained with wet soil and, in the quiet of the winter woods, her tension over Cian began to melt from her shoulders.

Keeva left her alone, snatching a rare doze on her cloak in the sun, as the guard set himself on the edge of the hill, digging under his nails with his dagger.

Drifting along in the daze of the plant-song, Minna hardly noticed the grey stones set upright along the path. She did not see the cloths fluttering in the rowan trees, or the sharpened stakes nailed with rotting shields. Then light hit her, and she realized she'd wandered out of the bare trees on to a hillside of dying bracken, bathed by sun. Frost still filled the hollows on the shadowed edges.

Clutching her bag to her chest, Minna glanced around. Only then did she see the mounted shields that ringed the clearing, their casings trailing tatters of leather. Warrior shields. She immediately turned, her heart striking out a warning. *A place of men.*

But before she could move, her eye fell on what the shields guarded. In the centre rose an immense hump of grey rock, like a whaleback surfacing from the brown grasses. And the low winter sun was picking out a vast expanse of carvings: the entire surface of the rock was inscribed with designs, many smoothed by years of wind and rain.

She slowly squatted. There were pecked hollows surrounded by rings, lines cutting the hollows, and spirals. The air in the clearing became hushed. Minna's arm was drawn from her side as if it had a mind of its own. *I will be solemn*, she said to the silent trees. *I will do honour.*

Tentatively, she found herself reaching for a spiral. Her palm spread across the whorl, and it was like dangling her fingers in a rushing stream, the current of energy dragging at her. She plucked her hand out and glanced over her shoulder. She wanted to leave, but then she remembered the hills, singing to her that time when she took Orla out to look for roots by the river. If there was pain in her dreams of this place, could there be something else, too? The song of the hills had hinted ... something. Something she would have heard, if that Lorcan had not come upon her.

Wetting her lips, Minna stared at her hand as it drifted out again to the spiral ...

... and instead of the grey rock there was a chariot racing underneath her. Her bare feet gripped the yoke just behind the flanks of two black ponies, which bunched as they ran. The warrior she was screamed as a line of armoured men flew by in a blur. She careened past a vast army, and she was a god, naked but for her sword, clinging to the jolting chariot, screaming fury and courage, knowing she would die, and not caring ...

She fell back on her haunches, gasping. She wasn't afraid, though, just assailed by emotion ... pride, freedom, exultation. She'd never felt such a fire in her blood; no pain, just joy.

'You found the hero carvings,' Keeva said, peering over her shoulder.

Minna scrambled up guiltily, but the maid just continued munching on a handful of blackberries, unperturbed.

'What are they?'

Keeva brushed the last berries from her hands. 'When the great heroes died, the ancestors carved symbols for them. That, there.' She pointed at the double spiral. 'You can trace around all the way in, then all the way back out. It's life, see: a cycle with no end, just another beginning. That's what my father always said. We come from the Mother's womb, we live, we die, we return to Her and then are reborn again. The endless spiral.' Her voice had grown uncharacteristically soft. 'On the islands we carve them, too, to remember the Goddess when so many forget.'

Minna's mind reeled. '*Reborn?*'

Keeva glanced at her, shrugging. 'When we die, we live in bliss in the Otherworld and then come back as babes again.' She looked down at Minna's bag. 'Did you get enough roots?' she asked cheerfully.

That night Minna was laying blankets on the floor in the middle of the night, unable to sleep as the girls tossed and turned. Her legs were still loose from the feeling of running that chariot . . . she stopped and stared into the shadows, her scalp prickling all over again. Then she tensed, glancing over her shoulder as footsteps came up the stairs.

'Lass,' a rough voice whispered. It was that man Donal, his bald pate shiny in the dim light. 'You must come with me now. The king orders it.'

Minna thought she had misheard, but then her hackles went up again. 'What do you mean?'

Donal seemed ill at ease, rubbing the back of his neck and avoiding her eyes. 'He needs you to attend him – he has a fever of some kind.' When she stared, wide-eyed, he snapped, 'Don't be foolish, girl, you won't be harmed. Hurry now!'

She had no choice but to follow, grabbing her cloak to throw over her bed-shift. Outside, the icy wind tugged at her hood, as torn banners of cloud streaked a yellow half-moon. His head down, Donal led Minna to Brónach's house. 'In there.' He gestured Minna to the door. 'He's in there.'

123

Chapter 20

Clenching his teeth against the pain, Cahir raised his head when the girl came in, and his eyes went wide.

Her boy's clothes and tightly-bound hair always made her look capable enough, and her face was angular and intelligent. Despite Maeve's whim to buy her, Orla said there was no contact between his wife and this girl now; the queen's thoughts had flitted on to something else. The girl cared for his daughters, she could heal and she was afraid of him. The perfect person to help.

Now this apparition came in her stead: hair a drift of black about her shoulders, face milk-pale, those stark features softened by the loose hair and lamplight. The fire picked out not the unearthly colour of her eyes now, but their shifting depths. And she was clad in a thin shift of linen with a lamp behind her, her outlined body definitely that of a woman. She looked young, vulnerable and very fair – and *she* was supposed to help *him*?

Cahir's certainty wavered. Perhaps she did not have the experience. Should he wait for Brónach after all? He shuddered at the thought of his aunt's bony fingers prodding him, her knowing eyes. The scent of his sickness soured the air, and the wound spasmed. Wincing, he leaned towards the slave. 'Girl, I require your assistance, but I *forbid* you to tell anyone you have even been here. Do you understand?'

The white column of her throat fluttered. After a pause she blurted, 'I will do so, but only if you swear you won't hurt me.'

Cahir stared, then his surprise dissolved into a dry snort of amusement. 'Ah, me.' He looked at Donal. 'What did you tell her, man? She looks like I'm about to gobble her up.'

Donal shrugged, said nothing. Cahir waved a hand at him. 'Leave us now, but stay outside. I want to know the minute my aunt appears, and if you see her, detain her for me until I can make my escape.'

As soon as Donal was gone, Cahir spread his fingers over his side. 'I am wounded,' he said slowly. 'Now it burns and I grow … concerned.'

Wounded? Minna's attention narrowed to the lump under his tunic, before she glanced at his face, noticing only then a sheen of sweat. *Infection.* That explained the sourness. 'But I don't understand why you called me, why you do not wait for Lady Brónach—'

'She sees too much as it is. But my daughters have told me you know some healing.'

And will keep my silence. That was the heart of the matter. She was a slave, and would hold her tongue out of fear. But if he had been wounded in an altercation with the Romans, why was that cause for secrecy?

To give herself time to think, she turned away. 'I will need more light, a hotter fire.' She stirred up the coals and fed them with twigs, then lit the lamps with tapers before returning to the king. Her hands trembled, but she settled her face into the mask of a healer, clung to that briskness.

The furrows around his mouth were deeper, his hair unbound and tangled with sweat. But it was only when she met his eyes that her healing sense spoke. In the firelight, his irises were flecked with gold and green, yet it was self-loathing that spilled from his black pupils. As soon as he met her glance, his lashes veiled his thoughts.

'Standing there mute won't help. You certainly didn't have trouble finding your voice before.'

Minna's fists curled. Then Keeva's words came back to her. *Make yourself useful to the nobles … you don't know what could happen.* She picked up the pot on the hearth. 'I am not mute,' she replied with dignity, going to the water barrel. 'And I have a name.' She could not help him with her whole heart while being seen as a *thing*, a possession. He might beat her, but still she had to speak. When she turned back, terrified and defiant, there was a definite spark behind his fevered glaze. *This is it*, she thought, *he'll just strike me and be done with it.*

But the king only shrugged. 'If that is what you need to fix this problem, Minna-the-slave-of-Eboracum, then I will call you anything you like.'

Flustered, she put water to boil and stood over him. He had a cup and jug in his lap, and when he poured the ale it splashed over the rim. She watched as he gulped, throat rippling beneath a dark pelt of stubble, then threw the cup on the rushes. Without looking at her he tugged off his plain blue tunic, wincing. 'Do, then, what you will.'

Cautiously, as if approaching a chained bear, Minna went down on her knees. To her dismay his torso had been clumsily bandaged, the linen smeared with dried blood. The cloth looked as though it had been used many times. She gently picked the knot apart and began unwinding, turning her face away when leaning close to his armpit. To her surprise, underneath the scent of infection he did not smell anything more than musky. The last part of the bandage was stuck down with dried pus, and as she eased it free he grunted.

Minna sat back swallowing, as Cahir stared straight ahead. He was letting her make of it what she would. And what was that?

She scanned the muscles over belly and chest, knowing enough of men to see it was the honed torso of someone used to rugged activity – sword-play, she amended, fascinated at the webs of random scars that marked his arms and hands. There was a tension in such muscles that was confronting, like a wild animal poised to spring. His ribs pushed against his skin in ragged breaths.

She lowered her eyes. Here were the wounds: two cuts of equal size and length, one under each pectoral muscle on either side of the abdomen. She knew immediately they were not battle wounds. Although she'd never actually seen a battle wound, it was impossible that any wild sword slash could replicate these symmetrical cuts. Minna padded her fingers with her skirt and rolled the flesh away from one, and Cahir stifled another grunt of pain. Because of infection neither wound had closed; their edges were angry red, the centres yellow. The skin was burning, but it wasn't the most serious infection she'd seen and would heal well enough with care.

Then her belly plummeted.

She saw now that the skin above and below the wounds was scored with other marks just the same; perfectly even, perfectly executed. They were older, running in a knitted ladder down one side of his belly and up the other. Some were still red, raised scars; others had faded to silver. Minna stared, aghast.

Cahir's faster breathing brought her back. Though his face was averted, his cheeks had coloured, and there were white lines of strain about his mouth. That was when she knew it was deliberate. She got unsteadily to her feet, turning to the fire and lifting off the pot with a stick.

'It's bad, isn't it?'

'No.' She levered off the lid, and steam washed over her. 'I can heal them. They won't get worse.'

After a pause, Cahir emitted a weary sigh, a sigh so full of pain that she stayed there, eyes on the fire. *He did it to himself.* A man like that, so tall and strong, would never suffer such humiliation unwillingly. She hastened to Brónach's workbench, her mind jumbled. *Groundsel and ivy leaves for a poultice. Yarrow ointment. Yarrow flowers, sorrel.* Nausea stung her throat as she ground the herbs and stewed them. He cut *himself.*

Struggling to regain composure, Minna knelt by Cahir and dared a glance at him, recognizing there a grim determination to hold everything in with that tight mouth. She dipped a cloth into the yarrow broth and put her palm on his chest to dab the wound. So she touched the king of Dalriada at last, skin to skin.

And all his feelings were suddenly pouring into her, flowing from his flesh into hers. Brutal pain, guilt, fury. He gasped and turned his head and they stared, falling into each other's eyes in shock. *He felt it, too.* Then his lips clamped down and he twisted away.

But it was too late, for Minna understood.

His fury was directed at himself, even though he wasn't suffering in complete silence – he spoke with the blade of his dagger, his flesh the vellum upon which he scored his shame. She dropped the cloth as his repressed feelings reached for her like a flame for a gust of air, then she broke the hold and hurried outside.

Donal stirred, but when she merely leaned against the wall, holding her belly, he turned back to his watch.

Minna drew the freezing air in deep, trying to cleanse her soul. It was some time before she could go back inside, and the only way to proceed was to move her hands as if they were separate from her body, carefully avoiding his eyes. She bathed the wound, pulped the poultice and applied bandages, then poured the fever brew. They did not speak.

When she had finished, Minna fetched her cloak. 'One week,' she murmured, her eyes on the wall, her cheeks sore from being bitten. 'I will need to change the poultice every day, then you can apply the salve yourself.'

The king nodded, face turned to the shadows. 'Donal will fetch you.'

She fled into the night.

Chapter 21

Cahir ordered five grain pits to be emptied and loaded on to ships bound for the Wall. After considering all alternatives, he had decided to pay the tax. There was nothing to be done – if he did not comply, the Romans would deliver to his people the same justice meted out to Finn.

In the night, he lay with one hand pressed to the wall as if he could force a path through it, showing him the way forward. In his mind, he conjured an entire plan to summon the warriors, encircle the dun, send a message of defiance to the Dux and wait for the axe to fall. He lived, vividly, the moment he would throw himself on a Roman lance and pierce his bowels, ending shame for ever. But his mind was bred to be cool, and he knew he would be condemning his people to instant death.

It was simple: he did not have the numbers of men for defiance.

What made Dunadd useful for trade made it vulnerable. He had forces mustered on all the approaches to the south and east; guards for the coastal forts, garrisons for the signal beacons on the headlands. But a full defence was impossible without tens of thousands of men, and in all Dalriada he could probably muster only eight thousand.

If that was not bad enough – his people looking at him with accusing eyes as the pits were emptied, the still gnawing worry about where Ruarc and his comrades had gone – Cahir had now been unsettled in a far different way.

His daughters had reported to him in their childish chatter the things the slave Minna had been saying in her sleep.

Cahir was so shaken that so far he had merely watched her as she went about healing his wounds. He knew her eyes denoted her as unusual; that his skin reacted to her hands. That was only because no one beyond his daughters had touched him properly for years, though, he told himself. He denied himself soft caresses, tenderness, releasing only bare lust when he bedded women. That was the price, his penance.

But this stranger's fingers moved like breaths across his skin, and the time he spent in the little schoolroom being salved were rare moments of peace. Sometimes, when he caught the girl's glances, he could swear he saw sympathy and an odd understanding there. Sympathy, for him! That made her unique in all Dalriada, he thought grimly.

And now this.

She cries out, Fa, Orla said. *We don't wake her any more, because we like to hear what she says. The Boar! she cries, and Rhiann's name sometimes, but Fa, she says other things, too . . .*

Minna and Keeva were turning back from the grain pit with the girls when a deafening shout went up from the walls, followed by blood-curdling shrieks.

Along with everyone else, they hastened to the gates and up the stairs to the walls. 'The Lord Ruarc is back!' came the cry. People crowded the palisade, crushing them against the stakes.

The king was standing in the middle of the gate arch. Before him, dancing around on his black horse, was Ruarc. Behind him was his friend Mellan and around ten other young warriors. Ruarc was dishevelled, his fine clothes muddy and blood-streaked, his face scratched and grimy. But he had paused to lime his hair, which was standing up in stiff waves on his crown and cresting down his back.

With a manic laugh, he untied something from his saddle and threw it in the earth at Cahir's feet. Everyone craned to see what it was. As it rolled and came to rest, the exclamations spread. Minna peered hard, then gasped and moved to shield Finola and Orla's eyes.

It was a severed head. Dried blood matted the long, black hair above blue tattoos on waxy skin. A Pict.

'What is this?' Cahir demanded.

Orla pulled away from Minna's hand, staring down with an avid glee. People's faces were lit with excitement, not revulsion.

Ruarc grinned, but his eyes burned with wildfire. 'What does it look like, my king?' He jabbed a finger toward the river, where a small herd of cattle milled about, penned in by circles of whooping riders. 'A cattle raid! There are the cattle, and here is the head of honour, one of five Picts we killed!'

Cahir's response was lost in the cheer that rose from the throng, whipped up by the appearance of the exuberant young warriors, spattered with gore but reeking of male pride and glory, their swords flashing under the sun. Orla and Finola jumped up and down beside Minna, giggling.

Then Ruarc looked down at his king and at last his smile faltered.

It was ridiculous, but in the middle of his rage Cahir nearly laughed.

Ruarc had set forth on a cattle-raid, just like the warriors of old, just as the bards sang in their sagas – though in those myths there was no need to consider consequences.

Still, as Cahir stood there before the restive stallion, he was shot through with envy. To have the freedom to swing his sword through the Picts like butter, and scream himself hoarse! His blood was Eremon's blood, and he too was stirred up by warriors on dancing horses, swords unsheathed, hair flying in the wind. *Lugh, give me strength. Put all that away.*

He had beaten Ruarc, and now the young cockerel had challenged him again. He held those blazing eyes. 'I thought we had settled this,' he said evenly. 'There, in the mountains. I make the decisions for us all. If you don't like it, leave or fight me properly this time – to the death.'

Ruarc's eyes flickered away, then abruptly he changed tack, tossing his golden mane. 'Why, my king, we only did this to honour you – to honour all our people!' He beamed that smile at all the spectators on the walls. 'We raided the enemy to make them remember us, to know we are not weak. If they think us complacent, they might attack to test us. Now they won't.'

Cahir studied him. Ruarc had got it out of his system, and was giving him a way out, too. He was not secure enough to challenge the king; but Cahir likewise needed his leadership of the young-bloods to make his kingdom secure.

'I value your sword-arms too much to shed your blood recklessly,' Cahir said at last, to a general murmur of approval. 'But if any of you put a single foot wrong again you *will be banished*. You cannot challenge the king, and that is final. You break your blood oaths if you do.'

Ruarc stared down, eyes bright. He went to say something then swallowed it.

'Secondly,' Cahir went on, 'though I acknowledge your bravery, you cannot keep these spoils. In disobeying your lord, the wealth is forfeit to me, to be distributed among the people for the long dark.'

Ruarc's throat moved again. 'Of course!' he cried, after only a moment's hesitation. 'This is all for the people. We did not do this for wealth! Regaining our honour – *their* honour – is all that matters.' He waved his sword over his head, and the people went wild, shouting and cheering.

Cahir watched with a half-smile. Gods, but he would make a fine king for the spectacle alone! *He'd* bedazzle the Romans into submission. Then he thought of the Dux's hard face and knew he would never be bested by someone like Ruarc. He would eat him for breakfast, and then come calling on Dunadd with fifty ships at his back.

Cahir held a hand up. There must be a way to cool all this hot blood. 'Your prowess, though admirable, will have inflamed our enemy. We are all in danger now of their revenge. So I am sending you to guard the hills, at least until snow blocks the passes. That is my will.'

At the moment Ruarc met Cahir's eyes, something passed between them that recognized this as the best way. Cahir sighed inwardly. 'In four days, we will slaughter one of the bulls and have a feast in honour of the gods who brought our warriors back safely.'

More excited murmurings ran across the crowd, and Ruarc broke into a triumphant smile. Cahir eyed him grimly. 'Let that fill your belly for the cold moons you'll spend on watch.' He turned away, walking stiffly. In his anger, he had been tensing too much, and now his wounds throbbed.

Minna usually changed the king's poultice when the girls were at lessons, but after the scene with Ruarc he did not come, and it was only at dusk that Donal drew her away from the king's hall to the empty schoolroom.

The wind rattled the darkened window as Minna knelt beside Cahir in the lamplight. In the week she had been treating him, she kept her gaze confined to his wounds. If she attached that flesh to the muscles that moved as he breathed, the sweeping lines of his arms and neck, or worse, the weight of his golden eyes on her, she grew clumsy and thick-fingered.

She had never touched a man, and now she had to touch one that looked like *this*. And she found, frighteningly, that the feelings she had deadened long ago were stirring because the other parts of her were being broken open, too. Since first she touched him, the pain in the dreams had sharpened, like a knife through her heart. Whispers fluttered around her incessantly at night, just below her hearing, as she clutched the sheets to her chin. She did not understand.

She could barely eat for the sense of foreboding that hung over the dun. And now he made her feel this – when he was a king, cold and hard, unreachable, and she should be terrified instead. *I do not understand.* She was going mad.

Her palms were slippery, and she rubbed them irritably down her trousers. Disconcertingly, Cahir was studying her. At last he cleared his throat, and then it came at her like an arrow. 'Orla told me about your dreams.'

Minna dropped the pot of comfrey salve into the folds of her tunic. 'I have heard the tales from your bard, my lord,' she stammered, retrieving it and clumsily putting the lid back on. 'The songs, the stories, the new things around me … they give me nightmares. That is all.'

His eyes fixed on her, like a cat about to spring. 'We know about such awake-dreams – there is no reason to hide them from me. I want to know …' He blew out his breath, and she realized how disturbed he was. Self-preservation flooded her. 'There is something you said in sleep, a war cry—'

'I heard it from Davin!'

Cahir caught her wrist so hard it hurt, his eyes flashing. 'Not the Boar of Eremon's lineage that my own warriors scream every day! It is a far older oath, used by those at Dunadd before my ancestors came from Erin. The oath of Rhiann's tribe: the Epidii, People of the Horse.'

Minna went cold, her lips moving in memory. *The Mare. The Mare.* A white horse on a blue banner, once raised alongside the boar in battle many years ago.

'See?' Cahir snapped. 'No one says these sacred words any more, no one even knows them except for the druids – and me. And there is more.'

Minna's nostrils flared as he pulled her closer. 'In your dreams you spoke of a hill: a crooked ridge that rears alone from a flat plain.' He paused, his face grim. 'It is the Hill of a Thousand Spears, our only description of this place, wherever it may be.'

'I heard it from Davin … I heard the tale one night—'

'Its appearance isn't in any songs. Again, it is druid lore.'

Minna subsided into silence, panting.

'I gained everything from Orla and Finola, Minna. They know more than you think, though they told me in innocence and, I have to say, love you well. But this does not detract from the real matter: you speak the names of my ancestors, shout the war-cries and see what few have seen, the greatest battlefield of all. So why is it that you, a Roman slave, summon my royal blood?' His eyes staked her there. '*Who are you?*'

His fist was holding hers captive, his breath hot on her cheek. It was the first time he had touched her with his fingers, and they burned. 'I know nothing. Please …'

Horror flared in Cahir's eyes. 'It cannot be that *she* told you to taunt me so? You are not her puppet after all?'

Maeve. 'No! I would never betray you …' she caught herself, '… your daughters. Never!'

'*Do you swear it?*'

It was as if his power had taken hold of her, and Minna was drawn inexorably towards him, though she fought it, horrified. 'I will swear on the spirit of the only person I have ever truly loved, my Mamo,' she cried desperately. 'I swear!'

For a long moment he searched her face, and she tried to lay herself bare, let him see she was no threat. She distinctly felt his awareness brush hers, as she had seen into him once. The world moved beneath her ... his breath was scented with berries and ale ... then she felt his fear of betrayal, sickening.

At last, Cahir released her wrist. His hands trembled as he placed them flat on his thighs, his face turned away. 'When Orla told me, I thought after all you were a spy. Anyone could have planted you: my wife, her father, the Dux Britanniarum himself, for all I know.'

Minna rubbed her wrist. 'I am no spy.'

'I can see that now. I would not be a king if I could not read men – or women. You do not have the skills to dissemble. There is no slyness in your eyes, and so far I have seen you speak always without thinking.' His voice was remote, but when he turned he was clearly shaken. 'We call you a dreamer, though I had not heard of this gift among the Roman kind. If anything else comes to you, you *must* tell me. It is vital, to me, to my daughters, if you care for them at all.'

Why? Minna cried inside. The dreams were her burden, her pain. What could they mean when he knew all these things already?

She found herself nodding, not trusting her voice, the touch of his breath resting on her skin.

Cahir walked slowly away from the schoolroom and took his horse down to the sea, abandoning himself to the gallop along the moonlit path, the wild wind tearing at the trees, the waves foaming far out in the darkness.

The girl Minna, whose touch made him shiver, who looked at him as if she knew him, was a dreamer, a vessel of the gods. And of all the people in Dalriada, the messages were now coming through her.

Cahir's own dreams had changed this past year, and he had startled sometimes when he was deep in thought by the fire, sure he had heard someone call his name. It was an echo that rose *up* through the air like a bubble from a deep pool – unlike any sound of Thisworld.

For years he had known something was stirring in him, long before this slave-girl ever set foot in Alba. He had ignored it, hoping and fearing at the same time that he was wrong. But now, to make it undeniable, *they* had brought a foreign dreamer here – a vessel with Roman blood, no less – to shock him into accepting it was real.

His ancestors had spoken before, in his dreams, in his shamed heart. Now they cried out their summons, and he knew they were demanding he heed it. They wanted him to remember what lay unfulfilled in his blood, the failure that weighed on him, crushed him until he couldn't breathe.

As if he could forget.

★

Minna was unsteadily making her way back to the hall when someone pulled her into a darkened yard, a hand covering her mouth. She bit back a cry when she recognized the smell of horse and leather.

She twisted free. 'What are you doing up here? Gods, they will kill you if they find you!' Frantically, she pulled Cian between the houses. 'Come, you must get back through the gate, and quickly.'

'Minna.' Something about his cracked voice arrested her. 'I had to see you.'

The moonlight fell on his gaunt face, bleaching his skin grey, turning his eyes into black, glazed pits. His bloodless lips moved. 'I have to go now – I can stay here no longer.' A shudder ran over him.

Alarmed, Minna chafed his cold hands. He didn't even notice her touch this time.

'They are murderers,' he hissed. 'Savages ... animals ... I cannot stand it.' She was confused, then remembered the Pict head rolling on the ground. 'The feast is in four nights ... You heard them, they will all be on the meadow and, before dawn, will be lost in drink. We can steal horses ... *we must run then!*'

His words struck her. 'So soon,' she whispered unthinkingly.

Cian stared into her eyes.

She should say, *of course, yes, run.* Her mouth even opened but nothing came out. And between one breath and the next, a vivid image flowered in her: the last time she stood on the crest of the crag gazing out over the marsh, when it seemed she was at the bow of a great, grey ship ploughing through a sea of rippling grass. The wind scoured her clean and the far hills sang to her, called to her ...

'They will not expect us to run in this season, but we can do it, we can.'

His voice reached her from far away. She should have felt excitement at the thought of freedom, but instead there was only a cold pang. As her silence lengthened, Cian said, 'Minna' in a darker tone.

But she could not reassure him. Her feet were rooted there as if tendrils of her soul had descended into the soil and she had no say over it at all. It was visceral, old, instinctive. Her heart beat with the knowing of the plants. Even the fear of Cahir's eyes and demanding words seemed fainter, instead stirring a hunger to know why she cried these things she could not know.

It was all madness; she must go home to Broc, to Eboracum. *But there was no home.* And Broc hadn't written once he left for the Wall, he didn't care – she knew he didn't, though she had shied away from this reality with all her will. He had handed her over to a man she hated, without a backwards glance.

As these thoughts ran through her, raising the hairs on her skin, the air heard her and whispered gleefully ... *yes, the blazing hills, the scent of soil, the light of Alba on the jewel sea ...* And into her heart something dropped, a tantalizing promise that the thing she had most longed for she would find in the cradle of this place, though she didn't yet know what it was.

The contradictions swirled about her, like clouds around a pinnacle on which she desperately clung. She was split in two: what her mind knew to be sense feeling wrong in her heart, unreal. Then at last it all dissolved. Minna's soul simply opened to her, and she had to face her own stark, baffling truth.

She was sick with the thought of leaving.

Cian searched her eyes and she saw the realization she could hardly voice to herself gradually dawn over him. His features slackened, like a wall crumbling, and for the first time she saw all the way into his naked self.

And all that was there was despair, an endless well falling down into eternal blackness. It sucked at her, wanting to take her with it.

She tried to speak, but he cut her off with a stifled cry. 'So this is why you would not go – they have seduced you, too!'

Minna found her voice as he backed up against the wall. 'No, that is not ... I did not know before but now ... so much has happened ...'

He struggled, his pain wavering before it was abruptly wiped out by a great flood of fury, like a dam breaking. '*No!* You are *Roman*, Minna. How can you do this?'

'I don't know,' she replied unsteadily. 'But I can't leave until I understand. I know this place ...'

'*No, you don't!*' he spat. The whites of his eyes were livid in the dimness, and his hand rose before him as if to ward her away. 'Oh, gods ...'

'Cian.' She tried to break through, snatch at his hands, but he flung her off.

'You are living in a fantasy, a world that doesn't exist! These people kill and burn and care for nothing and no one but their own blood lust and glory. *Nothing.* And that makes you not just foolish but a traitor to your own kind. *A traitor, do you hear me?*' He choked, the lump in his throat moving. "And I came back for you!" It came out in a wail.

She was thrust back by the disgust in his face, the storm of his emotion. She scrambled for her wits and at last clenched her fists by her sides, steadying herself. 'We need to speak when you are calmer, when you can listen to me.' She tilted her head up to him, pleading. 'Wait for me, and I'll tell you everything then, I promise.'

But Cian's eyes went wide with anguish, and he stumbled backwards down the alley.

'I need time!' she cried.

He paused. 'Time won't change what you've become,' he spat. '*One of them.*' He whirled, his feet thudding away.

The reality of what was happening crashed over Minna and she started after him. But a noblemen was passing, frowning at the disturbance, and instead she shrank back into the shadows, desperately trying to collect her thoughts.

Cian would come back, she told herself, pressing her shaking hands against the wall. After he worked off his anger, he would come back. He had to.

Chapter 22

LONG DARK, AD 366

Cian was gone.

For days Minna repeated this to herself, unable to believe it.

He didn't wait for the feast but stole Ruarc's stallion that very dawn, just as he said he would, slipping away as he watered it at the river. No one paid any attention to him, for despite his height he could move silently when he wanted, blending into shadows. Or so Minna heard, heartsick.

Ruarc's fury was incandescent. After a harsh interrogation, during which she only whispered that she knew nothing, riders were sent out to scour the bare woods. No trace of Cian was found.

And so Minna faced the coming of the snows without him.

The ground hardened, frost rimed the eaves and the water troughs froze. Clíona kept her busy drying and bottling elderberries, crabapples, rowan and late brambles, and roasting and grinding hazelnut meal. Mired in work, she found herself slipping into the same numbness as the cold land; her mouth forming the words when she taught the girls in the dim schoolroom, but her eyes blank.

Cian was Rome to her, like the memory of Broc with his clipped hair and Mamo, whose clothes had smelled of rosemary. A last whisper of family, an echo of her own tongue. *And yet she had turned away from all that.* She could hardly bear to face the confused tangle of feelings inside, like a skein of knotted threads. Or the loneliness that ached in her core, even though she curved both arms around her ribs, rocking her cold body to sleep.

The king had ordered rationing after the tithes, and soon people grew pinched on the thin barley gruel and dried strips of salt beef. The warriors were penned inside by rain and sleet, and fights woke Minna and the girls nearly every night. As the tension festered, her dreams became more vivid, until she was unable to tell the battle cries apart from the shriek of storms.

Then a rash of fevers spread through the dun among the malnourished, the old and young. As the number grew, Brónach grimly ordered Minna to assist her. She turned from dried berries to tinctures in goat-milk and draughts in ale, dosing people with brews in the night while the wise-woman crawled back to her bed.

The old woman was wasting away herself, her limbs gnarled as dead roots, disappearing from the dun so often that Minna was left to care for many alone. Each time Brónach returned she was thinner and grey-faced, and spoke more sharply. She appeared silently at Minna's shoulder as she worked the pestle, staring almost hungrily at her hands as they moved and then at her face, which Minna kept rigidly still.

At least the long nights of racking coughs and fevered children helped Minna not to think of Cian. For when she did, fear caught her heart in its teeth.

Three hooded riders emerged from the swirling sleet at the gate of Luguvalium, its stone walls frosted in the moonlight. The guards hurried up to the tower, helmets angled into the wind. 'Who goes there?'

One of the riders pulled a muffler away from his chin. 'The hawk flies farthest who sees keenest,' he called, giving the officer password for that month.

The cross-bars were slowly grated back, the gates creaked open and the riders clattered into the deserted marketplace across icy cobbles. The streets were dark, the freezing wind whistling under eaves and plucking at tightly-latched shutters edged in lamplight. Starlight glittered on frozen puddles and the central fountain, now a bowl of shining ice.

The riders made their way along the bleak streets, their horses' hooves striking the cobbles like flints, echoing along bare alleys. At last they reached the centre of the maze of laneways and shops, where a door in a high, stone hall was flanked by two Roman wall-lamps, their horn casings barely sheltering the struggling flames.

Inside, King Eldon was alone in his study, surrounded by papers, quills, inkpots and the Roman delights his family had filched over the years: fluted wine jugs, glass goblets, pewter plates, hanging bronze oil-lamps, and small marble statues. He liked to have them here, where he could feast his eyes on them in private.

With a satisfied sigh he stretched his legs to the glowing coals of the brazier, a grey hound twitching in sleep at his feet. The scroll from his daughter Maeve lay loose in his ample lap. She had managed to get a message to him in the depths of winter – that and its contents confirmed once again how much she was like him. So ambitious! If only his two sons had lived longer, they too would have fulfilled the family promise. With his wife gone as well there was only Maeve now, and so he was fortunate that she and he were of the same mind, their ambitions channelled through the person of her son, Eldon's heir. Not Cahir's – he would soon see to that.

He stared into the coals, the old excitement tightening his loins. Though he did not rise so eagerly any more, his groin still stirred with the memory of hunger, the greed for more. It was money and land he wanted now, of course, not flesh, as was proper for a civilized Roman man.

And why stop at the kingdom of the Carvetii, magnificent though it was? What sane king would do that? His family's long relationship with the Roman administration in supplying soldiers with grain and ale had brought wealth, but it was a system controlled by careful taxes and certain profit. The north, though, held out new and exciting opportunities to shovel more goods into the gaping maw of the Roman army – vast herds of cattle, their hides a ready supply of leather for military boots, straps, belts, shields and saddles; flocks of hill-sheep for wool cloaks, tunics and blankets, and to feed the markets on the continent. Dunadd would levy higher trade taxes if he were king, and he could take the pick of the Kernow tin, the Saxon amber and Rhenish wine before they ever reached Gaul or Britannia. And just as tantalizing, the Dalriadan kingdom had kin ties with Erin – *Garvan* had kin ties with Erin – and in Erin there was gold.

His heart was racing now, too, and it had been doing that too much lately, making him breathless. He thumped his chest impatiently and reached for his goblet of wine.

His hound sprang alert with a yip a moment before a timid slave tapped on the door, announcing messengers from the Dux. Eldon put down the wine, grasped for his gold pin and stabbed it into his cloak, and stood by his desk. Two soldiers appeared at the door. 'Yes?' he snapped briskly.

The two men looked through him, standing aside for a third. Before Eldon could speak again, the last man peeled back his soaking hood, brushing sleet from his grey hair.

'My lord!' Eldon exclaimed, unconsciously straightening, his belly thrust out. 'This is ... an honour.'

Fullofaudes merely nodded. 'I decided that such a matter required my personal presence.' He tossed his wet cloak over the nearest couch, amused by the irritation that flared in Eldon's porcine eyes, and how instinctively he hid it. Swiftly, the Carvetii king caught up the cloak, draping it over his slave's arms and trying not to look at the melting patches of sleet all over that fine wool.

'Bring spiced wine and pastries,' Eldon commanded his slaves in a ringing, pompous tone. 'And hurry.'

The Dux dismissed his own men to drink ale in the kitchens, then waited as the slaves came back and bustled about with wine and platters of food, while Eldon fussed over which table to array them on – the shale or the cedar-wood? Fullofaudes turned a ridiculously vulgar lamp over in his hands, then glanced at the new paintings that covered the plaster walls. The style was a crude apeing of those from southern villas; in fact – he peered closer – he could swear that Venus had three breasts, and that tiger over there was sporting a mane.

He suppressed a smile, turning as Eldon proffered a glass goblet of rose-hued wine, the steam scented with spices. 'So,' the Dux said, taking it and seating himself in the nearest chair – Eldon's favourite, judging by the slight pinch of the king's nostrils – 'you asked for my assistance, and here I am.'

Eldon eyed the mud from Fullofaudes' boots smearing the wool rug but said nothing, sliding into another chair. 'I did not expect you in person,' he stumbled. 'It must have been a terrible ride.'

'Then I hope it is worth it.' Fullofaudes kept his eyes on Eldon's twitching face. He had perfected the art of not blinking, and found it came in very useful with petty kings – as this one was, however grand his pretensions. The room was overstuffed with objects of clashing hue, shape and material, arranged by greed and vanity rather than any artistic sense. The Dux had been born on a farm in Belgica, but despite his humble beginnings and his long military career, he had realized at the outset that if one wanted to rise high in society one had to meet the powerbrokers on their own terms, to speak to politicians and noblemen of art, history and oratory as well as trade and the dispositions of soldiers. Poor Eldon. Fullofaudes was taken by a mischievous thought of the Carvetii king floundering amid the marble halls of Trier like a fat fish plucked from a dirty river.

'There is no question of worth,' Eldon said smugly, picking up a discarded scroll. He bestowed an oily smile. 'But I talk not of wealth, my lord – for of course you have no use for that, and I admire you for it.'

Fullofaudes suppressed a snort, sipping his wine.

Eldon's chins wobbled with excitement as he sat forward. 'But being the first and only Dux to take half of Alba and keep it this time – I think you'd be interested in that.'

Fullofaudes was, but did not intend to show it. He would give this man no hold over him. 'All of Alba would be better,' he commented drily.

Eldon laughed uncomfortably, then shrugged. 'I cannot deliver the Picts to you, not yet. But no Roman army has ever managed to take the west completely; they've only ever marched up the flat lands of the east and as soon as they reached the mountains, been forced back. But by gaining *Dalriada* we'd command a single territory all the way from the Province into the very heart of Alba, and your troops would be able to penetrate the mountains from the west, using all those harbours and deep sea-lochs to land ship after ship. The Picts have never faced that scale of threat. They would not only have to guard their southern borders, as now, but in all directions. We'd almost have them surrounded, and surely it would only be a matter of time ...' he paused for effect, '... before you claim the whole island for your emperor.'

Fullofaudes didn't blink. 'There's no question that I want the same as you, Eldon, so you can save your rhetoric.' He wondered if Eldon would know what that meant. 'I want you to tell me what you have in mind. But before you do that, I must make one thing very clear.' Now it was his turn to sit forward, and Eldon seemed mesmerized, uncaring now of his muddy rug or the spots of water marking his silk-covered chair. 'No one can know of my involvement in your plans, not even my men. That is why I could trust this visit to no messenger. I have the emperor to answer to in Gaul, and any action against a barbarian king *here* who is nominally an ally would be seen as rash when the Empire has its hands full dealing with trouble elsewhere.' Imprudence was not a reputation the Dux intended to forge for himself among his superiors. 'If Cahir had rebelled against the new tax, that would have been something else, but he did not.'

And so now, he thought, *you can do the dirty work for me, my friend, and I keep my own hands clean.* He dropped his voice. 'If anyone even finds out I have spoken to you, I would have to re-think all terms and arrangements with the Carvetii.'' He bared his teeth in a smile. 'All of them.'

Eldon gulped and nodded, breathing fast, the colour higher in his heavy, florid cheeks. *Too much wine and too many pastries*, the Dux thought with contempt. Eldon would do better to ride as he did, and eat sparingly if he would live to see his much-vaunted grandson on the throne of Dalriada.

'So,' Fullofaudes said pleasantly now, 'you will tell me all your thoughts.' And he held out his hand for the scroll.

On the day of the first snowfall, the Lady Riona appeared at the schoolroom as Minna was packing away the tablets, the girls having run ahead to badger Clíona for honeycakes.

Riona was agitated, her face alight. 'Minna,' she gushed, all her formality gone, 'I am with child.'

She beamed at Minna's stumbling felicitations, then pressed a bronze armband into her hands. When she protested, Riona brushed that aside, too. 'Nonsense. When a craftsman renders us a service, we gift them. I don't want to hear anything else about it.' For a moment the girl in her twinkled from her blue eyes. 'My mother-in-law is treating me like a princess, and my husband is bursting with pride. That is worth more than gold to me.'

'But ... what about the Lady Brónach?'

Riona cocked her head. 'I want to give this to you, and you alone. There, make an end of it now.'

After she departed, Minna stood before the window, staring at the armband outlined in her hands by that bright, snowy light. Slaves were not given gifts. She slowly touched the other ring about her neck, so familiar now she hardly noticed its rubbing in sleep, or the welt of shiny, hard skin over her collar-bones. Now she knew she would not notice it at all.

A spark of pride lit the darkness inside her, and Cian's disappearance began to hurt a little less.

She buried the armband beneath her mattress, far from Brónach's sharp gaze.

Then one day, as Minna and Keeva dressed geese for the pot, Clíona stood before her. 'One of the maids has started bringing up her breakfast, and she's got a fever,' the older woman announced gruffly, her eyes on the fire. 'I want you—' She checked herself. 'It would be good for you to come and see if there's anything to do for her.' Keeva's smile mirrored Minna's own shock.

Soon Minna came down with the same cough as the others, and it was still bad at midwinter. The druids and nobles left one dusk for the stone circle in the ancestor valley, conducting a rite to call the sun back from its wanderings. With a flurry, Clíona emptied the king's hall of men for the female servants' own ritual.

As one of the maids beat a tiny drum, and Keeva played a bone pipe, the unmarried maidens threw hazelnuts on the fire. How they cracked and leaped from the flames told them who they would bed, or marry. Minna sat wrapped in her cloak around the cheerful fire, listening to the squeals and lilting music, coughing. It had been deemed too cold for the princesses to accompany their parents to the ancestor valley, and so she had one sleepy child under each arm, nestled into her body, and the puppy gnawing a bone nearby.

When it was Keeva's turn, she muttered a name and tossed the hazelnut. After a time it emitted a pop and flew out of the fire in a great arc. The maidens all shrieked. 'Keeva, Keeva, who is he?'

'Whoever he is, he's going to keep you so busy in bed you'll have a whole tribe of lads and lassies!'

Keeva peered critically at the nut. 'The tribe he can keep, the bed I'll take.' More giggles ensued.

Minna's loneliness as the days grew shorter had been acute. But she was slipping into a fever daze now where the music and laughter about the fire felt right, and safe. Not like a prison. Keeva whispered in her ear: 'Don't tell them it's Lonán, or they will all be after him!'

Clíona came to Minna then before everyone and handed her a cup of hot mead, her eyes sharp with interest. She took it, thinking, *I am a traitor to my kind.* And when Keeva grinned at her she looked away and closed her eyes – only to find herself unwillingly remembering, as she often did, the silkiness of the king's skin under her fingers. Finola murmured in a doze, curling up in her lap like a kitten. *Traitor,* Minna said to herself again, more feebly.

'Minna!' She opened her eyes. A young girl had come into the king's hall with a squirming baby. The women's laughter died as Keeva leaned in, rosy with mead. 'She was asking for you.'

The girl squeaked, 'My brother has a rash on his nether parts. Mama wants you to make it go away.' She heaved the child into Minna's lap.

As Minna coughed on a pungent waft of urine, Keeva's black eyes gleamed. 'Looks as if our Lady Riona has a loose tongue.'

Cahir worked out his frustration training the warriors on the meadow.

The anger and shame over the rationing had made the men sullen and glowering. In answer, the king stalked up and down the lines of sparring fighters in his wolf-fur cloak, setting his face into wind, rain, snow, sleet and fog as if somehow it would scour him clean.

With angry bellows he flung spears at targets, exhorting the men on as he paced beside them, then striding in to break up escalating fights as their fury turned on each other. He waded in with his own blade, just to feel the weight in his hands and stare down one angry warrior after another. The tension smouldered like coals under peat.

Sometimes he broke off and went up on the walls to gaze over the struggling masses of men, hock-deep in mud. He would search, trying to see in the wavering lines and wheeling pairs a pattern, to discern any other message that his ancestors had for him – anything other than what was staring him in the face. But all he saw was chaos, and Ruarc charging through the midst, his wet hair flying and his eyes defiant as he paused to glance up at his king.

When it threatened to drive him mad, Cahir went down to the cliffs at night, arms wide, cloak rippling in the wind. There he cried to Eremon: *What do you want from me? Speak to me!* No answer ever came, only the sea-wind.

But when Davin sang another tale of Rhiann and Eremon one night, he found himself watching Minna the slave very closely. She was serving ale but as Davin began she paused in the shadows, and Cahir could swear he saw a glimmer of tears on her pale cheek. When she turned to the torchlight, her knuckles were white around the jug handle.

Then Cahir knew he was imagining nothing, and his blood *was* speaking. It was speaking through her.

BOOK TWO

LEAF-BUD, AD 367

Chapter 23

It was dawn on a freezing morning, and only Minna and Clíona were awake. The older maid was at the hearth, grumbling under her breath. How was she supposed to sleep with such flushes and itching skin? she demanded. 'Away with you!' she snapped irritably, batting Lia away from the pot, the pup now all gangly legs and twitching snout.

Minna fed twigs on the fire and sat back on her heels. 'I can make a good brew for that.' She cupped her hands and coughed into them. 'My Mamo used to drink it when I was young.'

Clíona eyed her as if she'd just suggested cutting her open. Pride wavered with need, then she sniffed, rubbing the small of her back. 'I suppose if it is good enough for the Lady Riona ...' She narrowed her eyes. 'You won't poison me, or make me grow hair where I shouldn't?'

Minna merely raised her brows, and Clíona dusted her hands down her dress. 'Then *only* if it doesn't taste like dung, and only if you don't breathe a word to anyone.'

'I promise.'

The porridge was simmering when a great thump on the doors flung them open. The other hounds leaped up from the fireside, growling, as a man stumbled in swathed in fur. He pushed the door shut, clawed his cloak from his chin.

Clíona's spoon clattered in the pot. 'Who—?'

'Niall,' the man cut her off. 'Dun of the Rock. Get me the king and the wise-woman at once.'

'What?' Clíona stood her ground. 'It's not even light, man! I'm not dragging anyone from their beds until you tell me—'

'Quiet, woman! I haven't ridden all night to be challenged by a

147

serving maid!' The man's cheeks were wind-bitten above a straggly black beard. 'This is a matter of life and death. Hurry, before my balls freeze to my arse!'

'Death?' Clíona bustled to one of the alcoves. 'Come to the fire, then, and warm yourself. There will be porridge soon.' She nudged a sleeping boy on a pallet with her toe, and set him to wake the king.

While he scurried up the stairs, Clíona tucked strands of hair back in her braids. 'What is going on, then?'

Niall hung his head. 'I will deliver my news only to the king.'

Cahir came down the stairs blinking in the firelight, buckling on his sword. His dark hair was rumpled, his tunic on inside-out. Minna dropped her eyes, stirring the porridge more briskly.

Niall immediately went down on one knee, his chest heaving. 'My lord,' he choked, 'the Picts have attacked one of our outlying duns, near the mountains. They have fled now, leaving many dead.'

Cahir's face paled. 'How many?'

'I do not know. The warriors stayed to defend the steading while their women and children fled to my own chief's dun.' His voice broke. 'They had to trek to us across the peaks in terrible cold, and many fell ill. The babies ...' He faltered.

Cahir gripped the man's shoulder. 'Go on.'

'The women recovered, but the babes are gravely ill. Some fever swept through them – and spread to the ones in our dun. Even my own child.' He looked up, pleading. 'We need help. We think the Picts are gone but we are not sure, and then the children ... we have been without a wise-woman for months and we cannot save them. It is the seal cough.'

Minna was on her feet. 'Seal cough?'

The man's gaze slid to her slave-ring, and Clíona flapped her skirt impatiently at him. 'The girl has the healing knowledge. The wise-woman trains her.'

The man shrugged wearily. 'Seal ...' He let forth a hoarse bark. 'They cough like this.'

Minna knew that horrid sound: the dog cough, the Romans called it.

Cahir rubbed his face as if pulling himself back from some dark dream. 'Peace, Niall. You are not alone now.' He looked at Minna, the pain exposed in his face. 'Go and wake my aunt and tell her we must leave at first light. I will rouse the warriors.'

She chewed her lip. 'She is not here,' she said in a low voice. 'It was fine yesterday, and I saw her ride out. She hasn't come back.'

Cahir cursed, his face darkening. His eyes were intense upon her. 'Then you must do it.' Minna went cold. 'You know this illness, I heard you.'

148

'I do, but—'

'Then this is my order. Hurry up.' He was already turning away, waking men from their pallets, sending the serving boys to inform the nobles.

Minna plodded through the snow to Brónach's house to get what was needed. There, beside the hearth, she sank on her knees, the strength melting from her. 'Lady, Mother, if you call me, if you need me, tell me what to do and I will do it.' Tucked under her chin, her hands were trembling. *The dog cough.* Mamo had always used a special root for that, imported from Rome. There must be something else she could use here.

She knew this couldn't be the proper approach to the Goddess, that she must be getting it clumsily wrong. But after a moment of fighting with her fear, something did come, as if placed in her mind by a deliberate, gentle hand. And that was all Minna had upon which to stake those tiny lives.

She came back to the hall with the little statue of Brigid clutched in one hand and in the other a packet of dusty, crushed leaves that she'd dug out from behind Brónach's jars, where it had been carelessly stacked with many others.

By now, Clíona and Keeva and the other servants were dashing back and forth, wrapping packets of food and helping to roll sleeping hides. As Minna appeared with a bulging pack, Clíona eyed her up and down. 'Gods, child! If you'll be on a horse you need more than that!' From the storage chests she extracted a thick hide tunic with the fleece inside, riding boots that laced over the knee, and a voluminous cloak lined with speckled fur that fell to Minna's feet.

Minna returned to the gallery to dress and tied the cloak high, covering the slave-ring. On impulse she curved Riona's arm-band about her wrist. These things seemed important now.

She descended to the hall where Clíona yanked her hood up. 'You'll do.'

A thought occurred to Minna. 'The queen!'

'It's the king's orders – what *she* thinks doesn't matter. Anyway, I'll deal with her and the girls. You go and do what you can.' She stopped as Minna's gaze slid towards Cahir. Muffled in his grey cloak of wolf-fur, his eyes shone topaz in the firelight.

Clíona grew still. 'Minna,' she whispered, and Minna dragged her eyes from him with difficulty. The maid was regarding her with an intensity she had never seen on that harassed face before. '*Who are you?*' she said, wondering, her gaze deeply searching. But Minna had no answer.

Cold rain drove into her eyes, and she had lost track of all time when they reached the Dun of the Rock on a windy headland to the north of Dunadd. The land had passed in a blur of misty grey, the trees lifting sparse branches to the sky. She clung grimly to the pony, thighs and tailbone aching, and by the time the light was fading once more the cleft of the pony's ears was engraved in lines behind her eyes.

They rode under a timber gateway into a muddy yard, where Donal helped Minna down. Pains shot up her legs and her nose was streaming. She stemmed it with the back of her hand, struggling to uncurl her fingers.

They were taken inside a hall and divested of damp cloaks. Minna was urged to a bench and given warmed mead. Cahir seemed oblivious to the cold and long ride; he listened to the news and then briskly gave out orders.

'I have fifty men,' he said to the young chieftain. 'Give me twenty more, leaving enough to defend the dun. We must search the hills and check the Picts have retreated.'

Revived a little by the mead, Minna stopped shivering. 'Where are the children?' she asked the women around her, who, she could see, were clearly distraught.

Cahir appeared at her side. 'The wise-woman Brónach is indisposed,' he told them. 'This young lady has been treating our own people since she came from the south. I have every faith in her.' He caught her eye. 'Her name is Minna.' Not *Minna the slave*; nor *Minna the foreigner*; nor *Minna the reviled*.

She placed the cup on the bench and rose, drawing her aching back straight as she met the women's red-rimmed eyes. 'Where are the children?' she asked again, strengthening her voice though her heart thumped. The king had faith in her. She remembered how Mamo sounded when she tended the sick; firm and in command because people were always so scared.

The chieftain's wife spoke. 'They are in the women's house.' Her voice was hoarse; she looked as if she had not slept for days. 'Many babes have already died. The others are beside the fire.'

Minna looked around. This hall was much smaller than Dunadd's, the hearth round, not long. 'How many are in danger?'

'Ten or eleven now.'

'And what has been done for them, lady?'

'There is little to be done, except be together and comfort each other. The coughing – ah! – you will hear. But there was only one wise-woman for many leagues around and she was carried off by her own sickness moons ago.'

'I have never seen so many die,' an older woman put in, shuffling closer. 'A few get the seal cough every year, but usually they recover. I've never seen so many at once, and never so bad. We put hot compresses on their chests, but this time ...' She sighed.

Minna took a deep breath, and as she let it out she forced the fear with it, as Mamo had taught her. Then she met the eyes of the chieftain's young wife, holding to her strength and binding it with her own. 'We need hides, as many as you can find. If they are not big enough to form tents, then tie them together. Then we need all the cauldrons and every other big pot filled with boiling water.' Minna swiftly unwrapped a bundle from her belt. 'Do you have more of this?' She held out the dried leaves and flowers she had taken from Brónach's house.

The women gathered around. It was grey-ear, one said, an early bloomer and already appearing in sheltered spots. The younger women with no sick children were dispatched to gather as much of it as possible.

Soon it was time for the men to go. Cahir drew her aside and searched her face. 'Can you do this?'

Minna allowed herself to meet his eyes and nodded.

He smiled briefly. 'Well done. Then we will return when we can.'

When the men had ridden away, Minna went to the children. Firelight illuminated the walls of the women's house and the knots of hunched mothers wrapped in furs. Minna knelt by one hollow-eyed woman and her baby, who was lying limp in her arms. She put her hand on his hot forehead. His eyes were glazed, and in between those pitiful barks he struggled to breathe, his throat dipping as he sucked at air. Minna's own chest grew tight, but she could not breathe for him.

Some of the women rocked silently, their eyes on the fire. When she went to touch these children it was to find their skin cold and their mother's arms their last cradle.

'Come on,' Minna murmured. 'Just a little more.' But the baby girl in her lap fussed and tried to pull away when she pressed the cup to her lips.

'Here. I'll hold her.' The chieftain's wife leaned in to the hide tent Minna had set up around the hearth, covering the bubbling cauldrons of water so the hide filled with steam. They dribbled more grey-ear down the child's throat, and were rewarded with a bout of spluttering and kicking.

In the dim tent, Minna smiled wearily at the other mothers. Steam, pungent with the scent of thyme, condensed on her nose and she dabbed it away. It had been too late for three other babies, but most were responding well.

She had not slept for two days, and nor could she yet, for there was another dun nearby where more children had come down with the same cough. Eventually she crawled out of the tent, blinking blearily, and donned all her thick riding clothes once more. The chieftain's wife sent a man with her as guide, and Minna set off again. Another day came and went, another dusk steeped in sea-fog that drifted in over the cliffs.

Two babies died at the second dun, but many more were saved, and at last there was nothing more Minna could do. As the ponies plodded back along the misty path to the Dun of the Rock, she hunched over her pain, closing her eyes. *Look!* she seemed to hear Lucius and Marcus cry, from the hill above the villa. *Minna! Hurry up!* That life had been so easy, after all, when she had thought it hard. They waved madly now, far ahead. *Minna!*

She startled awake as they halted in the yard of the dun, her hands tangled in the pony's mane. As the man helped her dismount, her legs buckled. Faces blurred before her eyes, frowning with concern. Someone asked her a sharp question, but when she tried to reply her throat spasmed. She couldn't focus.

In the hall, women came and sat by her, warming themselves at the fire. She needed to sleep, but could not leave them. One, holding her crying babe, pressed her face into Minna's hands late in the night. 'Lady,' she wept, 'my son lives, and we owe you our hearts. We will never forget.'

Lady. Slumped on the hearth-bench, she heard the word as if from afar. Lady.

'Minna.' It was Cahir, his hand on her forehead. 'I've been speaking to you.' She squinted up, trying to see him properly, but all the shadows and flames were whirling around her now. 'Gods! You're burning.' He turned his head. 'How long has she been like this?'

'I do not know, my lord. We've been so busy with the children. I thought she just needed to rest so I left her alone.'

'She's not resting, she's sick! Come, where can she lie down?'

'I'm ... I'm just tired ...' Minna protested weakly. 'But I need to see the children again.'

'You'll do no such thing.' And the next moment she was lifted and then gently lowered onto fur covers. A shudder took her, and someone chafed her hands. 'Her cheeks are hot, yet here she is cold.' Cahir's voice floated from far away. Minna's eyelids were so heavy ... she blinked, trying to force them open. 'You, heat her a stone for her feet.' People shuffled around her in a confusion of dark shapes, the edges blurred by firelight.

'Three nights and four days with no sleep, they tell me!' Cahir muttered. 'Foolish!'

Minna pushed at his hands, plucked feebly at her neck-ring. 'The babies ...' she whispered. 'No time for sleep.'

'Perhaps not then, but now there is nothing more you can do. Sleep and get well, please. You've done us a great service.'

She was tucked under furs; a hot stone was pressed to her bare feet. Then the feverish sweat turned to shivering, and a hand came down over her eyes, pushing them closed. 'Come, you must sleep. Gods, how contrary you are. You remind me of Orla.'

The words were gentle, just like Mamo spoke to her when she was sick. The smell of the fingers was different, but they urged her to rest. So Minna surrendered at last, tumbling down a deep hole. *A little sleep, a few moments, and then I can rise.*

The large hand moved from her eyes to cradle her forehead, and stayed there.

She was stumbling through a snowy wood on a moonlit night.

Ahead, the person she was chasing whisked out of sight whenever she turned towards her, melting away behind the bare, black trees. Minna tried to run faster, but the figure almost flew along the paths that wound in white scars through the undergrowth.

Wait for me! she cried. Despite the snow, she was conscious of a more distant sensation of burning and dampness, and a searing pain in her throat. Her nose and eyes were clogged, and she couldn't clearly see the outline of the person darting between the trees far ahead.

Her clumsy feet kept sinking into the snow and mud, tangling in fallen branches, and she sobbed with frustration. She felt heavy, confined, when she wanted to fly like a bird.

The figure ahead danced faster, faster, tantalizing and ethereal in the moonlight. *Wait!* Minna screamed again, her throat raw.

An answer floated back, urging her on. *No. You must come to me.*

Chapter 24

Minna woke to a freezing wind on her cheeks. She burrowed away from it into the furs in which she was swaddled.

Under her cheek, something firm rose and fell in a rhythm. Then she became conscious of a heartbeat, thumping in her ear. 'This cursed wind is getting stronger!' a voice rumbled from the same place.

Another answered, more faintly, 'I don't think we can make it by tonight after all, Cahir.'

'But she can't be out in this weather any longer – she's weak as it is. We must push on.'

Vaguely, Minna recognized the sound of a horse snorting, and something large heaved beneath her. 'Peace, boy,' Cahir muttered.

'If we push the horses direct into this gale, Cahir, they'll get tired and stuck in the drifts. We will be in a worse position then.'

Minna's throat convulsed and she coughed. She was too tightly bound and exhausted to raise her head, but grey light seeped between her eyelids.

'Are you awake, Minna?' Warm breath blew over her temple, and she made some faint sound of assent. It was soft there in his arms, and she relaxed against him, knowing his smell, his voice, his shape as something familiar and safe. Safe ... when he had forced her dreams from her, raised his voice ... that was strange ...

Cahir held her tighter. 'I don't know if you'll understand, but you are very ill and there was no one to help you. You were getting worse and I thought to get you back to Brónach.' He paused. 'And the gods take me if I've killed you instead.' He raised his voice. 'Does anyone know where we are? There must be shelter nearby.'

Another pause. 'I can just make out the Maiden Hill there. There's a hut we used to use for hunting, a few years back. It will be some shelter, at least.'

Cahir expelled a breath. 'Let's go.'

The stallion lurched, and there was no more talking. Sleet stung Minna's cheeks. She needed to rest again ... sink into sleep ...

'This time,' Cahir muttered, shaking her, 'you must stay awake. Don't slip away now; it's too cold.'

At last they halted, and she was lowered into someone else's arms. 'Look!' one of the men exclaimed. 'There is smoke on the roof!'

'Swords out then, two each side of the door.'

Minna heard a thump on wood, and after a silence another thump, more insistently. There was a shuffle inside, and the door scraped open. Cahir grunted. 'What, by the gods, are *you* doing here?'

Minna opened her eyes a slit. In the doorway stood Brónach, face white with shock. 'Nephew,' she murmured, dazed.

'I'm your king,' Cahir growled, 'and you were not there when we needed you – and now I find you hiding here instead!'

'The storm came—'

'I have no time for this. The girl is ill, from helping those who were *your* charge. Move aside.'

Despite the crackling fire, the inside of the hut was musty, with a bitter odour. No lamps were lit, and the glow of the hearth filled the room with bloody light. Minna was carefully placed on one of the small cots against the wall, as the men found shelter for the horses. The sheets smelled of mould, but Minna was shivering so hard now her teeth were chattering. Even though her senses were dulled, as she lay there she saw the change in Brónach.

The old woman's eyes were glassy, her unbound hair a wild tangle. She drew her woollen shawl around her shrunken chest. 'What happened?'

Cahir shot Brónach an angry glance. 'Many babies were sick at the Dun of the Rock, and she's gone too long without sleep and care. She must have caught the same fever.' When his aunt merely nodded, Cahir turned on her. 'You should have been there yourself, lady. And instead you are here ...' his eyes took in the room, 'hiding away while people die.'

The old woman flinched. 'I had other duties to attend to,' she muttered, swaying on her feet. 'Duties in the Otherworld, reaching to the gods—'

'Nothing more important than children! I make one demand of you, the only thing expected of you as a royal woman—'

'The only thing left to me, you mean!'

Cahir's eyes flashed. He towered over her, though she was tall for a woman. 'This girl fell ill fulfilling your duty, and you will make her well. *Do you understand?*'

Brónach's breath rattled in her chest. 'Of course,' she muttered, knotting her fingers in her shawl. 'I would do no less.'

'I would expect no less.'

While Brónach moved stiffly around the fire, the warmth of the furs sent Minna back into sleep. It was only much later she surfaced, as a bitter concoction was forced down her throat. She spluttered, and Brónach murmured, 'Take it, girl, it will help the fever.' The stale scent of her papery skin enveloped Minna.

Snatches of conversation filtered through her delirium. 'What did she do for them, the children?'

'She saved them. Had the women make tents … and steam to help them breathe.'

'Steam?'

'Yes. But let her sleep now.'

The voices disintegrated, and Minna was back in the wood, only this time she was closer to the shape flitting between the trees; so close she glimpsed hair beneath a hood, and saw the prints of dainty feet in the snow. A woman.

I'm coming! she cried. *Wait!*

She slept for most of the next two days, caught between fever and exhaustion. The king took his men back to Dunadd, but when she at last roused properly from that peculiar dream state the door was open and he was back.

Outside it was no longer stormy. The afternoon was unclouded, and shafts of sun slanted ruddy on the scraps of melting snow across the threshold. A raven cawed from the oak tree in the yard.

'I tell you it is madness.' Cahir was speaking in a low, angry voice, just out of Minna's sight.

'The evening is fine, and she will be in furs—'

'You cannot be serious!'

Minna turned her head on the pillow, and winced. Cahir and Brónach were standing before the fire. The old woman's imperious nose was outlined by the flames. 'It is a sacred pool of the Goddess, nephew, an old doorway to the Otherworld. The blessing of the waters on her forehead will heal her.'

'The cold will kill her!'

'It will not. She needs the blessing of the Mother – she will be safe, I swear it.'

Cahir hesitated, folding his arms.

'Trust me in this, nephew. Let me bless her at the pool, and then we can move her to Dunadd. I've run out of herbs now, anyway.'

Cahir gazed around the room. 'And yet there are jars and baskets everywhere, I see. What is it that you *do* here?'

Brónach stiffened. 'Surely that is my business.'

'Is it?' He cocked his head. 'It wouldn't be spells, would it, aunt? Trying to turn me into a salamander as a pet for my beloved wife?'

Brónach drew herself up. 'I would not betray my blood so; my work is on behalf of the people, whatever you choose to think. And there are no herbs of healing here beyond those I've used. It is the water that will cure her.'

'Bah!' Cahir held up his hands. 'She must be well wrapped, and stay out for a few moments only. I will carry her.'

As soon as Cahir went to stable his horse, Brónach's stillness fell from her like a discarded cloak. She sank on Minna's bed, twisting the purple ring on her finger in agitation. 'You seem past the worst, then. It must be youth.'

'I ... thank you ...' Minna faltered.

Brónach ignored her. 'What you did was clever – and I never told you to do it. You know more than I thought.' Her eyes were cold but watchful, like a snake.

Minna's breath laboured in her tight chest. 'It just ... came to me ... when I asked.'

'It just came to you,' Brónach repeated slowly. 'Came from where?'

When Minna only shook her head Brónach crouched towards her, her tangled grey mane falling about her withered face. '*From where?*'

Minna shrank back. 'A voice in my head ... no, a picture of what to do.' She forced herself to speak, for Brónach was the only one who might know what was happening, and why.

'*They* speak to you? *They* help you?' Brónach pushed herself up, pacing in swift strides to the fire and back. 'Can it be true? A slave, not even of the blood?' She paused, looking down at Minna. 'Then for everyone's sake you must indeed be touched by the Lady's pool. It is the only thing that can help you.'

Minna's heart leaped and then just as swiftly fell, confused at what she wanted. 'Will it stop me hearing things and ... and ... dreaming things?'

Brónach turned away, one finger tapping her crossed arms. 'Of course. The pool is where the Lady answers all questions, after all.' She approached the shelves against the wall. 'But first, have this draught for your chest, child. It will protect you in the cold.'

The pool had once stood in a clearing, but the crescent of dead birches around it was now overgrown with hazel scrub, feathered with catkins and tangles of ivy. A narrow path had been hacked through to the lip of a spring dammed by rocks.

Cahir placed Minna on the ground cushioned on hides, their breath misting the damp, freezing air. When he stepped back Brónach shouldered between them, resting her hand on Minna's head. 'Nephew, this is a woman's place – a goddess place. You must leave here or I cannot give her the blessing.'

An impulse to keep Cahir close seized Minna, but when she tried to form words they spun away into dizziness. She held her hand up. The outline of her fingers blurred and she blinked, trying to shake off the invading stupor. *What had Brónach done to her?*

The pang of fear that came then was dulled, and slipped away into the depths of the water. *The pool.* Minna's thoughts turned sluggishly. *This pool once received offerings of gold rings, and shimmered with sacred oil and drifted with flowers* . . . Her fingers gripped the rocks, the only solid thing. Everything else was fluid: ground, water, sky.

Cahir was arguing with his aunt, though Minna barely heard him beyond the roaring of her blood, and she could not look away from the pool. In the late sun it was a shield of copper etched with a tracery of bare birches, and in the centre, the pale moon of her face swam through the dark cloud of her hair. It called her. She heard little else now but the crystal singing of the water.

At last Cahir left and Brónach immediately leaned over Minna. 'Look hard into the pool of seeing then, Roman girl,' she hissed, 'and tell me what comes! I know there must be something, I smelled something in you all along. Hurry!' She forced Minna's head down, her bony chest against her back. Minna struggled as her nose hovered above the shining water. 'Go on!' Brónach urged. 'If they speak to you then they can make you see as well! Ask them. *Ask them and show me!*'

Minna whimpered, trying to force her head back. But the light on the water wavered and began to suck her in, and the black wells of her reflected eyes merged into one. Instead of the sky and clouds above there was only a swirling tunnel. A door opening, and she must pass through it. *I . . . don' t. . . I can't!*

Brónach crushed her against the rock lip as her mind fought, holding her on the threshold. But the singing was rising, high and clear. *Come!*

She wavered there for an age, but she had nothing to lose any more, nothing to keep her here. The voice beckoned, and finally, with a silent cry of surrender, Minna let go. Then there was no longer anything but that tunnel of song, of light, pulling her down into its depths.

Chapter 25

'Am I dead?' Minna asked faintly.

No. There was a smile in the air, if that were possible. *You are far from dead.*

Minna's heart gave a great bound. 'Mamo?' she whispered.

A pause. *No, child. But she is safe.*

'Safe? Where is she?'

She is resting, sleeping. Perhaps she will speak to you one day ... but not now.

'Then ... where am I?' Minna realized as she said it that she didn't feel afraid. She *should* feel afraid. But it was warm now, and the warmth was a blanket that would let no fear in. She didn't know if her eyes were open or shut because light was coming from all around her.

You are of the spirit now. It took this – effort, cold, exhaustion, sickness – to loosen the bonds of the body. To break open the shell and free the spirit.

'Then I *am* dead.'

Again the amusement. *No, dear one. Spirit and body can travel separately and still be joined, until the final sundering.*

'How?'

In dreams, in vision, in fevered sleep. While seeing, when you surrender.

An idea snagged and held. 'Then it was you in the woods, not Mamo?'

Yes.

'And you calling me, after Jared gave me the red flower ...'

You had to have the courage to let the body go and step through the doorway. I didn't want you thinking you would be alone when you did.

Emotions shouldn't exist in this place, but the loneliness that bore Minna down then was greater than any before. For she had tasted it from the day she was born.

You've never been alone. I have been close, in dreams. And ... in other ways.

'But ... what ...'

There is so little time. For now, open your eyes.

'My *eyes?*'

Do it, and see. Remember.

A tenderness in the voice touched Minna like a kiss on her brow. It felt female ... but young? Old?

Stop thinking. Open your eyes and don't be afraid. And the voice began singing sweetly, wordlessly.

When Minna thought of opening her eyes it seemed to happen, and she had to stop herself crying out. She was soaring through a blue sky, her arms spread – only they were not arms any more, but wings. Long feathers curled up at the tips, and a narrow head tilted so her keen eyes could gaze down. The breeze rushed under her, merging with the singing so she was lifted by both the voice and the wind. The sense of freedom was exhilarating, the power filling her chest as she cried, 'An eagle!' But no words came, only a screech flung from a feathered throat.

The singing continued as Minna dipped and banked. At long last the melody faded. *Yes, it is fine, it is joy.* No one was with her, no one flying beside her, but still she sensed those thoughts. *Do not lose your focus, though. Look down now.*

A land stretched beneath her, no longer covered in cloud or veils of mist, but a glorious melding of mountains, bracken, birches and heather. The air was clear as water, and smelled icy and sweet, of rock and streams and pine needles. It was Alba in leaf-fall.

It is beautiful. But study it closely.

There was Dunadd, and then the ancestor valley – Minna recognized the ancient tombs beading its length. To the north a long, silver loch was studded with islands. Swooping low over its ruffled surface, Minna saw the sacred mountain Cruachan rearing up at its end, a mighty monarch. *More,* the voice urged. *Go further.*

She was flying faster than any eagle could. One wing-beat took her over the soaring slopes of the mountain. She could see a long chain of lochs reaching to an eastern sea, and to the south a region of high peaks and deep-delved valleys. She tilted to left and right in great arcs as she followed first one valley then another, her wing tips nearly brushing the rocks.

Then ahead reared an imposing ridge of many peaks that irresistibly drew Minna down. A cleft in its slopes faced west, and there a gnarled rowan tree clung on, its branches bare of leaves. With a great uplift of wings, Minna landed on the thickest branch, making the tree dip and sway.

Before she could assemble her thoughts her beak stretched up, and from her throat issued a cry she could not contain. It was a demand from the king of the mountains, the great eagle, sent to earth from its eyrie. And though Minna heard it as an eagle's screech, the meaning of the words lit up her mind.

> *Awake, battle-lord,*
> *For the war-horns cry!*
> *Arise, for the sign is come!*
> *Take the name sword-wielder*
> *Blade-singer*
> *Shield-bearer.*
> *Hear your blood call you,*
> *Raise the boar above you,*
> *Make an end, battle-lord,*
> *The red-crests come!*

Minna found herself staring into the water, and there was the sky and the trees marked on the cold surface of the pool. Her breath misted the icy air beneath the bare branches, and the only other thing that moved was her blood, racing with the remnants of joy and awe. She stretched her aching neck and looked up.

The king and Brónach were both staring down at her, their faces frozen.

Minna shifted her gaze to Cahir, her mind untethered, and faltered at the horror in his eyes.

Then everything became confused. Cahir pushed Brónach aside to get to Minna between the overgrowth of brambles and thorn, crying out that the old woman had nearly killed her.

Brónach ignored him. 'You *saw*,' she whispered to Minna, fingers creeping to the moonstone around her neck. 'You saw – with no training, fasting or chanting. But how can the Mother reveal herself to *you*, an untrained slip of a girl?' The shock in her eyes was sharpening to anguish. '*How can this be?*'

The cold was coming up through Minna's palms now, spread on the icy soil, and she began to shiver. 'Silence!' Cahir roared to his aunt, gathering Minna into his arms and straightening. 'I will get her warm again, and as for *you* – leave this place. *Now.*'

The expression on Brónach's face was unearthly, eager and torn at the same time. 'But the words she spoke held truth, nephew. I sensed it, I *know* it!'

Cahir went rigid. 'The words she spoke are no concern of yours.'

Cahir carried Minna back to the hut and set her on the bed, wrapping blankets about her shoulders. Brónach gathered her belongings and left without a word, though she darted a single bright, hard glance at Minna from the doorway.

A heavy silence descended over the room as Cahir stood by the fire with his hands by his sides, his back to Minna as she crouched in the bed, shivering uncontrollably.

Her soul had been split open, and so her joy and wonder were swiftly eclipsed now by all the other things she had suppressed for months, freed by the tenderness in that spirit-woman's voice. And so came the grief for Mamo at last, undammed, uncontained and pure in its terrible power.

She turned her head to the pillow and fell down in darkness, weeping as if she would never stop.

Cahir crouched by the flames and fed them with hazel branches, listening to Minna's sobs being almost bodily wrenched from her. It was better to leave someone like that, sometimes – he remembered holding his daughters through such things.

He stayed squatting there as the fire caught and began to eat the wood, his eyes glazed. It took a long time for Minna's sobs to ease, but at last they faded, and she slept.

Cahir waited for her to wake as night fell, pacing the floor at first slowly, and then faster and more agitatedly as his thoughts gnawed on him.

When she stirred, he paused only to hand her a cup of water and then stood over her. He wanted to give her more time, but he could not. 'Minna,' he said, as she drank and lay back against the pillow, her face pale and bruised by tears. 'You must tell me immediately how you know that which you cried at the pool.'

Minna's fingers went to her swollen cheeks. Though she had wept until she could cry no more and should be empty, she found the absence of grief had left her full of wonder instead, and she felt Mamo close by, for she was no longer turning away from her.

'I don't know what you mean,' she answered slowly. The time by the water was now a blur. 'What did I say?'

Cahir did not hesitate, throwing back his head like a wolf howling.

> *Awake, battle-lord,*
> *For the war-horns cry!*
> *Arise, for the sign is come!*
> *Take the name sword-wielder*
> *Blade-singer*
> *Shield-bearer.*
> *Hear your blood call you,*

Raise the boar above you.
Make an end, battle-lord,
The red-crests come!

The delivery was both bitter and passionate, the words a summons that set her blood alight. But he didn't give her a chance to feel them, pointing at her accusingly. 'No one knows this but me. It is the most forbidden, the most private legacy of my lineage. How can you know this? *Why?*'

Her tongue wet her cracked lips. 'I ... it came from the vision ...'

He loomed over her, his face haunted. 'If you play me for a fool, Minna, there is no telling what I will do. If they put you up to this, Maeve, Brónach, anyone ...' He left that hanging, shook his head. 'The war cries and the Hill of a Thousand Spears were one thing; they are known by some, at least. *But no one knows this.* Do you have any idea what fire you play with?'

I would never betray him. Minna tasted that shocking rush of feeling, kneeling up on the covers. The exhaustion and aches were gone, washed from her by tears, and in their place her blood sang. 'No one told me anything, I swear. I was an eagle in the dream and I flew over Alba, and then the eagle cried those words to the sky.'

His fists clenched. 'If this is a joke, death is its price – even for you.'

Curiously, Minna was utterly unafraid, seized by the absurd urge to reach out and smooth that pain from his brow. 'I would accept death if I dishonoured you,' she said, her voice trembling, 'but I have not, whatever this means.'

After a long moment, Cahir groped blindly for the bench and sank to it. 'So it has come. The call was a whisper, now it is a roar.' His shoulders rose and fell in a great sigh of surrender. 'The sign of the prophecy has come, and I cannot hide from it any longer. *All the gods help me.*'

Chapter 26

Minna drew the blanket around her and knelt by Cahir's side. He was surprised at her boldness, but then saw that her bones had somehow shifted in the firelight, her eyes holding the shimmer of the pool. She looked older, as if something dark and pained had been bled from her and had changed her.

Her gaze was forceful. 'My lord, what is this ... prophecy, you called it?' When he hesitated, she rushed on, 'This is about me as well.'

So he told her. It was passed from Rhiann to her nephew King Gabran, and thence gifted from king to king's son. Only his father knew it, and he only told Cahir. But Cahir's throat closed up at the rest, and he could not explain the tangle of emotion that surrounded these lines of old poetry.

How his father had scorned them, and the boy Cahir followed his lead even though he felt inexplicably ashamed. How as he grew his rational mind argued it was just a story, while his heart continued to wonder and yearn. And then when the dreams came he pushed them aside, thought himself mad, while longing and fearing for it all to be true.

And now, at last, the promised sign had come.

For the prophecy *itself* was the sign it foretold, issuing from the throat of a stranger who could not know it; drawn out by the waters of a sacred pool. It was undeniable.

He made Minna tell him exactly what she saw, and when she'd finished he could not sit still any longer. '*They* sent this dream, these words, as they sent all others – my ancestors Eremon, Conaire, Rhiann. They cry out to me: I, their son, who have been so wilfully deaf and blind!'

She pulled the blanket closer about her shoulders. Draughts made the fire flicker, reflecting in her eyes. 'But I don't understand who the red-crests are.'

Pacing, Cahir placed a hand on the shelf by the door, staring into nothing. 'The red-crests are the Romans, Minna, named because long ago they wore scarlet crests on their helmets, though no more. After they defeated Eremon they withdrew for a time, but they always came back to Alba: back and forth, always hungry for our land, our blood. Then my grandfather gave them land for their outposts, and my father awarded them passage through our seas, signing the treaties that have become my shackles.' He sighed heavily. 'The Roman-kind used to march north with armies: now they creep with taxes, meting out secret deaths to those who resist. So the Empire still rolls closer, only in a different guise.'

'But my brother said there have been attacks on the Wall.'

He turned, his smile bitter. 'Others strike at them: the Picts, even some Erin kings. But I have not.' He looked down at his hands. 'These have been tied, and I have done nothing.'

What Minna said next stopped him in his tracks. 'But what *is* the prophecy asking?'

Cahir could only stare at her.

The druids said that when a door opened on the Otherworld, mortals were touched with the light that spilled through. And so this girl's water eyes revealed not innocence, or even a slave's fear, but pools of *sight* shining amid her black hair, filled with a transcendence he had rarely seen even in a druid's face. His last reservations disintegrated, and he entirely forgot who she was.

'The prophecy foretold that our line would free Alba of Rome. It was not accomplished at the Hill of a Thousand Spears – the story was not complete because it is *my* fate to fulfil it.' The words sounded like someone else's, as if Cahir were waking from a dream. It could not be true. *It was true.*

'No!'

'No? But a summons has come I cannot ignore. *Raise the boar above you.* The war banner.' He laughed harshly. 'Ruarc was right after all, damn him.'

Minna was hardly listening now, as if caught by something in the shadows. When her eyes glazed over a superstitious shiver ran up his neck. 'You must follow the flight of the eagle,' she said quietly.

The shiver turned to a thrill. Of course! He came back to the fire. 'From what I can make out, that path leads far north and east – into Pictish lands.' He gazed about the firelit walls, as if he could penetrate them with a clear gaze. 'And why there?' he murmured feverishly. There must be something ... he dared to hope ... could it be that there, at last, he would find an escape from shame, from bitterness? In answer his heart gave a bound. Eremon was bold as well as wise, old Finn had said. Cahir must be even bolder.

'The Picts ...' Her cheeks paled, as if she were only now waking. 'But it's dangerous!'

'And what have I got to lose?'

'Well ... your life!'

He shook his head bleakly. 'No, Minna, it isn't a life.' He squatted down. 'The druids train us to recognize signs. I am a king, and I've been called by the king of birds to a valley with a rowan tree, in the east. So *some* answer must lie there for me.' *And my atonement, my release,* he added fervently to himself, with a pang of terrible yearning. If that were so, nothing would hold him back.

Minna's mind ran swiftly ahead. 'Then I must go, too.'

When he frowned, she burst out, 'Don't deny me this, I beg you! I also need to find a reason. The reason ... for all this. Some peace, from the dreams. *Please.*'

Cahir sat on the floor beside her, crooking his arms around his knees. For a moment by the fire they were just two young people seeking answers to the restlessness inside them. 'You have been ill,' he said slowly. 'As a king I owe you my protection – and my heart tells me there is no peace on this absurd journey, only danger. But I am unsure of finding my way without you, since you saw the eagle's flight.' He sighed, raising a brow. 'It is too great a risk for you.'

'I don't care.' Her voice was bleak. 'I have no life here. I am a slave.'

He was shocked to glimpse the same despair in her he felt in his own heart, every day. An unconscious sense of kinship overcame him in a rush. 'We are both slaves in our own ways, perhaps; I to my dead father, you to my wife.'

And if I break my shackles, he found himself thinking, surprised at his own mind, *can I deny you the breaking of yours?*

The room seemed to hold its breath, the flames steady, the wind dying away. At last Cahir nodded. 'So be it.' The light in her eyes flared, penetrating him. 'I cannot refuse anyone the absolution I myself need.'

He got up, his blood already beginning to race. It was all going to change, at last. 'Minna,' he said hoarsely, after a moment. 'Do you know what my name means?'

She hesitated. 'How could I?'

'Cahir means battle-lord. Lately I've wondered if my father named me that in jest, for he wanted peace with the Romans at any price.' He turned to her, the fire warm on his cheek, and spoke softly. 'So it seems I'm supposed to wake up.'

Her fine jaw was outlined by the flames, and her eyes were glowing. 'Yes,' she whispered. 'I think I am to wake up, too.'

Chapter 27

Cahir, King of Dalriada watched dawn from the hill, drawing the prickling cold air deep into his throat. The sheltered hollows of the slopes were covered with green shoots, and catkins swung on the hazel trees. Pockets of snow still clung to the far mountains to the north, turning rose in the rising sun.

He filled his lungs again, exhilarated. His soul was already stretching its wings like a bird taking flight, following those who called to him across the sky. He did not know what revelation waited for him: after all, the cold facts of too few warriors and too many enemies were still the same. But he would be released from indecision and inaction, at least. He laughed to himself exultantly, like a boy. How his father would frown at such folly.

But Cahir could not stop this now even if he wanted to, and he didn't want to. He longed to be free. He needed to glimpse a life where he was not the failed king and lackey of the Romans.

He would be something more. He would be himself.

When he came back to the hut Minna was standing at his stallion's shoulder, tentatively stroking his arched neck. In the breeze her unbound hair mingled with his black mane, the colours indistinguishable, and her fearful posture had straightened into a grace Cahir sensed with his flesh, rather than his mind. She looked as if she belonged here beneath the spreading oak tree.

Cahir was taken by another stab of desire in his groin, that odd pull towards her, and he sternly curbed it. There were gulfs between them: he was a king and if she wasn't a slave then she was an enigma, an intrigue, a ... he did not know what she was. But he would not make her afraid for something passing, as all desire was. He needed her to get what he wanted. That sounded cooler, better.

She turned when his foot cracked a twig, blood rushing her cheeks. He did not know how he could have once thought her face bony. In the spring sunlight the lines seemed pure and fine now amid her streaming hair, the shape a heart.

'I want to set off in two days.' Cahir forced a smile, his pulse throbbing. 'If I'm going to be damned I should get started as soon as possible.'

She was unsure of him again. They had shared something impossible in the dark, the flames leaping amid the shadows, painting dreams on the walls. But now day had come. 'So you mean to go north,' she said quietly. 'My lord.' She added the last as an afterthought, but it had disappeared naturally from their conversation the night before, and Cahir was jolted by its return.

'Of course. I will gather a few men and pick a trail into the mountains.'

She gazed fixedly at the ground. 'And you will do this because of what I said?'

'Because of all of it, not just you. Now I see the entire pattern – my pattern.'

Her face changed. 'And is it not ... mine as well?' The words were deferential, but her eyes flashed fire from under her lashes.

'Yours as well,' Cahir said faintly. He wondered if she could see inside him, too; glimpse all his ugliness and guilt. That was not a good thought. 'Now I'm going back to Dunadd, and I want you to stay here. You should rest two more nights before being out in the cold. I will bring the men back tomorrow. There is enough food.' He reached to tie his scabbard on the side of his saddle, moving so suddenly that when she tried to step away they bumped against each other. Minna leaped back as if he'd burned her.

Cahir resolutely tightened the thongs. 'If I gather you firewood and you bar the door, you will not be afraid here on your own?'

Thoughts raced across her pale face. 'No, I won't be afraid,' she said, her voice still hoarse from her fever.

'And ... I trust you will be here when I return.'

She glanced towards the pool, the wind still whispering secrets across it among the overhanging trees. 'I will have no peace until I find that valley, just as you will not.' She looked back, spoke formally as if she had caught herself again. 'My lord, could you ask Keeva to look after the girls as if they were her own and ...' she coloured again, 'tell them I am sorry to leave them but will be back for them ... when I can.'

'I will tell them,' he said warmly.

After Cahir rode away Minna was still for a long moment. Then her arms came out and she turned a circle under the oak tree, its branches furred by buds.

She was alone. Her arms fell to her sides. She could run — she knew that's what Cahir had meant when he asked if she would be here. She raised her face to the weak sun and, as always, the knowing came to her heart there, as if drifting down in the dust motes. She would be haunted if she left now. Something tied her here, bound her soul, and she must find out what it was, to be free of it for ever.

As a child she had been afraid of the deepest pool in the river, and so one day Mamo stepped into it and held out her arms. Minna hovered on the bank, her toes curling into the mud. *Jump, and you will see it for what it is*, Mamo gently called. It took some time, but at last Minna jumped. The water went up her nose and she snorted and spluttered, but after a moment she and Mamo were laughing, water streaming from her black hair.

Minna opened her eyes, her throat tight at the memory. But her courage had always been stronger than her fear.

On the ride back, Cahir thought hard. If no one knew where he was going, the safety of Dunadd would not be weakened, but strengthened. He might be gathering an army, treating with the Romans, forming alliances with other tribes. He didn't trust Maeve and oily Oran, and there were perhaps many others he could not trust either, but fear of what he intended and where he might suddenly reappear would give them all pause for thought. A long enough pause to go and … well, to find his fate.

The ponderous words made him smile, trotting along the road in spring, sun in his face.

At Dunadd, he announced he was undertaking a diplomatic mission, but did not specify where he was going or for how long. At first Maeve wheedled, trying to extract the truth, but when he remained impassive she grew suspicious and then angry. In the end she screeched all manner of hateful things that left him completely unperturbed.

He left Finbar and a band of loyal warriors in charge of Dunadd. That only left the decision of which men to take with him, a small party who could move swiftly. Donal must come, of course, and Gobán, Fergal and Tiernan. But he wanted young men with him, too, the restless ones. It was a gamble, but he'd rather have them where he could see them. So Mellan came, with Ardal and Brogan — and Ruarc.

The attraction of a mystery adventure served to silence their questions. Provisions were packed — trailcakes of fat, berries and dried meat pounded together; strips of dried beef and fish; hard cheese; flasks of ale — along with sleeping hides, furs and winter clothes. Maeve watched these preparations through slitted, furious eyes.

A day later they were back at the hut. Relief swamped Cahir when Minna appeared at the door, her head high and wary on its slim neck, like a deer. Ruarc gaped at her.

'We will leave tomorrow,' Cahir said swiftly. Let the young cockerel be surprised for once. 'Tonight, we talk.'

And what was he to tell them? As night fell, they gathered around the fire. Their damp clothes stank as they dried, their boots and legs and shoulders crowded the hearth, and their spears and swords cluttered the walls. Minna stayed back, crouched on the bed.

Cahir gazed around at his men's faces, which were suspicious, eager and expectant in turn. Then he met Donal's gaze, his bulbous nose and lumpen ears defying his sharp, swift skill with a sword. Those mild, blue eyes were encouraging.

Could he really tell them about visions, dreams, prophecies?

'Some information has come into my hands,' he began at last. 'I cannot reveal it all to you now. But this is the heart – I need to cross the mountains into Pict lands. There is something there I must find.'

'The Picts?' Ruarc's voice was eager. 'Another raid?'

'No, it is not about fighting the Picts; indeed, I hope we do not have to. I intend to do this without them knowing we are there.' He met Ruarc's eyes. 'It is about the Romans.'

A pregnant silence fell. 'What about them?' Mellan asked at last, puzzled.

Cahir's pulse raced, and he stood up. 'I am reconsidering my position on our Roman ... entanglements.' He spoke briskly, injecting power into his voice, then gave them the barest of facts: that there was some link to their ancestors and Rome in enemy land. And he had to find it.

The older ones accepted his will, but the younger still looked suspicious, and he had to have them all on side. He realized he must show them who he really was after all – there was no other way. He braced himself.

'In vision, dream and voice, the gods have been calling me to take a new path for a long time – though they have not revealed their full purpose. Now, they have sent me an undeniable sign, something known only to me and my father, and all the kings before him.' They were hanging on every word. 'It is dangerous, though. If you will not come, I will go alone.'

Ruarc spoke up. 'So you want us to trek through the Pict mountains on the order of the gods, not knowing exactly where to or to what purpose? Is that what you're saying?'

'I am saying it is what I must do. I am asking you to provide the strength of your sword-arms. But it is your choice.'

'And this is about the Romans,' Ruarc persisted. 'Resisting them.'

Cahir had not voiced that thought so baldly to himself, for it set off an earthquake inside. 'Yes,' he said. 'Though I do not know how.'

Everyone was surprised. Ruarc's brows rose, as a smile broke over his face. 'Well, well. A chance to stretch our legs, skewer some Picts and thumb my nose at Romans is enough of a draw for me.'

The other young ones grinned, and Cahir's tension began to melt.

'But what about her?' Ruarc asked, indicating Minna. 'What's *she* doing here?' He glanced mockingly at her. 'Though I have heard she is handy with a blade.'

Cahir had nearly forgotten about Minna, intently listening on the bed, her face growing red at Ruarc's words. Though there was no way to explain what they had shared, his people were long used to believing such things as sight and foretellings: it was part of their soul, their stories. 'She is of the old blood, a dreamer. She was sent the greatest vision for me, and I need her for guidance.' At the uneasy and speculative glances, Cahir added sternly, 'This is my will: let that be an end of it.' He took up something from the hearth and squatted in the middle of them. In his hands was a strip of smoothed birch bark, on which he and Minna had scrawled a line map from her recollections, that first night. 'Here is the great glen, slanted north and east.'

Dour Góban pointed a finger at it. 'The Picts use the glen all year around.'

'Yes,' Cahir agreed. 'So we cannot take that trail, though it would be easier. This is what I propose instead. We follow the Loch of the Waters east and north towards Cruachan, then the glens to its south that lead over the dead moors, and across to the lochs and mountains on the other side.'

There was a pause. 'How far?'

'Where the mountains close in the north there is a particular ridge. Minna saw it; we will find it.'

Tiernan, a bluff, blond man with drooping moustache, sat back and took from his mouth the twig he'd been chewing. 'That's right through the most rugged country, Cahir.'

'I know, but there are advantages in that. One, it's inhospitable, so there are few Pictish homesteads. And two, this path is harder to travel than others, so we should be able to avoid their warriors on higher ground. The worst weather has passed now. It is possible.'

'Of course it's possible,' Ruarc said forcefully, his head down. 'I just hope it's worth it.'

Shivering in the sea-wind, Keeva hurried to keep up with Lonán as he strode into the port, which was propped high above the marsh on its rock.

After the nut cracking she'd certainly landed her fish, she thought, as the smith's apprentice glanced at her shyly. She wished he'd been a little harder to catch, but no matter. She'd discovered these last few days just how pleasing a smith could be in the bed-furs – strong muscles matched with clever hands.

"I told you it was too cold for you to come,' Lonán ventured, in his slow, considered way. 'You're such a little thing.'

'Don't call me little.' Keeva ducked around a cart tied up by the pier. 'You know I don't want you fawning on me like I'll break at any moment.'

Lonán smiled fondly at her retorts, which made her think she was getting more in him than hard, young arms and, one day, fine dresses and bronze rings. 'When we are wed, I can fawn all I like,' he said, with a surprising twinkle in his eye. 'I can do what I like as well, and you cannot gainsay me. Ever.'

Keeva exclaimed and slapped him. 'Don't go getting any such ideas, my lad! That's not part of any bargain we've made.'

Grinning, Lonán rubbed his arm even though Keeva wouldn't make a dent in it if she used all her force. 'Then I might have to think again. Elva might be a more compliant wife: I'm sure she said so.'

Keeva went to strike again, and, chuckling, Lonán took off at a run, his blond braids bouncing on his wide shoulders. There weren't many people out on this bitter day, only a few men carrying sacks and baskets on their shoulders from carts to sheds. It was still too early for ships, for the seas would not be safe for many weeks yet. Fintan the blacksmith had sent Lonán to see if there were any last stores of tin to buy from the overwintering Roman traders.

The tin forgotten, Lonán ducked in and out of the carts with Keeva behind him, both of them screeching like children. She'd just get near enough to grab his tunic when he'd dash down a different path, weaving between the houses.

Keeva had just caught up with him in a quiet backstreet when a door-hide nearby was flung back and two men strode out. Just before Keeva barrelled into them, Lonán whisked her out of the way into a nearby alley. He laughed and pulled Keeva into his arms, his lips lowering to hers, then paused when she paid him no attention. Instead, she was gazing over his shoulder, panting.

'What?' Lonán whispered. Keeva waved him into silence. The first man was that Lord Oran – Keeva distrusted his snaky eyes. Behind him was another man almost completely hidden in a cloak and hood. Keeva caught a glimpse of his face as he turned to murmur to Oran. He had pale eyes and a shaved forehead, now almost covered by his hood. A priest, here? The king would have a fit.

'What's wrong?' Lonán whispered again, and this time, to keep him quiet, Keeva did kiss him. Their lips met and Lonán closed his eyes. Keeva, though, kept one eye open.

So she saw the woman leave the house, her stained cloak held tight about her face, her head down. Despite her plain clothes, Keeva knew the ring on her finger: a carved carnelian from Roman lands. It was Maeve.

Keeva's thoughts tumbled, her mouth moving woodenly beneath Lonán's.

What was the queen doing in hiding, with the king away on his mysterious mission? He had told his daughters that Minna was still very sick and being nursed at the Dun of the Rock, but Keeva didn't believe it. Minna was with him, her heart told her, astonishing as it seemed. And when Brónach returned she had shut the door of her house and would see no one. Something odd was going on, Keeva could smell it. She was Attacotti, after all, and their blood was the oldest in Alba. Suspicion, worry for Minna, and a pang of loyalty for the king assailed her.

The Lord Oran clasped the priest's wrist – not very religiously, she thought – and there was a clink of coins being passed between them. Breathless, Keeva broke Lonán's kiss.

She had never heard that Christians paid priests for their god's word.

Chapter 28

Minna had never thought it possible to be so cold.
The winds funnelled down the hill-slopes straight from the clouded peaks, as the horses stumbled forward on frozen tussocks of sedge and heather. The bleak expanses of red moorland were dotted with black pools, their surfaces feathered by bleached grasses.

Bundled in sheepskins, she clung to her pony. Though she was too tired to walk she no longer ached, for she had much else to fill her, her senses heightened by the air on the back of her throat, in her nose.

Always her eyes were drawn to Cahir riding at the head, his chin high as if straining forward, his reins held easily in one hand. He did not seem to notice the icy wind tearing back his dark hair. The years had been stripped from his face. He blazed, his eyes on fire with fierce hunger, every movement imbued with a new power.

All the men followed that fiery light, even the younger ones responding to his commands instinctively because they were delivered in so sure a manner. They were baffled by this new king but infected by his excitement, and the mood was swift and light despite the clouds and glowering mountains. It was Ruarc's curiosity that mainly drove him, though, and he was still wary.

After a week they were in Pictish lands and moved more stealthily, the young men scouting the ridges during the day, while the others kept to the rocks and bare woods. At night they huddled in rock shelters with no fires, chewing strips of dried meat and trail cakes. The men ignored Minna as if they did not know what to do with her, sending cautious glances her way when she wasn't looking. All except Donal, who winked as he passed over her food.

Every day, when the men were watering the horses, Cahir unrolled the birch map and pored over it with Minna. 'I recognize this,' she would say, or, 'No, there were two rivers meeting here.'

Once, unsure of the path at the top of a pass, they had to wedge themselves into the rocks, pressed so close that Cahir's breath stirred Minna's hair. As she was trying to summon a memory of the vision, her brow creased, he glanced up with an unreadable expression. 'If anything happens to us, do what you must to save yourself, Minna. Run or hide until danger passes. Promise me.'

She hardly heard the words, drawn into his blazing eyes. Then the wind buffeted them, and she became acutely aware of his thighs bracing against the rock. At that moment the Picts seemed only a vague threat, for she was desperately fighting another battle – the way something inside her was dragged towards him whenever he was near, as if they were tied together.

By the time they met the mountains over the moor – the high spine of Alba – Minna didn't need to strain to hear the song of the land any more. It was all around her.

She easily ignored the cold, her chapped lips and cramped hands, for every time they crested a pass the grandeur of the peaks ahead took all awareness of her body away. She couldn't feel anything inside when the power of her surroundings was so complete. It only left awe; that, and nothing else.

The sheer heights poured with snow-melt streams, dwarfing the valleys along which they crept. And it was these peaks that raised her up each day in the frosted dawn, when every muscle cried out. It was this power that blessed her, healing her of all pain and weariness, her lingering cough and weakness.

The majesty of the hills *was* the song of Alba, and their royalty demanded surrender.

The decurion Flavius Martinus left the latrine with a scowl. Habitancum was one of the most northerly outpost forts, stuck up high on the Alban moors above the Wall. The wind swept incessantly along the stone trough of the latrine and his rump was no doubt now blue as a Pict's face.

'Sir.' A lanky figure detached itself from the gate and came alongside.

Martinus tensed, for the youth had no armour and his clothes were filthy, coated with what looked like weeks of mud. Still, the garrison had let him in. He squinted, then recognized the cub. 'Juggler boy, hail. Your ugly face gave me a fright.'

Whenever his troupe played the Wall this boy always had a grin plastered over his face. Martinus had diced with him, got drunk with him, and the damned pup had never stopped joking for a moment as he slid the Roman coins from the table-top into his pockets. But he was not smiling now: he was gaunt and haggard, his face bloodied by scratches.

'I need to speak with you.'

The decurion shrugged, re-adjusting his heavy cloak across his shoulders. 'Hurry up, then.'

'I have come to join the scouts.'

Martinus snorted. They stood back for a column of cavalry leading their mounts from the stables, the hooves clopping on the cobbles. 'And you think just by strolling in here, I will take you.'

The youth kept his bleak eyes on the ground. 'I was hoping so.'

Martinus rubbed his hands together in the cold wind. The dusk was drawing in from the moors already, and most of the streets were in the shadow of the high, stone walls. 'It doesn't work like that. Go down to Eboracum, sign up there and see where you get posted. Good luck.' He strode away.

After a moment the boy was loping alongside again. His eyes were eerily blank, and Martinus couldn't repress a sense of unease.

'I am the best rider you'll ever see,' the boy said, though it wasn't boastful, just distant, as if repeating something by rote. 'And I have travelled these lands for years, and I speak the Alban tongues as well as ours. I'm an asset.'

The decurion sighed with irritation. He was exhausted and short of temper after another raid by the blueskins this week in which he'd lost ten men guarding a Votadini quarry. *And how did they always know where his men would be?* It was uncanny; perhaps their murderous gods really did speak to them.

'As I said, it doesn't work that way,' he snapped. 'Now, piss off and leave me be.'

He was nearly at the headquarters yard when the acrobat cut him off. The fell light in his face made Martinus flinch. 'Commander,' he said, his low voice betraying a dark passion, 'I want to kill Albans more than I want to breathe. Sign me up – but don't pay me until you've seen me ride. I brought my own mount, and he's a beauty, bred for these hills.' As Martinus hesitated, he broke in, 'I know you need men. I've seen the graves along the road, and many of them are fresh.'

The decurion glared, but what he said was true. He'd lost many men this winter, and the administration in the south spent too long scratching its arse so he wouldn't get replacements for months, and his men would be in more danger every time they left the fort ... oh, blast it. Let the boy throw himself on an enemy spear and be done with it.

One less of his own men dead.

★

The cold bored deep into Minna's bones at night, and on stormy days the mountains were now glowering, angry gods wrapped in cloud. Their progress slowed to a crawl as they penetrated deeper into Pictish territory, and she began to feel that the hills had eyes. After two weeks they saw their first trails of smoke against the sky.

'This is a remote place,' Cahir said, as they huddled about their packs in a rock shelter. 'It is likely to be no more than a herder and his family.'

'We can't know that.' Brogan's sharp face was sullen in the fading light.

Donal sent him a keen look from under bushy brows. 'And there you were in the king's hall yipping at how you never get adventure, lad. What are you complaining about?'

Squatting with his hands on the ground, Ardal began, 'We're just saying—'

'Saying what?' Góban crossed his arms. 'It's no use dreaming every night of a sword in your hand and a Pictish neck before you only to balk now.'

'We're not balking,' Ruarc said. He was honing his sword with intent strokes of the whetstone, his golden head down. 'We just wonder what we are putting our names to.'

Cahir was standing by the entrance to the overhang, looking out. 'I understand,' he said quietly. All the heads swivelled towards him. 'I am claiming this deed, giving my name to it, and even I don't know where it will lead.' He turned, his eyes luminous. 'But it's better than lying under the heels of the Romans until my very breath is squeezed from my body!'

The young men stared in surprise at that passionate voice echoing off the rock. Minna could see their thoughts groping for understanding of this new lord before them. At last black-haired Ardal said defiantly, 'It's better than waiting at home.'

'Anything is better than that,' Mellan agreed.

'I promise you,' Cahir said then, meeting their eyes one by one, 'that you will share my thoughts, that you will know my heart at the moment I do myself. I promise you that for the life you have risked.' A silence fell after that, heavy with thought.

They had been caught in a flurry of sleet on the way to the shelter, and as the men set about eating, Cahir brought his own wolf cloak to wrap around Minna, who could not stop shivering.

She glanced up. 'You ... you will freeze.' Her hair hung damply about her face.

'No, I won't.' He tugged the cloak around her throat until she was nestled in wolf-fur, his eyes intent on his hands. 'You have much to learn of warriors: danger heats our blood. We do not go cold.'

Minna's breath stirred the fur ruff. He was right: he radiated heat. She sensed his swift heartbeat and fast breathing. 'And ... you are not afraid?' She was — it pressed on her every time she looked up to the peaks ahead and wondered if Picts lurked there, arrows nocked on bows. She almost felt the sharpness of their points as a tingling in the hollow of her throat.

'Afraid?' Cahir smiled, his eyes creasing at the corners. 'I forget you are Roman born. Your tales of the Christos say that death is the end. But when slain, we believe we are drawn into the bliss of the Otherworld through the gateway, and in time, once we have feasted with the gods, we are returned to our kin as new babes. We are the many-born, and so we are not afraid.'

Pride had kindled in his gaze, and Minna could not look away. Her beliefs were a mishmash of Parisii, with its longing for lost gods; the old Roman fear of Pluto's dark halls, from where no spirit returned; and the Christian heaven. Mamo felt that spirits came back to earth, too, though until Minna lost her she had never had cause to believe in such fiery hope. Keeva had told her that the tribes knew this truth, but it was only now, drowning in Cahir's eyes, that she fervently believed it.

'I do not want you to concern yourself with me,' she murmured. 'You have too many others to think of.'

His black brow arched. 'But I came to salute your bravery. The men are all impressed by how you keep up with us with no word of complaint — even Ruarc, grudging as he is.' Minna blinked, for the warriors hardly ever met her eyes. 'But if you'd rather not hear that ...'

A tide of heat rose up her cheeks. 'I don't think I'm brave, just stubborn. It doesn't take much to hold to a pony.'

Almost unnoticed, Cahir's hand still rested around the back of her neck, holding the fur against the freezing air. 'You'd be surprised.' His smile glowed, as ever, with a smouldering excitement. 'You have a warrior's heart — take comfort from it.'

'Said like a king,' she replied, shivering a little less.

At her words his face fell, the warmth in his eyes withdrawing. 'Not like a king, no.' His hand dropped away. 'I knew you would worry about being a burden, that is all, and you are not.'

Entirely bewildered, she watched him return to his men.

Chapter 29

Minna stood on the high pass looking north, the wind shrieking around her, stretching the hides against her icy skin. The men hastened ahead to the shelter of the glen below but she could not move.

'Minna!' Cahir came scrabbling back up the defile, sliding on the wet stones. 'What is it?'

She could not answer, holding to the rock, eyes closed, her body battered by gusts. In her mind, the eagle flew again through her blazing vision. Breathing slowly, she replayed its swoops and lifts, its turns and glides. *She was so close now.*

Over the past days a pressure had been building in her chest like a coming storm. Step by step, the immense, brooding land had scoured away all her human feelings. Step by step, her spirit had broken free of its shell to fly above her, tethered only by the winds.

As her bodily feet twisted on rocks and scree, her soul was swooping through the cloud-tops. Labouring in bulky furs, mittens and boots, she began to sense feathers splayed at the ends of her hands. Now, as she topped this pass, the hairs were raised on her skin. *Come,* the land called again, but with a swifter pulse of expectation.

'Come down before you freeze!' Cahir shouted.

'In a moment,' she whispered to herself. Her cheeks were going numb, but she was reliving the dream of the night before; the same voice hovering around her. *Your sight brought you, your courage held you. So hearken to me. At every step you must draw the Source up from the land, the air, the winds, the deep waters. It is a light that will illuminate all darkness. The Source will break the boundaries of your mind.*

Minna opened her eyes. The path ahead was hidden by swirling clouds but, as she watched, the veils of mist were drawn back for a moment, and there on the far side of a long valley reared the triple-headed peak she had seen in her vision.

'There,' she said, and the storm inside her broke, rolling with thunder. 'There!' she cried. Cahir leaned in to her, his shoulders hunched in his cloak. 'That left-hand peak,' she said breathlessly. 'We must find a path up the west slope.'

Cahir caught her arm, his eyes shadowed with concern. 'It is late, and there is sleet about the peaks. We will shelter and go up tomorrow.'

No, now. Now. Minna tore free of him ... and suddenly realized she was not looking *at* Cahir — but *through* him.

There he stood, solid as rock, and yet she could glimpse another world behind him: the sunlight warm, not icy, the slopes green under a clear sky. Her own world tilted, and despite the beckoning summer light of that other place she was felled by a surge of grief that took her legs out from under her so she had to catch at Cahir's arms.

Around them the sleet gusted grey and white, the sky clouded, but behind Cahir sunlight and shadow chased themselves across an emerald slope. 'We must go up now. *Please*. Only you and I.'

Cahir's gaze raked her face, and, wonderingly, he touched the tears that ran down her cold cheeks.

Together they crossed the valley and began to climb the steep slopes of the far peak.

Though it became gradually colder, Minna was by now lost in the keening chant of grief, an echo of something ancient that was all around her and inside her. It drew her on, her feet moving of their own accord, her eyes open but unseeing.

Halfway up she could smell the perfume of summer heather and mossy rock in sunshine. The other world was growing brighter and the song more piercing, the words wreathing her in a pain that was not her own.

At last she was struck down by that hurt, gasping, her legs buckling. Cahir turned back and gathered her into his arms. Then, cradled by him, she was called up the mountain.

Cahir laboured around the shoulder of the ridge along an exposed path, the wind gusting them towards its western face. He stumbled through broken boulders and across bleak slopes, then came to a stop on a ledge where the jagged cliffs fell away. His chest moved under Minna's cheek.

'So it is true.' A shudder went through his body.

A gnarled rowan grew from the cracked rock, its bare branches shielding a small patch of flat ground filled with blown snow. Cahir gently placed Minna on her feet, holding her as she swayed.

It was as her feet touched the ground that the Source flowed up from the earth like a molten river into her body, expanding in one rush of light, and all at once she understood. The Source was the essence of all things, not just the life of trees and beasts but the creations that fed life, the rocks and streams, the hills and lakes. It was the spirit that made a person utterly themselves, and all people One at the same time.

Minna closed her eyes and at last surrendered to that rush, breathlessly opening soul, heart ... and someone else's emotions stormed through her – grief, fury and despair – and she was felled to her knees.

Struggling to see, to move, she crawled to the centre of the hollow as the wind tore at her. Below, the valleys were hidden by clouds, and she and Cahir were alone on a pillar of rock in the whirling white. He knelt, the wind whipping his hair over his face. 'But there is nothing here!'

She shook her head, still able to see into the other world. There the sun was hanging low and red in a summer sky, and the hollow on which they now knelt was bathed in a still dusk. The rowan tree was young, its feathered leaves green and fresh.

And hearts were breaking there.

With a soft cry, Minna held out a hand, her eyes glazed. There was a dark-haired man weeping piteously, and a woman in a hooded cloak who held him. Beside them a hole had been delved by the man's sword, and now he straightened, hugging a tiny bundle wrapped in the same blue cloth of his blood-stained tunic. In spite of his grief, she could see the man had a noble face, and though he was young his eyes were old. Minna couldn't see the woman, for she turned with the bundle in her arms and laid it in the hole with a graceful tenderness.

Minna flinched as the grief impaled her, sharp and despairing. She spun towards Cahir. 'Dig! Dig here!' He crouched beside her, and she plucked at the sword on his belt. 'It's not far beneath. Hurry!'

Gazing into her wild eyes, Cahir didn't question. The ground was pebbled and icy, but he pressed his weight over his sword-hilt until the surface broke, and after a time the soil became softer and more disturbed. Minna pulled off her mittens and began scraping the earth away from the point, until she touched something and paused. Cahir dropped the sword and together they dug around the object. She knew what they would find before they saw it, her fingers instinctively shaping the ridges and curves.

There was a tiny cage of ribs rising in a delicate arch from the soil, and a small yellowed skull, eyeholes darkened with earth. The legs and arms were no bigger than Cahir's fingers, the hands tucked under the chin. A miniature scrap of tattered cloth still covered the lower body, blackened by frost.

For a moment Minna stared at it.

And suddenly her body was borne down and down, until her cheek was pressed into the icy soil next to the baby's skull. Its eye-holes gazed directly into her own. 'Mother ... Lady ... Christos ... M–Mamo ...'

Cahir seized her shoulder. '*Who is this*? Speak to me!'

Her fingers curled up under her chin as words were torn free from inside her, one by one. She didn't know what she'd said until they all hung there together like a shredded banner in the wind.

'It ... is ...me.'

Chapter 30

Minna shuddered all over, staring into her own dead eyes.
'It is me,' she whispered again, and when she said the
words they sank through her body as a chant, kindling all the
ancient, buried parts of her, like stars flaring into life as darkness fell. 'It
was my body once in another life. I *saw* it.'

'Minna,' Cahir breathed, then knelt and drew her head to his chest,
sheltering her with his cloak. But she barely felt him, seeing only the
dark man's haunted eyes as he held the baby. *Father*. And the woman
... she had disappeared before Minna saw her clearly. Her lips moved,
tasting the word. *Mother*.

'Then ...' Cahir murmured, awe-struck, 'you are one of the many-
born.'

Many-born. His words spun among the stars inside her, forming a pattern. The baby was dead, but Minna had come back, she had been born
again. She saw again the spirals carved into the rocks above Dunadd;
the endless cycle.

All the years of her life seemed to wheel around the ledge. The place
where she had ended was also her new beginning.

Trembling, she dragged herself upright. In the vision, the man had
pulled something from his neck and placed it with the baby, and the
woman added something else from her finger. Minna stared into Cahir's
eyes. Their sheen was dulled by the grey light, but they were full of
questions, his mouth warm, alive. His light drew her back. 'Look on
the baby,' she whispered. 'Look what is there.'

As Cahir bent over the grave, feeling in the earth with his fingers,
Minna tentatively reached out to touch the baby's skull. She closed her
eyes at the cold feel of bone, exhaling in a rush.

'Here!' Something was caught in the rotted wool at the child's neck, a black stone disc, shiny with moisture. As Cahir lifted it, remnants of its leather thong fell away. Brushing it with his thumb, he scrutinized the stone. 'It has carvings on it.'

Minna hardly heard him, for where the soil had crumbled away from the baby's finger joints a ring had fallen free. Hesitantly, she picked it up. It was gold. The disk on top was cast with an unusual design: two crescents set back to back, linked with a circle in the middle. *The cycles of the moon. The three faces of the Goddess.*

As she knew the herbs, so she knew this. The new moon crescent was for the Maiden; fresh and rising into life. The full moon was for the Mother; round and fertile with child. The waning crescent was for the death Crone, as the moon slides into its dark time. A woman's sign, for the moon's tides are female.

Cahir glanced up now, face tense with excitement. 'There are animals here. One is an eagle, I think – but the other appears to be a boar. *The* Boar. The sign of the royal house of Dalriada.'

They both stared down at the stone, but the pitch of the wind was rising now as if to hurry them along, and ice was invading Minna's veins. 'We must go now,' Cahir decided, touching her cheek with a frown. He paused. 'Do you want to take the child, Minna?'

She shivered, shaking her head: the baby had been placed here with love and honour, in a cradle dug by her father's sword. So while Cahir filled in the hole, Minna huddled against the rock under the rowan, out of the wind. Its twisted branches arched over her protectively as it had stood sentinel all these years over the grave. But how many years? *And who were those people?*

Filled with the grace of the Source, she only had to form the thought when her mind was flooded by pictures.

In a gilded hall three people stood by a throne. Above the throne, a hanging bore the design of a great eagle in gold on blue. One man was an ageing king with gold-brown hair and a striking hawk nose, and he was holding out the stone disk to the dark-haired young man Minna had seen weeping over the grave. *Father.*

Then the woman moved into the torchlight and Minna's vision was filled by that heart-stopping face: copper hair, a wide mouth and long, imperious nose, its severity softened by the upwards tilt of cat-like eyes. *Mother.* The ring shone on her finger.

'*This boar stone is not gold,*' the old king said. '*For gold is soft. It is of stone: hard, unbending, true and unchanging.*' He looked at the young man. '*It represents my bond to you, for that will be eternal, and never falter. My totem, and yours, joined together on a message stone. This declares to all who see it that we are allied in soul for ever.*'

The young man's eyes shone. '*What does the writing say?*' There was a lilt to his speech that Minna found familiar.

The old king looked at the woman, and she held the stone up to her grave, blue eyes. Her voice was deep and musical. '*It says: Calgacus of the Caledonii pledges allegiance and brotherhood to Eremon of Dalriada.*'

Minna's head reared back against the rock. Eremon, her father. And that made *her*, the woman ... Rhiann, the Epidii princess. Cahir's ancestor.

'*No untruth can ever be written this way,*' Calgacus said. '*So no man will ever be able to dispute that you speak in my name.*'

His face glowing, Eremon took the stone and drew the thong over his head. '*I thank you, lord.*' His voice was husky with emotion. '*I have no gift in return but that of my own oath. Yet I tell you now: it is as eternal as this stone.*'

The scene faded and Cahir was on his knees before her, sheltered from the driving wind. Choking, Minna held out the ring and stone, a storm of confusion roaring through her. 'They are yours – take them, take them!'

He stowed the stone under his tunic, but looking intently at her closed her fingers over the ring. 'In my heart I know the boar is meant for me, but this is a noblewoman's ring, Minna. It was given to the child. If what you say is true ...' he swallowed, as shaken as she, '... surely it's yours, not mine.'

The ring vibrated in Minna's fist, but with that tingle of power came dread. She couldn't wear this, couldn't *be* this. It was a seer's ring.

'Go on,' Cahir urged her softly, his eyes grave. 'You must put it on, for the gods brought us here and gave it to you.'

When she still didn't move he took her left hand and slipped the ring on, and it nestled into her skin as if it belonged there. A seer's ring; her mother's ring.

Minna's ring.

Night had fallen.

In a cave in the valley below Minna lay wrapped in furs, staring into the shadows, seeing nothing of the walls or the men squeezed into the narrow cleft of rock.

Cahir had allowed them to build a fire this time, for after he carried her down the path from the peak she could not stop shuddering. Now she was safe, the men all ignored her and crowded about their king, firing questions at him.

Her eyes sank closed as their urgent voices enveloped Cahir. She couldn't think beyond her father's face, weeping, and her mother cradling them both. She kept seeing the gaping eye-holes of the skull. Loss burned her throat, her chest.

Gobán had taken the stone and was tilting it to the firelight. 'Gods, what *is* this?'

Swiftly, Cahir told them how the grave had been found. His voice boomed off the rocks around Minna, yanking her awake.

'So it's an eagle,' Brogan said, extracting the stone from Gobán and holding it to his narrow, clever face.

'And there are lines around the edge,' Mellan added, peering over his shoulder.

'It is *ogham*.' Cahir strode to them eagerly. 'The sacred druid language, I am sure of it.'

Ruarc frowned. 'But what does it all *mean*?'

There was silence, because no one knew. But Minna did. Now the Source drew her up, poured warmth in so she could be strong; the Source woke her mind, would not allow her the sleep of exhaustion. 'I know.' All the heads turned towards her. 'I know what the stone says, and who made it.'

Cahir stepped forward. 'Minna ...'

Looking up, she could see a corona of light about Cahir's head and shoulders that followed him as he moved. The crown. She shifted her gaze to the men, and saw into them, one by one. The bloodlust that could kill a man and revel in the honour, of course. But also the flutters of softer memories, of swords polished, and the glow of home fires; babes held in rough hands and the joy of a carefully honed point piercing a stag's flank. And over all, young and old, a heavy cloud of bitter disappointment that was the weight of the Roman yoke.

She glanced at Donal. There she glimpsed a woman's face, drawn and dying, and afterwards nothing to fill Donal's hands once her flesh had withered; nothing to make him look down the years ahead and rejoice – only his king and a wild hope he had never even voiced to himself. That something might change.

Minna rose to her feet, clutching the furs about her, and words were drawn up from her belly as if they were not her own. Holding Cahir's golden eyes, she told them of Calgacus of the Caledonii and Eremon of Erin.

Her voice was faint at first, faltering, but as they listened and there was no mockery in their faces, it strengthened. The men's expressions gradually changed, too, as she spoke, until she was surrounded by a ring of eyes shining in the firelight with awe and wonder. *Wonder*, from hardened warriors, when men had only ever sneered at her before? But that was her life before. Before Dalriada.

For Minna remembered *these* men listening to Davin's tales of dreams and legends in the hall with rapt faces. And in the wind and rain it had been Tiernan's stories of gods and great deeds that kept them warm with no fire, and young Ardal's soft singing that sent them to sleep. The sight was a gift, Cahir had said, and so these blooded warriors hearkened to a slave-girl simply because she was god-spoken, and because she had won their king's respect. In the cave, they gave her theirs.

The light around Cahir had been leaping higher with every word of hers, like a bonfire. Now it glowed about the men as Minna sank back to the hides, exhausted, and Cahir walked slowly to the far side of the cave, his head down.

'But,' a bewildered Mellan asked, 'who is this Calgacus?'

No one answered, until Cahir spun around, his eyes glittering. 'I know. I sat night after night with Darach and the druids around their fires, wanting to know everything about our past that was still remembered. When Eremon walked this land the tribes in the east were not all one people known as Picts – they had separate names and separate kings. The Caledonii were the strongest, and their most revered king was Calgacus. Since then, those eastern tribes have merged under one ruler, Gede son of Urp.' He glanced at Minna, and she felt it as a touch on her face. 'What I did not know is that Calgacus was allied with Eremon in the most binding way possible.'

The air rippled. Ardal frowned. 'The Picts and ... us?'

Cahir spread a hand on the damp cave wall, looking at the cracks as if they held answers. 'Our ancestors fought the Romans at the Hill of a Thousand Spears. Now a thought whispers to me ...' he took a deep breath and it rushed out, '... that Eremon fought with the Picts under Calgacus at that very battle.'

'It could not be!' Ruarc burst out. 'We sing of that place; we drink to that memory!'

'I think it is.'

Minna's hands were pressed across her heart. The dream she had had the first night at Dunadd of a man in battle, his despair as hordes of Romans poured down a slope towards him. *'My prince, look to the east. More Romans have come!'* Eremon. Her father.

'How could we have been allied with the Picts?' Tiernan pulled at his long moustache in agitation. 'They are our enemy – I have spilt their blood with my own sword.'

'Now we are enemies.' Cahir's face was blazing. 'But perhaps not always. Perhaps we and the Picts fought together once; faced the Romans and nearly won.'

Minna braced her hands on the earth floor, for the shimmering light around the men had risen up into flames behind her eyes, the currents shifting towards an unknown future. She sensed the paths of fate wavering, twisting.

'What are you saying?' Ruarc demanded of his king, clenching his fists.

Cahir looked at each of his warriors in turn: Ruarc, Ardal and the young firebrands, and his steady men, Tiernan, Góban, Fergal and Donal. The sparks leaped between them, the silent communication of warriors and hunters, and Minna found herself urging them, *Give him his honour; let him take it up with you behind him!*

'It is time,' Cahir said deliberately, 'to free ourselves of our oppressors, lest we die of shame in our beds. Our ancestors call us: it is time to fight Rome once more.'

They were all silent with astonishment, the atmosphere taut, on the edge. Then Donal suddenly blew out his breath, his eyes alight. 'We thought you'd never ask.'

Cahir blinked, and a grin dawned over his face. 'I never thought I would either.'

Ruarc and Mellan looked at each other, stunned, and then a babble of voices and laughter broke out as it all spilled from them at once, voices young and old rising together. *Yes, heed the gods! Take up arms! Mount an attack to force the Romans to battle, to wrest back Dalriadan honour, Dalriadan life-blood!*

And as Cahir's warriors demanded what he most wanted to give – his secret desire to redeem himself – he stood in their midst with hungry eyes and said nothing, drinking in their acclaim as a man who has thirsted and nearly died of it. The cave rang with their shouts, the grate of swords drawn, the tips thrust together.

Minna sat still amid the furs, gazing into the fire as the rock walls sang. The paths of fate settled around her, taking up their new form.

Chapter 31

Cahir sat at the cave mouth beneath the stars while the others slept. He was exhausted after the hours of discussion, but he would not miss this night for slumber. It still wasn't clear what to do with this stone, but right now he didn't care, for every hour that passed took him towards a new hope.

He could just hear the muted murmur of Ardal and Ruarc down the slope, standing watch, but when a light pad of feet sounded behind him he did not immediately turn. He had to brace himself first, and only then could he look at Minna as she knelt and gazed up at the stars, her breath misting the mountain air.

The tension tightened as the silence drew out. 'Minna,' he murmured at last. He tried to speak, then shook his head. 'You are of our blood.'

Her throat was outlined by starlight, so he saw her swallow with difficulty. 'It's more than blood. My soul was here with them. If the stone was theirs, then so was I.'

'But you are of my *lineage*.' He struggled to think through the storm in his body, for after the calls for war he felt alive as never before, and with her beside him again the pull in his belly was exquisite. He had repeated the litany in his head so many times: there were great barriers between them. Only suddenly, there were not, and he had nothing sure to cling to any more.

The anguish in Minna's eyes stopped his thoughts. 'I've known this ever since I stepped on to Alba's soil. Nothing felt right inside me.' She grasped the slave-ring around her neck. 'But now I am caught ... between.'

Without thinking Cahir reached to uncurl her tight fingers from the metal, and the jolt of that touch ran up his arm. 'You are Alban now, because of what you've done as well as what you are. You have proven your allegiance—'

'But I did not mean to leave them, Broc and my ...' Her face twisted, her waves of dark hair shadowing her white cheeks. 'Are they my people any more? I don't know.'

He caught both of her hands, making her look up at him. 'Minna, *we* are your people now, as you are ours. It is beyond my comprehension ... but it is true.'

'*You* can say that.' Minna searched his eyes, her fear raw, naked and terrible in her face. 'You have your dream, while my parents are gone for ever. *So what does that make me?*'

Her brow, nose and jaw were starlit curves, and Cahir stared at them, knowing it wasn't just desire that gripped him now, not a sharp, swift heat but a shifting of the very world beneath. She had given him his future.

'I will tell you this, as King of Dalriada.' His voice was unsteady. 'I cannot accept one truth from your visions and not the others. You are of the royal blood of Eremon and Rhiann, and you will stand in my hall as an honoured lady and take the place torn from you. This I promise, for the service you have rendered me and my people.' It sounded stilted, when he really wanted to take hold of her and set free the fire coursing through him.

She turned to him, wondering, her face shining with tears. 'I had not thought ...' She trailed off, and Cahir gritted his teeth to hold all that tumult of feeling at bay inside him: that she was the only one to see all the way into him and not turn away. That he *knew* her when first she touched him.

She broke his gaze to retreat to the safety of the stars. 'Nothing from before can make sense any more.'

'No,' Cahir said, watching the silver light graze her cheek. 'Not any more.'

The next morning the men gratefully turned back for Dunadd, relief and excitement quickening their movements. The horses picked up on it, tossing their heads and whinnying.

Minna, though, had woken to a day of shadowy bleakness, her soul left empty after that tempest. For the Source had gone from her, like a lamp guttering out.

After two days she was mired in too much doubt to feel anything. No more dreams came, no more voices telling her why she had found the stone and ring. The grave had illuminated Cahir's path, but left her own dark – he had gained something, while she had only discovered what she had lost.

When she looked upon his glowing face, she knew it was worth it, but a small voice in her cried out that she would be a vessel for other's fates, but not her own. *Foolish . . . foolish!* she berated herself. She wanted to cling to the memory of her father's face, her mother's smile, to take joy in them. To feel the wonder for ever. But she was so cold instead, cold and shaking.

As the triple peak fell away behind the mountains, the rocks closing about the valley, she glanced back, clinging to the pony's mane as all the warriors gazed forward.

At night, stretching an arm across her forehead, Minna's mind conjured up many other visions — Maeve's furious eyes, the contempt in Brónach's sharp face, the knowing smiles behind her back. It was not enough to stand up in Cahir's hall and say she was some kind of kin. Who would believe it? Who would accept her? The fear began to gnaw like the cold.

She wondered later if she had not been struggling so she might have sensed the whispers from the moon. If she'd listened, she might have heard a warning.

One moment, there was only the night sky and the sleepy murmurs of the men wrapped in their bedrolls. The next, the rocks all around were moving and guttural voices split the air.

Between one breath and the next, Cahir and his men flew from their hides, their swords already drawn. Minna had a confused impression of babbling men in shaggy furs descending on them from all directions, before Cahir bellowed a war-cry and his men caught up their shields and formed an instinctive knot about him, swords up.

Donal paused to shove Minna into a cluster of boulders, and she hit her head as she fell. By the time she scrabbled around, screaming men were clashing with each other all over the narrow defile, lunging and pulling back. Moonlight and shadows flitted over their features, making it hard to see, but then she recognized the wild, curling tattoos from every Roman child's nightmare, marking those white, snarling faces. Blueskins.

One Pict was already down, then two, as the patches of snow were spattered by blood, dark as pitch under the moon. Minna stared at a severed hand that fell near her feet with fingers spread, a tattoo curling up the wrist into the shredded flesh, and abruptly she was scrambling backwards, wedging herself into the cleft between two rocks as bile stung her throat.

The moonlight bounced off the frosted rocks and white ground, and by its light, Cahir circled one ragged bear of a man, lunging in then leaping back. His sword drew wild arcs which were met by his opponent time and again in a clash of metal, and Minna stifled a cry when Cahir slid on the ice and the Pict darted in with a stab that was barely blocked by a desperate swing of the king's shield. She tasted blood on her lip, panting.

Around these two the others fought in pairs, almost evenly matched. Then Tiernan was struck down by a blow to the neck, his long moustache matted with blood, and Minna shoved her fist into her mouth, gagging. He told tales at night, and he had begun to smile at her, his eyes sharp but kind ... The Pictish victor was standing there unchallenged for a moment, blood running from his chin. Then slowly he turned and met Minna's stunned eyes, before lunging towards her.

With a yelp she tried to squeeze through the cleft between the boulders. She had her shoulders through the gap when the man grabbed her ankle and hauled on it, and her head struck rock. In panic Minna scrabbled at the icy stones, but the man pulled her again, growling, and her skull was pounded again, sending stars around it that exploded in darkness.

When she came to she was crumpled like a rag on the ground. The noise of fighting had faded; there were only babbling Pict voices. Minna's head sprang up, thoughts flying to Cahir despite the flare of pain from the blow that made her whimper. A clutch of bodies were on the ground, but she couldn't see who was who. As she tried to clear her head, the stink of wet fleece enveloped her and a cold blade was pressed to her throat. A Pict loomed over her, his eyes glinting in the moonlight.

'Don't move!' came Cahir's faint voice, before it was cut off by a grunt. With a gasp of relief, Minna twisted towards him but was pulled up by the point of the blade.

Amid a confusion of shadows, one attacker held Cahir at the tip of his sword, as the big man who had fought him fingered his fine bronze torc, both jabbering excitedly in their own tongue. Other Dalriadan warriors were also being held at bay – Minna counted seven standing, each with a sword or dagger at their throat. Mellan had been on guard, but he was there, thrown to his knees. She couldn't see who else had died besides Tiernan.

The Pict leader barked something and his warriors answered, spitting in the faces of their captives. Minna's captor dragged her head back by her braids, callused fingers cupping her chin. He grunted something to the big man, who was studying Cahir's sword now while others picked over the Dalriadans' clothing and weapons like crows on a carcass, holding them up to the silver light, squinting, relieving them of daggers, whetstones, bows and swords. The tattoos marking their cheeks and foreheads broke their features into leering patterns of light and dark.

The Dalriadan warriors were dragged to their feet, their arms bound with lengths of flax rope. They snarled, struggling, until Cahir managed to yell again, 'Do not fight, by my order!' With a growl, the big warrior turned back and struck him across the mouth to silence him, as Minna tried to tug free of the arms that held her. Though he stumbled, Cahir recovered and drew himself erect. 'There is no chance if we run,' he said steadily, staring the Pict leader down. The man glowered and spat at Cahir's feet, then hauled him along on the rope. The horses were brought behind, tossing their heads, their eyes wide and white.

Minna was about to follow when, without warning, her captor seized her around the waist and flung her over his shoulder, holding her legs so she couldn't kick. Agony lanced her head again but she instinctively struck at his back, making him snort with amusement. She writhed furiously for a time as he continued to laugh, holding her even tighter, then collapsed in despair over his shoulder. His shoulder-bone dug into her belly and she had to grit her teeth as she was jostled down the path that descended into the valley.

Chapter 32

'I would advise you to tell me who you are.' The Pictish druid Taran sat erect on a carved stool in his chieftain's hall.

Before him huddled the war party of *gaels* – the strangers, the Picts called them – whose tracks his chieftain's men had fortuitously come across while hunting a rogue wolf on the highest ridges. The Pict warriors were circling the seven men and one woman, spitting at their feet, their jeers drowning his voice. Taran glanced at them. The old chief, gnawing a bone by the hearth, saw the druid's cold look and shouted at his warriors until they subsided.

Taran sighed. One youthful lapse of judgement and here he was, posted to this barren outpost, far from his king's court in the north. 'There's no point keeping your silence.' The *gael* words were stilted on Taran's tongue. Many druids learned the enemy language from captives; it was only prudent for situations such as these, though he never imagined he'd have cause to use it.

The tallest *gael* with the nobleman's torc and upright bearing would not speak, his head turned away, though it was to him Taran directed his questions. Now the black-haired girl glanced at the man again, fear clouding her light eyes, and the other men darted furtive glances at him, too.

Taran rubbed the shaved dome of his forehead as if it would prod his brain awake. 'The thing is, I am torn. The warriors here want your blood, and it is an easy thing to give them. I, however, see your jewels and the quality of your swords and know you are noble, and therefore of value. Surely your people would pay much for you to be kept alive? If you keep your silence, by dawn you will be dead. It's your choice.'

At long last, just as Taran was regretfully realizing he'd have no chance to find out much about *gaels* before these were killed, the tall man stirred. When he turned to Taran, to the druid's considerable surprise, there was no aggression in his face, and certainly no fear. He looked as though he'd been thinking, gravely and deeply.

He straightened, and Taran, fascinated, stared at the trickle of dried blood at the corner of his mouth. 'What if I tell you not who I am, but what I am here for?' The man enunciated each word of the *gael* speech carefully.

With a spike of irritation, Taran realized it was for his benefit. 'That would be a start.'

'Then allow me to withdraw something from my tunic without one of these crows skewering me. It is no hidden weapon – your men pecked us clean.'

Taran's fingers drummed the chair. 'Urben,' he called one of his own warriors, 'stand behind him with your dagger at his throat. If he threatens us, slit it.' Then he gestured with his chin. 'Show me what you will, then, *gael*. You intrigue me now.'

Slowly, the man reached into his tunic and drew out a flat black stone on a thong.

'What is this?' Taran sat forward.

The *gael* leader held the stone to Urben, who brought it to Taran. The druid turned it over in his long, sensitive fingers. 'What ... is this?' he repeated. His breath wheezed, as it did whenever he grew excited. There were faint lines around the edge of the stone, and two images. His eyes weren't very good, though, so he couldn't see the detail.

'It is a message stone from the old tales – a pledge between my people and yours.'

Taran held the stone for a moment and closed his eyes. He sent a probe of awareness into the cool, smooth disk, opening his inner eyes instead. A whisper tickled his mind. *Old. Lost. A king's pledge. Caledonii. Caledonii* ... His eyes snapped open. 'Where did you find this?' The chieftain's ears pricked up, and some of his warriors crowded behind Taran to peer at the stone.

'In your lands. We were brought to a hidden valley by a vision from our gods.' The man paused, his breath releasing. 'On my oath, we came not to attack, only to seek this, though we did not know at the time what the vision would reveal.'

Taran peered at the stone. He could barely make out the *ogham* lines, but the eagle ... The whispers came again. *The girl. The girl knows.* He saw her gaze fixed on the stone with those unmistakably Otherworld eyes. Abruptly, he swung towards her. 'And what does it say?'

The *gael* leader made a movement to silence her, but the girl stirred as if she had been in trance and answered automatically. 'It says Calgacus of the Caledonii—'

'Stop!' Taran flung up his hand. She could not say the name aloud, not here. Heart pounding, he lifted the stone and turned to the lamp sputtering behind him. Now he made it out. *Calgacus of the Caledonii pledges allegiance and brotherhood to Eremon of Dalriada.* He felt it like a fist in his belly, though long training kept his face still. 'It is an old form of language, and … an old name. A very old name.'

'We didn't know the words at first,' the *gael* leader interrupted. 'Yet the visions showed me—'

'You?' Taran glanced at the black-haired witch. 'You saw it, girl, I can see it in your face. It was your vision.'

Slowly, the girl nodded, her eyes on the tall man. Taran brushed his thumb over the carvings. One side the eagle; Calgacus's eagle. The druid lore had preserved the old king's name and symbol, even as it was banished from all thought and memory for everyone else.

The chief had come alongside him. 'We will give them to the gods at dawn—'

'There will be no deaths.' Taran was trying to keep his excitement under control.

'By my oath there will be! I am lord here.'

'And I am here by order of the brethren,' Taran shot back. 'And with this gift these men have now passed from your realm into mine.' As the chieftain's men braced their spears, Taran met the old man's eye and forced druid power into his own. 'They bear something that will be of great interest to King Gede, as well as the chief druid. You may dismiss the latter as an old mutterer, but do you really want our falcon king swooping upon you from the sky in wrath for disobeying me?'

The warriors in the firelit hall became hushed. Bristling with fury, the chief glared at the *gael*, then at Taran, and eventually threw up his hands and turned away.

Taran rose and addressed the leader. 'Your men will stay here, but you and the girl will come to my hut and tell me everything about how you found this. Now!'

They followed the young, stooped druid, Minna almost sick in the belly with relief. They would not be killed; not yet.

A pungent lamp filled with mutton-fat swung from a rafter in the druid's hut. The other poles were hung with strings of wild garlic and all manner of odd bits and pieces, including the skulls of sheep, fox and bird and clusters of eagle and hawk talons. A table was scattered with coloured rocks, twisted branches smoothed by wind, and the corpses of small animals preserved in bowls of brine.

Minna felt the change in the air as she entered. It was thicker and hazy, vibrating in a way that made her scalp prickle. This power was different from that of her dreams, as if its substance would not meld with her own. The power of men.

'This eagle is an old sign,' the young druid wheezed, sinking into a rush chair by his fire. His face was thin and serious. 'One we no longer use.'

'And the boar is of Dalriada,' Cahir said quietly.

The druid glanced up. 'Yes,' he agreed, tilting his head. The long, dark hair below his shaved forehead was braided with speckled hawk feathers. 'So I have heard. But I have *not* heard of any such binding pledge between your people and mine before.' He hesitated, his piercing brown eyes shifting to Minna. 'If you have manufactured this for your own purposes ...'

'We have *not*!' she cried. To think of all they had gone through for this, with Tiernan dead, and, she had learned, Brogan, too. The pain of those deaths was ground into Cahir's face. Then he took a firm hold of her arm and her indignation died.

He turned calmly to the druid. 'We came far and risked much to find this valley. We did not know there would be a message stone, or that it had anything to do with the Pict kind. We hoped to gain what we came for and return home with no blood shed. We have put our lives in grave danger in so many ways – why would we lie?'

'To get yourselves out of a tight place, now you've been caught raiding.'

Cahir let Minna go, and she immediately threw herself down by the druid's chair. 'You said it is a secret name of your people, an old form of *your* language. But I was told druids never write anything down, that their lore is held in their minds and passed on by word alone. So there *is* no way we could know what this said unless the stone is truly old and made by your druids.'

Taran pondered this, his face pale, as Cahir broke in. 'You must feel this truth.'

At last the druid sat back, shrugging. 'So you have found a stone buried many years ago. What of it? What has this to do with today?' His glance was shrewd and testing. 'Unless there is more, like your name, perhaps.'

Cahir stiffened, folding his arms. 'As a warrior, that is for me to give when I will. Yet you are right. There is more. This stone has opened a new path for Dalriada that involves your people and your king – and the Romans.' He paused, his tongue sliding over his cut lip. 'It involves the Hill of a Thousand Spears.'

The druid's eyes flickered with a revulsion he swiftly masked.

'So you have heard of that, too,' Cahir said softly, and Minna sensed the tension rise in the room.

'That place is linked with the name on the stone,' the druid forced out. 'Calgacus was a king of the Picts long ago. But he died, and all are forbidden to speak of him now.'

'Well, I will speak of him!' Cahir was unable to hide the passion in his voice. 'It is time to speak of what your own king has long fought for, and his father and grandfather before that. Ridding Alba of the Roman kind!'

The druid's face lit with surprise, then calculation. 'But not you, *gael*. All know the Dalriadans lick the Roman boot while *we alone* continue the struggle. So what right have you to speak of resisting Rome?'

Cahir kept a rein on his temper. 'What you say was true once, but the wind has shifted now. My king has new thoughts, which I have been given leave to speak of to your king only.' Minna's ears pricked up at that; he had been keeping his own counsel for days. 'The stone joined us a long time ago. Perhaps ...' He paused. 'Perhaps our interests can align again.'

The young druid stared at Cahir for a long time. At last, his gaze dropped to the boar stone. 'None but druids have spoken this king's name for three hundred years. This eagle sign was scratched from the boundary stones before they were buried, along with the secret shame of our defeat. Never have my people and the *gaels* been linked by anything but bloodshed.' Abruptly, he rose to his feet. 'This stone and what it means is beyond my authority. I am travelling north for Beltaine to see my brethren at King Gede's dun – and you will come.'

Minna went cold.

'He needs to know of you, and judge himself what your punishment will be.' His mouth lifted. 'He will get from you what I cannot, believe me.'

It took all of the druid's powers of persuasion to make his chief agree to the loss of the prisoners. The old man stormed about, whipping up his warriors into a baying frenzy, but no flicker of fear crossed the set features of the Dalriadan prisoners, not even when they were prodded by jeering Picts.

Only Ruarc showed his temper as a Pict dug him in the ribs with a sword hilt, Ruarc landing a kick that crumpled the man to the floor. Chaos erupted. The fallen warrior scrambled to his feet and struck Ruarc across the face, and swords were drawn with shouts of rage. It was the young druid who waded in, holding them all with the force of his trained voice, preventing the blades making contact with flesh.

Eventually Ruarc sank back, meeting Donal's eyes with a lift of his chin. Then something in the older warrior's face reached him and he sat straight and silent like the others, glancing neither left nor right. In that moment, Minna's fear was eclipsed by pride. Somehow, through days of sleet and wind and exhaustion, these rough men had become her people. If she had to die, she would rather perish surrounded by such bravery. Perhaps they would help her to be brave, too. She huddled around her knees on the floor, one hand pressed to the cold place inside her belly.

The Picts eventually drifted away to their own beds, leaving only guards. The druid returned the stone to Cahir and headed for the door. Outlined in the square of darkness, he turned, the wind swirling his robes about his legs. 'I will offer names first then, *gael*. I am Taran. On foot to King Gede's dun will take four days.'

Their musty bedrolls had been thrown by the fire and the coals banked, leaving the hall nearly black. The men were settling down on the other side of the hearth, by unspoken agreement leaving Minna and Cahir alone. Every now and then one of the Pict guards paced past, brandishing his spear, and the Dalriadan murmurs sank into whispers.

In the dimness, Minna wriggled into her hides next to Cahir's pallet, as aware of his nearness as the Picts looming over them. Because she couldn't see much she could hear her heart even louder, thumping in her ears. *King Gede.* A cold feeling snaked up her spine whenever she thought of him.

Next to her, Cahir was pounding his cloak into a pillow with agitation. All at once he turned on his knees, startling her. 'Why did you say you saw the visions?'

Minna peered at his outline in the half-dark. He was sitting on his heels, his ears cocked to the guards rustling behind, but his eyes intent on her. 'Because that was the truth,' she said.

'I was trying to protect you – you had no right to speak without my leave.'

His anger silenced her, and she stared at the shape of him, her throat tightening. He was going north now to speak about wars, king to king, if they lived at all. There would be no place for her there. Of course.

Cahir's hissed curse came at her like a slap. 'Gods! If you call attention to yourself this way you share my fate. It was a foolish thing to do!'

There was a charged silence where the air seemed to vibrate, because they had nearly died, and now they were alive, blood racing. Then she jumped when the touch came out of the dark, fingers tracing along her cheek. 'I do not want you ...' Cahir began, his voice failing.

Her heart finished it. He did not want her harmed. Another curse came, muttered low in his throat, and out of nowhere his lips were suddenly pressed to hers.

The kiss was swift and hard, and Minna was dizzied by the alien taste of last night's ale on his mouth, the scent of his skin. *He is a king. He has a wife. I am nothing, nothing.* So her mind hammered out in the moment before it was drowned by the sensation of his tongue softening against hers.

One of the Pict guards came closer – she heard his footsteps – and Cahir broke away, catching her head between his hands. 'I knew!' he whispered fiercely into her mouth. 'I knew when you first touched me this lay between us.'

I knew. Minna's fingers tangled in his lips, but the Pict grunted something guttural at them and they sank back in their hides, their hands barely touching.

Minna lay in the dark, searingly awake, sensing Cahir tense beside her. And her heart drummed something else now. *He has no love. I am his blood, his breath. I am his.*

Chapter 33

'**M**ithras!' the Roman scout breathed. 'They are right in our sights!'

Cian did not answer. Lying on his belly in the undergrowth, he was peering through a hawthorn brake, his palms slick around his bow.

The blueskins were usually the ones who became part of the silent forest, attacking suddenly from the shadows. But on this squally day above the Wall one of their ponies, heavily laden with booty from pillaged Votadini farms, had stumbled while crossing a stream and crushed its rider.

Cian and his fellow scouts had been alerted by the screaming of the horse with its broken leg, and though its throat was swiftly cut they were on the trail by then. They watched the Picts drag the injured man away from the stream into the trees and crouch there jabbering, agitated. The downed man seemed important.

'Enough,' Cian's comrade muttered. 'They'll kill *him* in a minute and be off before we can get them.' He wriggled backwards to the larger troupe of soldiers hidden in the woods. The sound of the rushing stream had covered their approach.

Cian's pulse was galloping. This was it: his first fight with the Painted Men. A vein in his forehead throbbed.

The signal was given – a cuckoo's call – and the Roman soldiers sprang out of the bushes as the Picts shrieked, fumbling for their weapons. Cian steadied himself against an oak tree as his first arrow cleaved the air, burying itself in the chest of one blueskin and felling him. Three others met the same fate before the Romans crashed into them, fighting hand to hand. Cian dropped his bow and seized a short sword from its scabbard. Then, with a screech that flew up into the grey clouds above, he barrelled into the fray.

Abruptly, all noise ceased and time slowed.

Pale faces loomed all about him, features twisted with hate, lips spittled, the skin carved up by tattoos. Blades lunged at him. His nerves strained to break into blind panic as the faces kept coming ... the swords coming ... as they did in his dreams. *No. Don't you dare.* Cian screwed up his face. *Don't you dare be a coward. Don't you dare run.*

Instead, he wrestled his fury into action, used it to steady his legs and brace his arms. *Mamaí. For you, Mamaí.* He saw his mother's face, white and sunken – and so at last the rage flowed freely.

Cian struck and spun as he had been taught to do once long ago and never forgotten, and his blade sliced across an exposed neck. The give of the sword into flesh shocked him, as did the scarlet spray of arterial blood.

Then a Pict caught the edge of his mailshirt with a dagger, hauling him back to awareness. He hacked again, and another of the feared warriors went down. The sight of blood welling across the blue tattoos did not make Cian feel sick now, but elated. Something hot bloomed in his chest, and he was yelling until he was hoarse, his sword a blur in his hands.

His lithe grace and acrobat's skill was a weapon in itself: he could react faster, turn on a heel, duck and roll and weave. *It was beautiful ... as more men fell, their bodies broken ... and exhilarating ... as he* hacked at one man long after he was dead, sawed the head off and held it up by the hair, panting.

All the Picts were slaughtered now, and there in silence Cian's own troupe stood, gazing at him. His hair was soaked with blood, his mail running red. In the eyes of the other soldiers were both horror and respect as they stared at the severed head clutched in Cian's fingers. Yes, respect.

Cian threw the head on the ground and turned away for the stream, his head buzzing, his breath like a rushing wind.

King Gede's fort, the Dun of Bright Water, was built on the northern coast at the end of the great glen. As they dropped down from the high ground it became warmer, the breeze tinged with salt. The trees were coming into leaf, the new bracken unfurling through the dying brown of last year.

After that one, searing touch, Cahir and Minna had to avoid each other or expose themselves to the sharp eyes of the Pict guards, Taran and not least their own men, who darted many speculative glances at them. But every now and then their gazes met, hot and bright, before flickering away. They had barely escaped death, but they might die even so – this could be all the time they had – and the mingled fear and danger brought every nerve of Minna's body alive.

If only her inner eye was so. They did not know what would be done with them, and though she prayed and strained for some glimpse of their fate – anything – her voices were silent, her dreams confused. She was bereft, and had only Cahir's gaze to cling to, brilliant and unwavering across the campfire. To be worthy of him, she must set fear aside.

The valleys opened out to wide marshes rippling in the cold sea-wind, clouded by squawking eddies of white and black birds.

There were scouts to deal with, and watchposts to pass, and it was afternoon by the time they came along the ridges of higher ground that eventually led to the king's fort on a headland surrounded by crashing sea. From a rise inland floated the clear note of a hunting horn.

'That is my king,' Taran said, suddenly nervous. 'We will go to him immediately.'

The king's party was ranged around the crest of a hill that dropped sharply to the marshes below. Warriors lounged on horses or stood among milling hounds. The Picts were thickset, dressed for the northern wind in rugged fur cloaks pinned with enormous, boastful brooches, arms decorated with wide, bronze bands. Above black, bristling beards and moustaches, florid cheeks were painted with blue whorls and spirals.

As Taran greeted the king's guards, Minna's eyes were drawn to the figure sitting alone on a horse at the cliff edge.

The man's wrist was stretched out, his eyes on the marsh, and a moment later his nobles let out a deafening shout of approval as an enormous bird shot up over the cliff. It was a falcon of some kind, its plumage snowy-white, a smaller seabird caught in its talons. To Minna's astonishment, the falcon – its wing-spread twice that of a man's arm – dropped the limp bird at the hunter's feet and landed neatly on the pad bound to his wrist. Murmuring, the man fed a sliver of meat into the dagger-sharp beak and slipped a hood over its head.

Taran had been deep in conversation with other druids in white robes, and now a guard with a bow slung over his back went and whispered in the man's ear. Gede, King of the Picts turned in his saddle and stared down at Cahir.

He was slightly older than the Dalriadan king, his dark red hair threaded with copper and silver. In contrast to the rough appearance of his nobles, everything about him was neat and precise. Gede's hair was caught sleekly, bound with a golden ring to direct it in a ruddy horse-tail down his back. His beard was clipped to a sharp point, dyed scarlet.

Minna darted a swift glance from lowered eyes. Curving tattoos entirely covered Gede's cheeks, jaw and brow – and the pattern formed the face of a falcon. A ferocious bird-eye was angled on each cheek, ruffled feathers drawn above his brows, and his sharp, dyed beard was the beak. His eyes were a cold blue, his flesh as spare and honed as his gaze.

With a swift movement the Pictish king dismounted. She could see now that he was not tall, and when the wind flattened his long tunic and cloak it revealed a wiry build and narrow shoulders.

Gede passed the falcon to a retainer, then rested his hand on his bridle as if to show off the rich coral and amber decorations. He had only to turn his head slightly before a white-haired druid hastened to his side.

Gede quelled his revulsion as the old druid Galan addressed the interlopers in the *gael* tongue. The merest glimpse of unpainted skin was enough to blot out the cold sun. Who were they, and how dare they enter his domain?

He glared at the young druid who had brought them, satisfied to see him pale at his king's displeasure. Druids! They were always skulking about with secret plans that served their own dark arts more than their king. There was only one way to deal with trespassing *gaels* – a sword across the back of the neck.

Gede smoothed his anger so he could think, focusing on Galan translating his words to the enemy leader. 'Long has it been since any *gael* trod these lands.'

The man sent Gede a look of insolent pride. 'True enough,' he replied through Galan. 'But when my people last rode these shores we came as sword brothers.'

Sword brother! Gede's hand tightened around his horse's bridle. 'Of what do you speak?' he demanded.

The tall man paused. 'I speak of the Hill of a Thousand Spears.'

Galan the druid caught his breath as he translated: Gede knew that place, and how it was forbidden to speak of it. A cloud of shame hovered over it, blotting out all memory.

'That is a place where our people's blood was spilled,' Gede said sternly. 'Who are you to name it as your own?'

The *gael* leader paused, standing straight and unafraid – and he should damn well be afraid, by Taranis! Gede strode forward and challenged him. 'No man can come into my presence who has not named himself! No man can order me who has claimed no rank. No man can gain admittance to my gates without offering the oath of his lineage.'

'Indeed?' The *gael* held his eye for far too long. 'Then know that I am Cahir son of Conor, King of Dalriada in Alba, direct in line from Gabran himself.'

Gede was too well-trained to react, even though a bolt of fury and triumph went right through him. *By Manannán's breath and balls!* The *gael* king, fallen into his hands as if from the sky? The gods could not be so generous.

Taran hastened forward. 'My lord,' he stammered. 'I did not know, my lord. He would not tell me—'

Gede silenced him and smiled coldly at this Cahir. 'You risk much to come to my hall, with the blood of my people on your hands.'

'No more than the blood of mine on yours.' He paused as it was translated. 'And yet once long ago it was all spilled together at the Hill of a Thousand Spears.'

Galan hissed. 'He speaks sacrilege, my lord!'

The *gael* king continued. 'I speak only truth. My people were *there*. They fought with the Picts – the Caledonii as you were then known – side by side against the Romans. As our young druid friend can tell you, we have proof of this: that our people and yours were allies once.'

The Pict warriors around Gede muttered. *Allies*. The word thundered in his mind. His men were a dark wall of bodies, gazing at him angrily. Why was he allowing this?

'The *gaels* infect our shores like creeping mould, like the rotting of flesh in a wound,' Gede retorted scornfully. 'They can claim no blood brotherhood with us.'

'And yet our people died fighting together once. I have proof.'

Gede's skin prickled, and Taran slid to his side. 'They have found a stone, my lord,' he murmured. 'It is a message stone, and yes, it tells of a binding alliance between an old king of the Dalriadans and ...' he gulped, took a breath, 'and King Calgacus, my lord.'

'*What*?' Galan hissed. 'That is a forbidden name, my son!' He glared at his young druid. 'Was your exile in the mountains not cold enough to quell your runaway tongue?'

Taran went white, as Gede held up his hand. 'Peace. Whatever he says, it is right he brought the *gael* king and placed him into my hands.'

Then he smiled.

Chapter 34

When they approached the Dun of Bright Water, the sand around the headland was shining wet with the receding tide. Boats were scattered over the beach, with fishermen mending nets and farmers tilling seaweed into the fallow fields behind the dunes.

The defences of the dun itself were formidable. Across the promontory, immense bastions of multiple ramparts had been raised, with deep ditches delved before them. The gates and their rearing towers were painted, gilded and streaming with banners, the rock tunnels they passed through carved with curling designs. The ramparts bristled with spears, as heavily-armed warriors lined all the palisades and towers and paced the walkways, watching the sea and land approaches.

Inside, the enormous fort was on two levels: the lower ringed by high, cliff-top walls that faced out to the crashing waves, the upper crowned by grand buildings and the king's hall with its soaring roof.

They climbed up wide stairs flanked by armoured warriors and eventually reached the hall, which was draped in gold and blue standards showing a falcon poised for the kill, with outstretched talons and spread wings. Rows of spears in the ground fluttered with pennants of brown and white feathers, and the double doors were hung with bundles of human skulls, yellowed with age.

Minna went to follow Cahir inside, but the Pictish guards at the door lowered their spears to bar her way. She did not think she imagined their expressions, as if she were a deformed thing that had crawled from shadow to sun.

The old druid barked something, and Taran hastily stepped forward. 'Women are not permitted in the king's hall except to serve food,' he said. 'And certainly not present for matters of state, even if your situation is rather ... unusual. You will be taken to the women's house for now, where servants have orders to attend you.'

She looked desperately to Cahir, but he only nodded with a tight smile. 'We are protected by the laws of hospitality now, Minna. They are sacred all over Alba. Gede could not harm me at his hearth.' He glanced at the leering skulls. 'Even if he wanted to.'

The women's hall was a small roundhouse with looms set near the door for light, and baskets of wool and fleece by the hearth. Other tools of women's work were scattered around: spindles, coils of coloured thread, needles and awls, piles of soft leather.

Receiving Taran's instructions, the three servants inside set aside their sewing and weaving, and bustled back and forth filling a wooden bathtub behind a screen. One pulled the bedraggled twine from Minna's braids and another went to tug off her filthy clothes. She snatched at each piece as it was removed, self-conscious and then ashamed when the slave-ring came to light. The women peered at it, chattering in their own language, and she dropped her eyes.

One of the women spoke briskly, pointing at her linen shift. She glanced at the steam, her skin suddenly crawling with the film of dried sweat, blood and grime, her hair lank and itchy. At last, staring at the wall, she allowed her dirty shift to be peeled from her.

In the bath they scrubbed her hair and limbs, then rubbed her dry with rough linen so her skin glowed. Then they wrapped her in a thick wool robe, gave her bread and honey, and pointed at the bed before leaving. She bolted the food and nervously curled up. After a short time, even though she grimly fought it, she couldn't help but fall asleep.

When she drifted into awareness, she knew that dusk was not far away, for though the door-hide was down a hint of rosy light crept under it. She also knew that someone was watching her.

She lay for a moment gathering her wits, then turned on her side with a yawn. The eyes peeping through the wicker bedscreen lowered with embarrassment, before a young woman stepped out into the open.

'I was just making sure you were rested,' the woman explained with a flutter of her hand. She spoke the Dalriadan language in a voice so stilted and soft Minna had to strain to hear. She was a few years older than her, with narrow, slightly bowed shoulders.

'I am.' Minna sat up with the furs around her chin. 'Thank you,' she added politely.

The young woman's brown hair was caught in a net of gold thread, and her dress was blue and intricately embroidered. Her fingers were twisting themselves into knots, but when she noticed what she was doing she folded her hands. 'I am Nessa, Gede's queen.'

'Oh!' Minna couldn't help the exclamation, but she would have imagined someone more haughty as a match for that king.

Nessa seemed to read her mind, her mouth twitching ruefully, which changed her whole face. 'I did not mean to intrude while you slept.' She perched on the end of the bed.

'No ... I thank you ... for your hospitality.' Minna wondered how to speak, what to say. 'It was a very fine bath,' she offered at last, and could have cursed herself for a fool.

The young queen's grey eyes were startled, then amused. 'My women said you were very unusual, lady. They said ...' Nessa paused, then rushed on, 'that you had hair like the night sky and eyes like the sea.' She glanced at her as if worried she might have caused offence.

Minna couldn't hide a nervous laugh, for the directness of Alban women continued to amaze her. And she called her *lady*. 'My name is Minna. Just Minna.'

Nessa tilted her head. 'And the servants from the king's hall heard the druids whispering that you speak with the gods.'

Minna was taken aback, then thought it better this queen swiftly knew some of her strange truth. She touched the tender skin beneath the iron ring. 'I was captured from the Roman Province, lady, as a slave. In leaf-fall.'

The queen nodded, still scrupulously polite – then Minna remembered she walked at a king's side now, and this woman knew it. 'We don't have slaves: it is a Roman fashion,' Nessa said carefully. 'But would it be ... presumptuous ... to ask where you are from? Only if it causes you no distress, of course.'

She was further disarmed by this respect. 'Eboracum.'

'Ah, I have heard of this place – this silk thread comes from there.' The queen touched her sleeve matter-of-factly, as if she did not value her rich clothes.

Minna, however, was burning with her own questions. 'Lady, how do you speak the Dalriadan language?'

Nessa smiled. 'My father rules a dun in the west, and when I was a small child I was taken by the *gaels* after a battle, as a royal hostage. I lived in one of their northern duns.'

'But that is terrible, to be sent away from your home!'

Nessa shrugged. 'It was always going to happen, one way or another. My mother is of the Pictish royal line, and so therefore am I. Our noble blood runs through women, not the men as in Dalriada, did you know that?'

Minna didn't, but she nodded anyway.

'Then things change – people die, others have babes or lose them – and eventually I was needed back to bestow on a husband, and then a son, the kingship with my royal blood. Not that the *gaels* knew that! My people paid a ransom of gold and cattle to retrieve me. But this is all long ago – there are no hostages now. Just ... deaths.'

Minna watched the pain flicker over her grey eyes like clouds.

A knock on the wall outside interrupted them. Taran strode in, hovering awkwardly, glancing with unease at the women's things scattered about. 'Lady,' he addressed Minna. His manner was very different now. 'King Gede requires your presence in his hall.'

'Me?' Minna repeated blankly.

The druid glanced at her, exasperated. 'Are you not the one who spoke of your visions to me so passionately? Now my king wants to see you.'

'But ... but I have to get dressed.'

'Then I will wait for you outside. Hurry.'

When he had gone, Nessa looked down at Minna, fear tight around her eyes. 'I will lend you a dress,' she offered. 'You do not wish to feel vulnerable before Gede son of Urp.'

It took Minna a moment to remember she was speaking of her own husband.

Every surface in the Pict hall was painted or carved with wild designs: lines quartering spirals and circles; stags, boars and wolves; salmon and geese alongside unrecognizable beasts. There was a lavish use of gilding, and the hangings and cushions glowed with clashing hues and silver thread. The entire expanse of the encircling wall was covered in shields, spears, scabbards and crossed daggers, fracturing the firelight and the flames of the torches in Minna's eyes.

Blinking, she sought for Cahir, who was at King Gede's right hand with a cup of ale in a gold-rimmed horn. He looked grim, his glower only deepening at her appearance. His own men were ranged behind him, while Gede's nobles took up the ring of hearth-benches. All of them were staring at her.

Minna's fingers knotted in the crimson folds of Nessa's dress; her knees, hidden by the heavy fabric, were quivering alarmingly. Then she touched the priestess ring, drawing strength from it.

Suddenly, Cahir broke in. 'I said this is not necessary.'

The old druid frowned. 'My king deems it so.'

Taran stepped between them. 'Lady, this message stone is powerful, as are the forbidden words you have spoken to us. I ask you to state before my king – it was *your* visions that led you to this?'

Minna stared into Cahir's set face. His eyes ordered her to deny who she was, to protect herself. But the druids wouldn't believe him without her, they would know. *Jump in*, Mamo whispered. *Jump into the dark water. It will hold you, as will I.*

'Yes,' Minna said, but her voice seemed faint in the immensity of that hall. Then her glance fell on, of all people, Ruarc. The flickering torches lit up his defiant eyes, and Donal's thinning pate, and the gold in Gobán's beard. Ardal raised his chin as he folded his arms. They sought to give her courage, because of their pride in their king which she must sustain.

'They are my visions,' she said more strongly. 'I was drawn to the valley and shown a grave from long ago.'

'Whose is the grave?' Gede demanded.

Minna closed her eyes. 'The child of Eremon of Erin, the Dalriadan king's most revered ancestor. I saw him place the ... the baby there. He put the boar stone on her breast.'

The Picts muttered among themselves as this was translated. Another man spoke up, stocky and brutish as his king was sleek, with ragged dark hair and a beard forked into peaks. 'And this so-called royal child was laid in *our* territory?' he scorned.

Minna glanced again at Cahir, his mouth covered by his fingers, his eyes narrowed. She shifted her gaze to a wall hanging, and began to speak as Taran translated.

Cahir tapped the chair with one finger, the only thing betraying his emotion.

The red dress brought a glow to Minna's skin and a gloss to her dark hair, which was caught back in some kind of gold net. With the donning of the noble clothes, something had come to the fore in her bearing that was hidden before. A bronze belt moulded the cloth to her narrow waist and swelling hips, and Cahir's desire heated his anger. He wanted to admire her and throttle her at the same time. Even the way she tilted her chin destroyed any chance he had of pretending she was some bed slut who meant nothing.

As she spoke, the Pict druids leaned together and murmured animatedly, waving their hands. Gede, as usual, betrayed no feeling in his hawkish face.

Minna suddenly turned on Taran. 'Perhaps the battle is why the child was buried in your lands. Whatever it was, there was trust enough between your people and ours for them to mark it in stone for ever, enough for them to go to war together.' Her nostrils flared.

Minna! Cahir despaired. He could have accomplished this alone. But the druids were having none of it.

The chief druid came stiffly to his feet. 'We know the stone is old, and what it says, and the name of he who is not named. The letter symbols are sacred to druidkind, and no untruth can be so written. But there is one more vital test, girl. We wish to know more of these visions of yours. You will *see* for us.'

Cahir shot out of his chair. '*No*. She has given you what you need of the past – now we must speak of the future. That is my realm, my risk.'

The old druid faced him with a sneer. 'You ask us to accept something that goes against all our lore, from a slip of a slave-girl? You seek to turn years of enmity on its head because of a grave offering lost to the years?' He pointed at Minna, his hand trembling with age. 'If she truly is god-blessed, then she must be tested by the Water of Seeing, for it reveals only truth. My king will accept no less than this show of faith.'

Cahir saw Minna's face set with determination. Before he could move, she strode before Gede himself. 'I accept this test.'

'No!' Cahir repeated. '*I will not allow it.*'

Her lips compressed and she lowered her eyes – though he wasn't fooled. 'My lord, your subjects are expected to show their loyalty to you, each in their own way. It is what you demand of them. So why will you not demand it of me?' Despite her tone, her eyes flashed up and twin flares of indignation passed between them.

Gede's evident amusement silenced Cahir. The Pict king eyed Minna up and down, then said something to Taran.

The druid coughed, embarrassed. 'My lord wants to know what slave speaks thus to a sworn king, and what king would suffer it?'

Minna and Cahir were both caught out. Then the words that came to Cahir's lips shocked him, rising from what had always been a barren place and filling all the aching, lonely reaches inside him. He instantly knew he could no more deny this impulse than deny his own fate – for she simply was his fate. Since the night in the hut by the pool, when Minna had uttered the sacred war cry, he had been ruled by feeling and instinct alone, and so he was taken over by this now like a rush of flame. In a heartbeat, the flare rose and consumed all he had been before, and in its wake the tension in him utterly surrendered.

'She is no slave, but the seer of my hall.'

Minna's eyes widened with confusion, but they were tender, shining, and suddenly it seemed as if he and she were alone. 'And she is my *lennan*.'

Cahir barely registered the grunts of surprise that came from the direction of his own men. But then the old druid let out a phlegmatic cough, and he and Minna were wrenched back to a room of hard-eyed Picts, the walls ablaze with firelit weapons.

'Royal kin makes no difference to us,' Galan huffed. 'Only the Water of Seeing can prove whether she is seer or not.'

Minna dragged herself away from Cahir's charged gaze. 'I will undergo that test,' she repeated. 'Whenever you desire.'

'Now,' King Gede announced, on his feet in one swift movement.

His chief druid nodded. 'She must be at the pool at moonrise.'

'She should rest another day before facing any cold pool, or any spirit test at all,' Cahir protested.

The druid shrugged bony shoulders. 'Tired, rested, it matters not if one is truly a seer.' His unblinking eyes rested on Minna. 'She should know that when the mind is dulled by the privations of the body ... *then* can the visions come more clearly.'

Minna touched Cahir's arm, softly. 'I will go now and prepare, if you will it,' she said to Galan.

'At moonrise,' the druid confirmed. 'When the tides run high in sea and blood both.'

Chapter 35

Pictish guards escorted the Dalriadans to a guest lodge then flanked the inner doorway. Cahir held Minna back, hidden by the screen of the porch. Above them, a pitch torch flickered and dipped in the sea-wind.

She knew he would try to argue again, but there was something more important to address. She caught the front of his tunic, the strength she had found before all those warriors beating in her breast, sweeping all shyness away. 'Do not say a single *thing* about being careful or being tired or straining myself. What is this *lennan*?'

For a moment he struggled to find words, then merely cupped her cheeks. 'It means sweetheart ... lover ... but more than that.' He took a deep breath. 'It is the wife, Minna, taken for love, not treaty. The second wife, but some say the true wife.'

Heat surged up Minna's body. She tried to clear her throat and failed. 'And is this not something you ask someone, whether they want to be a *lennan*?' she whispered hoarsely. 'Or do you just make your mind up and get around to telling her later?'

Cahir's hands buried themselves in the silky strands of hair that escaped the net. 'I didn't have a chance to tell her, because it came to me all of a sudden. But now she can say no if she wants.'

Minna's breath caught on a laugh that was half a sob. 'But we are not ... lovers.' Her blood leaped, wilful and swift.

'Then that is your decision, too.' There was a fire in his eyes she had not recognized before, and it turned her belly.

Slowly, conscious of the Pict guards standing so close, her thumbs traced the angle of his high cheekbones, moulded the fine hollows and curve of his brows. His eyes shut briefly, as her fingers brushed his wide, full mouth with a shy wonder. 'My decision,' she repeated. And it came to her in a rush that she had choices now, where before she had none. Not like a slave.

She buried her face in the curve where Cahir's neck met his shoulder, breathing his skin, touching her lips there. Giving him her answer.

There was little time until moonrise. The warriors ate a meal of roast venison and bread, gathering close by the hearth to talk unguarded. Her cheeks still warm, Minna darted glances at them from the corner of her lowered eyes. In a moment, everything had changed.

Mellan and Ardal were not even trying to hide the speculative, wondering looks they sent back and forth from Minna to their king, though they swiftly turned away when they caught her eye. But a smile was playing about Donal's mouth. Seeing that, Minna felt the tension begin to leave her body. She dared a glance at Ruarc. He sat back, arms folded, but though he never once looked at her, his eyes on his king were fierce and proud, not hostile. Perhaps all it took was a woman nearly killing herself by cold and exhaustion, Minna thought, the mingled bubble of joy, shock and fear inside making her light-headed.

She ate nothing, instructed by Taran to fast, though she sensed the Water of Seeing waiting for her, moving and shimmering with her thoughts. She dragged her attention back to the men.

'What I want to know, Cahir, is what you will propose to Gede once they are happy with this,' Gobán broke off and turned slightly to Minna, his head sketching the merest nod, '*seeing* business of ... of the lady's.' There was only a faint stumble and, ever gruff, he frowned it away. The ale had veined his nose and heavy cheeks.

There was a distinct gleam in Cahir's eye as he answered. 'It depends on what my lady *sees*,' he said distinctly. Then he placed both hands on his knees, looking at each man in turn. 'But I promised I would share my heart when I knew it, and now I have seen Gede, the pieces have already come to me more clearly.' They all leaned forward, heads almost touching, the firelight aglow on their eager faces. 'Neither Gede nor I have ever had the numbers to resist the Romans as an army – Gede could never do more than raid the Wall. No people outside the Empire possess that power on their own, not the Saxons over the northern sea, though they shake their axes, nor the Attacotti in the Western Isles. The Erin chiefs might have it, though they squabble among themselves too much to band together. But think on this.' His voice dropped. 'Gede told me he has made strong trade alliances with the Saxons that he thinks he can easily turn to military support, for they are greedy for plunder and glory. So they will follow *him*. The Attacotti are already our allies, and the Dalriadans in Erin under Fergus are our kin. They will all follow *me*. It is the merging of our two peoples – Pict and Dalriadan – that will draw in the others and create the greater force: an army of five peoples that spans the northern sea.' He sat straight, pride in his shoulders. 'Nothing like this has ever been wrought before.'

'Not even by Eremon,' Donal said softly.

Cahir met his eyes. 'No.'

Excitement ran among the men like wildfire.

Her knee against Cahir's, Minna savoured the power flowing from his flesh to hers. When had their hearts become so entwined they soared or fell together like this?

It was the kiss. She had understood at that moment that she had been drawn across the wild moors not just to this land, but to his side. If Alba was her fate then Cahir was, too. All along, she had been returning to him.

The druids gave her a robe of coarse wool to wear over bare skin, and Taran said she must go barefoot as well. When she emerged from the lodge, the night air chilled her skin and the pit of her belly. As the druids closed about her with torches, Minna cast one glance at Cahir. His eyes reflected the flames. 'I will be close behind you,' he said, and only then could she let go and not look back.

The moon was a ship of bronze sailing over the sea from the east. The sea-wind buffeted the walls, lifting Minna's unbound hair from her neck. Behind her walked Gede and Cahir, side by side.

Then the entrance to the Water of Seeing yawned before her, a black doorway in an outcrop of pale stone within the walls, not far from the king's hall. Steps led down into the darkness.

Taran stood before her. The druids had begun singing under their breath, their torches wavering lines around her. 'So you leave Thisworld for the Otherworld,' he intoned, then whispered, 'Do not fear: even if you cannot *see*, we will not let you die from the Water's cold. And if you are who you say you are, then you will surely not travel so far that the cord breaks and your spirit become lost among the other worlds.' His teeth gleamed slightly. 'The moon will no doubt still be up when you emerge.'

After these barely encouraging words, Minna walked carefully into the blackness and progressed down slippery steps that were cut into the rock, her toes curling over the edges. The light from the torch-bearers sparkled on pale flecks in the dark, mossy walls. The druid singing vibrated off the stone in discordant harmonies that shattered all clear thought, and she felt the song summoning the power of the rock, the earth, the sky.

The water.

At the bottom of the stairs lay a small chamber of curved walls and vaulted roof barely the height of a man, its entire floor forming the pool. As she came down, the draught from the stairs riffled the surface, black and impenetrable but sheened by the torches.

She came to a shivering stop on the lowest step, slimy with weed. Wavelets lapped over her ankles, the water biting cold, for it had never seen sun. Taran moved to a narrow ledge that edged the chamber.

'Daughter.' Galan's deep voice boomed from the rock walls all around. The smell of pitch was sharp in the dank air. 'You must enter the place day never comes, and emerge with a vision. As your body is of water, so this pool will melt the bounds of your flesh and allow your soul to be one again with spirit. But if your soul is too weighted with darkness, you may sink and not come up, and the water will claim you.'

They are just ritual words, Minna cried to herself. *Taran said I would live and see the moon.*

'So, *gael* child: do you come to the Water of Seeing with a clear heart, with no blemish upon it of lie or betrayal or dishonour or hurt done?'

Unexpectedly, Cian's face appeared in Minna's mind, his eyes stormy with pain. 'I have done no hurt intentionally,' she whispered. 'But ... I have hurt, nonetheless.'

The druid grunted, the sound amplified by the enclosing walls. 'The Water will accept you if hurt was done while you followed your higher truth, and that is all. Was it so, child?'

She saw Cahir now, his smile tender. Behind him were Alba's hills, clothed in the flame of leaf-fall, and Alba's sea, dark as night. *Cian, I am sorry.* 'Yes,' she whispered.

'Then the Water of Seeing lays before you. Step down into the pool and lay back in the water. You will be held.'

She stared at Taran, his glazed pupils large and black in the flickering light. Behind came the ponderous footsteps of the old druid passing her, and both entered the water up to their chests. The druid singing on the stairs intensified, and the surface of the pool shifted.

Bracing herself, Minna stepped in, and though her feet went out from under her and she gasped, Taran held her shoulders. The water was so icy it burned, sucking all the air from her lungs. Panting, she sensed the two druids tip her back, supporting her head and feet. She closed her eyes and struggled, for the cold was a band of iron around her body, stiffening it. A hoarse whimper escaped her.

'You must merge with the water, child, take the cold into your flesh, slow your blood,' the chief druid murmured. 'Do not fight it.'

She blinked away the biting pain. *This is what seers do*, came the thought. *This is what they train for.* Rhiann was a priestess; she would have done this with no cry of pain or fear. But Minna had not been trained.

Above, the torches sprinkled the dark, moist roof with points of fire, like stars. 'Surrender,' Taran whispered. That had always been hard for Minna, for the fight in her heart and soul was instinctive. But she closed her eyes and fixed on an image of the pool seeping into every hollow of flesh, muscle and bone, slowly weighting her as if she were a hide bag filling with water, until her skin dissolved and she became only fluid.

'Good, good,' Taran breathed. The pain had lightened to a vague, numb hurt now. Then, so low she almost couldn't hear it, Taran joined the singing, and as the water *became* her, the vibration of his voice travelled through it to envelop her with song.

Her breathing grew slower, and she realized she was growing warm: the resisting flesh surrendering, melting into spirit, losing the sense that said: *I am one thing; and that, another.* Her heart struck her ribs, a beat that makes blood flow ... the warm blood in which she floated ... the womb blood ...

Behind Minna's eyelids, a diffuse, golden glow appeared, brighter in places with points of fire. 'See the true pool,' the chief druid murmured. '*This* – not the water – is the font of all seeing. Do you see it as light, as an opening?'

'I see,' she whispered, tears running down her chin. 'I see.'

The druid said something else, but the meaning was lost as Minna was abruptly pulled into a whirling circle of colour and light, all sounds receding. The light writhed, then resolved itself into the figures of men fighting, arms and legs striking out, bodies falling. It was a battlefield – *the* battlefield. Above her she saw the crooked ridge of what she knew now as the Hill of a Thousand Spears.

She floated above the desolate scene, as below a tall warrior in a magnificent helmet was struck from the platform of his jewelled chariot, his horses collapsing in their traces. It was King Calgacus, his mane of golden hair matted now with blood. One eye was nothing but a pulpy wound, but he regained his footing and began to swing his massive sword around his head in great arcs. The men he faced were covered with polished plates like fish scales, helmets red-crested.

A soldier came up behind the golden king with javelin poised, and Minna saw that Calgacus's guard had been cut down around him. Only one was left, a bard caught in the web of the chariot harness, watching the Romans advance on his king. He was weeping. Minna tried to shout a warning, and found she was voiceless. But below her it was the bard who screamed, and the king heard him and whirled, bringing his long sword across the enemy behind and slicing into his neck. Blood sprayed over the king's face, and as he faced the other red wolves who circled, he smiled and licked the blood from his chin.

Then he threw his head back and roared a challenge, and all the

Romans ran at him, snarling. He ducked and struck out, and one, two, three went down. They lay awash in a sea of blood at his feet, and so more soldiers were drawn by the scent, and more again. Calgacus bellowed, and in answer the Romans piled in on each other in their eagerness for his death.

He disappeared beneath them, and Minna found herself reaching for him, trying to save him ... and the noise and stench of battle were suddenly released to her senses. She heard the screams and groans, the whinnies of horses; smelled the urine and sweat. She felt the blades enter *his chest his arm his belly his neck his eye his spine his leg his feet his heart* ... and she lived his desolation at the loss of everything.

But even this was eclipsed by an even greater flare of pride that he died on his own terms. *Calgacus the Sword, King of the north, last to fall for Alba.*

So were his thoughts, before all went dark. And Minna wept.

After a time, the lights came for her. In that moment, she knew she had been drawn here to this place-of-no-place for herself as well as for Cahir and his war.

They whirled about her, diaphanous as silk veils; a slow-turning cloud of spirit-lights. *Do not be afraid.*

Though she desperately strained to recognize the speaker, it was not the tender guide of her eagle flight. This was a melding of more than one voice, shimmering layers of different souls: one deep and wise, the other silvery and light. *Do not be afraid, daughter.* But she knew them.

The spirit-lights spun closer, gathering momentum until a column encased her in a whirlwind of light. Were these the whispers that haunted her sleep? Invisible fingers pressed her eyelids closed. *Do not think. Feel.*

The voices began to sing, mingling in an old melody that spun a cradle of sound around her. The fingers turned Minna's palms upwards, though she could see nothing but light. Dizzied, she tried to form words. *Who are you? Why are you here?*

The answer came immediately. *Speak not. Fear not. You are safe, and your Sisters love you.*

Her soul spun. *Sisters.* She knew that name, and it was not about blood kin, but ... *soul kin.* An endless longing overtook her, and she knew she had borne it from birth, and it had festered like a wound on her soul. A longing to be one with many others, not alone. To be a single note in a song greater than herself. To share warm bread around a dawn fire.

Minna's palms fell open in supplication. *Let me come to you,* she pleaded. *To be one again.*

We are always one. We are all beloved of the Mother. A drop of water landed in one palm, and she felt the smoothness of a river pebble in the other, warmed by fire. Or was she someone else, and this a distant memory? *You have merely fallen into forgetfulness, into sleep. But you will awake now, Minna, daughter of the Goddess. Awake, and know your true self.*

As she slipped back down the tunnel of light, her body calling, she heard one last thing, proclaimed as if by a chorus of women around her: *The One who was filled is awake, and now must become Many.*

Chapter 36

C ahir spent the night pacing, his muscles aching. Minna was safe in bed now but she slept strangely, tossing and murmuring.

Nor could he ease himself by hammering out a war plan with Gede. The Pict king had disappeared with his druids to confer, all of them set-faced after Minna's revelations, and Cahir had been left to pace and think, and pause every now and then to gaze down at his *lennan*.

He wondered again where that urge to bestow such a precious name on her had come from, for in speaking before witnesses he had made an irrevocable decision. But it must already have been made inside him, the path simply laid at his feet. And perhaps his mind had just caught up with his emotions at last.

Cahir pulled a tendril of black hair away from Minna's alabaster cheek and intently tucked it behind one ear. What man would not desire her? She was a unique beauty, a seer, and as kings were emissaries of the gods an Otherworldly mate was entirely fitting. Such matches were valued by his people, lauded in song and tale.

He stood for a moment and smiled at himself, because it was really about so much more, and so much less. Love, unlooked for and utterly surprising.

He turned, his smile fading as he thought of Maeve. She was Roman, a Christian – she would not accept a *lennan*. His fingers brushed the loom against the wall, threaded with a half-finished bolt of checked cloth, and he chewed his lip. He was king, she would *have* to accept it. And anyway ... he stopped at the end of Minna's bed. How could he care for Maeve's rages when this mysterious girl with the water eyes had just described the dying moments of the most famous Pict king; a tale only one bard had brought back from the battlefield, a secret hoarded by their druids for centuries?

Calgacus did fight at the Hill of a Thousand Spears, at Eremon's side, and he was blinded before he fell. Among the Picts there could be no argument now that she spoke the truth. What Gede would do about it was another matter.

Reliving the wonder of the dark cavern and the flickering water, Minna's soft voice echoing from the walls in her trance, Cahir breathed hard as he stared down at her pale face.

A stór. My beloved.

At midday Minna woke.

Cahir sat on the bed and held her hand as her eyelids flickered open and colour flooded her cheeks. Without thinking, he leaned down and pressed his face against her forehead.

When she was fully herself, he told her everything that Taran had told him. Minna stared at the wall as he spoke, unmoving.

'... At the battle, thousands upon thousands of Pict warriors were slaughtered, and in the moons afterwards, the women and children struggled to survive. The warriors were decimated, there were not enough men ... it was chaos. People died of famine, then from the cold of a long dark that seemed to have no end. The shame and grief was so great they have blotted it from common memory. The bards were forbidden to sing of it, the druids from speaking it. They could not bear for the tale to be remembered.' He paused. 'The same battle is in my ancestry, but it does not carry that darkness.'

She turned to him, and Cahir was so entranced he fell silent. If he saw a light there before it was nothing compared to what was there now; not strength this time but peace, as if her eyes had opened on another world of great beauty he could not see. 'Rhiann, my mother, gave your prophecy to Gabran.' Even her voice was richer and more resonant. 'She spoke of it with pride, found hope even in defeat. She preserved the tale.'

Cahir brought her fingers to his lips. 'She must have been a seer of the highest order.' His eyes roamed her face. She was still his Minna but different, timeless. What had happened to her in her dreams? 'The boar stone was a strong talisman and would have wrought much on its own. But this ... you have given them a message from their gods which is undeniable. The druids have acknowledged you as a true seer.'

Her face was more open than before, and he saw the reverberation of *seer* ringing like a bell through her soul. Her lips formed the word.

'Minna.' He searched her eyes. 'Are you still mine?'

She was slow to absorb that, as if still far away, but then a smile bloomed over her face. 'Certainly, if you are mine.' And unexpectedly she reached up and drew Cahir's lips to hers, and as he overbalanced on the bed she turned on top of him, her hair hiding them in a black, fragrant tent.

'You are sick,' he protested.

She smiled radiantly. 'I am not sick – I feel ... I feel awake.' She laughed. 'So awake.'

Her hip was tucked into the groove between his legs, and there was no way to hide how his body was responding. And here she was, an invalid. '*I'm not sick!*' she laughed again. Giving up, Cahir buried his grin in her mouth, tangling hands in her hair. It still smelled of moss and cold water.

Their tongues met; she was tentative at first, hesitating in wonder before giving herself up to response. Then the heat grew, became hungry, and Cahir felt he was falling upwards into the melting wetness of her mouth, craving her taste and smell. His fingers moulded each delicate bone in her spine ... he could snap her in two, but he would cradle her instead, and the vulnerability made him groan, and she pressed closer.

A noise outside broke them apart. For a moment Cahir could only lie there, dazed. He had to take her to his bed. But where? In the middle of an enemy dun? Aye, he could see himself buried in her, lost in her ... and then having to be a king, a commander, sparring with Gede. And yet it would release him, clear his head. Make him whole again.

'See?' Minna raised herself on one elbow, her lips swollen. She was not glowing now, but dangerously on fire.

'See what?'

'I'm not ill, I am alive! Now you can let me out of bed.'

A pause, as he traced the soft skin of her arm. 'I might, I might not.'

A trail of goose-bumps rose under his fingers, and their gazes met, incandescent. Then the noise outside became a knock. With a chuckle Minna scrambled under the covers as Cahir hastily got up.

Brimming with laughter, Minna glanced at Cahir at the last moment before Nessa entered the women's house.

He had bathed and shaved, revealing the wind-burn across his cheeks, his chapped lips. But with every step away from the cave, ringing with his men's voices, the lines of his old pain were smoothing out. It was as if a deeper layer of sight had opened to her in the Water of Seeing, revealing his noble beauty and strength. Her heart contracted.

Everything was more vivid suddenly: the flames of the fire shimmering violet, the touch of the wool blanket on her bare legs. Something happened when the voices filled her ...

'Oh!' Nessa cried in dismay, spotting Cahir. Her hand shot out to grab a little boy who had toddled into the room at her feet. 'My lord, I am so sorry, I thought your lady was alone.'

Minna glanced at Cahir again, stifling a smile. 'Please, lady, it is all right.' She extended an unsteady hand. 'This is Cahir son of Conor, King of Dalriada. And this is Gede's queen, my lord. Queen Nessa.'

Nessa dipped her head and murmured a platitude while Cahir bowed. 'Please stay seated.' She gathered the toddler into her arms. 'I will leave you—'

'No, no,' Minna protested. For as the laughter died and she looked upon mother and son, the firelight seemed to flare into a nimbus of gold all around the babe's head, while Nessa's shoulders hunched about a secret, dull as lead.

'Stay,' Cahir also urged the queen. 'I have not slept well myself for two days, lady. And I could do with time to speak with my men.' As Nessa slid the boy to the ground, Cahir glanced down at Minna, his eyes caressing her. 'You should also sleep again, *a stór*.'

'Ba! Ba!' the child cried, chasing a twine ball across the floor.

After Cahir took his leave, Nessa sat gingerly on the bed. Minna's eyes alighted on the bowl in her hands covered with a linen cloth. 'Is that food?' she asked hopefully. With a shy smile, Nessa unwrapped a hunk of honey bread and wedge of yellow cheese.

They were silent as Minna chewed. She swallowed, watching the little boy crawl across the rug after the ball. 'That is a most beautiful child, lady,' she observed.

'Please, do call me Nessa.' Her eyes lit up proudly as she turned her head, following him. 'That is my son. His name is Drustan.' In the firelight, the babe's curls were tinged with copper.

'And he has his father's hair.'

Nessa's smile faltered. 'That he does.'

The glimmering Water within Minna shifted, though she held her tongue, smiling ruefully instead. 'Well, I am in bed again. You must think me a very boring guest.'

'No, no! You are quite the talk of the dun ...' She trailed away apologetically.

Minna could imagine what she had heard. Slowly, she brushed the crumbs from her lap. 'What do they say?' she asked frankly, meeting Nessa's grey eyes. The peace was running warm and strong in her, and though they had fallen into talking in an easy way again – Minna and a queen – strangely it didn't jar, or feel odd.

Nessa nervously smoothed the folds of her dress. 'I'm not speaking of you behind your back, but the servants gossip and ... it is hard to avoid.'

'I don't mind,' she said softly.

The queen smiled, relieved. 'Then they say you had miraculous visions in the pool – though the druids will not say what – and that your king claimed you as his *lennan*.' From the upwards dart of Nessa's eyes, it seemed she thought more of that.

'The visions were of resistance against the Romans, an ancient battle – and the prospect of coming war. Now it is in the hands of your husband and my ... Cahir ... to decide what is to be done.'

Nessa absorbed that, her eyes on her son's head as he plucked at the frayed edge of the rug. 'Gede will agree to go to war if that is what your king wants. He will always wield his sword, given the chance.'

A ripple of contempt ran beneath the queen's words, and in the silence that followed, secrets slipped among the shadows like wraiths. The gold-haired child stopped tugging and stared into the dark corners beyond the fire.

Nessa glanced apprehensively at Minna now, and Minna instantly read what lay in the queen's eyes and knew she did not want to be set apart ever again. 'You don't need to fear me, lady,' she said simply, the grace so new on her tongue, in her voice. 'I am just the same as I was.'

Nessa looked away, her cheeks crimson. 'I'm sorry. I'm not very good at talking to women. Gede discourages friendships with the nobles' wives and ...' She gestured sharply, frustrated and helpless. 'I am allowed no ladies of rank as companions. Only the servants.' That was odd. The whispers rustled in the shadows. Abruptly, the queen stood up. 'And I nearly forgot – that is why I came to see if you were awake! There is a leaf-bud fair today and it's sunny. I know you are probably feeling too tired, but ...' Her brows arched hopefully.

'*Yes!*' Minna grinned. 'I am *not* tired. My limbs are twitching and I need to move or I'll go mad. I've slept for a night and almost a day as it is. Please let us go; you must free me.'

Nessa brushed Drustan's hair as he stumbled against her leg. 'Only if you are well enough. I'll be in trouble from your king if not.'

Her only answer was a snort, for Minna was already throwing back the covers.

Placing her son in the hands of a serving woman, Nessa gave Minna a simple dress of green wool, and Minna swiftly bound her hair in one braid over her shoulder. Along with the fur cloak for the wind, she took the other roll of honey bread to eat as she walked.

The meadow outside the fort gates sloped down to the white beach, the grass crowded now with people. It was the first fair since the long dark gave way to sun. People bartered what they had made in the previous months: leather belts and shoes, bolts of wool, fur edgings and embroidered hems, crocks of cheese and jars of honey, brooches and strung beads.

Filling her lungs with salt air, Minna wandered among the stalls, glad to stretch her legs. They were wobbly at first, but strengthened quickly, her shoulders loosening as if they had been bowed for months. She walked beside Nessa with her head raised, and saw the glances come her way, and the whispers.

Men traded from carts while women spread their wares on cloaks. Strips of meat sizzled over fires, and girls slapped dough with bare hands, laying bannocks on griddles. Children, shaking off the long dark, chased each other down to the beach to dig up shells and seaweed.

Minna breathed. It was all so vivid, as if she had been asleep for months. The sunlight on the sea glittered, the waves rushed up the sands with a loud hiss. She could taste the roasting meat on the air.

Then all at once she felt compelled to turn around. They had wandered up a rise near the gates, and so she could gaze right out across the marshes and woods and low hills, seeing far to the south and west. There was a dark line on the horizon. Minna shaded her eyes.

Nessa was at a jeweller's cart hung with beads. As the trader spoke, she ran a string of chunky amber through her fingers, feeling its weight. The crowd flowed around them, but Minna could not force herself to move. The chatter and laughter and cries of children receded. *The Caledonii mountains.*

The water within her moved again, and in her mind she glimpsed a pale horse, ears tilted towards those same hills, walking at the head of a murmuring sea of men. An army: vast, faceless. And on the reins, a slim hand and a gold ring.

The salt-weathered trader held the beads up to the sun, exclaiming something to Nessa. Minna barely heard the answering murmur, for she was caught by a terrible sense of doom, a memory grey and thick as the clouds hanging over the army. Did Rhiann go to war at Eremon's side, then, to meet their fate at the Hill of a Thousand Spears? Her eyes glazed, Minna brushed the incised surface of the ring slowly with one finger.

When she at last looked down, rousing herself, it was straight into a pair of iridescent green eyes, set in the wizened face of an old woman on the far side of the fair. Their gazes locked.

'Minna.' Nessa's voice startled her. 'Which do you think is prettier? The blue or the green?' She had bought the amber and was now holding up a string of glass beads.

Minna murmured something vague, jarred by a sense of recognition when she looked at the old woman. But she had never seen her before. *Sister.* The word was breathed into her ear by the breeze.

She was halfway across the fair before Nessa caught her up. 'Where are you going?'

The old woman was on the edge of the fair, in a space left around her by the other traders. She was sitting cross-legged on a tatty cloak, her pure white hair hanging about her shoulders like a fall of snow. On the cloak sat little scoops of leaves, knots of bark, dried roots and crushed powders.

'A herb-woman,' Minna murmured.

'She is the wise-woman,' Nessa hissed, 'and her mind is unsound. Leave her, Minna.'

But her feet were moving without conscious thought, and then she was squatting in front of the ragged cloak, smiling a greeting. 'May I?' she said in Dalriadan, gesturing at a knot of leaves on a curl of birch bark. The old woman nodded, her bright green eyes curious. Minna crushed a shred between her fingers to smell it.

The herbalist was slight, but her limbs were strong and gnarled as driftwood, wrapped in layers of fringed wool that flapped in the wind. 'It is ... mountain ... leaf,' the woman replied in the same language, the words faltering as if being drawn up from distant memory. Her voice was as weathered as her cheeks. 'For boils. Drawing pus ... breaking open.'

She knew the *gael* speech. Minna nodded, surprised. The druids still retained the tongue, though, so others might. Those seaweed eyes were bright with mischief as the woman cocked her head. 'What were you looking at girl, eh?'

'What do you mean?'

'In the air, over there. You were seeing something. I saw you. I *smelled* it.' She reached out one bony finger and touched Minna's forehead, right between her eyes.

The skin prickled, and Minna rubbed it away as the old woman sat back with a sly smile. Teal feathers dangled from a lock of white hair at her temple, and there were shells on a thong around her scrawny neck. 'Darine saw the light around you. It shimmers like the night-banners that hang in the northern sky. You saw something, and it made you sad.' She cackled knowingly. 'You can *see*.'

Minna's breath was snatched from her. She looked at those eyes and she knew her, and yet didn't know her.

Then the old woman wasn't looking at her any more but up to the sky, her awareness clouded and distant. 'You remember the sword-king,' she whispered. '*They* tell me. You remember the old battle.'

She stifled an exclamation. 'Calgacus?'

'That's the one!' The woman grinned. 'The eagle king lived near here to the west. But *no one* knows that except the druid priests – and Darine. Darine knows many such things, if anyone would ask. Darine has travelled to east and south and even lands of the *gael*.' She pointed with her chin at the people jostling all about. 'But *they* don't care. They have forgotten everything.' Her green eyes were suddenly sharp, inscrutable. 'You have remembered, though, and those with sense run away from such memories, *gael* child. Are you touched in the head like me?'

Minna smiled tightly. 'There are questions I need to answer. I am just searching, that is all.'

'Ah ... searching. We are all searching.' She stared off into space, sucking her lip through a gap in her teeth. 'Darine does not see, but she hears. There are mutterings and mumblings all around, even here. The fey ones speak.' Abruptly, she began batting away something invisible. 'Aye, aye!' she muttered. 'I hear, I hear!'

Minna was just edging back when Darine's eyes pinned her there, clear again. 'They say to invite you to my fire now. To show you something.'

Her pulse quickened. 'Show me what?'

Darine looked affronted. 'How should I know?' Instantly, she was on her feet, lithe despite her age. 'Come, come.' She began gathering up her belongings, pouring leaves and roots back into earthen jars, packing them in a basket. 'I live down there on the sand, in the dunes. Close to the sea, I like. Away from all the people, the stink, the smoke.'

'Come to your home ... now?'

Darine sighed. 'Aye, I can't be doing with the visitors either. But you try ignoring the spirits, girly, and see if they leave *you* alone.'

Her words penetrated Minna, and suddenly she knew why she came out this day. Her lips moved slowly, but her heart beat faster. 'I don't want to ignore her. I have to reach out to her.' Her: the spirit woman who held out love, and then took it away.

Darine glanced at her sharply. Nessa said Minna's name again, taking her arm and drawing her away. She did not miss the glance exchanged between the queen and the old woman: Nessa afraid, Darine smiling slyly while touching her head with respect.

'We must go now.' Nessa was frowning. 'Come, there are other stalls to see.'

Minna glanced back at Darine packing her herbs, muttering to herself. 'You go on. I will take tea with the wise-woman.'

'*Tea!*' Nessa squawked, then lowered her voice. 'But ... you can't. She is a witch,' she hissed.

'She is learned in herb-lore,' Minna replied calmly. 'You know I have been learning the healing skills. There are things I need to speak of with her.'

Guilt flickered over the queen's face, before she turned her cheek away. 'You shouldn't go. It's not safe.'

'Why? She seems harmless enough.'

'*Harmless?* She makes potions and spells and—'

'Nessa.' Minna touched her hand. 'When people say those things it is only because they don't understand. She brews healing draughts, nothing more.'

Nessa's nostrils were pinched. 'Nothing more.' She sighed and stepped back. 'Then be careful.'

'Of course, and will you send a message to Cahir telling him where I am, and that I will be back this afternoon before dark?'

Minna hastened after the old woman Darine as she ambled off along the sands, wondering at the racing of her heart.

Chapter 37

Gede watched as the *gael* king entered his hall behind Taran. The man betrayed no anxiety about what had transpired. Gede had to admit that everything he had heard about this Cahir was being overturned.

A Roman lover. A coward. A gelding with no will of his own. That is what people whispered.

But this man had surprised him. There were no fanciful Roman touches about his person, no brooches, no ridiculous attempts at a toga, no perfumes to make him stink of Rome. And nothing obsequious. If there was one thing Gede hated, it was oily words and smiles. The fact this king spoke plainly and his eyes were proud had made Gede – unwillingly – sprout the merest kernal of respect for him.

Or perhaps wariness. This king was a stronger enemy on his flank than Gede had ever supposed, based on their sporadic clashes over the years. Over time the Roman Province had provided far richer pickings, and it had been to this that Gede increasingly applied his resources, merely setting a watch on the *gaels*. He would have given more thought to that defence had he known this Cahir was not the plump, perfumed king of his imagination.

Taran stood by to translate as Cahir took a seat and accepted a cup of ale. Gede gestured to Galan, who rose from his bench.

'The girl was accepted by the Water,' Galan stated gruffly. 'What she saw is known only to the druid-kind.' He glanced at Gede, betraying anxiety. 'We accept that what she said is true. There was an alliance between the *gaels* and our people.'

Gede recognized that flicker in Galan's eyes and was satisfied. A king who instilled fear in his druids was a strong king indeed. He rested his chin on his gloved hand. He had taken his gyrfalcon out to the cliffs this morning, giving himself time to think. A few hours in the cold wind and he had been resolved enough to deliver his verdict. He would not show impatience to this Cahir, though. It would not do to show any emotion at all.

'And?' The Dalriadan king's ale was untouched. He stared at Gede, black brows framing golden eyes with an intensity that was almost disrespectful. 'This means that you will agree to the alliance I have proposed?'

Gede's hackles rose at the implicit demand. 'The stone is a true message, the visions are real, but these are the bond of an ancient king who, though he died gloriously, ultimately failed. Would *you* let matters of state be decided on such evidence? The man is dead, and his cause with him.' He was deliberately provocative, enjoying the gasps of his druids.

Cahir frowned, and Galan hastily broke in. 'My king.' He bowed stiffly to Gede. 'To the brotherhood, this was a bond sanctioned by the gods, an oath witnessed by the gods. The carving states this alliance was intended to be unbreakable through time.'

'And what of it? Calgacus is not here now.'

Galan looked perplexed. Gede had not been so aggressive earlier. Well, he believed in keeping people unsettled – it was easier to control them that way.

'My king.' Galan summoned his druid dignity. 'We spoke of this. Among the brotherhood this word *is* sacred, even now. But the fact that the girl was gifted with the secret lore seals it. The gods would not have sent this vision if this lore was dead, if this story was ended. She saw our most glorious king because his word is meant to be heeded, I am sure of it.'

'*Our most glorious king?*' Gede raised one eyebrow. 'Why, Galan, I assume you are speaking of me, your lord?'

Galan's withered cheeks quivered as he chewed his tongue. Perhaps Gede had made his point strongly enough now. He had only meant to send a message that he wouldn't be bossed about by druids or cowed by enemy kings.

'This Eremon of Dalriada and Calgacus rallied troops together,' Galan ground out. 'They speak from the Otherworld for one reason only: there is an opportunity here, great king,' Gede did not miss the sarcasm, 'to revisit our approach to the question of the Roman kind and the Empire beyond the wall, to go forth in open battle at last, in unity and strength.' He glanced at Cahir, who was on the edge of his seat. 'The gods brought the *gael* king to you over mountains and through snow. They demand you heed them!'

Gede flung himself to his feet, trying not to show his agitation.

'My lord.' The Dalriadan king was keeping an admirable hold on his temper, and in that moment Gede almost felt kinship with him. They faced each other. 'Leaving aside all questions of visions and prophecies, it is still very simple. You have raided the Romans for years: why?'

Gede's eyes narrowed. 'Plunder. Why else?'

Cahir smiled wolfishly. 'I do not think only for plunder.' He took a step closer, and Gede's second-in-command Garnat moved forward, one hand on his sword, the other forking his black beard. Gede did not flinch. Taran was struggling to translate swiftly.

Cahir dropped his voice. 'You hate them, and it makes your skin crawl that they hold sway over any part of Alba at all. You know they are hoping to consume Dalriada, and if I have to stand alone, and I fall, you are wondering how long your own lands will stay free.'

Gede drew breath. This was much more interesting than the bleating of druids. 'You seem to claim a great knowledge of my mind.'

'I say this because it is how I feel. We are both kings of Alba, we want to keep our people safe. But you restrict yourselves to raiding because as strong as you are,' he nodded at the lavish decoration, the walls encrusted with swords and shields, 'you do not have the strength for a full-scale assault on the Wall and the lands below.'

Gede was forced to look up at the taller man. The Picts had attacked the Province only three years ago, but the *gael* was right, damn him. They were all raids, nothing lasting. 'Perhaps I do have the strength, but have not seen the point, if it would only bring fire and Roman swords swarming over my duns.'

'You would have done it if you could,' Cahir persisted. 'The Picts have never given the Romans quarter, and I admire that.' He spoke with a dignity that robbed his words of any weakness. 'What we need is the strength for a strike which knocks out the northern command, to cripple them so greatly they cannot strike back. We need them so terrified, so riven and harried, that they leave Alba for ever. It has happened before, in Germania, when the tribes there repelled Rome. It can be done; we just need the numbers.' He stepped forward, his eyes blazing with thoughts of war and armies.

Unwillingly, Gede felt himself drawn into that excitement. How the man spoke! What he saw in his face was just what Gede felt when the falcon landed on his arm, screaming to the sky – the same foolish pride he had brought under control on the ride back to the dun. 'I have allies among the Saxons.'

'Yes. And I among the Attacotti and in Erin. But never have we all acted together.' Cahir's eyes bored into Gede, making it hard to turn away. 'Never have we acted as one. And this is what I offer you. To set aside our differences and the pain of our past—'

'You presume too much!' Gede retorted, gripping the back of his carved chair.

Cahir was relentless. 'Set it aside *for now*,' he emphasized. 'Just long enough to form the greatest army Alba has known – indeed, perhaps that the whole isle of Britain has known!' He leaned forward, his hand contracting into a fist before Gede's face. 'Long enough to *win*.'

The man had taken command of the situation, and Gede would not have it. He strode to the edge of the hall, so all eyes had to follow him. There his gaze roamed over those shields, battered and nicked from fights long past; and the swords, each one a hero's, polished to a high shine. What else did a Pict king exist for but to fight when a challenge was thrown down? He had come to the same conclusions as this king on the windy cliff-edge, but for slightly different reasons.

For the great Calgacus was still lodged in druid memory, in the memory of the stones, *even though he lost.* Gede, though, would win, and rid this land of the Romans. Then his legend would eclipse that of Calgacus of the Caledonii. Gede would have no other king's name above his own.

He composed his features and turned, glimpsing a shadow of pain and anxiety on the Dalriadan king's face. So he had his weaknesses, too. 'I have thought long on this,' Gede said, his voice raised. 'I have consulted my warriors.' He glanced at Garnat, hungry, too, for war. 'If I can bring the Saxons, and you can bring the Attacotti and the Erin men, then yes, we will have a force that the Romans cannot repel. This is an opportunity that only a fool would let slip through his fingers, whether it is with old enemies or not. And I am no fool.'

Cahir bowed his head in gracious acknowledgement. But he was breathing hard.

Gede strode back to the hearth, and though it made his flesh crawl – so ingrained was the long hatred of the *gael* – he held out his open wrist for Cahir to clasp. It was a gesture that said the opponent was unarmed; it spoke of trust, however tenuous.

Cahir took the proffered wrist, their arm-bands grating together. Their faces were close, and Gede made sure his eyelids did not so much as flicker. 'Then you have your alliance, King Cahir. For the benefit of both our peoples.'

Darine's hut nestled in low dunes by a salt marsh, a dome of branches and earth, its thatch roof weighted with nets and stones. Driftwood branches were arranged in a circle before the door, decorated with strips of seaweed like the banners on a king's hall. Bird skulls lined the roof, staring down from gaping eyeholes.

Inside there was no lamp, but by the light of a smoky fire Minna saw the walls were stuffed with moss and dried grass, and bunches of herbs were tied to the roof beams. It smelled of salt and fish.

Still muttering to herself, Darine put water on to boil. 'Get the dried blackberries from that pot there, *gael* child.'

Minna was reaching over the barrels in the indicated corner when she knocked the lid off a tall basket, then exclaimed and stood back. The basket was brimming with bronze torcs, arm-rings and finger-rings, ropes of amber and glass beads. She merely stared, wondering if this was another vision, then clapped the lid back on.

'You found my treasure,' Darine said, when she sat down.

'Yes. You have so much. Are they gifts?'

'Gifts, yes.'

Darine wore no jewellery but for the pierced shell beads on a thong and the feathers in her hair, but gathered in that one basket was the wealth of a mighty chieftain. 'You are given valuable gifts.'

Darine's smile turned sly. 'I do valuable things.'

Minna thought about that. 'You mean things people don't want others to know you've done.'

Darine beamed. 'Quick, too.' She poked at the tea-pot. 'The men come to me to curse an enemy, make a woman open her legs, put a poison on their blade. The women come to make a babe nest in the womb – or to rid themselves of one.'

Minna frowned, and Darine laughed. 'When you open to the Source, girl, you must accept its light and dark both. You want to help people, then you risk the terrible along with the great. There may be beauty, noble deeds and honour, but also guilt, frustration and terror. You can feel the flight, the freedom – aye, I see you have! – but the journey there can wander through some barren valleys. You must be able to push through fear, doubt, illusion and weariness, or you will see no visions. Find your courage, or turn your back on it altogether.' She cackled, sucking the gap in her teeth. 'And if so, get fat with puppies instead, mend your man's shirts by the fire, grind grain until your back bows. It's your choice.'

Minna's snatches of vision were full of blood and pain, but she would never forget the love and grief she saw mingled in Eremon's face as he held that tiny body on the mountain. She knew what she would choose.

Darine poured the blackberry tea into two horn cups, her mossy eyes sharp across the fire. 'Who are you, then, and why do the voices want you here?'

Minna curved her hands about the cup. 'I'm from Britannia, not Alba. I was enslaved and sold to the *gaels*.'

The old woman arched sparse, white brows. 'You bear the blood of the red-crests?'

'My grandmother said we were of the old blood, too. She taught me how to speak and told me the old tales.' She smiled encouragingly at

Darine. 'Tales of Deirdre and Cuchulainn of Erin—'

'Ah, Cuchulainn!' Darine's eyes misted over. '"For dread of me,"' she murmured, quoting the famous hero, '"fighting men avoid fords and battles. Armies go backward from the fear of my face."'

Mamo had told Minna the very same thing. The room was silent as Darine searched Minna's eyes, and though she felt as she did when Brónach probed her, this was not sickening. 'Power you have,' the wise-woman whispered. 'Aye! The flame is in you, child, burning bright.' Then in an eerie sing-song, Darine began to chant:

> Three times three the king's sword fell
> And bright was the blood on the plain of spears.
> One eye taken, one eye blazing
> Yet the bard was the blind one
> As tears took him
> His song branded on his throat.

Calgacus's death. For a moment Minna was transported back to the Water of Seeing.

'I am not supposed to know,' Darine whispered, conspiratorially. 'The priests keep it to themselves. But I have lived long, so long that when I was small the memory of the battle was sharper. I heard the druids then, as I crawled into the groves at night when they whispered their secrets. I gleaned many things that women weren't supposed to know. Slowly, I gathered them and kept them here.' She tapped her head.

Minna blinked the steam away. 'Then you must know much about plants. About . . . voices. And visions.'

Darine rocked, nodding. 'I am the oldest, child, the last to remember anything. The plants have voices, too, did you know? They sing to me of their life, snatches of chants, things to hum over the fevered babe, the dying man.' She sighed. 'But it all leaks away from me year by year, and soon I will lie down and let the long dark take me.'

The cup burned Minna's fingers. The knowledge could not just *leach away* into nothing. 'But . . . but there were shepherds of the Source,' she murmured, the knowing flooding her. 'There were . . . *women* . . . who held and nurtured it, sang it alive, sang it to sleep through the long dark. Many women together, chanting, holding the vision as one—'

Darine cried out and clamped her hands over her ears, scuttling back. 'How can you speak of this pain? Now they cry out to me. They fill my head and make it burn.'

Minna stared, alarmed, until the wise-woman raised her face, tears welling in her eyes. 'You make me ache for them,' she whispered.

Minna placed the cup down. 'Ache for who?' But she knew.

The old woman's breath laboured. 'The Sisters. The priestesses. The Order of the Goddess that once was.'

Sister, the whisper came again.

'Darine, what happened to them? Where are they?' Her words spilled out, sharp with grief. '*Why do they speak to me?*'

'They ... they reach to *you?*'

She nodded, and Darine stared into the fire, rocking. 'It is ... hard to speak. I ... cannot ... it hurts too much ... I cannot speak.'

Minna shuffled closer on her knees. 'One who walks in the Otherworld used to come to me in vision,' she said urgently. 'But now she has fallen silent, and I don't know everything she was trying to tell me. I need to reach her.'

The room was still, as Darine curled up like a mouse in the nest of her white hair. 'There used to be a way,' the old woman forced out eventually, 'to journey among the visions, to step into the Otherworld at will.'

'What way?' She was leaning forward.

Darine shook her head. 'I know only a memory of long ago, my grandmother. *Saor,* it is called. It frees the spirit.'

Saor. The word rang through Minna. 'But *what* is it?'

Darine gasped in pain, her fingers pressed over her ears. 'No ... it hurts ...'

Minna firmly took both her elbows and drew them down, held her forearms. Their eyes locked. 'You are not alone any more.' That grief was terrible to see, and almost instinctively the healer in Minna surrendered and allowed Darine's pain to flow through her own heart, to ease her. *A grief of ages. A mountain of loneliness bearing down, squeezing the life out of old flesh, the fire out of a weary soul. An unbearable loss that should have been shared by many, not one alone.*

Instantly, Minna found Darine's unshed tears flowing down her own face, and the old woman stared in wonder, touching them with her finger. Her wrinkled lips moved, her throat at last released. 'The herbs, they have plant-souls ... *Saor* is six mingled ... just the right amounts ... They help the spirit and body part, so that the spirit can journey far.'

Minna could hardly breathe, tasting the tears on her lips. She sat back on her heels, releasing Darine.

'But *saor* is very dangerous,' Darine whispered, her eyes huge and glazed with memory. 'There must be skill, training, to ensure the silver cord of the spirit does not break and the body die. You must breathe life into the cord ... breathe, and never let it break.'

She was absorbing this when the old woman suddenly twisted, pointing up at the roof. 'There, the one with the little blue flowers, like teardrops, and the woody stem there, with no flowers, the leaves grey and shiny.'

Minna swiped at her cheek and staggered up, touching each plant as the wise-woman named it. She had seen many of these at Dunadd, yet never felt they were anything but medicinal. *Freedom*, something sang in her veins, sweeping away grief. *Saor.*

'And the one with the leaves like a cow's ear, but not all of it ... just the seeds ... and ... and ...' Darine's voice faded. 'There is more, but I don't know them.' She slapped her cheek in frustration. 'I don't know them all!'

'It doesn't matter; it is a start.' Minna pressed the leaves to her nose, and folded each one in the hide pouch at her waist. Three, of six. The doorway beckoned. She knelt before the wise-woman. 'You have done me the greatest honour. I didn't know there was such a thing as *saor*, but now—' She stopped herself. *Now I remember.*

Darine's wrinkled cheeks were wet. She dragged herself up and, moving stiffly now, traced the branches of the herbs on the rafters, lingering over the designs carved in the posts. Minna's gaze followed her fingers and paused. There in the wood was the same design as on Rhiann's priestess ring: the three faces of the Mother.

'If your heart knows, then it is only fitting, they are telling me, that you also know the story of the Sisters.' She glanced at Minna, her eyes bleak. 'For it is not only the druids who have their secrets. There is another story. Many may have told it once, but under kings like Gede women were no longer welcome as holders of the Source, and gradually the knowledge was lost. Almost lost.' Her voice was so faint Minna strained to hear her. 'My great-grandmother knew, and her daughter, my grandmother. And me.' She turned away. 'I will tell you how the Sisters met their end.'

Chapter 38

Minna walked back along the darkening beach at dusk, all feeling scoured from her. Darine's tale had burned her heart to cold ash.

Three hundred years ago, the elders of the priestess order lived together on an isle in the western sea, the Attacotti homeland. The Sisters warded the Source that ran through the earth; the male druids the power that fired the sun and stars. Earth was for women, because of its tides and cycles. Sun and sky were for men, for the rain that seeded the soil, the sun that energized all growth. That was balance, but it was gone now.

The Roman general Agricola grew afraid of the reverence in which the Sisters were held by the Alban people. He resolved to attack the island and kill them.

But the elder sisters had foreseen the Roman attack. They knew that only a great outrage would bring together all the warring tribes of Alba in alliance, and so they stood with compassion in their hearts and let the Romans destroy them, because that sacrifice would lead the tribes to become one. All came to pass, and because of that slaughter, Eremon and Calgacus were able to bring the tribes together at the Hill of a Thousand Spears.

But the Albans were defeated, Minna had cried.

Even that was foreseen by the Sisters, Darine replied. They knew that Roman strength and greed would need to come to its zenith and be on the wane for them to be banished, and it was the gradual strengthening of the tribes into one people over many centuries that mattered most, not one battle. After all, she said, it is many threads that make a cloth; many lives that make a fate for a nation. But the story of the Sisters and the Source was not over yet.

They knew their order in its ancient form would not long remain intact. It would be crushed by the great battle, and lost during the dark years afterwards. The priestesses would die out, and, in time, women would forget what they held buried in their souls.

Here Darine's voice dropped to a whisper.

So the wisest ones took all the knowledge of the Source – the memories of other lives, the rites and songs, the knowledge of plants and of people's hearts, the ways to journey between worlds, the skills of vision and prophecy built up since the dawn of time – and they kept it safe in the only vessel that would survive time itself.

Darine did not know what that was. It could be a secret pool that held the images of times gone by. It could be an object made of gold or crystal. It could be an old story remembered by some distant bard. Was Minna supposed to find that, too? It was too daunting to contemplate.

'So,' Darine finished, 'the Alban tribes became the Pictish nation. The land made way also for the Dalriadans who came from Erin, linked by blood to Dunadd. Now the warriors of Alba are strong again, but riven by enmity and suspicion. Athough they do not know it, they are waiting for the one to unite them once more, take them forth again with a vision of the gods on their banners. And this time, the Romans will be vanquished from Alba, and Alba will be freed.'

Waiting for someone. The sea-wind brushed over Minna's cold cheek, and she shivered as she ploughed through the sand, pulling her cloak closed.

Cahir.

The dun was flaming with torches. As Minna passed the king's hall she saw servants dashing back and forth with bowls and baskets, harried.

Nessa was waiting for her in the women's house. 'Hurry!' she cried, when Minna came in with the sea-wind in her hair, her eyes far away. 'Gede has called a feast and we are meant to attend him.'

'Why?' She whirled to Nessa. 'Is there news about the alliance?'

'I have no news. They tell me nothing besides the fact we have to attend Gede. And we are late!'

Making no mention of Darine, Nessa made Minna sit so the serving maids could brush her hair, threading gold braid through the black plaits and pinning it around her head. They dressed her in another of Nessa's robes, deep-blue wool bound by a gilded leather belt, and both she and the queen hastened to the hall.

Inside, Minna barely heard King Gede murmur a rebuke to his wife, for she could not look away from Cahir standing at his side.

Someone had lent him clothes fit for a king. His green tunic was ornately embroidered around the hem and sleeves, elegantly framing his broad shoulders. His trousers were of close-fitting leather, outlining his long thighs, and his dark hair was gleaming, braided at the sides to reveal his sun-browned, lean face that bore a new strength, a certainty. Most of all, when his golden eyes met Minna's they were euphoric.

Nessa scuttled behind Gede's chair, drawing Minna to the women's side of the hall. They sat on a bench half in the shadows. Ale cups were being filled by maids hurrying about with stone jugs, and others bore platters of oysters, mussels, fried fish and roast pig from the beast spitted over the fire. Fat dripped from its flanks, sizzling in the flames.

Ruarc, Ardal and Mellan were with a group of young Picts to one side, dicing and drinking, with some fierce boasting thrown in, which neither side could understand. Donal, Gobán and Fergal kept to themselves, watching Cahir's back with sharp eyes.

At last King Gede gestured for silence. 'By the glory of Taranis Thunder God and Lugh of the Sun, we drink to an alliance made this day between the people of Gede son of Urp and the people of Cahir son of Conor.'

Cahir's eyes burned into Minna's. Gede had agreed.

'The Dalriadan king bears a token of an old pledge between our peoples. Now we pledge to join again, to set aside old enmities to attack the enemy of all Alba.' He paused. 'And that enemy is Rome!' An enormous drunken cheer went up.

The noise assaulted Minna's senses. She gripped the bench, and in her mind another vast army marched over the land, spear-tips waving, feet drumming. *Mother, pray we do the right thing, that I have seen true.* But when she focused on Cahir she could not regret anything, for through this he had found himself. And found her.

'Our alliance will draw together the four peoples of the north,' Gede was saying. 'Pict, Dalriadan in Alba and Erin, Attacotti and Saxon. Such a force can be forged into a blade of iron that pierces the heart of Rome!'

More cheering and foot-stamping ensued among the young, drunken Picts, though others glowered, the big man who always guarded Gede one of them. The Pict king shouted a toast, his smile a savage baring of teeth, and through the noise, Minna tried to send tendrils of her new sight towards him. But as she probed, searching for cracks in his mask, her seeing suddenly hit a wall; inside, Gede was an impenetrable tangle of feelings and thoughts. He glanced around the room, his eyes passing over Minna like a shadow, then moving on.

Cahir replied to the toast, and before their warriors the two kings joined hands once more. Then all the Picts were on their feet, men stumbling for more ale, the bard tuning his harp. With a timid smile Nessa told Minna she must go to her son, and Minna watched her retreat, concerned at her paleness. She had no time to think, though, for Cahir was there before her, holding out his hand.

'Come,' he said, and she was drawn in his wake as he shouldered his way through the crowd.

Outside, a swollen moon rolled over the sky between the clouds. Cahir's eyes were alight as he drew Minna up the steps to the walls of the dun. The Pict guards glanced at them and went back to their watch. Further along the walkway was an empty tower that stared out to sea, and a moon-trail led far into the hissing darkness of the waves.

'He listened to you.' Minna searched Cahir's eyes. The moonlight flickered through the racing clouds.

'To you.' Cahir tucked wisps of hair over her ears, holding her face.

'I have hardly spoken to him—'

'It was the vision, Minna, more than the stone.'

'But he doesn't seem a man to hearken to visions, or dreams.'

Cahir shrugged. 'Of course, I do not trust him – I never will. I will use him, and he will use me, and that is the extent of our brotherhood. But that is enough, for neither of us can do this alone.' Gede did have the fire in him, though: Minna had at least seen that. He wanted this as much as Cahir did.

Her arms went around Cahir's waist and she buried her face in the warm hollow of his throat, thoughts of war and death suddenly receding far away. But when he pressed lips to the tender place behind her ear, a flame ran over her skin. Just that one, small touch, the whisper of her name, and she was a torch in his arms.

In fever, and icy water, the remnants of the child in her had been burned away, and it was a woman's instincts that ruled her now.

He parted her lips with his tongue, and she devoured what he gave, letting herself sink into him, that heat and sweetness that was like honey and silk enveloping her whole mouth. When that ravishing kiss moved to her neck, nipping the skin, she felt the strength go out of her legs, holding to his arms as the world reeled, his muscles hard with tension under her fingers. Her hips ground into his as if she had no will over them – she wanted more than kisses now, which did not consume in the way she yearned to be consumed.

Cahir cupped her breast through her dress, and she tensed. Her nipple was exquisitely tender, and as he stroked it all feeling rushed there and she whimpered, moulding her body to his, thigh to thigh. He made a raw sound in the back of his throat as he claimed her mouth again, and she seized his free hand and cradled it to her other breast.

Crushing each other, they stumbled back against the watchtower,

Cahir's shoulders braced against the wood. 'Gods! I could take you now, but *a stór*,' he shuddered, 'I don't want the first time to be … I want to savour you, to show you—'

'But I need you,' she said thickly, her lips bruised. Her fingers traced the moonlit line of his bones.

'I need you as well, but not like this, not in this dark place.'

Suddenly the hunger released her and she was trembling all over. 'But it aches!'

He laughed unsteadily, raking back his hair. His eyes glittered in the moonlight. 'It's a sweet ache, though, you will see. I haven't felt it for … much too long.'

Minna sighed and pressed her forehead to his chin. The stubble scratched her, but even that small sense was exquisite, and a tenderness swamped her, a feeling as strong as the lust. Her mind raced to when they might have the time to explore this, and be consumed … and that made her think of Dunadd again. She could not help it, for all thoughts and paths led back there.

She leaned back and gazed up at him, suddenly cold. 'What is going to happen when we return?'

His smile faded. 'It will be different,' he said bluntly, taking her hand. 'Difficult, perhaps.'

She said nothing as he smoothed a finger over each one of her nails. 'Minna. I need to ask you again because this war is *imagining* and *hope* no longer, but real.' He stared intently at her hand, his eyes veiled. 'Are you really willing to be my *lennan*? Women can take their pleasure with any man, but being a king's *lennan* is like being another queen. The people will look upon you as that, for though you are not the legal wife, the love I bear for you and the honour I do you brings its own power. You do understand what you are accepting?'

Maeve's petulant face came to Minna. 'Yes.' She touched his bent head lightly, curved a hand about his neck. 'And it is you I want – to be bonded to you.'

He looked up at her, the moon caught in his eyes. 'It is about more than love.' The power in his voice held her. 'If we do this, you will be held accountable for the decisions I make. There is no way then for you to claim innocence in the face of our enemies.' He swallowed, breathing hard. 'So if you choose not to risk this, *a stór*, I will send you wherever you want to go – even back to Britannia.'

She shook her head, smoothed his tight jaw. 'If I turn away from you, I turn from a land that has claimed me as its own. Don't you see that? I am one with you: we share the blood and the dream. If I foreswear you I deny my own soul. There is no going back for me.'

Cahir expelled his breath, his fingers caressing her hard skin beneath the slave-ring. 'I have my reasons for not striking this off right here and now, Minna. Wear this a little longer, and trust me when I say you will be free.'

Sunlight rippled over Keeva's naked body as she stretched out on Lonán's cloak. Unfurling leaves fluttered above them in a cold wind, but in this hollow among the bushes it was sheltered.

They were in the woods to the north of Dunadd, a deserted place because hidden in the trees was a cluster of standing stones, some fallen, some hunched upright, splotched with lichen. Keeva often came here to escape all the bustle at Dunadd – after all, they weren't raised by *her* ancestors, and it was the one place no one ventured.

Lonán rolled on his stomach, touching a nodding hyacinth to Keeva's small, bare breasts. She smiled lazily at him.

'You are a shameless Attacotti maid,' Lonán murmured, still blushing. 'In the middle of the day! Master Fintan would have my ear if he knew that collecting firewood entailed this.'

But he had looked so intent and serious with that load of wood balanced on his shoulders. Keeva trailed a finger over one of his soot-blackened palms, the thick fingers blistered and cut. 'I didn't hear you protesting too loudly.'

'You make it hard to say no,' he mumbled.

'Do I?' With a sly grin, Keeva picked up one of those misshapen, burnt fingers and ran her lips and tongue over it.

'You'll leave me with no strength for work this day.'

But Keeva had paused, Lonán's finger slipping from her mouth. Voices were floating from the clearing of the stones. 'Hawen's balls,' Lonán hissed, grabbing for his trousers. 'We're not meant to be here, and you know it!'

'No one comes here but druids.' Keeva was on hands and knees peering through the bushes. Lonán grunted as he pulled on his trousers.

'Goddess,' Keeva muttered.

Lonán was madly lacing his boots. 'What?'

'It is the queen.'

'So?' Lonán grabbed for his tunic, which had been flung into a patch of primroses.

Keeva threw him a look. 'It is the queen and that Oran man again, and the priest we saw in the port – I'm sure of it.'

'Gods!' Lonán tossed Keeva's dress over her bare buttocks. 'All the more reason to get out of here then. Hurry up!'

'Wait.' Keeva's face was grim. 'There are Dalriadan warriors there; I don't know their names. But they are not the king's men.'

'Keeva, we must go.' Lonán was tugging on his tunic. Keeva glared at him. *He* did not live in the hall. He did not know anything about the anger between queen and king, Ruarc and Oran, Carvetii and Dalriada, beyond the fact that he made swords and shield rivets and daggers for them all. He didn't care about Minna's baffling disappearance with the king.

Keeva felt sick; something wasn't right. Her decision made, she flung herself down and started wriggling through the undergrowth towards the voices. Behind her Lonán hissed her name, but she ignored him.

The ground was slimy with last year's leaves, and she got close to the stones without making much noise. In any case, the people gathered there were speaking intently and did not hear her. The queen was sitting in shadow on one of the fallen stones. The dangerous-looking priest was a silent, hooded figure beside her. Oran was addressing a group of grim warriors, around a score in all, crouched in the bracken.

'You have been handpicked,' he was saying in Dalriadan, 'and I trust we have your complete loyalty.' Some of the warriors shifted uneasily on their heels, others lowered their heads. Oran stared at them one by one. 'Know that the payments you have received are only a fraction of what you can expect once we control the dun and port.'

Keeva pressed into the ground. *Goddess.*

'It had better be a lot,' one man said, shifting his shoulders as if shrugging off a weight. 'This is no small thing you demand. It is treason.'

Maeve glared at the man. 'Treason is a word much open to interpretation,' she retorted. 'It is my father who will arm those ships, and he is the King of the Carvetii—'

'But this raid isn't sanctioned by the Romans, is it, my lady?' one of the warriors interrupted quietly. 'So we could be damned by them as well as our own king.'

Oran smoothly took over. 'Both the Dux and the queen's father have been trying to make your king see sense for years. He refuses, and in so doing puts all his people in great danger. They are in danger from the Picts, because he persists in rejecting the protection of the Roman army; and from the Romans themselves, who grow impatient with his indecision. Now is the only chance we have to put right what has been wrong.' His nostrils flared as he raised his chin. 'So it is not *treason* to topple a foolish king; it is wisdom, and as we intend to install the prince Garvan as king, the line of Dalriada will still claim this throne. However, *this* young king will command allies that can protect Dunadd and allow it to prosper, bringing in more riches, more trade and better access to the markets of Roman Britannia.' He paused. 'More access to riches for *everyone.* And as loyal queen's men, you will be highly favoured.' His eyes strayed to Maeve, and they exchanged a small smile that turned Keeva's belly.

There was a long silence. 'We've already agreed,' one man muttered. 'No more speeches for us.'

'Then we will turn to facts. The ships will dock at Beltaine in two weeks among the first trading fleet – any earlier and they would have attracted undue suspicion from the coastal duns.' He shrugged. 'Waiting for the seas to be safe was the risk we had to take. The original plan was to catch our king fox in his den,' again that smile towards the queen, 'but Cahir's continued absence is neither here nor there. When he returns with his paltry guard of, what, ten men? – he will ride straight into a trap, and find himself dispossessed.' The man in the hood laughed softly – he was no priest, Keeva thought – and Maeve's eyes lit up.

'Still, we cannot afford to give that mule Finbar the opportunity to resist. The takeover must be swift and complete. With the port secure, we can ride on Dunadd. You men inside,' he indicated them, 'will make sure the gates are kept open. There will be enough confusion to buy you time – the king has left a dun seething with resentments and uncertainty; indeed, many of the warriors are not sure to whom they give their loyalty at all. That is his great weakness, and our advantage.' He met each frowning face in turn. '*So will you seize this moment*? Are you ready and willing to set this tribe to rights? It is now or never.'

The warriors agreed dourly, with no signs of excitement or pleasure. Forcing her thoughts through a storm of rage, Keeva had the presence of mind for one thing only.

She peered at every traitorous Dalriadan warrior and marked their faces, hardly daring to breathe.

Chapter 39

Cahir and Minna sat with Gede in his hall as their men prepared to depart. Their swords had now been returned to them as a mark of the alliance, and Cahir sat more easily with his against his thigh.

The gnawed bones from the feast had been thrown on the refuse pits, the spilled cups righted, the benches swept. Gede sat beneath his wall of shields, stroking the ears of an enormous grey hound that stared at Minna from unblinking golden eyes.

'This has to be done with the greatest surprise,' Gede remarked through Taran, who stood as always at his shoulder.

'And yet to muster such an army takes time. It will be hard to hide.'

'Hard to hide, yes, but essential.'

Cahir nodded. 'I will suspend all trade to and from my port. My mission to Erin can be taken in secret. The men should be mustered on land in small groups that only join when we leave the mountains for the plain that leads to the Wall. And the rest go by sea.'

Gede folded his fingers around his chin. 'There is something I have not told you. On the east coast, I have certain Roman scouts in my pay.'

'In your *pay*?'

'They were native recruits from the Votadini.' He sniffed. 'The Romans have ever been complacent about their allies, as if no one would ever think to reject the Empire once they were in it.' He smiled slyly. 'Have you never wondered why our recent raids were so successful?'

Cahir whistled. 'Then we must use them to find out how the Dux is positioning his forces now leaf-bud has come. Our best approach is to strike before he can rally his troops.'

'My thoughts exactly.'

Cahir paused. 'If you have this intelligence, then I do not think we should wait until the longest day. The longer we take to muster, the greater the chance that word leaks out to the Dux, and instead of his Wall forces alone we are faced with the entire army of the Province.'

Gede nodded. A guarded respect had grown between them. 'I will send messengers to the Saxons and extract what information I can from the scouts. Let us say by the end of the Beltaine moon we should be at the Wall. I will send you word when I have more detailed information.'

The Beltaine moon. Minna glanced at Cahir as they went out into the sunshine. Only a few weeks away. So little time to draw him into her soul, so she never forgot what he tasted like, how he smelled, his voice.

She farewelled the queen in the women's house. Her old shift, tunic and hide trousers had been burned they were so filthy, but Nessa had given her long wool dresses for the journey home, and new riding breeches. Her fur-lined cloak had been cleaned with salt, the tanned outer rubbed with wool-fat for the rain.

Nessa squeezed her hands. 'I am sorry you are leaving, Minna, and that I've been so grim. You must think me weak not to stand up to Gede. I am ashamed of it.' Her eyes fell on Drustan, gnawing on a pig-bone. 'But he has ways of holding me.'

Minna chose her words carefully. 'It is not right that you are so alone.'

Nessa pulled away, turning to the doorway to gaze out at the sun. 'Gede has made this a dun for warlords, their wives hidden away in their forts. He said he is sick of the interference of women.' She turned and smiled bleakly. 'That is why I crept in to see you that first time, just to hear and see something of the world outside.'

Minna regarded the queen with pity. 'Then I wish you were not so far away.'

'I wish so, too.' She took a breath, picked up a package of rolled linen beside the loom. 'Before you go, though, I have a gift for you.' She placed the package in Minna's hands. 'Promise you'll open this in private, and if you're wondering what they are for, remember that my heart is not so cold I do not know what new love is. Remember that whenever you smell them.'

Minna was too moved to answer, until Nessa touched her arm. 'Safe travels.'

'And you.' Impulsively, she hugged her, the queen's body thin and awkward in her arms.

When the Dalriadans rode away from the Dun of Bright Water,

Minna glanced back to the only person who climbed the walls to watch them go. Nessa raised a hand in farewell, and it glimmered white against the dark timber, small as a bird.

They rode along the great glen by the chain of dark lochs. Far above, the crests of the peaks still held snow, but on the low ground all the trees were in leaf and bracken covered the slopes.

Taran and a few Pictish warriors rode as escort. Cahir and Minna took their leave of the druid when they came to the deserted border-lands.

'You proved to be guests of a higher order than I was expecting,' Taran observed to Minna, hunching into his cloak as the cold wind pulled at it. His brows arched. 'But I doubt I will be forgetting anything about you now, Minna of Dalriada.'

He was the first person to name her so, to name her home. Her heart was still pounding as Taran took his leave of Cahir.

The Picts parted from them then, waiting at the head of a long loch while they carried on west.

West, towards the Dalriadan sea.

'But should I not go to Finbar?' Keeva whispered to Clíona, as they huddled in one of the dark alcoves in the hall.

Clíona slowly replaced the lid of the flour bin. Her face was as pale as the ground grain. 'Are you sure of what you heard, child?'

'Yes! Everything, just as I've told you.' Keeva sank onto the bin. 'Oh, gods, this is terrible!'

'Hush!' Clíona glanced around. 'You don't know who is listening, and if the queen gets wind that you know, that I know, we are both dead. *Dead*, Keeva.'

Keeva nodded, pressing her hands between her thighs.

Clíona was thinking fast. 'You must not breathe a word of this, for we have no way of knowing who is on *her* side.' She almost spat the word. 'We can only speak to Finbar.'

'But what if he is betraying the king as well?'

'Och, stupid girl!' Clíona threw her hands up. 'Finbar has been the royal family's most loyal man since I was a chit your age. It isn't pos-sible – and if he has turned traitor, then we are already lost. Now, put your cloak on and hide your hair, and seek him out for a private audience.'

But Keeva's face was stricken. 'I've just remembered: Finbar has gone to check on the outlying duns now the weather has broken. He's not here.'

'Well, we can't trust anyone else.' Clíona smoothed back her hair, steadying herself. 'And we cannot send you to chase after him, and draw attention to ourselves. We'll just have to wait for him.'

Keeva was on her feet. 'We need the king back, and quickly. Where can he be?'

Chapter 40

'How is he?' Martinus crouched by the tossing, moaning man stretched out on the army surgeon's cot.

The surgeon dipped a cloth in a bowl of vinegar and honey. On the tray beside it, the lamplight flared on a collection of forceps, scalpels and saws. 'The arrow went in deep and got lodged behind his back muscle. It took some digging to extract it, but it had already festered. Another day in the hills and he would have died.'

The youth tossed again, flinging out one arm. His torso was bound by a bandage stained with pus and blood. '*Minna!*' he cried hoarsely.

Martinus pursed his lips. 'Is it the fever making him babble so?'

The surgeon combed his beard with his fingers. 'The fever burned for days; I thought I would lose him. He's past that now, so I gave him henbane to sleep. Though it was enough to fell a larger man, he's exceedingly restless, as you can see.'

The commander smiled thinly. 'He's my best fighter; of course he's restless. I've never seen any soldier with such blind courage – he's killed twice as many vermin as anyone else.' The surgeon made no comment, clearing up his instruments. 'So when will he be fighting fit again? I need him back on the supply lines.'

'Fit?' The surgeon frowned. 'Sir, he's been very badly wounded, and the fever has wasted him. It will be a week before he is even eating properly.'

Martinus shrugged as he made for the door. 'Just patch him up and send him back out there as soon as you can. At least it wasn't his sword side, so it matters little if the muscle knits well or not, as long as it's whole.'

When he had gone, the surgeon sighed, feeling the patient's head.

The boy writhed on the sweat-soaked pillow. 'No …' he muttered under his breath, 'I ... can't ...' Suddenly those blue eyes sprang open, looking straight through the man leaning over him. 'I can't do it any more,' he said plaintively.

The army doctor peered closer. Was the soldier still in the delirium? He must be. Though he had spoken clearly, his eyes were glazed. Another draught of spiced wine might help. He busied himself at the stove.

Behind him, Cian's cracked lips moved in a whisper. 'Minna. Don't leave.'

Cahir pushed his warriors to reach Dunadd by the fire festival of Beltaine. They led their horses by moonlight along the shores of the great glen, and rose when the sky was barely light.

They were close to Brónach's hut on the mountain when a figure appeared on the slopes above the track, sliding madly down between the trees. Cahir had his men formed up around Minna, swords drawn, by the time the man burst into the open. He was small and wiry, dressed in brown and muted green so he could hardly be seen against the forest.

'Thank the gods you are back, my lord!' the man puffed, as Cahir's horse nervously danced backwards.

'What has happened?'

Sweat was pouring down the man's red face. 'I will tell you, but come into the woods where no one can see. We have been keeping a lookout for you for weeks.'

Dread crawled over Minna's skin as she listened to the man's explanation. A rebellion had been mounted by Maeve and Oran, a plan for Roman trading ships packed with Carvetii soldiers to enter the port on the day of Beltaine, before the evening feast, taking advantage of the bustle to go unnoticed.

That was in two days.

A serving girl had overheard the plot, then told Finbar. The queen's men had set lookouts for the king, too, but Finbar had sent his best scouts much further from Dunadd, so they would spot the king first. Finbar knew Cahir would not miss Beltaine, he said.

'And his plan if I did not come?' Cahir's face betrayed an immense rage, though his voice was steady.

The scout gulped at that look, shifting his bow on his back. 'He was going to lie in wait for the attack – to gain proof, my lord. He did not wish to act against the queen without you here, on hearsay alone.'

'Sensible,' Cahir said coldly, but when he turned even Minna stepped back from the ice and fire in his eyes. 'We also do not want to scare the plotters off. We must have proof of this treachery so I can expel them all, at last.'

Minna gaped. He was going to allow the ships into the bay?

'Do you know the name of the girl who heard this?' Cahir demanded of the scout.

'I ... ah ... it was the little dark-haired Attacotti, my lord. She told the maid who supervises the hall.'

Minna breathed out with relief. *Keeva and Clíona.* Cahir swung towards her, one brow raised. 'Keeva would be loyal,' she confirmed. 'I am sure of it – she often spoke of the Romans with hatred, and of the queen ... badly. And I know no woman more passionate about Dalriada and the kingship as Clíona.' Her cheeks warmed as all the men listened.

'Very well.' Cahir braced his shoulders. 'Mellan, ride to all the north duns within half a day's ride. Every available fighter must be armed and back here by dawn – as many as you can get. Any not ready, leave behind and ride like *banshees* are on your tail. Meet me by the place of the otters at sunrise.' He spun around. 'Ardal, do the same for the south, avoiding Dunadd. If you are hailed, ride on and don't let them see your face. Go now!' After all these weeks, the men moved in tandem with his thoughts and did not question. Mellan and Ardal remounted and thundered away.

Cahir beckoned to the scout. 'The girl Keeva, did she see who else was involved?'

The man nodded vigorously. 'They picked sailors from the port as well as warriors in the dun. The girl has already named who she can to Finbar.'

'Good.' For a moment Cahir gazed into the dappled sun between the oak leaves, then faced the scout. 'Listen carefully. We must disarm the traitors before an alarm can be sent to the ships, turning them back. Go and tell Finbar I am here, and will ride to the walls of Dunadd when the sun is halfway down the sky today. In the meantime, his men must shadow those traitors in Dunadd, and mark where Oran and Maeve and their men are. I want Finbar's guards in the crowds, ready to seize them at my signal. Have him also man the port with our own warriors, in disguise. Once the traitors are captured we must evacuate the port.'

'We have been trailing the traitors for days already, my lord.'

'Good. We must also disable their lookouts so I can arrive at the dun undetected. Go back and gather the men you need to accomplish that. Now, Donal.' Cahir drew him forward. 'I am certain the clifftop beacons will be in Oran's hands. Go to the Dun of the Cliff and pick a small force of men, then take the beacon back by stealth. Góban, do the same on the south headland. Whatever happens, Oran cannot have an opportunity to signal the ships and stop them from landing. Understand?'

Donal and Góban swiftly left, grim-faced. 'Fergal, Ruarc, we will give Finbar a few hours, then ride to Dunadd together. Go up to the hut now and water your horses, clean your weapons and helmets.' He smiled at Ruarc. 'This is one time you can look as impressive as you like.'

Ruarc was staring at Cahir as if he were a ghost. 'You want *me* to go with *you*?'

'Certainly.' Cahir held his eyes. 'I want all those young bucks who idolize you to see us united. When we get to Dunadd, you will order them to seize the traitors as I will order my own men. If they see us standing strong together, they will not falter.'

Ruarc swelled with pride. 'As you wish, my lord.' It was the first time he had ever called Cahir that.

When the men had dispersed, Cahir and Minna were alone in the woods. He pulled her close. '*A stór*, when we ride to Dunadd I want you to stay some way behind us. If it turns bad, whip the horse and fly as fast as you can.' His eyes burned, angry but not disappointed with this news. He wanted this confrontation.

She clutched at his tunic. 'What do you mean if it goes bad? The people support you—'

'We don't know that – we don't know anything.' Cahir gripped her face, thumbs under her eyes so she could not look away. 'I warned you, Minna. If Maeve gains the upper hand, if I am killed, you must not be captured. This plot bears the stench of the Dux, not just of Maeve and her father, I can smell it. They will hurt you, or worse. Promise me you will run.'

She gagged on her protests. Here it was, then, the reality behind the glory of Mamo's tales, the stories of men riding to war – here it was. Terror like a vice on her chest, wondering if she would see him again, or if his life would be ended in a heartbeat by a blade, or an arrow. It wasn't glorious, it wasn't proud!

'Minna! Are you listening?' Cahir shook her, and she forced herself to nod.

He cursed then and kissed her, holding her so tight she couldn't breathe.

Cahir, Minna, Fergal and Ruarc galloped across the meadow towards Dunadd with the sun stretching low across the grass. Inside her cloak and hood, Minna clung to her pony's mane as it followed Cahir's, bumping along so her teeth rattled in her jaw.

The guards along the walls caught up their spears when the four riders – three of them armed warriors – clattered across the bridge to the dun, but no horn shrieked a challenge. Finbar had done his job. Though people milling about the entrance hurried inside at their urgent approach, some men pushed themselves between the timber gates to prevent them shutting: the traitors, confused but obeying Oran's orders.

Cahir reared his black horse before the walls, throwing back his wolf-fur hood and holding up his sword. Shock ran among the warriors crowding the walls and gatehouse, the women and children. 'The king! It is the king!'

Finbar was on the palisade directly in front of the watchtower, his eyes meeting his lord's, a nod of understanding passing between them. Cahir turned to Fergal. 'Ride as fast as you can to the port and find Finbar's men now. Maeve and Oran are to be seized and held captive, the others disarmed. Hurry!' Fergal wheeled his horse and set off along the river.

'Warriors, hear me!' Cahir cried up at the walls of Dunadd, spinning his horse and trotting it back and forth. 'Treachery is being done this day! The conspirators are even now within these walls, even now at the port waiting for Roman ships to invade our lands!' Gasps punctuated the air. 'But I have returned in time, and we know who they are.' His sword stabbed high above a face lean from weeks of deprivation, scoured by wind. 'They are led by the queen, Maeve of the Carvetii, but these are *Dalriadans* who do this, warriors sworn to *me*! Traitors, I name them now, and I order them seized and held under guard! Follow Finbar!'

There were shouts as Finbar disappeared down the stairs, and scuffles broke out on the walls and behind the gates. Finbar's warriors had their swords out now, and metal clashed against metal, as women squealed and grabbed their children, fleeing further inside. Some of the traitors tried to slip out of the gates and were hauled back.

But the greater part of the Dalriadan warriors were undecided, caught in confusion. They milled about the walls and muttered among themselves, their eyes darting from Cahir to the fighting inside the dun.

All of a sudden Ruarc kicked his horse level with the king, flinging his helmet to the ground so his golden hair spilled out. '*What is this, my brothers?* Here I stand by my king's side, as loyal to his name as this treachery is vile. I say take hold of these men who would sell their people for greed, who taint the blood of every one of you in the eyes of the gods. Hurry! We have no time to lose!'

Ruarc's youthful voice was a stirring clamour, his appearance cutting through the confusion like a knife. Suddenly the warriors on the walls were screeching their rage, racing to join Finbar. The shouting intensified, and the gates were flung fully open.

By now the children and women had been dragged inside the houses, and Cahir kicked his horse through the gates into the yard. Minna's pony leaped after him, but just as she got inside, a man tumbled off the wall above. His body thudded at her feet, her pony stumbled, and she slid off its back into a pile of hay outside the stables. Lying winded in the tangle of her cloak, she stared at the dead man's face, and the bloom of blood over his chest.

'Do not kill the traitors yet!' Cahir cried, leaping to the ground. He spared a glance for Minna and, seeing she was unhurt, gestured her back against the wall. 'Take them alive if you can.'

It was over almost as soon as it had begun. A group of bruised and cut warriors were herded out by Finbar, swordless, and Finbar and Cahir embraced as the warriors clustering the walls and streets cheered.

Then Cahir took Minna's arm and pressed her up the stairs out of the surging crowd. 'Now the real test begins.' He was scanning the men. 'I make for the port, and I won't be back tonight.'

'Take care.' Minna stared at a spatter of blood across his arm, her head swimming from the fall. 'Take care you come back to me.'

Cahir glanced down and, astonishingly, grinned. His face was flushed with triumph. 'We have the advantage, my love, so do not worry.'

'Do not treat me like a foolish girl, Cahir! Who would not worry?'

His grin widened, eyes sparking. 'Not a girl, no.' He looked as if he might kiss her, then merely squeezed her hand and raced back down the stairs. 'To me, all of you who ride! We must away to the port and lay ambush for the invaders at dawn. *To me!*'

Minna ran up the stairs out of the way as dozens of horses were loosed from the stables, men throwing themselves up bareback, brandishing swords. As the tide of warriors flowed out of the gate and over the marsh, the dun suddenly emptied, women rushing out to watch them go. Minna hurried up the path to the crag, scrambling up the rock steps past the king's hall to the cliff edge. There she stared into the flaming heart of the sun, watching Cahir streaking away along the trade path.

'Minna, Minna!' Orla and Finola flung themselves at her, screeching like wildcats. She hugged them back, trying to answer their questions, as Lia leaped and yapped, running around in circles chasing her tail. Then Keeva and Clíona came up behind them, and she extracted herself long enough to catch Keeva's arms. 'You saved him!' she cried, nearly insensible with relief. 'I can never thank you, never.' She looked over Keeva's shoulder to Clíona. 'The king knows of your part in this, too, both of you. I swore to him you would be loyal – I knew I was right.'

The words poured from her, and she did not pause to think what change had been wrought in her since she left. But Keeva, who had opened her mouth to cry a greeting and then shut it, held Minna now at arm's length.

Clíona was also staring in profound shock. 'What happened to you?

We heard about the children in the dun.' She clucked and shook her head. 'You have been the talk of Dunadd for weeks. Saving all those babies and then disappearing, and the king with you ...' She trailed away, for once speechless.

'Minna,' Keeva said slowly. 'The king?'

Then Minna realized she had instinctively spoken of Cahir with passion in her voice. 'I cannot explain now,' she stammered, suddenly becoming aware of Orla's green eyes fixed on her face.

Clíona and Keeva exchanged glances, then Keeva shrugged, trying to smile. 'Tell us later, if you wish – I am just glad you are back safely, whatever happened. When I heard what I did, at first I didn't know what to do ...'

Keeva blurted out the whole story, as Orla and Finola clung to Minna's legs and the sun sank. After fielding another torrent of questions, at long last Minna glanced up to steady herself, and there grew still. On the other side of the king's hall, a lonely figure was standing looking out across the marsh, huddled in a dark cloak.

Brónach's cold eyes shifted from the horizon to Minna's face and there paused. By the jolt of recognition she knew that, of all people, Brónach understood exactly how she had changed.

Chapter 41

The band of Finbar's warriors who had cordoned off the port were hidden in the woods. They recognized Fergal immediately and signalled him to halt. In twos and threes they then crept in among the narrow streets, and seized the small group of traitors before they could defend themselves.

Maeve and Oran, holed up awaiting the dawn, were run down and captured as they tried to escape across the winding channels of silt at the river mouth, dragging the prince Garvan with them. By the time Cahir arrived the port was already his.

Dusk was falling, the sunset gilding the water. The headland that shielded the bay from the sea was already steeped in shadow. Cahir ordered the Dalriadan traders, fishermen and farmers, and all women and children evacuated to Dunadd. Any remnant Roman traders were put under guard, as were Cahir's wife and son, whom he could not yet face. Nearby he quartered Oran. The so-called priest – in reality an assassin provided by King Eldon – killed three of Cahir's men with the dagger under his cloak before being brought down by weight of numbers and impaled on a spear.

Cahir tried to put them all out of his mind, his rage at Maeve and his pain over his son held in check by cold thought until this rebellion was dealt with and he could release it.

On the morning of Beltaine, the sun rose over a choppy sea, whipped up by a southerly wind. Cahir stood helmeted and armed, his wolf-fur cloak thrown aside to reveal his polished mailshirt and long sword at his waist. He raised his head and sniffed the wind: this would fill the sails of any craft heading north.

The sheltered bay was cut off from sightlines to the ocean, which was why Cahir kept beacons ready on the cliffs to sound an alarm for raiders. This morning the raiders would come, but there would be no alarm.

When the sun was a handspan over the eastern hills, a man on horse-back came galloping down the track from the southern cliffs. It was Donal, puffing from the effort, his cheeks so sun-burned they merged into his ruddy moustache. 'The ships have been sighted,' he reported to Cahir.

'Well?' The king turned to the man curled on the sand at his feet, his arms bound behind him.

The fisherman squirmed. 'There will be two ships, with double masts and red-painted sails.' He bit his lips, shuddering too hard to continue.

Finbar cursed and kicked his rump. 'Come on, out with it!'

The man scooted away from Finbar's boot. Cahir did not move. This traitor had capitulated as soon as he lined him up with his companions the day before, screeching that he had been forced – he didn't want to go against his king – that he would tell them everything in exchange for his life.

Now Cahir glanced at Donal, who nodded. 'Two masts, there are, my lord. Red sails.'

'Good,' Cahir said encouragingly to the traitor. 'You are pleasing me. Go on.'

The man shot a pleading look at his king. 'That is how we were to know them. But when they land, four men will come off first, just four. The others will pour ashore only at the signal.'

Cahir squinted at the sunlight now shining on the mudflats at the rivermouth, then turned to his men. Ruarc, Mellan and Ardal were back together again after the latter two brought fifty men apiece in from the outlying duns, giving him a force of three hundred in all. 'Here is what we do. I want Eldon's men thinking all is well when they land, so we need to draw them off the ships. Set a score of men without armour or weapons to pose as fishermen and carters on the pier and nearby streets. The rest are to hide anywhere they can.' He turned to his younger warriors. 'Pots of coals are also to be set up behind the first line of houses, and good archers alongside. If they don't come off at once, we will fire the ships.'

As he turned away, the fisherman whined again. 'And me, my lord? You must spare my life, as you said? I have told you everything, every-thing!'

Cahir paused and gazed down at him coldly. '*You* offered this in-formation in exchange for your life. I never promised any such thing.' Without a backwards glance he strode away, ignoring the wail of defeat and terror that rose like a gull's cry above the waves.

Under full sail, two sleek ships with painted eyes on their bows glided into the bay of Dunadd.

Ahead, all seemed normal to the commander of the Carvetii forces, a Roman centurion with many years of service to the Dux under his belt. He squinted at the shore. Cookfires hazed the thatch roofs of the port. Men went about their business, unloading fish from *curraghs*, heaving sacks into carts. Log-boats trailed nets as they criss-crossed the river mouth. Washing flapped on ropes between the houses.

The furthest house to the right was set on a spur of rock, and flew a long, tattered banner of red wool from its roof. So the signal was in place; all was well. The Dalriadans shuffling about had no inkling that their lives were about to change.

The commander slid down the ladder into the hold, where the Carvetii warriors crouched in rows. 'Keep your swords hidden. Wait until you hear my whistle, then get ashore as swiftly as you can. It is imperative we take them by surprise.'

A greater number and size of ships would have alerted the Dalriadans that these were no traders, so they could only bring eighty men in total. King Eldon had informed him there was only a small guard in the port itself, however, and the rebels would have dealt with them by now.

Tucked around the corner of a storehouse, his helmet pulled over his brow, Cahir watched the ships tie up on the pier.

'I assume you won't charge out at the front,' Donal muttered in his ear.

'Why, Donal,' he murmured, 'you would deny me my blood-right? This is treason against the person of the king, as well as the tribe.'

Donal snorted. 'We haven't come so far for you to be cut down by a lucky stroke from some Carvetii pig.' He paused. 'Anger makes one hasty.'

'Anger makes one swift,' Cahir countered.

'I think the lady would prefer it if you didn't risk your blood on this day.'

Cahir glanced at Donal from the corner of his eye, amused in that heart-pounding, light-headed way that comes with the rush of energy just before a fight.

He turned back to his vigil. For too long his hands had been bound like those of the prisoners. He had been forced to hold his head high, while shamed inside. Now, at last, it could come to this simple thing: his sword against another's, muscle sparring with muscle. There was no substitute for the pleasure gained when a man's awareness could narrow to that pinprick of focus – kill or be killed. So simple and pure. 'I will run as fast as my legs carry me. If you are too old and can't keep up, that's your problem.'

Another snort, but then men were disembarking from the first ship. One. Two. Cahir's palm was slippery around his hilt, so he wiped it down his leg, taking care not to show the blade to the sun. Three. The war-cry rose in his throat, held back like a hound on a leash.

Four.

Four men who, to his practised eye, possessed the lop-sided body strength of fighters, not traders or sailors. Time slowed, as everything happened at once.

As he heard their commander's whistle, Cahir put back his head and released his voice. 'The Boar!' he bellowed, just as Eremon had cried of old. The shout was taken up by men all over the port, rising in a wave that broke over the shore. Donal shot out from the cover of the shed, his sword whirling above his head. Warriors poured out of every side street, cloaks thrown aside to reveal their blades.

As Cahir sprinted for the pier, his legs pumping, arrows of fire began arcing over his head. Some sizzled into the sea, some set alight the barrels and posts on the pier, as black smoke crawled into the sky. But many found their mark, and in moments both ships were alight, the masts spears of fire, the ropes throwing flames across the decks.

The men from the ships were white-faced with fear, shouting over the tumult to their comrades to throw off the ropes and row. But there was no chance, as those onboard were driven out by the smoke and flames, men flinging themselves into the shallow water and stumbling to shore.

Cahir struck and twisted, his blade passing through flesh and into ribs, buried in the space between vertebrae. He caught a slash across the forearm but savoured the burn, for the man was dead in the next stroke and he was spinning to face another.

There was only the chance for two more kills, for the Carvetii were outnumbered, having expected to face a village of farmers and women, not warriors. To Cahir's right, Donal, Finbar and Fergal were mopping up a knot of men who had run down the beach, moving as one after long years of fighting side by side. To his left, Ruarc was a golden god, taking on two men and laughing, while Mellan and Ardal danced around him with their own opponents.

The fire was still crackling on the ships when it was all over.

The messengers rode back to Dunadd after sunrise. Minna went to Orla and Finola and woke them, her heart heavy.

Carefully, she explained what had happened to their mother; that she would be leaving to go back to Luguvalium now. Then she left a pause. She knew the girls had not been close to Maeve, that they felt desperately unloved. But she was their mother.

They stared up at Minna with round eyes. 'I don't want to leave the hills and our ponies,' Orla announced at last, brushing hair angrily from her brow. 'Or Lia, because the Romans don't like dogs much.'

Minna regarded her gravely, holding Finola's hand. 'I know you don't want to leave, and you do not have to. You are princesses of Dalriada, and your place is with your father.' They had to make their way through this in their own way.

Orla's lip quavered, and she babbled on as if she did not hear Minna, her eyes glazed. '*And* I could not leave Davin, or his harp, could I? Or the songs, or the river, or the woods.'

Minna shook her head, as Finola crawled silently into her lap and curled up there like the puppy, trembling.

The sun was high, and the Dalriadan traitors were lined up on the beach on their knees, Cahir pacing before them. These were the ones who had been taken at Dunadd's gates.

To one side stood Maeve, her hair tumbled from its curls, her plump face streaked with tears and saliva. A bruise shadowed her jaw; Cahir did not much care who had inflicted it. Oran's neat clothes were rumpled and stained with blood where he had caught a sword-nick on his wrist during capture. His carefully bland face was now twisted with contempt.

Cahir's mind was buzzing, but he needed to keep a grip on his emotions. If he executed Maeve and Oran, Eldon would attack with a greater force and begin a blood-feud. Cahir could not afford to have the Carvetii king anywhere near his lands while he mustered his army for the Roman attack.

He stopped. Maeve's eyes bored into him with fanatic hatred, and he itched to strike her down. But that was the impulse of an angry young man, not a king. A king kept a cool head. And Garvan was still under guard. Cahir would have no chance to heal *that* rift if the boy's mother died by his father's hand. He knew he had no choice but to banish Maeve to Luguvalium.

Eldon had broken oath with him, and he felt very certain the Carvetii king would lick his wounds for some time, at least long enough to give Cahir a breathing space. And before Eldon could decide his next move, the combined forces of Alban and Erin Dalriada and the Attacotti chiefs – thousands of men – would arrive at his gates and that problem would be solved.

Cahir stood before his wife. In an icy tone he said, 'Lady, you are a traitor to your king and to your people. But you will be pleased to know that, despite your life being forfeit, I have decided to spare it.'

Maeve's face clenched, and she tried to spit at him. 'Traitor?' she screeched. 'They are not *my people* and you are not *my king*! And despite *this* I still tried to do the best for them, to bring you into the real world but you would not heed me—'

'Lady!' Oran interrupted. Cahir saw the relief in his eyes when he heard they would live. He really thought Cahir would kill them – because that is what he would have done, in a heartbeat. 'There is nothing to say now.'

'No, there is not,' Cahir agreed, slowly exhaling. 'These are your charges: threatening a rightful king with death; bringing an enemy force onto Dalriadan lands; and supporting the Romans, would-be conquerors of our people. As you so succinctly put it, Maeve, you are not of us, of Dalriada. With your contempt you made that plain from the day you arrived. So now, Dalriada *expels* you.'

The word had a satisfying ring to it, Cahir thought, as his men smothered smiles and Maeve spluttered. Before she could speak again, Oran nudged her into silence. She shifted her glare to him.

Cahir wasn't finished. 'You came to me with a payment, a dowry, but you have forfeited this now by your treachery, so your own return to your father is the mark of our divorce.' *That* tasted well in his mouth. He nodded at Ruarc, Mellan and Ardal. 'Keep them under guard and ready a boat.' He smiled broadly at Maeve. 'A small one, open to the sky. One that has carried many fish, I think. And four guards and two sailors. They can leave tomorrow.'

If Maeve had not already lost all decorum, she did now. Yowling, she writhed in Ruarc's arms. In the end, he and his sword-mates dragged her bodily away, Oran prodded along behind at the tip of a sword.

Cahir turned from the shore and briefly closed his eyes. So it was done. The tension that had kept his blood pumping for two days now was leaching away, leaving exhaustion in its wake. But he had much more to do.

Tonight was Beltaine, a most auspicious time to announce the change in himself, his kingship and the fate of Dalriada. The time, at last, to be with Minna in the brief flicker of light before war closed in.

He braced his shoulders and met Donal's eyes. The men lined up on their knees all had their heads down, the white skin on their necks exposed. At each end of the pitiful row, Cahir's men rested their weight casually on their unsheathed swords, murmuring to each other.

He steeled himself from pity. There could be no weakness, no quarter given. 'Kill them,' he ordered, accepting into his heart the wails of fear from the captured men. This was a price he would pay for his kingdom.

When the bodies were tossed on a pyre, and the bloody sand kicked into the sea and washed away, Cahir gathered his trusted warriors together. 'Go now,' he said, 'into every house and every byre in Dunadd, every dun within an hour's ride, and tell the people there exactly what has happened and what we have won. And call them to attend the Beltaine rite this night to hear from their king's mouth what the gods want of us now.'

Chapter 42

Cahir rode back to Dunadd alone in the still afternoon, smoke smearing the horizon behind him. It was well his horse knew the path, for though the king stared straight ahead, he was not seeing the marsh with its spangled pools, or the glimpse of his hall on its crag ahead.

All he could see was Garvan's tear-stained face.

Father and son had conducted an audience alone. Cahir knew Garvan had been left with his mother too often, and now he had cause to rue that mistake, for he'd been shocked by how Maeve had poisoned the boy's mind against him and Dalriada. It took some time to understand his own folly: he simply had not foreseen that he, of all people, could sire an heir so lacking in Alban pride and connection to his blood.

As they spoke, the boy's coldness turned from sneers to shouting, Maeve's words spilling from him like a gush of dirty water. Cahir listened and said nothing as his own shock bled into anger, and then pity. For his son was repeating his mother's feelings when his quivering mouth and stilted voice betrayed something else.

Gently Cahir had to probe for it, stripping away the assertions, cornering the child with unwavering firmness. At last the exhausted Garvan broke, and the truth came out, and what was underneath was not hatred at all. Grinding his fists into his eyes, he looked at Cahir with the hurt of a wounded animal. 'I cannot be you, Father! I cannot! So I won't be!'

Cahir didn't understand. 'You are my son and heir—'

'I am not!' Garvan's face was swollen with tears. 'I can't fight like you, I don't look like you or sound like you – I'm *not* you and I never will be *enough*.'

This was why he wanted to be Roman? Cahir tried to reach him, but the boy hunched into the wall and turned his face away. And that was how Cahir had to leave him in the end, with instructions for Fergal to bring him back in two days when his anger had cooled.

Now Cahir nudged his stallion into a trot across the marsh, the wind cold on his set face. Garvan was the heir – he must be brought back into the fold. With Maeve gone it could be accomplished, given time. It was as he approached the gates of Dunadd that he forcibly put that pain aside.

For it was Beltaine night, and already the wood for the bonfire was being carted down the valley to the river meadow. Cooksmoke curled from every house with the scent of honey cakes. Beltaine ... this was the time for Minna, at last, and tonight that would be all that mattered.

Urged on by the lean in his body, the horse broke into a gallop.

While Clíona bathed the girls in the queen's hall, Minna sat on their bed in a linen shift. She had climbed up to the shadowed gallery because she didn't know where else to go. Everyone was treating her with hesitation, their eyes darting sideways to her when they thought she wasn't looking.

That morning, Orla had picked some of the may-blossom that was festooning the woods all around the dun with clouds of fragrant white blooms. Minna sat now twirling a sprig in her fingers, her mind racing. She felt a stirring in the air and earth around her, an expectant, breathless weight, heralding ... what?

She was so absorbed in the flower, her brow creased, that one moment she was alone and the next Cahir was there. He was muddy, his clothes smeared with charcoal, his eyes red-rimmed from smoke. But they glowed, despite his grimy face.

'What are you doing here?' he croaked.

Minna gazed at him uncertainly, until suddenly he smiled. '*A stór,* this is not your bed any more.' And taking her hand and the lamp, he led her to the bedplace she had rushed past with Brónach on that first day at Dunadd. There were no dressing tables or mirrors here, only a single chest at the foot of a bed which took up the entire space under the eaves, covered in furs. Cahir unbuckled his sword-belt and tossed it to the bed, and then sank backwards on it with a groan.

Minna pulled off his muddy boots and sat by him, taking his hand. His knuckles were grazed, the folds of skin stained with something dark. She looked at the dried blood, and hesitantly touched it.

He followed her eyes, then stared at the roof. 'Minna,' he said softly, 'when you were a girl and you thought about your future love, was he a farmer coming in from the fields, drawing your child into his lap? Or a merchant, perhaps, in your city house, shutting up shop to gather around the fire?' His eyes roamed over the thatch. 'I am sure you never thought of a man with blood on his hands, with so many baying for his death, who in one day nearly lost a kingdom, then gained it again.' He smiled bleakly at her. 'You're much too clever to want that.'

She recognized the strain in his voice, and raised his bloodied hand to her mouth to kiss it before folding it around the sprig of flowers. 'I did not think of any man at all – for you were entirely unimaginable.'

His smile melted the weariness and pain in his face, and he drew her with him to the bed, pushing the scabbard aside. He smelled of musty horse, his dark hair stiff with salt in her fingers. Tilting up her chin, he kissed her, his fingers tracing her eyelids, brows and cheeks as if committing them to memory, and she sighed as his lips moved to her throat, arched back for him.

When he straightened, his eyes fell on the blooms crushed into the folds of her shift. 'They are the Beltaine flowers – may-blossom. Did you know?'

She nodded breathlessly. 'Orla picked them at the river. I think it was her way of coping, to talk and run and not meet my eyes.'

Cahir touched the blossoms with a finger. 'My daughters love you. That will overcome anything.'

She slid a hand across his belly and rested her head on his shoulder. 'I almost didn't notice how the land has changed, how leaf-bud has come. I couldn't think of anything but you, and whether you were safe. But then I felt it today, when I waited on the walls for you to come back. I smelled the air, saw the woods white with flowers.' She hesitated. 'We went away in the cold, and now everything has changed. It is not only Orla and Finola who must accept this.' She thought of herself, the servants, and also Brónach, who the day before would not speak to her, turning her shoulder and stalking away.

'That is what Beltaine means, Minna. It is change.'

She stared into the lamp-flame. It flickered as if someone murmured to her. *Yes.* 'The land comes alive, throws off dark and cold for light and warmth – I feel it running in my blood.'

He searched her eyes with wonder. 'You *do* know, don't you? I always wanted to feel the heartbeat of the land which the bards sing of – a king is supposed to feel that.'

Minna pulled herself up, her hair pooling in her lap. 'But a king can only be bound to his land by the goddess of the land.' The flame dipped before her eyes. 'Davin said so once.'

'And the goddess was supposed to be his queen.'

But that had not happened here, and the harvest had been bad for years. Cahir kissed the tender skin of her wrist, drawing her back. 'Minna, Beltaine is also the feast of fertility.' He held her eyes. 'I hurried our return because I wanted to tell my people of my new course *tonight*, when they will feel its truth. And I need you by my side as Beltaine queen.'

He spoke as if she might refuse, and fear did flicker like a shadow over the lamp-flame. But the air was whispering gladness to her. She touched the fragile may-blossom and felt the blooms in the woods opening, the sap in the trees rising, the quickening of the land around her. And suddenly she knew what this night would bring. 'We must join,' she said wonderingly, shifting her gaze to his golden eyes. 'We must be one in body, this night.'

He breathed out, pressed a hand to her cheek. 'I know what I ask of you. But it is said that a great love between the Beltaine queen and king will bring fertile blessings to the land, if they give themselves up to the power of the night.' He hesitated. 'It isn't what I wanted for the first time, for we must share ourselves with the world as well as each other. Do you understand?'

'Yes. And as I am a maiden, this brings its own power.' A chord struck inside her: did Rhiann do this? She touched the blood on his fingers again and shuddered as if waking. 'You need this protection – you need all the power we can summon for this war. My blood will mingle with your seed and draw it to us. It is how it must be.'

He was disconcerted by her far-away tone, though she was merely awed by its rightness, as if she had been looped into an unbroken thread stretching into the past.

'I don't want it to be all about a sacrifice, Minna,' he broke in, taking hold of her arms. 'I want it to be us, too.'

Minna smiled softly at him. 'But can't you feel that?' And she took his hand and placed it over her breast, so he could sense how her heart raced.

At dusk Keeva came to ready her with a group of serving girls.

'I am sorry,' Keeva whispered to her, 'but the king has ordered it. We must make you the Beltaine queen, and this night pays respect to the fertility of maidens.' She sighed, gesturing behind her. 'And here are the maidens.' Keeva was the only one unperturbed by Minna's change in status.

She smiled anxiously. 'As long as none of them bear anything of the queen's.'

'Gods, no!' Keeva grinned, pulling her up. 'What fool do you take me for?'

They bathed her in the queen's hall, stripped now of everything Roman, everything of Maeve's. As the maids drew hot cloths over Minna's skin the steam rose around her, and suddenly she understood she was not being readied as a mare is groomed for her stallion. She was washing away all traces of what she had been, and becoming something else. Something sacred.

They dried her with scented linen and wrapped her in soft wool. Orla and Finola hovered solemnly nearby, awed by their glimpse of this intimate woman's rite. Only one thing was wrong: the cold metal of the slave-ring on her warm skin. She touched it, but Keeva drew her fingers away with a knowing smile. 'Do not worry. Put it out of your mind.'

So she gave herself up to the soft hands combing her hair, drawing it into long curls. Keeva stood back, scrutinizing her. 'Perhaps oil of myrrh?'

'Not myrrh!' Minna would always associate that scent with Maeve. Instead, she suddenly remembered Nessa's gift, and how she had spoken of new love and of scent. 'Orla.' Minna turned to her. 'There is a small package beside your father's bed. Go and get it for me.' Orla dashed off. The gift, unwrapped in Minna's lap, proved to be a collection of small blue bottles. When she pulled out the stoppers they were perfumed oils: wild roses, musk and honeysuckle. It was an extravagant gift.

Keeva beamed, ordering the maids to rub every inch of Minna's skin with oil: under the curve of her breasts, in the dip of her waist, down her thighs. She stood naked, enveloped in the rich scents, the smoothing touches sending her out of herself into another place, and so, miraculously, she felt no shame or shyness.

For Cahir had named her *many-born*, and she knew in that moment she had once stood in another time, dark-eyed and dusky-skinned, while servants oiled her body beneath an awning of scarlet silk, making her ready for a husband. Her blood pulsing, she focused on the memory of hands on her skin and gold on her arms and ankles. *Every sensation must be felt.* She heard the murmur from ancient teachings. *Open the maiden's body slowly with sense and touch and smell, and the silken gateway will be entered without pain.*

They finished as Riona appeared at the door with lengths of cloth over her arm. Minna noted the swell of the babe under her clothes and their eyes met, though Riona's smile was uncertain.

'Greetings, Minna,' she said formally. 'I have been ordered to bring you a dress of mine.' She tried to dispel her discomfort with a laugh. 'I don't fit into it any more, and I can't blame the baby, I have to say!'

Minna fingered the cloth in awe. There was a shift of white linen and a long-sleeved underdress of cream wool. Over that went a sleeveless robe of fresh green, with a belt wrought of gold leaves. 'The belt is not mine,' Riona added swiftly. 'The king chose it from the treasury. Along with this.' She indicated the girl who had come in behind her, holding on a cushion an astonishing headdress. On a fillet of gold, vines of bronze wound about berries of amber and garnet, trailing gilded leaves over the wearer's forehead. 'I have not seen it since I was a child. I think it belonged to the king's mother.'

Minna could not speak, while the serving girls whispered behind their hands. Riona's curiosity was naked. They would all wait and see what this night brought, her look said, before they knew how to address her. She was being set beside the king as Beltaine queen. But why?

The fillet was placed in her hair, and rings with bells slipped on her fingers and ankles; they chimed as she walked. Lastly, Finola and Orla wound the may-blossoms all through her dark tresses with their small fingers, and she touched their faces and kissed them.

Outside, a horn blew. Minna straightened, her blood flowing faster, bringing her back from the past.

Cahir addressed his people on the darkened meadow. Somewhere, hidden in the shadows under the trees by the river, Minna waited. But he had to win his people first.

His warriors and fast riders had done their work spreading the news, and the moonlit grass was a shifting sea of people; a crowd of perhaps two or three thousand. Nobles had been summoned from all the outlying duns, as swift as their horses could carry them, as well as every farmer and herder and their wives and babes from the nearby glens.

Here it would be decided, then, if they heeded his words.

He drew strength from the presence of his men at his shoulder: burly Finbar and Gobán with hands folded on swords, legs braced; Mellan looking belligerently around, wary for any slight; Ardal smiling secretly behind his black hair. And Ruarc, adorned with so much bronze he was on fire, staring out into the crowd as if daring anyone to disagree.

'My people!' Cahir's voice carried far in the cold air. 'You know the treachery that I faced on my return, and how the Carvetii attack was foiled by the bravery and loyalty of our warriors. We are safe, and the traitors, including the former queen, have been dealt with.'

That part was easy. People were fired up by the shock of the raid, the rage and then relief, the excitement of the bonfires and dancing to come – and in no small measure by the mead they had already imbibed.

'This you know, but you don't know why I left and what happened on my journey. Now, I will tell you it all.' With a breath he drew into himself now all his power, his awe, his memory of the night in the cave when his men acclaimed him, and the light in Minna's eyes when she spoke the visions.

Above all, he summoned the power of the prophecy, and when he cried it to his people, he now heard the echo of all those who had first chanted it, who had wanted him to remember.

At long last, he knew Eremon was at his shoulder.

Seated on the white mare beneath the oak trees, Minna heard the shouts growing louder. *Dalriada! Dalriada!*

The cry went on, and the pipers and drummers standing by for the dancing joined in as if it were a song. Peering through the leaves, she glimpsed the torchlight gleam once on Cahir's sword as he held it up and pierced the sky. *Dalriada! Dalriada!*

He had won them. Though she had not heard his words, Minna knew he had spoken like a god, invoking what his people longed for: freedom, pride in their blood, and a strong king who would fight for them. Like his men, their mood had been hidden, buried so deep they did not know their own hearts. They never believed it could be different, and so swallowed their anger and frustration like a bitter root, shoved down where it did not choke, only festered. Waiting for their lord to wake from his pain and release them from theirs.

'It is time.' The maidens escorting Minna had been silent, but now Riona, who had taken charge, gestured Donal to lead the white mare forward.

As they came out of the trees under the stars, the attendants in front and behind began chanting a low, throaty song. They walked with a sway in their hips, slowing the pony to a rhythmic walk so Minna also began to sway in the saddle, the slow, sensual movement passing from the pony's stride through its flanks to her own flesh, rocking her. The gold leaves in the headdress brushed her forehead, white flowers fluttered from her hair and, with every step, the bells on her ankles chimed.

The girls around her clapped in time to the song, and Keeva, holding the saddle, glanced up, her mouth forming the words. It was an old chant about the Maiden of the fields. Where she trod, the earth bloomed, and the god that took her and made her his own became king of the land. Soon, Minna found her lips and throat moving as well, the words winding about her soul, demanding to be sung. The movement of the pony and her body sent her into a trance.

And then she was approaching a dark sea of people, and the sea parted, leaving a river of grass that wound its way to Cahir's feet. As if in a dream, Minna looked out over the thousands of white faces, their breath misting the air like a cloud, before fixing her eyes on Cahir where he stood on a wooden platform between two flaming bonfires. The bath, the oils and the singing had all conspired to loosen the bounds of Minna's body, and there on the horse, surrounded by the people, something greater began filling her. Something more powerful than herself.

As she reached Cahir she heard the whispers and murmurs growing all around, rumours of her healing skills and the miracle of the sick babies, passed from person to person.

As soon as the horse was before him, Cahir raised his hands. 'And so you may wonder what great seer saw these visions I speak of; who brought your king back to his strength.'

Minna could not draw her gaze from him. The corona of light was more than a crown; it was a flame engulfing his whole body. He was a god. On his head he bore a war-helm of domed iron now, on top a crested boar wrought in polished bronze.

'Here is your seer!' Cahir was drunk with a savage joy, and she tensed as he extended one hand towards her. 'Minna of Eboracum, the slave-girl that was!'

A cacophony greeted this revelation: shock, excitement and disbelief. Heart pounding, Minna held to the shine of Cahir's eyes as if she were drowning.

He told them what she had done, and seen, just as she had repeated it faithfully to Darach the chief druid when he probed her that afternoon. Some people grew restless after Cahir's telling, as if they might argue, but then their eyes flew between Minna and the king. Vibrating with the sense of the Other, Minna felt the understanding sink through their minds. Minna and Cahir *were one*.

'And what say you, chief druid?' Cahir spun towards Darach.

'My lord,' Darach offered, unblinking. 'We have examined the stone, and tested the girl; we have consulted the stars and the entrails of a raven; and we conclude that her visions are true.' He smiled enigmatically. 'The gods are apt to provide their messages and signs through unexpected means. As to the other, the question of war – all people know the Romans are no friends of the brethren.'

The king replied with a gracious nod, while Minna's belly churned. 'So the choice is made,' Cahir boomed, 'to fight for who we are, to listen to the gods, to do their will on earth and regain our pride. In the coming days, I will answer all your questions until there are none. But for now, know that my own choices have also been made.'

His eyes were at last on Minna, warm and liquid, and Donal's hands were on her waist lifting her down, and in that moment the old warrior, irreverent as always, caught her eye and winked. She looked at Cahir's hand extended towards her and could not move, until Keeva bowed and nudged her on. And so she let Cahir catch her fingers and draw her up on the platform.

She saw nothing for a long moment but the blaze in Cahir's face, and behind him, the shining points of his men's eyes in the firelight.

'My people, I bring you one who is not only *seer*, voice of the gods, but one of the many-born who once long ago was of my royal blood. Now she has returned to us.' Cahir paused, his smile tender. 'And so I also name her my *lennan*, dearly beloved of the king.'

Her heart was a bird caught in a snare, beating wildly, and in that moment of disorientation Cahir delivered his last surprise. With a turn of his head he beckoned someone forward, and Minna could only stare at Fintan the smith as he emerged into the firelight, a hammer and chisel in his broad hands. Lonán followed, hoisting a block of wood and wad of linen.

'As I take her as my *lennan*,' Cahir announced, 'and the seer of my hall, so I free Minna of Eboracum.' There was an exclamation of pleasure from Clíona, and this was taken up by many others in the crowd. Smiling, Cahir raised Minna's trembling hand to his lips and then led her off the platform.

She saw only a blur of wondering faces as Lonán set the block down and Cahir unclasped his cloak and spread it on the ground. 'Lady.' Fintan bowed. 'Do not be afraid, for if you kneel there, and we put this pad under your ring, I can strike it off with no pain at all.'

She didn't trust herself to speak, and under a great silence she knelt and laid her head on the block, fixing her eyes on the rising sliver of moon as the smith positioned his chisel on the hinge of the ring. The Lady had given Minna strength when the hated ring was bound around her neck, and now She was here to see her freed.

'Breathe out,' Fintan instructed, and swiftly struck the chisel with his hammer. Suddenly the iron ring was in pieces on the ground.

There was a clamorous cheer, as Cahir raised her to her feet and held her there. She was swaying, light-headed. 'As we strike off the bonds of Roman slavery from Minna of Eboracum, now Minna of Dalriada, so we strike off the Roman shackles from our own necks!' Cahir cried, and before everyone he circled her waist and kissed her.

At this, the people went wild. *This* was the excitement they longed for after the dreary season of endless dark. Their brooding king had been transformed into a figure of legend, and he had a maiden by his side, not the hated Carvetii princess.

Minna smiled even as her eyes stung, her mouth curving against Cahir's in a secret joy they shared alone. The musicians could no longer be contained, and the pipes had immediately broken into song, backed by urgent drumming.

'Lord.' It was Darach. Behind him, dancers had joined the music, for there seemed nothing more to be said, and much to celebrate. 'We will bless the cattle now, driving them between the fires, but the betrothed couples await you to be wed.' He hesitated, glancing at Minna, then merely nodding gracefully. 'My lady.'

Cahir looked down at her, his excitement flowing free. His people had acclaimed him this night as if this was his true crowning, banishing all pain. 'It is really your blessing they await, *a stór*, not mine.'

'Mine?'

'You are the queen of the may this night, and they have not had the royal blessing of love for many years, or felt the earth quicken as it should. But it is quickening now.'

Yes, Minna cried, as she was taken to the bonfires and showered with more hawthorn blossom. Cahir blessed the betrothed youths with the flat of his sword, and as the druids gave Minna a bowl of rowan ash, milk and honey, the first of the girls was bending her head before her. It was Keeva ... Keeva and Lonán, of course. This blessing would seal their marriage, and those of all the others waiting in line.

Her world stood still. She must summon the Source and call it home, as Darine said the Sisters once did. Closing her eyes, Minna blocked out the shrieks of merriment and bawling of the cattle, surrendering all thought, all feeling to become the vessel. *I am yours, my Goddess, in service to your people. Give now of your Source, to make the land, your flesh, fruitful, so that your people may prosper.*

The ancient vow was released from her heart, transforming the world around her. Suddenly, she could feel the Source pooling under her feet as a vibrating warmth. In her spirit-eye it became streams of light running together into one river that flowed up her body. She swelled with it, expanded, her skin glowing, and in that heat, that light, that surrender, another presence came and filled her body.

The Goddess. The energy of Mother. The single essence of all goddesses as one, worshipped by different names but the same – an immense love, compassion and grace that overflowed from Minna in tears, for she could not contain it all.

The light was a flooding wave, pushing her far out across the world, and swirling within its currents was all knowledge, all the answers to every question. Minna's own soul, a bobbing flame, was carried along in the tide. She was so close to it all ... so close to knowing everything ... she could put out her hand and capture it, know it ... why she was here ... what she was ... *who spoke to her in dreams ... who loved her ...*

She heard a gasp. Her eyes flew open and she was back, looking directly into Keeva's upturned face.

The maid's clever smile was gone, transfigured with awe. Overcome, she clasped her hands together, bowing her head. 'Lady,' she breathed, and this time Minna knew it was not given as a formal address to the king's *lennan*, but to the Other who walked in her body.

As her own spirit stood aside, awed, Minna saw her finger dip into the ash paste without volition and draw a spiral on Keeva's forehead. 'Be strong and open in heart,' her voice flowed, wise and deep as oceans. 'Be fruitful in body and compassionate in soul. The Lady's blessings on your union.'

When Keeva got to her feet, for the first time Minna saw tears in her black eyes as she reached for Lonán's hand. Then, one by one, the maidens came before Minna, and their men before Cahir, as a reverent hush descended on the hill. The silence spread to the dancers, who began to slow, and the musicians and those drinking at the ale kegs, who fell into whispers.

By the time she marked the last girl, the pool of the Source in Minna's belly had moved lower, pulsating. As the land was burgeoning, flooding with sap and new life, so it was coursing through her body. And when Cahir dropped his sword and turned to her, she looked into the face of the God, his eyes alight with stars.

'Take me to the ancestor valley,' she whispered, both of them moving blindly towards each other. 'It must be there.'

He led her to the horse and lifted her up, and all the while the awed silence spread around them. The sea of people parted once more, their faces shining, as Cahir rode back across the river meadow. Hands reached out to touch Minna's dress and catch the flowers that fell from her crown. Eyes glowed in the light of the bonfires.

Cahir rode past Dunadd to the north, the Source thundering in their blood. Clinging to his waist, Minna melted into his warm body as if they were already one. The moon was just high enough to light the path, drawing them on.

He left the horse by a circle of buried stones and, taking her in his arms, plunged into the dark woods. Where he walked, the forest came alive: she could see the Source spreading in his footsteps, gilding the branches and leaves, their edges coated with dew.

At last the moon pooled in a hollow of grass guarded by birches. As he rested her down on his cloak, she could smell the primroses and hyacinths. He had brought her to a bower that was a sea of blooms. *The Maiden of Flowers.*

Silently, Cahir set aside her crown, drew her robes over her head and slid her shift from her shoulder, pausing to lay a reverent kiss on her skin. The may-blossoms fell about them like snow, crushed in the folds of their clothes.

Though the heat of passion was in them both, Minna knew how sacred this loving was. Their bodies would transmute the Source so it showered the earth with new life, and as she blessed the betrothed couples, now it was her task to bless the Sacred King. She must become the channel for the Source to enshrine him.

So as he bore her to the ground, she twisted out from under him, bidding him lie instead as she rose to her feet. There she paused and gazed down, summoning instinctively all those women she had been in before-lives, letting them fill her until desire soaked her flesh. For as she had been Rhiann's child so she had been other women, who loved in other places, and that was why she wasn't afraid: their passions were clamouring for release.

Cahir gazed back, moonlight shining in his eyes, opening all of himself to her. He looked no less a man for showing his vulnerability, a fear that even now, at this moment, she might see into him and find him wanting.

She sank to her knees beside his scarred body, stroking his powerful limbs as the ancient words came to her tongue to anoint him. 'Be crowned, oh king, by the light of the land, the love of the land, the will of the land.'

The scents of the oils wafted about her, and there was a loosening between her thighs, warm and wet, as she touched Cahir in every place she had been oiled. Gasping, he moved under her and stroked the glow back into her own skin, polishing it, kissing her limbs one by one as if they were each a sacred offering.

When at last he entered her and filled her, she knew it was the union of all things, for all the men he had been, and all the women of her soul.

But though the joining was bigger than them both, when Minna was astride him, wrapped around him, it was Cahir's hands that came to rest on the small of her back, and fitted there perfectly.

Chapter 43

It was a breath before dawn, as night fled through a veil of glimmering mist. A timeless moment of dreamy touches and delirious joining, another melding of bodies that had continued through the night as if they could not bear to be parted. The divine nectar of taste and scent and warm skin, before the sun rose and they had to be human again.

As the mist turned gold, Minna nestled against Cahir's naked back in their nest of cloaks, his hair wet with dew like a god of the woods.

And she stared up at the trees, sore and replete, and she knew. She had walked as a goddess, she had so very nearly touched the knowing, but been drawn back for others before she could truly *see* her own truth. So it was clear now she must journey further herself, with her own will. Further and deeper.

And for that she needed the *saor* of which Darine had spoken. She needed Brónach.

That day Cahir expelled all traders from the port with the tale there was an outbreak of a plague in Dunadd. Messengers were secretly dispatched north, east and south bearing armbands cast into boar's heads as a sign to muster Dalriadan warriors to the king's standard. It was soon time for Cahir to sail for Erin, to convince his brother king Fergus to join the rebellion.

Minna stood with him on the cold beach beside a long, oared boat wallowing in the shallows. As the men shouted to each other, tossing in barrels of food and bundles of weapons, Cahir wrapped his cloak about Minna and drew her into the curve of his body. 'You will be safe here while I am gone, *a stór*,' he murmured, his eyes shadowed. 'But will you be content? Or am I leaving you to the vixens? I don't know how women reckon these things.'

She forced a smile, bracing her shoulders. The women still looked askance at her, but that did not matter when she ached for him like this, in her marrow. '*Content* is a fine sentiment, but really ...' She glanced over his shoulder to a stern-faced Ruarc directing Mellan and Ardal to store their swords and shields.

Cahir smiled, tired but completely sure of himself. 'I suppose it isn't a time to feel happy.' He kissed her ear, murmuring, 'But if I could take you to my bed for a moon, that might do it.'

When she looked up his eyes were burning, intense beneath his black brows, and she knew her own matched them. They had been consumed in the forest, but the miracle was there was no end to that fire; it came alive again each day, and each night when they exhausted themselves among the bed-furs. She could not stop the heat in her face, and he laughed. 'My little wildcat,' he whispered, his full mouth brimming with a tangible excitement.

'I couldn't keep you there for a moon,' she said hoarsely, stepping back. 'There's nothing you want more than to ride to battle; I can see it in your face.'

He merely grinned, and she was almost suffocated by a rush of desire, for with love came the panicked urge to keep him close. She opened her mouth to tell him about her own task, and then changed her mind when she remembered Darine's whisper in the salty darkness of her hut. *Saor is very dangerous.* That was not what he needed to hear.

She closed her eyes, tasted his mouth one last time and pushed him away with a light, playful hand. 'Go now, so you can come back to me sooner.'

With a new determination, Minna headed straight for Brónach's house. The old healer was avoiding her so assiduously she made no appearance for Beltaine, but the time for that had ended.

When there was no answer to her soft query, she lifted the hide and stepped inside. Brónach was there, rigidly staring into the coals of the fire, a blanket around her shoulders. 'This is my house,' she said clearly, without turning her grey head. 'It is still my domain.'

Now she saw her properly, Minna was appalled. In the nearly two moons they had been travelling, Brónach had become bowed and bony, her flesh almost eaten away, desiccated. Her hands on the chair arms were like claws, stained green, brown and purple in the creases of her wrists and fingers and around her long nails.

'Lady Brónach.' She had to clear her throat. 'I regret to intrude, but I must speak with you.'

'Speak with me?' Brónach's voice was toneless, her eyes on the fire. 'Since when did you wish to speak with *me*?'

Minna sat on the hearth-bench, for once picking her words carefully.

'I can understand if you are disconcerted by all the change that has occurred.' That received a bitter snort. 'However, I value your insights, and hope I can learn from you.'

Brónach winced as she rested her head on the chair, gazing up at the roof. Her eyes were feverish, the whites red-veined. 'You think yourself so wise, girl – as all the young do. Yet you still don't know what you have done.'

'I never sought to disrespect you.'

An explosion of mirth led to a fit of coughing. The cough was loose and full of phlegm, and, with a swift glance, Minna saw how the old woman's hands shook. 'I am not here to supplant you,' she said, praying for patience. 'You have the age and wisdom I do not – you are a princess of Dalriada.' She knew better than to reveal what she had discovered of her own ancestry on the mountain. 'Our skills combined make us better able to serve these people. Surely you must see that.'

The opening wavered there, a chance for surrender and grace. Brónach's lip merely curled. 'These are pretty words that mean little. As little as my years of pain and effort mean to the gods!'

'You are a good healer,' Minna persisted.

'Am I?' Brónach raised a sardonic eyebrow. 'When I cannot even look children in the eye, while you call forth their adoration?'

Minna sighed inside and rested her chin on her hands. 'Lady Brónach, in the north a wise-woman told me of a preparation called *saor*.'

Something flickered over the old woman's face and was gone.

'It is an old concoction of six herbs. The woman said the *saor* loosens the bindings of the body to enable a spirit to travel into the Otherworld.' Brónach had gone still, her eyes masked. 'I know most of the ingredients, but not all.'

'You seem to glean what you need from the very air.'

'Sometimes,' Minna agreed carefully. 'But I think ... when I want something for myself it is harder.' She sat straight, forcing strength into her voice. 'If you help me, perhaps we can find it again.'

The old woman looked up to the sprigs of herbs on her rafters. '*Saor*,' she repeated, and her voice wavered. 'I could never find it. There are too many plants ...'

Minna did not betray surprise. 'It might be that one herb-woman cannot discover its secrets alone, that for some reason we must work together.'

Brónach smoothed her sparse brows with her fingers, thinking. 'You dangle this ... *saor* ... to placate me.'

'No.' Minna held her eyes. 'I don't. Work with me, and see how it can be.'

'And if I say no? What if I set myself against you?'

Brónach was testing her, but she had been tested by many these past months. She stood as proudly as she could manage, making the old woman look up. 'Lady, I am sure you've heard I am the king's *lennan* now. I share his heart, his bed and his confidence. He will pursue this course against the Romans, and he has his warriors' backing. It might not be wise to set yourself against us.' She couldn't believe how calmly she spoke, but she felt strong here in this place of healing, and suddenly she knew. Rhiann once lived here, on this very spot. She sensed it in the vibration of the air, like a low heartbeat, coming up through the earth.

Their eyes locked, and it was not Minna's that at last fell. 'You leave me little choice, Roman girl. But at any rate I am intrigued by this *saor*.'

You want it, Minna thought fiercely. *You could never walk away without knowing what it is.*

'Why do you do this?' Brónach suddenly cocked her head. 'I took you from your sickbed and forced you to look into the pool. Why don't you hate me for it?'

Minna considered that. 'I understand you were not in your right mind. And I saw in that pool what I desperately needed to see. That vision brought me to love, and gave Cahir the alliance with the Picts.' She smiled calmly. 'Perhaps I should be thanking you.'

Brónach said nothing for a moment, then snorted, her mouth a grim curve. 'You have learned more of king-craft than I thought. And because of that, I will help you. Too much sunny temper would only irritate me – if you've gained some bite we might get along.'

Minna smiled to herself, opening a pouch at her waist and unrolling the withered leaves she had taken from Darine.

Brónach only had one of Darine's three plants in her stores, for they were badly depleted after the long dark. From speaking to the grandmothers crouched by their fires – those few crones in the dun much older than Brónach – they found a possible fourth, once used for toothaches and flavouring old meat. When Minna crushed the leaves and smelled them something chimed in her, and her eyes met Brónach's over the hearth-fire. The old healer nodded and folded the plant into her pouch.

For the remaining plants, they had to roam outside the dun to the sheltered slopes and hidden glens where the rarer herbs were sprouting undisturbed from the cold earth. The people left them alone. Being seen in serious conversation with the king's aunt only enriched Minna's sudden elevation, and the awe and discomfort in people's eyes was now turning to respect.

Brónach's manner to Minna remained brisk – but in relation to the task itself she revealed a brutal hunger. She pushed her wasted legs up hills and deep into the woods, and hunched over the drying and grinding late in the night.

Once they had narrowed their choice to eight possible plants, they began brewing decoctions of seeds, roots and leaves in differing combinations, while Minna made notes of their trials in Latin.

They tried drying, fermenting, boiling swiftly, steeping slowly, and different parts of the plants mixed with sap, vinegar, wine or honey to release their pungency. Sometimes, sitting quietly in the steam, Minna felt a strong instinct that something was right, and sometimes she did not.

'We'll have to test this,' she said one day, of a dubious-looking brown liquid. 'It should be me – I am the youngest and have the stronger body.'

'It should be me,' Brónach snapped. She was exhausted and drawn, grey-faced. 'I am old, and will die soon anyway.'

'You have been dosing yourself for years with different things,' Minna protested. 'They will have less effect on you.' In the end they were too tired to argue, so both tried it.

The testing consisted of small amounts of each herb before bed. Minna thought that if she received a vivid dream of any kind, then the herb was doing something to the bond between her spirit and body. Brónach, who despite Minna's protests hardly slept, insisted they both try it during the day. 'It should make you feel as if the world has shifted: a little sleepy, slow and light-headed, as though the outline of your body is blurred.'

As the days unfolded, they discarded some combinations and refined others. They inflicted upon themselves nausea, retching, headaches, blurred vision, racing pulses, sleepiness and dry tongue. Nothing was severe, but it was taxing, and Minna saw how it was leaching the last dregs of Brónach's health. However, the old woman would not let her bear the brunt of the testing. With that feverish light in her eyes, she only drove herself harder.

Minna lay in bed at night too agitated to sleep, stroking her fingers through Orla and Finola's hair as they curled into her side, staring at the roof. She asked for something to guide her, but would only wake unbearably thirsty, a lump of loneliness in her throat.

By the seventh night they had six different draughts ready, one of each herb. Minna sat before Brónach's fire with a line of glass flasks that were in turn lurid green, straw-hued, murky, or red-tinged. Behind her, Brónach was slumped on cushions against the bench, coughing. They had both reached the limits of their energy. The old woman's skin was papery and white, every breath laboured. Her grey hair had fallen from its braids, and her robes were stained by plant juice and dirt.

'I feel these are them,' Minna murmured, rubbing the small of her back.

The effect on Brónach was instant. 'How do you know?'

Minna couldn't explain. When she passed her palms over a bottle it was like a string plucked on a harp, vibrating her hand, and together the six flasks sent a perfect, harmonic chord into her heart. 'It just feels right,' she said defensively. Their tempers were strung out now, along with their bodies.

'I have no more ideas, anyway,' Brónach whispered, her gaze boring into the vials. 'That is all I have ever heard about.'

'Well, I am sure of it.'

'Then let us try it now.' Brónach's hand reached out, shaking with tremors.

Minna instinctively blocked her. 'No, we are both exhausted; we're not thinking straight.'

'We don't need to think—'

'Yes, we do! The wise-woman Darine told me that it wasn't just about finding the *saor*. The taking of it is dangerous.' She spread her hands. 'I feel ... inside ... that we have to take the time to prepare. Sit quietly, breathe, call upon the goddesses.' Her eye strayed to the line of little figurines. 'Surely *you* must see that. We have to be calm and aware, open, ready—'

'I am ready! And you will make *me* wait?' Brónach dragged herself up by the hearth-bench, wheezing. She pointed a long, bony finger at Minna. 'Do you have any idea,' she hissed, 'how hard I worked for all that you have gained so easily? The nights I fasted and went without sleep, dosing myself with any plant to try and see in the sacred pool, as my ancestresses did.' She lifted her hands, twisted talons. 'I brought this age on myself by pushing so hard. I nearly died from cold and lack of food, because *I* wanted to discover all the secrets of the old ways. I have spent my whole life searching for them, and all I get is fragments, glimpses!' She swung to her workbench, raking fingers through her grey hair. 'I nearly made it through the veil so many times. I was so close ... I heard them ... saw their faces.' She stopped, sucked in a grating breath. 'I need to see more now. I *must*.'

'And you will, but not like this.' Minna staggered to her feet. 'It is too dangerous.'

She heard the indrawn breath, and saw Brónach tense. Then the old woman whirled around and Minna was stunned to see, after all these careful days, every mask stripped from her wasted face. 'What right do you have to command me? You, a foreigner, an ignorant, naïve nothing of a girl who gains visions without even trying, who *senses* the healing ways that I fought for years to unravel?' She strode to Minna and gripped her chin. 'And now you will keep me from what I have sought?'

Bitterness flooded into Minna from her hand: the pain of a shrivelled womb; the trap of an austere life, offering neither escape nor belonging; the desperation to seek another way, though by then it was too late, for the bitterness had formed a dank prison too thick for vision to penetrate.

'I'm not trying to keep you from anything except death!' She twisted herself free and rubbed her aching jaw.

'You are, you are!' The last sense slipped from Brónach's eyes, and they became wild and glazed. 'You are trying to steal what is mine, my glory, my triumph, as you have stolen everything!'

'This is not about glory; it's about helping people—'

'*I will not let you take this from me as well*!'

The hatred almost flung Minna back against the wall. Had she been too preoccupied to see this unravelling before her very eyes?

Brónach stiffened at her expression. 'Oh Goddess ... you *pity* me now? *You*?' A bowl came to hand and, without warning, she threw it across the room so it shattered on the hearth, sending shards flying up. 'I will not allow this! Get out of my house! Get out!'

Minna slid along the wall to the door. 'I *will* go outside,' she said with barely restrained fury, 'because we are weary and not in our right minds. But I'm coming back when our heads are clearer.'

'Yes, go.' Contemptuously, Brónach turned her head. 'I can no longer look upon your face.'

Outside, Minna stalked down to the village gate and paced the walls, gulping down the night air. The warriors on guard peered at her in the faint starlight, then tipped their spears to their brows with respect. Even that barely penetrated her storm of frustration.

In her anger she had taken no cloak, and the wind sliced straight through her thin shift until she began to shiver uncontrollably, hunching her shoulders. When she could stand the cold no longer she strode back, head up.

She could not let Brónach get the better of her, or nothing would ever be resolved.

When she flung up the door-hide of the house, she stopped as if she'd walked into a wall.

Brónach was sprawled on the rug, her limbs splayed, her body spasming. Forgetting everything, she dropped to her knees and held her stiff shoulders. 'Brónach?' As she bent close Minna smelled the bitterness on the old woman's breath and looked wildly around.

By the glow of the dying fire she could still see the vials on the hearth-stone – empty. All the *saor* had been taken. She shook Brónach by the shoulders. 'Wake up!'

There was no answer. The old woman's eyes rolled back, the whites showing as the spasms hit her. A trickle of bloody foam ran from the corner of her mouth. Minna raced to light the lamps on the workbench. She needed an emetic to expel the potion – the bitter plant with blue flowers that old women called purgeweed. She knocked pots and bottles in the rushes and scrabbled for the stoppers.

Brónach was moaning now, grinding her teeth, and when Minna rushed to her side and tried to prise her jaw open it was rigid. She pinched her nose until her mouth gaped and poured the purgeweed down. The old woman gagged and writhed, but Minna grimly held her mouth shut. More went down.

Suddenly Brónach went still. Minna piled cushions up and dragged the old woman over them onto her belly, gathering towels and an empty pot. She had counted through both sets of fingers four score times when the old woman's torso suddenly stiffened. A ripple ran through her twisted body. As Minna grasped her shoulders, her mouth opened and a stream of vomit came gushing into the empty pot, sharp with bitterness.

Brónach moaned, turning in her hands, but Minna held firm as another spasm came. There was no food in the bile – how could she have missed that Brónach was not eating?

All of a sudden the old woman went limp, her chest deflating. Her rigid body became a dead weight in Minna's arms, pulling her over so she was sprawled on the floor. Alarmed, Minna slapped her cheeks. 'Brónach, stay here with me!' In desperation, she thumped that bony chest.

Brónach's body spasmed again, the bitter vomit spattering Minna's dress and bare arms, and then she fell limp once more. 'Brónach!' The old woman's head lolled back, her neck nerveless.

With a cry, Minna laid her down and pressed her head to her chest. There was only a last rattle, and then no heartbeat. Nothing.

She sat back on her heels, as silence descended over the room like a shroud. Slowly, she reached to touch the old woman's waxy skin, her fingers quivering. Brónach had found a way to cross between the veils after all.

Abruptly, Minna began to shake. *Light and dark,* Darine had said. *Accept its light and dark both* ... She put her hands over her face.

Chapter 44

The Lady Brónach had a funeral as austere as her life had been.

Few came to the burning at a remote beach, fewer expressed sadness. There was a turnout of nobles as befitted her rank, and the chief druid droned a blessing, sprinkled her forehead with sacred water and lit her pitch-soaked pyre with a rowan branch.

Minna watched the flames licking about the old woman's grave face. Now that her features had smoothed out she could perceive, perhaps, a hint of triumph at the edge of that thin mouth.

Fear settled in her bones as she walked away from the smoke. Alone, she had to traverse that same path of death now. She had to know.

With great deliberation, Minna remade each ingredient of the *saor* from her notes. It was a purification rite, she realized now, and must be done with sacred feeling, not hunger or frustration. With mindfulness.

She set the goddess figurines in a circle around her and the purge-weed close by. She changed into a fresh robe and bathed her hands and face.

Then she asked Keeva to take up a seat outside, and only disturb her if she had not appeared by moonrise.

Keeva eyed her warily. 'I will do that of course, but what if I hear nothing, and you are lying there ... dying?' No one knew exactly what had happened to Brónach, only that she had accidentally taken the wrong herbs and, sickened as she already was, succumbed, even though Minna tried to save her.

Minna forced a brave smile she did not feel. 'I will be very careful, and I am not sick, or old. If at moonrise it seems something has gone wrong, you will know by my face. Take the purgeweed and make me drink it, no matter what happens.'

Keeva's black eyes went wide. Her fear was at war with a desperate curiosity to know what she was doing. 'As long as the king does not have my head.' She sat down on the bench outside, grimly folding her arms.

Cross-legged before the vials with her eyes closed, Minna wavered on the precipice for an endless time. This felt familiar, sitting in this quiet place, and she knew without forming the thoughts that she had to breathe from feet to head to relax her body into trance. But her heart pounded and raced, for she kept seeing Brónach's death throes in her mind.

She fought and wrestled with herself, with that fear, and understood then Darine's warning: *There must be skill, training, to ensure the silver cord of the spirit does not break and the body die. You must breathe life into the cord ... breathe, and never let it break.* At last her fingers closed about the first vial, the liquid dense and dark green, and she dipped her finger in to taste it. It was sour, and redolent of soil and rock. A thrill ran up her body: she knew the taste. *She must trust.*

'I call on my Mothers to help me,' she whispered. 'My mother Rhiann of the Epidii, and the Great Mother of All, who sent me visions and looks down on me as the moon. Lend me your grace to mix this *saor* well, and conduct myself in a way that does you honour.'

She smelled each vial one by one, deep into her belly where her instincts were strong. She breathed, slowing her racing mind, and, with her eyes closed, began mixing the herbs. Fingertips brushed glass, tingled when the right flask was found. Nostrils flared, drawing in scent, adjusting, stirring. Brónach did not do this, Minna kept telling herself. Brónach took all of it, in the wrong amounts and the wrong order. But she would feel her way through.

She knew she was done when her hands hovered over the vials and then came to rest in her lap of their own accord. She opened her eyes and gazed into the cup. *Saor.* Her mother had taken it. It looked like nothing more than dirty pond water, but this was a tool, she understood now. *Saor* did not give the visions; it merely freed the spirit to see clearly through the veils, unhindered. One still had to have the courage to walk in the Otherworld, to pass through darkness.

With fluttering fingers, she picked up the cup and, in one swift motion, drank it down.

The *saor* was musty and grainy, unpleasant yet absolutely and impossibly familiar. Minna stretched out on the rug and waited. Nothing obvious happened, and it was only when she started that she realized she had been staring unblinking into the fire.

Her limbs had gone numb. Her mind floated. She curled on her side, the movement making her aware of the odd sense of her body, as if it were only tenuously connected to her thoughts. *Curious*, she thought dreamily. *But I really must ...*

And she was falling.

A light that was her rushed down a tunnel and flung itself out into night as a spirit taking wing. *Silver cord.* She heard the echo of Darine's voice. Then, looking back, she saw that the spirit was a thread, not a point of light, unfettered and free to spin in the void. The silver thread of light wound back through the worlds, through the stardust and the veils of mist, to that body by the fire that was hers.

Minna felt as if she knew these things and was telling herself again.

But, oh, her spirit soared, and it was such freedom to spin among the Otherworld stars, a joy like nothing she had known. For she was not one separate being, but joined with everything around her; part of the One when she had always felt so alone. A revelation. She was taken then with an unbearable temptation to let go of all thought and melt back into the All-That-Is, the everything, like the other lights dancing around her.

It is always this way, her knowing said. But that is why you must remember who you leave behind, and what you need to do. You have to know yourself, that you have a human life to continue. She saw Cahir's face now, pale and trickled with blood over one eye. That is why you must remember. You need to know if he will be safe.

Soaring through the void, Minna struggled to remember the sacred breath. *Breathe.* She fought, then drew it in and released it again and again, and every time she drew in the Source and breathed it along the cord, the silver thread grew brighter and stronger.

Yes. It was always the same fight: to hold to her will when she could give up and dissolve; to know when to surrender. To travel far, she must trust and let go, but to come back she also had to hold an image of who she was in this life, and how she wanted to return.

It was hard. Sometimes the thread nearly broke – for she forgot life and Cahir and Minna, and longed to soar for ever – and sometimes she was being tugged back at dizzying speed to the firelit room and her body, because she grew afraid and faltered.

But onwards, she must go. Onwards, to a place in a snowy wood set out of time. Summoning courage, she exerted all her will and held to the image in her heart.

Her feet were on snow, running. Trees lifted black branches to an endless sky of no colour. Then the singing made her pause.

It floated through the trees, one woman's voice, earthy and rich. And as the notes wandered up and down, Minna's mind was filled with waterfalls spilling down soaring mountain-sides, and ocean swells, crested with white foam. The singer's thoughts, memories, sung into being.

A loneliness more vivid than grief filled Minna and she ran faster, her breath in time with her heartbeat. The singing drew her on ... *Bracken blazing on a hillside; frozen pools on high moors; an eagle, circling.*

She finally stumbled into a snowy dell, recognizing it as the place she and Cahir had loved on Beltaine night. Now, the flowers were under snow, the birches as pale as the ground. In the hollow the woman had come to a halt with her face turned away, her cloak blue as violets against the white.

The singing faded.

Minna took a step, and then another. The woman was as still as the trees, as the birdless, empty sky. Minna plunged through snow to her side and, without thinking, took hold of the blue cloak. Then, and only then did the woman turn, and Minna was face to face at last with Rhiann.

Her fine features and pale skin were framed by copper hair, wisps of it trailing across her cheeks. Her face was ageless, but her eyes ... Minna could hardly look in them, for they opened on glittering clouds of the same stars through which she had journeyed.

Then that faded, and they were just human, and tender, and Minna simply sank on her knees in the snow, burying her face in the scented folds of the cloak.

A touch came on the crown of her head, a blessing. *You had to seek me for yourself, and so it has made you strong.*

Minna crushed the cloth to her eyes. *Mother.* She smelled honey and soap, and something deeper that stirred an ancient memory. It was a voice singing in her ear, low and breathy. The scent of warm, milky skin. *Come to me*, it sang.

'Then ... it was you all along, drawing me on. And you who sang to me ... I remember, when I was small ... but it could not have been this life, not this time.'

It was before, when I carried you up the mountain to the rowan.

Minna's mind was drowning in questions, but she wanted to stay here breathing in that smell, and do nothing else.

A smile lightened the air. *Now I am yours and you are mine, and Alba needs its priestesses once more. I sang to call you home.*

Chapter 45

It was late in the night, and Fullofaudes sat with his officers around a table in the fort at Iscarium, the tribal capital of the Brigantes between the Wall and Eboracum. Along with his men, the Dux basked in the firelit warmth of the command quarters, letting the hum of laughter and thunk of cups flow over him as he read a secret dispatch that had just been brought to him. The words had been pressed into wax in a wood tablet so they could be erased.

His officers were filled with restless energy, for they had spent a long winter locked up indoors. Now spring was here again and they were making ready to travel north, back to the Wall.

Though they all hated the northlands and feared the barbarian danger, they longed, like him, to be back in the saddle, breathing air free of the fug of winter, the smoke, the greasy meat and stale pottage, the stink of piss pots and sour sweat.

As Fullofaudes read, he kept his face absolutely still. But his muscles tensed, his legs bracing on the floor beneath the table. Eldon's plan had failed in spectacular fashion. His daughter had been expelled from Dalriada and the Dux's man had been killed – though thank the Christos there was no proof that Fullofaudes had been involved.

Swallowing another gulp of ale, Fullofaudes rose, seemingly unhurried, and stood over the fire, leaning one arm on the mantel and staring into the flames so they all blurred together. The outcome of this was much worse than a few dead men and a scorned queen. Cahir was obviously an unusually intelligent barbarian, and surely would guess Fullofaudes had some involvement in this. So any element of surprise had gone, and with it a certain amount of Roman threat and power.

Abruptly he swung around. On seeing his expression his officers fell silent.

'What is it, sir?' one asked, pausing in the act of peeling an apple with his knife.

Fullofaudes took a deep breath, throwing the closed tablet on the table. 'It seems that our friend Eldon has over-reached himself,' he said evenly. 'Stupid fool decided to attack Dalriada when Cahir was away from his fort. The Carvetii were pathetically under-resourced, of course.'

One of his officers let out a whistle and put down his ale cup. 'And what happened?'

'The Dalriadans got wind of it and set a trap for him.' He told them the rest – what he could tell – and the faces around the table that had been laughing and bright with ale now fell into more sober lines. Fullofaudes thought fast, then gripped the back of an empty chair and speared one man with his gaze.

'I want two extra *vexillationes* units and two *auxilia* units to come back north with us,' he ordered. 'Draw them from different forts so we don't deplete one over the others.'

The man just looked at him. 'Now, sir? It's not even dawn yet.'

'Well, I want the messengers out of the gate *by* dawn!' Fullofaudes snapped, and at the tone of his voice they all jumped to attention in their chairs. The first man scrambled for his helmet and sword and strode out, and Fullofaudes turned to the next. 'You have good relationships with our allies the Votadini. I want you to ride to Traprain yourself, taking only a few men with you. Request the Votadini king, in person, to strengthen his defences and double his scouts both along the coast and to his west. They must watch Cahir now as well as the Picts, and report back on any hint of change – anything at all.'

The Votadini acted as a buffer state between the eastern Wall and the Picts, but had become complacent in their wealth and Roman status, despite their dangerous neighbours.

As the man rose, Fullofaudes said, 'Wait.' He gazed around at them all. 'This information is not to leave this room, under any circumstances.' He took another deep, steadying breath. 'I want two of the old forts re-garrisoned in secret, even if we have to get the troops from Nectaridus in the south. One can be the outpost in Votadini territory, and the second in the hills at Vindolanda – full complement of men, half cavalry, to be held in reserve. No one will be allowed in or out of those forts, and they are to hide their strength and numbers as much as possible.' He remembered himself and braced his shoulders, raised his chin, spoke briskly to engender confidence. 'We will all ride at dawn – I want to get back to the Wall as soon as possible.'

All the officers were on their feet now, the clink of cups and sound of laughter replaced by the jingle of mail, buckles and sword-belts, the thud of heavy boots and scraped-back chairs.

When they had gone, each with his specific orders, Fullofaudes stood by the fire and opened the wax tablet once more, scanning the last lines again, his pulse throbbing slowly in his neck. Cahir had given out that there was plague in Dunadd. All traders had been expelled. Dalriada now showed a blank face to the world, which unsettled him more than any wild Pictish attack.

An uncomfortable prickle ran along the back of his neck, as the logs shifted in the grate, casting up sparks.

By the time Cahir sailed back to Alba with Fergus's oath of support, warriors had already begun pouring in from every far-flung glen, the remote mountains and the Attacotti islands. Every boy who could lift a spear came, and old men thought past their prime, who would hold a sword or bow one last time.

They came in streams, all flowing to Dunadd.

For days Minna had been at the mountain hut on her own, and the evening she returned she walked the pony out of the ancestor valley and there pulled it up short. A river of fire poured down the glen, lapping at the slopes and the peaks. The campfires of the warriors, more than she could have imagined. Dry-mouthed, she gazed at this enormous weapon she had caused to be forged.

Rhiann's words kept coming back to her in snatches, as if remembered in a dream. For one moment Minna had been with her in the hollow of snow, and the next the cord of her spirit was tugging her urgently back to her body by the fire. She woke sick to the stomach but holding to a memory of Rhiann's voice, telling her what she most wanted to know: *Your fate in this life was bound to our son Cahir, and it is his destiny to free Alba. We were only the vanguard, but he is the host.*

And here was the host. The pony's ears twitched as Minna's legs tensed on its back, and she sought to sit straight in the saddle. Since taking the *saor* and returning she felt as if her skin had been stretched over new bones and expanded flesh, barely able to contain her any more. Along with Cahir, she had wrought this scene of fire and force with her visions, *her words*.

As the nights without Cahir had drawn out, she had found herself seeking a reason for that in the dark hours, a salve for the guilt that so many would die. She had been drawn to the mountain hut, staring into the cold, black pool beneath the birches where she had seen the vision of the eagle. And as she wondered, so Rhiann's words had been there, floating up from the memory of the Otherworld dream.

The Source in Alba was expressed through love of the sacred land; the songs and stories; the honour of clan and family; the care of all living things. If the Romans conquered, they would make Alba like Rome, stamp out the druids as they did the Sisters, destroy the rites, the dreams. The Source must be protected or Alba's very soul would die.

But as Minna had woken Cahir, so she was the one who must mourn for all who would perish at Alba's hand. Only she could sense the souls, and know how to bless their passing to come. And so she had spent days singing into the pool, chanting the funeral dirges for those who would yet die.

Rhiann had charged her with this: her first task as a priestess, to rebalance the Source. For that is what she was; what she would be. Now she was a Sister. Now she was not alone.

By the time she reached Dunadd, she could feel the momentum of the Source building beneath the ground, shivering in the air. The village resounded with the clang of weapons. Men shouted greetings to each other as servants hurried back and forth stabling horses, hefting packs and swords and spears. And Cahir was back.

Passing Fintan's forge, Minna saw the bloom of fire, and lamplight falling on Lonán's sweaty arms. Doorways spilled light and women's voices, tense and expectant as children screeched and scampered about with excitement. On the wooded ridge to Dunadd's south the pillars of the druid temple were outlined by bonfires, and Minna heard drumming from afar. The king was there, the gate guards said, with all the chieftains of Dalriada.

The king's hall was crowded with unfamiliar men demanding food and ale, always more ale. The benches were jostling with drunken warriors polishing scabbards, arguing, kicking the hounds out of the way.

As Minna had stared into the pool, singing and weeping, she had seen glimpses of this war. She had lived the blood-lust, the bowel-loosening fear, the fury of a warrior in battle.

Now, as she passed through the hall, the whispers following her, the eyes wondering, she understood that this drunken oblivion was not so strange after all.

Cahir had called a council of chieftains inside the temple. Outside the ring of pillars, druids circled the bonfires, chanting and throwing herbs on the flames so sparks shot high in the night sky.

The hill was surrounded by a crescent of banners, painted with symbols of stag and fox, bear and wolf, horse and eagle. Now, one by one, the chiefs stood before him and presented their numbers and their oaths.

Cahir sat very straight on the chair brought out for him, his hands flat on his thighs. As the numbers grew, he had to force himself to stay still. The Attacotti had come with three thousand fighting men from their islands to the west. Their lord was Kinet, a short man with black hair and piercing eyes, fanatically loyal to his sea and wind gods.

This, added to the hordes mustered by the Dalriadan chiefs from every dun, and the men pledged by Fergus in Erin, would field a force of fifteen thousand men. The Picts would also bring fifteen thousand; the Saxons five thousand, though Cahir and Gede had decided to hold them in reserve, mustered on the Pictish coast, in case they had to face more Roman forces further south.

Thirty-five thousand, to march on Britannia.

This was the only night that Cahir had the opportunity to see the western force gathered together, for come tomorrow they would be sent south in groups, moving secretly through the mountains, re-grouping north of the Clutha for their rush on the south. The younger druids would go with them, blessing them with sacred water and rowan, watching the clouds and stars for signs.

His hand on his sword, Cahir now stood up before the chieftains. The shadows thrown up by the flames leaped eerily around the temple pillars, open to the sky. His gods' faces watched him, carved into the oak.

The chiefs and their guards cheered him for long moments, and he absorbed that acclaim deep into his beating heart. 'A message has come from our ally, Gede of the Picts,' he said when they fell silent, in a voice that soared across the throng. 'The Roman scouts in his pay will soon confirm the positions of their forces for the end of the Beltaine moon.'

Gede would take most of his warriors in a great fleet down the east coast, Cahir down the west. The western commanders would travel by any sea-going craft they had been able to appropriate – traders, curraghs and fishing boats – and would meet Fergus of Erin north of Luguvalium before taking the town.

They must be a swift blade that comes out of the shadows, and strikes before any cry escapes.

Minna stabbed the needle into her palm and caught herself from cursing. Orla and Finola were curled among the pillows beside her, sound asleep. It was very late, and the noise downstairs was only just beginning to die as the oblivion of ale took over. She peered at the cloth, holding it up to the lamp-light and frowning.

'It can't be that bad,' Cahir said behind her.

She dropped her sewing. 'I fear it could.' She looked up at him, and they were silent for a long moment.

With a smile, he took the lamp, and Minna pulled the furs around the girls' shoulders, leaving Lia nestled between them. At their own bedplace, Cahir turned to her. 'So what is this, *a stór*?' He peered at the crumpled piece of linen in her hands.

Minna held out the stringy piece of cloth. 'I wanted you to carry something from me, and I have nothing that my own hands can make. You already have your great banners ...'

Cahir unrolled it, and, when he said nothing, she added hastily, 'It's for you to tie around your neck or your arm, with the boar stone. You see,' she felt herself going red, 'I have no family symbol, and I am Dalriadan now anyway, but people have said – Nessa said – that I remind her of the sea ... so ... I decided to embroider this.' It was an admittedly crude seagull outlined in blue on white, with a black beak like her hair, above a green sea. The gull was a wanderer, too.

His face grave, he curved a hand about her cheek, and she closed her eyes, absorbing the sensation of the sword calluses scraping her soft skin. Then he kissed her, at last giving her his greeting, the hunger leaping between them. It was some time before he broke away and said thickly, 'I have something for you, from Erin.'

It was a long necklace of crystal beads, tinged with green so they shone like ice, like water. They matched her eyes, and she left them on when he undressed her, hanging between her breasts, cool against the heated skin.

Cahir's hair was damp from the river meadow as he urgently caressed her, murmuring love into her skin, the vibrations sending jolts along her nerves as his mouth traced her ribs. She could feel the suppressed fire in him, the battle excitement building. But when his mouth closed over one nipple, the warmth between her thighs made her forget all else. Forget that she was losing him.

The lamp guttered out.

Her touch flowed from the soft places under his arms across the hard planes of his back. He was leaving, and so she must take him into her as if somehow she could keep him safe within the halo of her body's light. Desire and sorrow were wound together with choking intensity.

He sensed the drift of her heart and slid down her body, nestling between her thighs, his tongue shocking the heat back to her core. When he rose up and sheathed himself in her he paused for a moment at their greatest joining, as if he would never part.

Moved by a great reverence, Minna sensed the light growing behind her closed eyes, a glow that enveloped them both. This was sacred, too; an act that blessed them both. Cahir gasped, and she smoothed back his unbound hair, drawing her legs together so she could feel all of his skin from breast to flank.

'I love you.'

Cahir kissed her palm, moving within her like the sea. 'I know. I have seen it in your face.'

'But it's dark,' she whispered, tears standing in her eyes.

'Then I can feel it.' He dipped his head, his tongue drinking from the scented hollow of her throat as he buried himself again. 'Can you?'

he whispered. 'Can you feel it, *mo chridhe*?' My heart. He murmured into her hair, winding endearments around her like a soft mantle.

She couldn't answer, though, her body cleft by loss as well as his warmth. This might be the last time he loved her, when her skin was only just coming to know the moods of his touch. She needed more, for that flame to be exhausted. She needed years.

The terrible longing intensified the joy, and they were drowning in a rush of breath and pounding hearts, sweat on skin, and her cries that he swallowed with his kisses, as if tasting them.

And at last there was no more to say, for the love lay between them unhindered and unbound, and held them as the darkness did.

Chapter 46

'I will write to you.' Beneath the brow-guard of Cahir's boar helmet, his eyes scanned the warriors crowding the port. Two weeks after Beltaine and the bulk of the army had slipped away on foot through the mountains. Day by day Dunadd had emptied.

Minna wrapped her arms around her chest, huddled in her cloak, trying to look as if she were not dying inside. 'Write? I thought you despised Roman learning.' She raised an eyebrow. 'So now you speak *Latin*?'

Cahir grinned, but he was also avoiding her eye. '*I* don't, minx – I've rounded up a trader who does, though. A British trader.'

'Poor man.'

'I can't trust messages will get to you over land, but sea-traders can avoid the armies. And you will receive news in my own words.'

'That would be wonderful.' She looked away, blinking in the harsh sunlight.

All of Dunadd had come to farewell the king. Minna stood by Cahir's command ship, a plank trader with square sails that was tied against the pier, shifting with the swells from a north-westerly wind. Around it, boats of all sizes cluttered the bay. The shoreline was jostling with people; the scent of fear and nerves was as sharp as sweat in the air.

Leather jerkins had been greased, mail and spear-tips burnished, hair limed into ferocious peaks. Ruarc was resplendent in bronze and iron armour and a gilded wood scabbard, his leaf-green cloak caught by an enormous brooch. On his head was a helmet as ornate as Cahir's own, winged like a seabird.

Women and children lined the beach. Orla and Finola were standing at the end of the pier with a grim Clíona: Orla was fighting to look brave, her mouth pursed; Finola was less successful. Garvan was also there, sporting a defiant scowl, though Minna had seen the confusion in his eyes. However, despite his best efforts, Cahir had enjoyed no success in softening his son's heart yet.

Nearby, the noblewomen did not wail and wring their hands but stood in a silent group, bejewelled and finely dressed, their faces proud. Minna summoned her courage; she had to be like them.

Gobán strode by, shouting Cahir's orders to the men loading the boats. War horns brayed, pipes skirled. Finbar and Donal stood by Cahir's side, for it was to them he was entrusting Dunadd, along with a significant contingent of warriors to guard the fort.

A deep voice boomed out now, trained to reach across the water with a precise volume and clarity: Darach. Cahir removed his helmet and bowed his head before the chief druid. The bustle of movement faded, replaced by expectant silence. There was only the cry of gulls, the slap of the waves.

Darach sprinkled sacred water on Cahir's brow with rowan-wood, then turned to the four directions, arms raised. 'Lugh, son of the sun, we ask you to bestow your light on our son Cahir, King of Dalriada, so that he may see his path clearly and follow it. Manannán, lord of the sea, we ask the waves, your steeds, to bear these ships swiftly to the Roman shore. Hawen, boar god, make keen the edge of these blades, and strong the arms that bear them. And the lord of death, he who is not named: if you claim your sons then feast them on the Blessed Isle as befitting their bravery, and return them to life with us once again.'

When Darach had fallen silent, Cahir raised his head, his face shining. A younger druid came forward with his great sword in its battered scabbard and handed it to Minna. She had been told what to do, but never could she be prepared for this.

She bowed her head over Cahir's sword, struggling to hold it up. 'My lord.' Her voice sounded small amid that vast crowd. 'As your *lennan* I arm you and send you to war. In this way, may the blessings of the Goddess also be laid upon you and your endeavours.' *And bring you safely back to me*, she added silently.

Cahir placed his hand over the scabbard. 'My lady,' he acknowledged, and stood with his arms out so she could belt it on him as the noblewomen had done for their warriors. It was awkward, but she must not let the tip touch the ground. Every eye was fixed on her as she self-consciously sank to her knees to fasten the buckle, leaning around him. His breath brushed her brow, sending a tremor through her, and when the sword lay against his thigh he helped her to her feet.

A deafening cheer went up from the warriors, echoing back from the hills and across the water. Those on the ships struck their swords on their shields, making a noise like rolls of harsh thunder. In the midst of that roar, Cahir held Minna's eyes. 'Can you see it?'

Confused for a moment, Minna smiled softly. His love. 'I can see it.'

Then, to her surprise, Cahir did not kiss her formally on both cheeks, but claimed her mouth instead, impetuous and passionate. The cheering swelled, and Minna could still feel the last hint of warmth on her lips even as he turned away to board his ship. The boar banner rippled over his head in the wind, and his men closed about him. He was hers no longer.

She stayed there as the ships left the bay, the banks of oars rising and dipping, the sails filling out as they reached the open sea. Only when the command ship disappeared around the headland did she take a shuddering breath.

She could not turn back to land, though. She knew all the noble-women stood there, watching to see what she might do now that she was alone here. As she paused, struggling with herself, a touch came on her shoulder.

It was Riona, smoothing a cloak across her swelling belly. 'Lady,' she said, her voice raised to carry, 'if you would be so good as to come to my mother-in-law's house, she would like to share a cup of mead with you. One of my nephews has a rash, and she requests your help if you would give it.' Minna swivelled to shore, with a grateful smile at Riona.

There was a moment of indecision as together they reached the knot of noblewomen. Then one with a babe-in-arms detached herself and strode boldly towards Minna. She nodded respectfully, and, as the child began to wail, Riona broke in. 'The Lady Breda is worried for her son.'

'He cries all the time,' the woman murmured, jiggling the boy on her hip. 'And he holds his belly. I fear ...' her haughty face twisted, 'that he is not well.'

So this would build the bridge. Minna straightened, and reached out for the child.

BOOK THREE
SUNSEASON, AD 367

Chapter 47

Fullofaudes raced his horse along the ranks of men, its hooves spattering mud around his ears. He pulled up at the lip of the hill so abruptly that the horse shied.

At first the Dux said nothing, gazing into this cursed mist that had fallen over the rolling hills below the Wall. It was only now being burned off by a rising sun. 'Do we know the numbers?' he bellowed to his officers, sitting on their mounts beneath his standard.

Their faces sported the same carefully blank expressions, but Fullofaudes saw in their eyes the stark fear he was trying to suppress. 'Not yet, sir,' one said, clearing his throat. 'We can't see far enough, so I have sent riders along the fringes to determine the extent of the enemy force.' Fullofaudes watched his lips move. *The enemy force.* Tugging off his helmet, he ran his hands through sweaty hair, conscious of the grime coating his face and muddied armour. He was not his usual self, precise and hard: he was undone.

The first message had been a brutal shock. He received the news in Brigantes territory, after quelling another riot about taxes. A sudden attack had been launched by Picts landing at the eastern end of the Wall. So many warriors had stormed the shores that the forts had either been taken or abandoned. Fullofaudes thundered back north with cavalry and infantry units drawn from his hinterland forts, furious but ultimately confident.

Now, after three days, he had gained no sleep, and his mind and body were struggling. More messages had come in, relentless messages, and with each one his world had darkened around him. What he had thought was another sporadic raid, like the Pictish one three years ago, turned out to be something entirely different.

A force had not only landed in the east, but an even bigger one had invaded the west, with scores of boats and columns of warriors pouring down from the northern moors and across the Erin sea. Two armies, west and east, swarming together like ants.

Then more riders came in. Luguvalium fallen. His outpost forts destroyed. His scouts scattered. The Wall burning. He barely had chance to abandon his positions and regroup his forces here in the hills, to stop the barbarians heading any further south.

Worse was to come, though. When Fullofaudes summoned his reserve troops he discovered that four *vexillationes* of cavalry, two thousand men, had already been annihilated by a night raid on one of the recently reoccupied outpost forts to the north. How did the Picts know where they were stationed, when he had ordered its occupation a secret?

That question still gnawed on his exhausted mind, but there was no time to digest its implications. This behaviour went against everything he knew about the northern peoples – that they were squabbling beasts whose infighting did his work for him. This was something not seen for centuries; they had joined together in a great alliance, the first since Agricola's days. And unless the Dux was willing to abandon the north of Britannia to their fire and swords, he must accept the terrible challenge of open battle.

Spurring the horse to the edge of the ridge where the ground fell to scree, Fullofaudes peered into the mist, which was breaking now in ghostly swirls. He could just glimpse dark masses of men on the farther ridge, although as yet they were silent, like wraiths emerging from another world, another time. He curbed his fears and his wandering mind once more. They were men, and they could die.

His scouts came galloping back, milling about on sweaty horses behind him. Unable to see clearly, they had ridden perilously close to the enemy flanks on west and east, hazarding a rough count of men. As they stammered the numbers to him now, Fullofaudes did not turn around in the saddle. Ten, twenty, *thirty thousand or more*. It could not be. He had seven thousand, if he was lucky, the rest spread over the Province, guarding the borders and coasts.

Fullofaudes knew he was on the edge of an immense precipice. Dread and disbelief clawed at him, threatening to break him.

Then the drizzle began to lift, revealing rank upon rank of tattooed faces, wild hair and beards, tattered banners and shaggy cloaks. The dark, endless masses blanketed the opposite ridge, covering the ground for miles around.

'Dear God ... Jupiter and Mars ... Mithras ...' he gasped, calling on every god he knew.

*

'... by Hawen, lord of the boar ...' Cahir murmured.

In a misty, birch-clad bowl of the hills, the Dalriadan king and his commanders stood in a reverent circle around two of Darach's younger druids. One held on his open palms the sacred talismans – two boar tusks, yellowed with age.

Cahir stared down as the druid stepped around the circle, coming before the warriors one by one. The tusks were Eremon's, gifted to Gabran to replace the ones Eremon and Conaire sacrificed at the Hill of a Thousand Spears. They were for Hawen, the boar god: his own cruel weapons. All these years they had been kept in a fur-lined box in the druid temple, and in Cahir's memory never been taken forth. For they were battle tokens, and his people had not been to open war for centuries, only skirmishes and raids.

Now, they had been brought forth for him alone: Cahir son of Conor.

The second druid held out Cahir's sword to the warriors, chanting under his breath. Ruarc took the sword and, briefly closing his eyes, his lips moving in a vow, sliced the meat of his palm. Making a fist, he squeezed blood in droplets over the yellowed tusks, his face transfigured. One by one the other warriors did the same, and Cahir took their fervent, unspoken oaths into his heart.

At last the sword came back to Cahir himself. He nicked his own skin and watched the blood mix with his men's, smearing the tusks. This was to bind them all to him and to their ancestors. This was to give them victory.

Every nerve singing, Cahir strode away through the smoke as the druids burned the entrails of a deer, their arms spread to the sky. Ruarc hurried to his side, matching his step. 'Where shall we range the spears, my lord?'

Cahir took his helmet from under his arm and put it on. The iron strips at cheek and neck were cold on his skin, steadying his heart. 'The Roman cavalry are always on the wings. Put ours on our right, then ride over to Gede and get his to the left.'

Ruarc nodded and loped away. The wooden spears had been his inspired idea, for the Albans could not bring horses by sea and therefore were at a disadvantage from the Roman cavalry. One night, around the feasting fires after the taking of Luguvalium, Ruarc suggested felling tall, young trees and sharpening their ends into stakes, their tips hardened in the fire. These could be placed at the warriors' feet, hidden in the heather, and when the cavalry charged they would lift them up and block the onslaught. His king agreed, and Ruarc had detailed men on felling and sharpening duty at once.

Cahir watched Ruarc go, his lime-stiffened hair a golden mane around his head. Now they were taking action, he had become a focused, settled presence, and a critical link in his chain of command to the younger warriors.

He was yanked back from these thoughts by Alban war-horns screeching discordantly along the ridge above him – there must be movement in the Roman ranks to the south. He made his way over the hill to his boar banner, staked out between two poles in the still air, the scarlet boar rushing to the attack across its white background. His heart soared to see it.

Silently, his men finished preparing him, for the arming of a king was a sacred act. Mellan helped Cahir don his mailshirt, and Gobán buckled his sword-belt at his waist. They checked the laces of his boots, tight around the knee so they would not trip him when he was running. Finally, Fergal took up Cahir's war shield and fitted it over his knuckles.

Weighed down by iron, Cahir adjusted his stance on the edge of the ridge, bracing his shoulders. Below him, as the mist lifted, the Dalriadan and Attacotti armies flowed down to the plain on the right of battle, the west. In the centre were Fergus's Erin warriors, and on the far flank, the east, the Picts were gathered in their thousands. And all so eerily silent, beyond the coughs, the mutters and curses, the clank of armour and weapons.

No, not silence. An instinctive denial shot through Cahir. Too long had his men been voiceless. Now they faced an honourable battle, in full strength, and just like the heroes of old they must cry their courage to the gods.

Slowly raising his wood and hide shield above his head, Cahir struck it with the hilt of his unsheathed sword so it boomed over the murmuring throng. He drew a great breath, then bellowed it out: 'The Boar!' *Thud.* He struck the shield again. 'The Boar!' *Thud.* 'The Boar! *Thud.* 'The Boar!'

Around Cahir heads turned, and in moments up came thousands of shields borne aloft, and swords shimmering in the mist, and the Dalriadans broke into one war chant: *The Boar*! The blows of the swords formed a primal drumbeat, urgent and stirring, gradually growing faster and louder. It was a racing heart; pounding blood. Mellan leaped on the spot, waving his blade, screaming at the top of his lungs, and the young men followed, yowling like wildcats.

The chants and drumming spread, first to the Dalriadan warriors of Erin who cried out the same, sharing the blood of the boar; and then to the Picts, though their war cries were unintelligible at this distance. It didn't matter, though, for the din rose and ebbed together, soaring and crashing, the spears being pounded up and down alongside so the light caught in blinding ripples across the ranks.

With a savage smile Cahir stood silent now and let the sound penetrate his body, lifting him up to the heavens. And the last lines from the prophecy came into his head:

> *Hear your blood call you,*
> *Raise the boar above you,*
> *Make an end, battle-lord,*
> *The red-crests come!*

Cian stood among the massed Roman infantry, and, as the war shouts of Alba rolled over the plain, he felt the blood drain from his muscles. Wearily he tried to grasp at strength, at anger, but his body and soul were too brutalized for even a tattered remnant of that feeling. Instead, he stared dazedly at the massed wraiths now growing clearer as the mist lifted.

Finally it blew away on the wind and revealed to his exhausted eyes a sea of men that covered all the hillslopes to the north: an ocean into which he could only cast himself and drown.

'We are dead,' someone hissed next to him.

Cian spared him no glance, by habit shifting his grip on his short-sword, though he felt no fear, only despair. There had been too many months of raids in freezing cold and dark, Picts lunging out of black woods and sleet-filled valleys, swords honed. Too many men whose blood had spattered his own flesh – enemy and comrade, Alban and Roman – staining it for ever.

He had thought to expunge all pain and doubt in the heat of fighting; that he would cleanse himself. But the opposite happened. His wound still cramped, as though his body carried a memory of being broken. He was thin and stooped, his bones sticking out from the fever that had wasted him. But worse, when he at last returned to duties his battle-lust was bone-dry. Instead of the empty silence he craved, Picts stalked his dreams, blurring into Dalriadan faces and then to Minna, dark-haired and sorrowful. The shades of the men he had killed were piled on his shoulders, weighing him down.

Cian licked his dripping chin, wondering distantly if his sweat mingling with the rain meant that at least his body was preparing itself for battle, even if his heart could not. Crouched in the misty darkness before dawn, he had decided that today he would seek a final release. His own death was the only path remaining now.

The barbarian war-chants, rising and falling, built a pressure in the air like a coming storm. For a moment Cian thought of the sound itself growing strong enough to fell him, so he could simply lie there and stare at the sky as the other soldiers poured over and crushed him.

'Whore-sons.' A soldier spat the words, a gob of sticky mucus just missing Cian's boot. They called this one Red, for his copper hair and stark freckles. He was running his finger over his sword-blade, rhythmically, obsessively, ignoring the blood that beaded the tip. 'At least we've got them in one place at last. Here we can make an end; the Dux will fix it.'

He glanced at Cian, his sharp, sour face even more pointed from a lack of good food, and from looking over his shoulder and never sleeping. His thick hair was sodden, stuck to his drawn cheeks. He was Red, but they also called him black-heart, for his hatred for the blueskins outmatched anything Cian could muster. For a soft southerner – from Eboracum way, that's all Cian knew – he had turned as savage as the enemy. Red didn't even realize there was no difference now between himself and those he skewered on his spear. But Cian knew.

'What the hell is keeping him?' Red growled, peering through the last tatters of fog to the Dux's command post.

'We can't attack first.' Cian summoned some distant memory of tactics. 'Let them come on and expend themselves across the boggy plain; then we can approach from high ground.'

Red snorted, his finger flicking along the sword-edge like a licking tongue. Blood dripped on his knee. 'What would you know anyway, *pretty boy*?'

Cian turned his back, shuffling his stance on the muddy slope. The sun was slicing through the breaking mist when at last the Roman trumpets blew, and men were herded into formation by their commanders. Lines were straight-drawn, swords unsheathed from waists, helmets adjusted, spears braced. Prayers ran through the men like a wind, the Christos named along with the old gods of Rome, and the more ancient gods of Gaul and Britannia.

Officers strode back and forth, shouting last orders – in contrast to the barbarians who were spending their final moments whipping each other into an ever-greater frenzy, so none would feel fear and pain, so they could run at twice the speed, spear with double the strength.

Cian dragged his thoughts away from that maelstrom of noise. *Where were the cavalry?* Perhaps the Dux wanted to keep them in reserve. As if there might be a later.

The Roman horns blared again and were answered by the shriek of the barbarian war-trumpets, as if two great eagles fought in the skies above. The lines of soldiers around Cian pulled in tighter. The barbarians broke ranks with an enormous mass shout and onward rush to the ridge. Cian was pushed forward by the weight of his comrades and was suddenly stumbling down the slope. There was no turning back.

But he didn't want to turn back. He wanted to let the wave take him and bear him down into the void.

When the armies met, the clash of arms, shields and bodies resounded off the rocks with the roar of a hundred-year storm battering the coast.

Fullofaudes watched through narrowed eyes, his desperation becoming despair as he saw the barbarian tide wash over his ranks, his lines wavering then breaking, before being shored up by the more experienced soldiers. *Seven thousand to thirty* ... He must not think like that; there must be something he could do, some strategy that would enable his force to prevail.

Shouting at his commanders, he heard the horns screech and saw the scouts racing back and forth, passing on orders. Men were pulled out, reformed and forced back into the line. Throngs of soldiers and enemy warriors struggled in a turmoil below him, their weapons a frenzy of blades, the heather and turf slippery with blood. Screams, curses and shrieks pierced the air, as if the harpies of legend flew above in their fury, wafting about them the stench of death. There was so much blood that the hot, copper smell of it even reached Fullofaudes on his hill, drifting over the dank dew of morning.

He watched, but after barely an hour it was inescapable: his army was hopelessly outnumbered, their regulation armour a desperate island of order and civilization in the midst of the clashing colours, ragged furs and tattoos of the tribes; the fury of a wild sea overwhelming the stalwart land. No, it would not be!

His last chance was his cavalry reserves. The barbarians had none, and horses were all but invincible against infantry, his five hundred riders the equivalent of three thousand on foot. Orders were bawled from the hill, then passed via trumpet signal, and in moments the cavalry came thundering around the shoulders of the slope, one wing on the left and one on the right. His senior officers gathered around him, all of them straining to see.

The more far-sighted shouted in despair a moment before Fullofaudes realized what was unfolding before his disbelieving eyes. As the cavalry bore down on the barbarian warriors, they held firm almost to the last moment, and only when it looked like certain death for the Albans there rose from the ground a forest of stakes, each the length of three men, their bases dug into the ground and sharpened tips held up at an angle to meet the oncoming charge.

The Dux's oath left his lips a moment after the cavalry crashed over those stakes, racing too fast to avoid the collision. Horses were lanced through bellies; men through their necks; others flung free of their saddles to break their limbs on the ground. Fullofaudes could only watch as his prized cavalry soldiers were torn off their wounded horses, each fighter disappearing under a mass of hacking barbarians. He wanted to turn his face away, to rail, to cry out, but he could not.

'Send all remaining reserves in,' he barked to his officers, their faces white as bone, as their horses wheeled restlessly at the smell of death.

Drawing his sword, the Dux spun his stallion. 'We have to throw everything at them. Let us make a good end.'

He made to kick his horse down the ridge, but one of his officers blocked him, appalled. 'Sir, you cannot join the battle! You cannot – it's a rout.'

'It is a rout,' the Dux agreed hoarsely. 'So we will fling *everything* we have at them.' He paused, pinning them there with his gaze. 'Come! We must not let the men waver and flee. Show yourselves and your courage! For Rome!'

With that exhortation, he spurred the horse down into the pits of hell.

Fighting back to back with Ruarc, Gobán and Fergal close about him, Cahir saw that every knot of Romans was surrounded by triple their numbers of Albans, and he was flooded with jubilation.

He cleaved the terrified ranks of the enemy before him, striding through swinging his sword two-handed, taller and heavier than they and able to scythe through them like fallen wheat. It wasn't the most elegant fighting, but it was glorious and reckless.

Blood was a hot wash down his face, and its taste on his tongue pricked at an animal part of him that knew it meant victory. He did not falter. Freed of mist, the sun ignited the sheets of polished iron cladding the warriors around him, reflecting back a blur of light, and sweat ran down his skin underneath the armour, washing away all restraint.

In the midst of the chaos Cahir unleashed a roar from his very soul, and as he stabbed and spun he felt more power and grace surging through him, utterly unwearied.

As if summoned by his passion he *felt* the presence of Eremon and Conaire and their men at his shoulder, formed of the dust motes and hazed sunlight around him. He sensed them behind him, eyes bright with battle ardour beneath helmet-guards, their spears a forest, their swords a wall of iron. Their spirits poured strength directly into his heart, and it flowed to every part of his body. Cahir fought as he had never fought before, as if he were filled with the endless sun and wind and sky.

'The Boar! The Boar!'

Cian stumbled down the hillside, his arms spread wide like a sacrifice to the screaming enemies before him. But he surprised himself.

Though his blackened soul craved the release of death, his body retained the instinct for life. He heard a war cry wrenching itself from his throat, and, as the armies collided, he was suddenly ducking and weaving through a tempest of bodies, blades and lances. Part of him watched in detachment as he slashed and lunged with his sword and oval shield, a guttural growl punctuating each wild swipe and twisting leap. His acrobat's grace was reawakened, his movements a dance, seductive in its deadly rhythm. *Block with the sword, shield up across the arm, sword point into that exposed flank.*

Inside he railed at this crude desire for another breath, another day of sun and wind, a need that overrode all sense. But without conscious thought, his arms and legs knew what must be done.

Battle days are full of ironies.

Red, who so desperately wanted to continue inflicting his hatred on all blueskins, took a blade in the guts in the first few moments of battle, clean and simple. Cian saw him go down, a look of absolute disbelief on his face, before he was lost under mud and blood and tramping feet.

And Cian, who had started the day praying for death, found himself overwhelmingly alive. He heard manic laughter, and realized that it was coming from his own throat.

He would have dropped his sword quite gladly, throwing back his head and screaming that mad laughter to the blue sky. But a snarling Pict came for him with a broken lance, and his sword was swinging around of its own accord. After shattering the lance his blade tip went in under the Pict's arm, and sank into the soft place above the ribs.

Screaming now, Cian clutched the hilt with both hands and drove it home.

Cahir and his men retreated back to the ridge to view the battle's progress. Wiping sweat away, they gulped ale from flasks and caught their breath. Gobán leaned on his spear, muttering to Fergal, but Ruarc stayed at Cahir's side, his sword resting over his shoulder. Blood spattered his boyish face, and he made no move to rub it off, his eyes wide and white amid the gore.

'Hawen's blood and breath!' Cahir exclaimed, pointing to the middle of the plain. Ruarc raised his eyebrows. 'Their Dux has joined the battle. I didn't think he would ever come down off his hill and fight like a man.'

Ruarc grinned. 'It's because they know they are beaten. Ha! At least he has the balls to die with his army.' He flipped his sword back into both hands.

But Cahir was already one step ahead. 'Then we will make an end!' he cried, turning away for the slope.

Ruarc charged after him. 'Let us take him, my lord!'

'Come!' Cahir shouted over his shoulder. To the side, in a small valley that split the hills, the druids and horseboys were catching and corralling any spare mounts that came riderless from the chaos. Ruarc saw Cahir's intention, and a wild grin split his face as they ran for the most fiery stallions, those still tossing their heads, nostrils flaring.

Ruarc bellowed to Mellan and the few other young warriors nearby. Screeching, they followed their king, leaping onto saddles, hauling the horses around. Cahir galloped back into battle with a dozen riders at his shoulder, their eyes intent on the Dux, far away across a sea of ducking heads and slashing swords.

The Roman infantry, their famed discipline unravelling, fell back before the snorting horses and wild-eyed riders who bore down on them with blades swinging like scythes. There were no more rigid lines, just knots of Romans surrounded on all sides by shrieking Albans.

Again and again Cahir lost sight of Fullofaudes, as he leaned down to hack at men who tore at his bridle, blocking blows to the stallion's bowels and legs with his shield. His knuckles were bloody and his wrists bruised from the many strikes he deflected, his back cramped as he twisted, sweat running into his eyes. But he shrugged it all away with an elated laugh, kicking the battle-trained horse up so it reared and struck out with its hooves. His men were close beside him, the flailing legs of their mounts cutting through the ranks, and the press around them soon melted away so they were able to gain a clear space and dig the horses in the ribs to a gallop.

Like arrows they streaked around the flanks of battle, as up ahead the eagle standard of the Dux dipped out of view, then waved upright anew. The Roman infantry and officers had pulled into a tight group around their leader, but they were beset on all sides by howling Alban warriors.

Hearing the approaching war cries, the Dalriadan and Pict fighters leaped back as the riders collided with the Roman foot soldiers, and then closed about them again as Cahir and his men jumped to the ground to fight hand to hand.

On a small knoll, the Dux was wielding his sword with grim efficiency, wiry and strong for his build, but his guard was no match for the numbers of enemy piling on top of it, or the Albans' greater height and reach. At length, Cahir pressed through a mass of lunging, rearing horses, his eyes fixed on the Dux in the centre of his men.

Cahir could not drag his gaze from that hard, Roman face which had haunted his dreams; the merciless eyes that had condemned Finn and so many others. Striking out left and right with a cold rage, Ruarc at one shoulder, Mellan at the other, the last of the Roman officers were soon piled in tumbled heaps at Fullofaudes' feet, and he was swinging his sword against air, his standard shredded on the ground.

Cahir strode up boldly, one hand wrapped around his bloody swordhilt and one tearing off his helmet, dropping it to the ground as he waded through knee-high heather and broken bodies. Fullofaudes looked upon his revealed face, his eyes widening.

Surrounded by jeering Albans, he knew there was no point in fighting any more, and his blade went loose in his hand. With a contemptuous flick of his sword-tip, Cahir dashed the weapon from his fingers so it fell uselessly on the bloodied turf.

And they stared at each other as the last throes of battle raged on around the knoll: in the Dux's cold, grey eyes helpless rage and defeat; and in Cahir's, a burning victory.

Chapter 48

Minna sat in the hall with a salt-stained scroll from Cahir in her hand. The unread contents burned her fingers, and she could barely make any conversation in Latin with the little trader who had offered to bring news to Dunadd, and, in so doing, flee the war.

At last he left to return to his ship. She raced up the stairs and threw herself on Cahir's bed, ripping open the stained vellum. She unrolled the scroll and held it to the lamplight, her hands shaking. The writing was spidery, the ink already fading:

Forgive my informality, my love, for we have little time. But praise to the gods! We have enjoyed a great victory over the northern army of the Dux Fullofaudes, taking him by surprise. Fergus of Erin joined me in the west, and we took Luguvalium in a decisive victory and then subdued the Wall forts one by one until we joined Gede's army in the east. The Dux had by then gathered most of his forces, but it was to no avail as we crushed them in one charge, our numbers and our anger ruling the day. Gede's men killed the captured Fullofaudes, though it might have been better to keep him for bargaining. Our two armies have split once more to continue south on a wide front, east and west of the central hills. We are targeting the forts that guard the roads, and we will no doubt have to face more forces that the Dux was gathering from the south, and perhaps the southern commander as well, this Nectaridus. I have no more time, and must send this now. Please convey this news to Finbar.

You are in my heart as ever. As I sit here in the rain, I think always of the last night.

There was no name, but it was from Cahir. Only he knew of that sacred love-making in the darkness. Minna hugged the scroll to her breast, smiling into the lamp-flame.

When she came downstairs, Donal and Finbar were huddled around Cahir's chair, deep in what looked like a grim conversation. Donal saw her first and greeted her, unsmiling, while Finbar continued scowling.

'A message came from the king,' Minna said, looking from one to the other. What had happened? 'He writes to you that he has triumphed in the first, great battle.'

'We have already heard the rumours from the port, lass.' Donal's eyes lit up, though his smile was stiff. 'That is fine news indeed, fine news.'

'Then ... what is wrong?'

Donal glanced at Finbar. 'As you know, the Prince Garvan refused to return to his father's hall after his mother ... ah ... departed.'

Minna had barely crossed paths with Cahir's son. Quite naturally, he blamed her for the change in his mother's fortunes and refused to sleep under the same roof. He spent his time with the other boys too young for war, exercising their horses and playing at weapons, sleeping in their houses and refusing any food from his father's hearth. She had hoped, probably in vain, that once the sting lessened they might one day forge some kind of mutual tolerance.

Finbar crossed his arms. 'The boy has run,' he said simply. 'Four days ago. He's taken his horse, stolen a sword and armour, and gone. The woman of the house where he was sleeping didn't notice – said the boys were thrown together like a litter of puppies on her floor and how could she count them every day?'

'Gone?' Minna repeated blankly. 'Gone where?'

Finbar's mouth pursed sourly. 'To war, where else? The other boys said he was chafing to go; said he was the heir and he wasn't going to be left behind, and he would earn his own glory to be king.'

Donal rested his foot on the edge of the hearth-bench. 'As to what side he wants to be king for, that's up for debate.'

'It doesn't matter whether he's gone to join his mother or his father,' Finbar snapped. 'The king will still spit-roast us for this.'

Donal shook his head. 'Cahir charged us with the defence of this dun, not to act as nursemaids for a prince who should know better. He misjudged the loyalty in the boy.'

It wasn't bad judgement, Minna thought with a pang. It was guilt on Cahir's part, and a desperate hope that got the better of him.

'We've already sent out scouts,' Donal wearily told Minna. 'But he's got four days on us, and he's a fine little rider.' His mouth tightened. 'Finding one boy in such chaotic circumstances is going to be near impossible.'

Finbar nodded grimly. 'If the scouts don't find him, we must hope the boy has headed for his mother, and she can keep him safe within stout walls. At least then he can make his mind up at leisure whether he wants to be King of Dalriada, or King of the Carvetii.'

Minna eased the hounds-foot fungus from the base of a log and put it in the bag around her chest. 'Come,' she urged, 'I told you once what we use it for.'

Crouched on the log, Finola screwed up her face.

Minna waited, as the wet bracken slowly soaked her trousers. Even though the druids had just celebrated midsummer, rain had been drifting in the last few days, soft and misty from the sea.

Sometimes she thought of Garvan, cold and shivering under dripping trees. There had been no sign of him, though men had searched for days. More often she pictured Cahir, pushing her love towards him as if she could keep him safe. She wanted to take the *saor* again, to see something of him, but she didn't think it was safe to try too often, for it depleted the body as well as the soul. And every now and then, she was surprised to find Cian's face in her mind, though she had no idea where he might be – far away, she hoped, for his sake. She sent prayers to the Mother for him as well, though she knew he would only scoff.

She clambered up on the log beside Finola. The oak trees in this little hollow were festooned with moss, and ferns curled over her feet. Nearby she heard Orla singing as she chased butterflies, and scuffles from Lia's paws. 'We use the brown mushroom when there are pains ...' she prompted Finola.

'In the tummy!' the little girl finished, her solemn face lighting up.

Minna beamed. 'Good. The Lady Breda's children have griping pains in the belly, and I think it might be those horrid little worms.' She tickled Finola, and the child squealed and laughed. Though the youngest, it was she who showed an aptitude for the herbs, healing and dreams, while Orla, with her quicksilver emotions, preferred music and words.

'Minna!' Orla suddenly called in a sing-song voice. 'Someone's coming, a man on a horse.'

Lia began barking, as Minna lifted Finola on her back and tramped through the bracken to the rough-hewn track. Orla was crouched in the middle of the path, holding back the lunging puppy from one of Dunadd's mounted guards. Minna let Finola slide to the ground.

'Lady.' The man seemed perplexed. 'The Queen of the Picts is here demanding to see you. She arrived by sea this morning and came to Dunadd. I left to find you, but she insisted on accompanying me. She is not far behind.'

'Queen Nessa is *here*? Did she say why?'

'She said she will only speak with you, lady.'

Minna dropped Finola's hand. Nessa would never risk such a journey on a whim. She strode blindly past the guard, then began to run.

The track dropped from hilly ground to the marshes, and she saw Nessa walking a borrowed horse not far behind, accompanied by a warrior of her own kin. Nessa gestured the man to stop, then walked the horse on some way before pulling up, raising her hand.

Minna's impulse was to keep running, but each leg felt as if it were sunk in mud now, and she could only walk on unsteadily. As she approached Nessa, the bowl of the land began to echo with a soft, discordant song.

'Why are you here?' Her voice was faint. 'What is wrong?'

Nessa's chest was fluttering, though she had not moved. 'I have something urgent to tell you that I could entrust to no messenger. I come because of the friendship we share.' She was struggling not to cry, her mouth twisting.

'What?' Minna whispered.

Nessa's eyes tightened with pain. 'It is about Cahir. He is in terrible danger – but not from the Romans alone.'

The faint song all around Minna became a drum, beating out her heart's life.

Chapter 49

Minna paced before the hearth in the king's hall, her knuckles pressed to her mouth.

Finbar, Donal, Keeva and Clíona were all there, and Nessa sat in Cahir's chair, her feet in a basin of hot water. Riona had stumbled upon them and, seeing Minna's expression, taken her own seat.

'Tell them what you told me,' Minna whispered to Nessa. 'I cannot put the words together.'

Nessa gulped, addressing Finbar. 'After Gede left, I began to venture among the people more, because of things Minna said to me ... the way she made me feel ...' Her shoulders fell. 'I have been out both day and night, walking and listening, and taking more interest. The dun is nearly empty of fighting men, but I learned much from those left.' Her eyes rose, large and frightened, to Finbar's face. 'One night I was by myself on the walls, when everyone thought I was abed.'

Minna turned away to the fire. *Cahir.*

Nessa rushed on. 'I heard the captain of the defences speaking with another warrior. They didn't know I was there. The guard made some remark about how bored he was and the captain said: "No matter. We'll soon have leagues of new territory to divide up – you can be chief of your own fancy dun." They laughed then, and I thought they were talking about Roman lands, after the war. But then the first added something I can't even repeat about ... Dalriadan women.'

There was a shocked silence from everyone. Minna's eyes closed tight, her back to them. 'Tell them what it means, Nessa.'

There was a pause. 'I sent my man Urp among the men, and he found out ... he found out ... that Gede doesn't intend to only win the Roman lands. He wants all of Alba, too. He wants Dalriada.'

A muffled expletive burst from Donal. Then Finbar's voice came, hard as iron. 'Gede is in the south fighting Romans. What is he talking about?'

Minna spun on her heel. 'The only reason he agreed to the alliance was so that Cahir would help him destroy the Romans. And then ...' she had to spit it out, 'when it was done, turn on Cahir and betray him.'

'*No!*' Riona was aghast; Clíona and Keeva white with shock.

Donal bit off a curse as he and Finbar both came to their feet, their fury palpable.

Nessa buried her face in her hands. 'I am so ashamed. That my own husband, and king, could plan such a crime.'

'How will it happen?' Finbar demanded, impatient with Nessa's tears. '*Where?*'

'I don't know.' Nessa dropped her hands in despair. 'I only know that once he has the victory he needs over the Romans, he will find a way to turn on Cahir without implicating himself and m–murder him.'

Minna grasped for the nearest roofpost, pressing her back to it. Keeva was on her feet, holding her arm. 'Sit down before you faint.'

'No, no, leave me.' She was seeing again Gede's sardonic smile at the feast. Why hadn't she seen him for what he was? Instead, she had been too distracted by her own new gifts – gifts that had limits, as she had not realized then. She turned and leaned her forehead against the cool wood. Gede was so tangled he was almost impossible to read, but she should have tried harder. She had failed Cahir. *You have murdered him.* 'No,' she whispered.

'And your warriors agreed to this?' Donal demanded of Nessa. 'Betraying those you have fought beside breaks a sacred oath. It dishonours their swords, their shields, their very blood.'

'I know,' Nessa stammered. 'And though it offends many, enough are content to receive Gede's spoils and forget their shame.'

In the silence that ensued, Minna raised her face. 'He cannot get away with this. I will not let him.' Fury was bracing her now; that Gede would seek to take from her what she had so long sought.

Donal's face was set. 'We must get a message to Cahir at once, Finbar.'

'If he's taken the western part of the Wall, then there will be men stationed there who will know where he is. We could relay a message—'

'*Relay?*' Minna's voice cut in harshly. 'Use warriors as messengers and they are targets for attack – one goes down, and the message is lost.'

As they all stared, surprised at her vehemence, a sense of familiarity came over her. Facing down men and declaring she would make up her own mind to go into danger. *Yes*, Rhiann whispered to her. *Listen to the past. It was me.* But Minna did it now for love, and there was nothing stronger. Cahir was her anchor; she needed to be with him no matter what happened.

'And what do you propose instead?' Finbar asked disdainfully. He had not seen Minna in the cave in the north; he had never understood what she was or had become.

'Have you forgotten where I was born?' She returned his look. 'I am Roman by blood. I've already travelled those lands, walked those roads. I speak Latin, and can pass as Roman or Dalriadan. *Can you?*'

'Minna!' Nessa cried, as the implications sank in.

'Now, lady,' Donal began, groping for the authority of his sword, which he then discovered he had left aside. 'The idea of *you* undertaking this is nonsense. With a few men I can travel far more swiftly—'

'*Wait!*' Finbar stormed. 'Donal, what are you blathering about? We will send men to Cahir, aye, but there's no sense in you going, and damn well no sense in this girl going. She's the king's *lennan*! Do you have any idea what he would do to us?'

She placed herself in front of him. 'A party of Dalriadan warriors is more likely to be attacked than me. If we meet any Roman soldiers then I am simply a Latin lady trying to return home – there must be many people on the roads fleeing the armies.'

'Madness!' Finbar raked hands through his grey hair, making it stick out. But the faces of the women told a different story. Keeva was grinning, eyes alight. Riona looked admiring, and Clíona wryly resigned. Only Nessa was appalled.

'And there is another thing,' Minna declared, with a last burst of inspiration. 'I have been named by Cahir not only as his *lennan* but as his seer. I received visions from your gods, your ancestors who guide his kingship. Your men may need the connection between us to find him in time.' She paused, then added softly. 'And *he* will need me.'

She met Donal's eyes as his indecision dissolved into amused horror, like a kitten had just sunk its claws into his hand.

'This is ridiculous.' Finbar turned on Donal. 'Utterly foolish!'

Donal merely sighed. 'If she says she wants to go, brother, I don't see how we can stop her. We weren't appointed *her* guards, after all.'

Minna hadn't actually thought of that. No one guarded her any more.

Finbar crossed his arms across his barrel chest. 'Well, she can't go without an escort, and I do have say over that.'

Donal shrugged. 'I will go as her escort.'

'Ha!' Finbar jabbed a finger at him. 'You always wanted to join this battle. That's what this is really about, isn't it? Admit it!' Donal smiled and shrugged again. Finbar glanced at Minna, eyes narrowed. 'We need all our men to defend this dun.'

'We won't need many,' Donal argued. 'The fewer the better – then we can lay low more easily.'

'Of course it's far too dangerous, Minna,' Nessa suddenly interrupted. 'What are you thinking?' She sniffed, dashing away tears.

Minna knelt before her. 'You, of all people, must understand – you came all this way for me.' She took Nessa's hand. 'My heart is bound to Cahir's. I cannot sit here while he is so threatened. *I will go mad.*'

Nessa's eyes searched hers, and at last her mouth softened.

'If it were *my* man,' Riona said stoutly, 'I would go to him, too. In the old days the women went to war, didn't they?'

'Yes,' Keeva put in eagerly. 'Oh, Minna, the bards will sing of you—'

Donal stifled a squawk. 'She's not going to war! She's travelling in the wake of an army. If the king thought that ...' He trailed away, speaking so glumly that Minna smiled at him. Then her eyes came to rest on Clíona.

'What are you looking at me for?' the older woman sniffed. 'You'll only do exactly what you want to do; I can see it in your face.'

That was the truest thing said. For the first time in Minna's life no one could stop her. She was an entirely free woman, and as Cahir had made her so, even he could not gainsay her. She clambered to her feet and faced Donal. 'Are you really willing to do this for Cahir, for me?'

'I am more than willing.' Donal's face showed clear admiration.

'Pah!' Finbar sat down. 'Let it not be on my head, then.' But though his frown remained, he raised no more objections.

As the others dispersed, Nessa spoke Minna's name in a soft voice, and she turned from speaking with Clíona about provisions. Dwarfed by Cahir's chair, Nessa was limp, head down. 'There is something else I must tell you.'

Minna sank warily to the bench beside her. Nessa's eyes had almost disappeared into hollows, her face was so strained. 'It's my fault this happened.'

'Of course it isn't.'

'It is!' Nessa hissed.

Minna waited until Clíona left, and lowered her voice. 'What are you talking about?'

Nessa's eyes shifted to the fire, her lip quavering. 'I have to tell you about the real history between Gede and I.'

She thought of the secrets she had sensed at the Dun of Bright Water, and felt the weight of that darkness descend between them again. 'Tell me,' she said.

It tumbled out. Gede once had an elder brother, called Drustan. Their warlike family seized the kingship by force at a moment of weakness, even though they were not prime candidates for the throne. They demanded Nessa as Drustan's bride to bestow her royal blood through marriage, legitimizing his claim. This would also strengthen the claim of any son that came after him. Nessa dutifully bore the son – little Drust.

Minna's skin began to prickle over her arms, her neck. Suddenly Nessa burst out, 'But I did not know it would end that way!'

Her mouth went dry. 'What would end?'

Nessa turned her head. 'When I first came to the dun Gede would watch me, and then he began catching me alone, wooing me, kissing and touching. I never had such soft words from Drustan, only coldness, and, young fool that I was, I grew mad with desire for Gede. I thought he loved me. I didn't know he could ever do such a thing.'

Minna's heart beat slowly, as the darkness fell over her. Nessa curled up like a dying leaf, barely able to whisper how Drustan went away to raid over the Wall, and there died, though not from a wound.

Gede killed him, his own brother.

Then he came back north and claimed Nessa, but it was not for love after all, only for the throne, the blood.

'Then how could you wed him?' Minna's words were squeezed from a tight throat.

Nessa buried her face in her hands. Gede implanted his seed in her before he went to war with his brother. When he came back, and Nessa surmised what he'd done, she got rid of the child with Darine's herbs. Furious at being denied his own royal son, Gede said if Nessa ever told the truth of Drustan's death he would say *she* had done it, freeing herself to marry him. She flung back that she would tell the truth if he did not leave her body alone. They had been living in mutual loathing ever since.

Minna's mind was spinning. 'But how would anyone believe you killed Drustan if he was so far away on campaign? And did no one see Gede attack his brother?' Her mouth formed the questions, but a terrible thread was already unrolling in her heart. She grabbed Nessa's arms, her thumbs digging into her flesh. '*How did Gede kill him?*'

Nessa swallowed a sob. 'I'm sorry ... sorry I did not tell you before.' She closed her eyes. 'He did it with poison.'

Weariness had no hold over Cahir.

He strode tirelessly at the head of his army, his triumph a storm in his blood. He saw more keenly in the clear air, as if all the veils of shame and disappointment had been stripped from his eyes.

It had taken some time to gather his men together after the great battle, but now they were marching with the Attacotti and their Erin brothers in one enormous flood down the west side of the central hills. Fortunately this route took him away from Gede, who had chosen the east side.

For though the two kings raised cups of victory ale together on the battlefield, and Gede smiled and spoke rousingly amid the cheers of their combined forces, his eyes when they passed over Cahir were always cold, with speculation in their depths.

Cahir was heartily glad to turn his back on the Picts and head south, for they had news that the forces of the Count of the Saxon Shore – Fullofaudes' southern counterpart – were being recalled from their bases on the coasts.

Other battles were coming, and Cahir did not want coldness and watchfulness. He wanted to lose himself in passion and fire. He wanted to breathe freely for the first time in his life.

Chapter 50

Minna hunched miserably in the stern of the *curragh* which ploughed through the waves.

As the fishermen and six warriors rowed into a south-westerly wind, her belly was reliving its previous sea journey on Jared's ship. She spent her time beneath a pile of cloaks, shivering and retching over the side.

Donal tried to point out practically that no healthy man ever died from sea-sickness, but after she cocked one bleary, vengeful eye at him he let her be. After that, only desperate thoughts of Cahir stopped Minna wanting to follow her bile down into the dark, foam-laced waves. Everything stank, from the tar of the hides to the fishy smell of ropes and sails.

Finally, on the sixth day, they sailed into a broad estuary from the open sea. It was low water, and in the morning light the inlet was a vast plain of glistening sand and mudflats, edged with marsh grass. Far away to north, east and south there rose mountains, blue and hazy in the sunshine after days of rain.

The fishermen said they must stand off for high water, for it was dangerous, with the swirls of sand sculpted into underwater sandbars and treacherous bore tides. 'I think it's wiser to land north of the Wall anyway, rather than row straight up to the walls of Luguvalium,' Donal pronounced after consulting with the other warriors. 'Two rivers join this inlet: the southern leads directly to the town; the northern just leads into the marshes behind the town. I think we should take the northern river.'

Minna sipped water, her thoughts suddenly roaming back in time to Broc. It was ludicrous to wonder if she might see him, for the frontier was hundreds of miles long. But she was closer now than she had been for so long. What was he doing? Was he involved in the great battle? She didn't know, and she wasn't sure if she wanted to. When she thought of him, there was a blank space inside that frightened her, as if she couldn't feel him anywhere. Her eyes on the glittering water, she held that ache in her throat, knowing the unbridgeable gulfs between them now, thinking of the boy he had been. There was a tug in her heart towards those memories. But that's all they were, memories. And as for Cian, she pictured him far away in Gaul, or even Rome, watching silver tigers in the arena. She slowly wiped her quivering lip. She knew he was clever enough to have fled far from Alba, far from this danger. 'Cahir's letter said they had taken Luguvalium,' she croaked.

'True,' Donal was saying, 'but there might be remnant Roman bands close to the town still, and our boys will have their hands full with the civilians as well. I can't take that chance with you. Nor do we know what has happened to the Carvetii nobility.' The shadowy presence of Maeve reared up between them. Was she being held in the town? 'No, we'll land where it's quiet, give Luguvalium a wide berth and circle about from the north through the empty lands to the Wall forts further east. They will have a better idea of the lay of the land.'

They beached to wait for the tide in a tiny cove on the northern shore. Watching Minna crawl on hands and knees to retch up the water, Donal said, 'You know, lass, aside from your stirring words that day, I'm not sure I should have let you come.'

She wiped her mouth and pulled her cloak around her with shaking fingers. '*Let* me? I don't think you had a choice.'

Donal grinned. The wind stirred the tufts over his ears into a ruddy halo, and his balding pate was burned an angry red. 'Aye, but imagine me saying that to Cahir. "Sorry, my king, but she *made* me do it – that bitty slip of a girl."' He sighed. 'Make no mistake, he'll have my innards roasting over a fire shortly.'

'Donal.' She squinted out at the sun on the mudflats. 'It is not only men who can be brave and bold and foolhardy. It is not only men who can risk themselves. When Cahir took me as his seer, it wasn't just a name.' She buried her chin in her shoulder, voicing the thing that whispered to her in the dark hours, when her guilt grew into a monster. 'If he dies, I do, too. I am bound to him.'

Behind her, Donal was silent. 'However he bellows,' he said quietly at last, 'my king would do well to have you by his side. Whatever comes.'

When the estuary was covered with water once more they pushed off again. Before they left, Minna went behind the rocks and changed from her stinking tunic, stained with vomit, into a dress of blue wool from her pack. Around her neck she looped the crystal necklace Cahir had given her, and wound her hair up with bronze pins. Though her clothes were barbarian, she thought she could pass as a Roman lady without much scrutiny.

They rowed to the northern rivermouth, the banks of the inlets deserted islands of saltmarsh and bog, carpeted with moss and, in drier parts, thrift and grass. There were no sounds but the calls of the gulls and the wind scratching the leaves of the scrubby trees. The fishing huts they passed, covered with seaweed, were abandoned and smokeless. They glided past one settlement that was nothing but scattered ashes.

The silence became oppressive. The wide skies and endless snaking channels were lonely, the braying of geese swallowed by the emptiness. Then the salt-flats eventually gave way to abandoned fields, and still there was no sign of life. Minna sat in the bowels of the *curragh*, her knuckles white as she gripped its side. The sun was behind their heads when they at last coasted around a bend and saw a village. Clusters of half-burned houses surrounded the river, and the air was tainted with smoke.

Ashore, a horse whinnied.

Squinting, Minna could just see men picking over the remains of the buildings. Their hair and clothes were dirty and smoke-blackened, merging into the background of mudflats and low hills. Then, as if struck by a flint, the sun moved between the hills and trees, and lit up metal armour.

Warriors. She felt herself blanch as Donal growled an order and their men stopped rowing, their oars dripping in the air. But there was no halting the boat unless they made a lot of noise with reversed oars, and so for an endless moment it glided forward like a swan.

Ahead, a wooden bridge spanned the river, and it was lined with warriors, the slanting sun picking out the chainmail, their gazes fixed on the *curragh*. Minna's eyes flew over them. She saw leather jerkins, battered helmets, lances, bows and swords – but all warriors looked the same from afar, barbarian and Roman alike. *Was their hair long or short … did they bear the checked tunics of the tribes, the tufts of fur and skin tipping spear-hafts, the bronze mounts on helmet crests?* Donal rose to full height in the bow. He would know, he could tell …

His curse pierced Minna's breast, just as a man on the bridge bellowed a challenge. 'Halt, or we'll shoot!'

He spoke Latin.

Chapter 51

Minna clung to Donal's arm as the men on the bridge trained their bows. 'Pull over now!' the commander yelled. 'Down your weapons *now*!'

'They are not ours.' She could not form words properly, but Donal grunted agreement, scanning the shores to either side. The Roman soldiers were already swarming along the turf banks, their spears braced.

She fought panic, grinding her fingers into Donal's bones to steady herself. Then something forced its way out. 'Don't shoot!' she cried in Latin. 'We are no raiders!'

The captain paused. 'Name yourself, or we'll stick you with so many spines you'll look like bloody hedgehogs!'

Minna let go of Donal to draw herself up, glimpsing the fury settling over his face. She made herself stop thinking so wildly of Cahir. 'My name is … Ana Lucilla,' she replied hoarsely, digging up a friend of Mistress Flavia from her memory. The man on the bridge squinted down.

'Hold away from the shore,' Donal muttered at his oarsmen, eyeing the soldiers on either bank. The oars dipped, steadying the boat in the current.

'And what the devil are you doing sailing in like this, girl, in such rough company?'

She braced herself on the mast. She had made up stories for Marcus, after all, all the time. 'I was with my kin in the south when news came of the attacks. I have to return to my father.'

'Bloody hell!' The man barked a laugh. 'You've got nerve. This place is crawling with savages, don't you know?'

'We've been at sea,' Minna ventured, hoping the man was simple, or tired, or both.

'It's fortunate for you then that we just wrangled this town back from those bastards, though whether you've got any family left alive is another matter.' He shrugged, and spat into the water. 'People fled by the cartload.'

She made no reply, hoping her terrified expression spoke for her. The soldier stepped back from the edge of the bridge, though his shoulders did not relax. 'Get those clods of yours to lay down their weapons. You can land ... there ...' he pointed, 'but as soon as they ship the oars they put their hands out or we'll spear every last one of them. Got that?'

Minna whispered the translation to Donal. 'Is there anything to—'

'No.' Donal cut her off. 'If we land, you buy us time. I don't know what for, but time.' Slowly, with a look of pain, he unbuckled his sword-belt. 'Ah, lass.'

'Don't say it,' she replied through clenched teeth.

As the boat hit the shallows, the Roman soldiers splashed out to take hold of the bow. One by one, the Dalriadans stumbled over the side into the water. Grimly, Donal ignored all the spears to lift Minna and struggle to the bank, placing her gently down.

The commander had by now made his way down to them. He and his troop were filthy and ragged, some outfitted with pilfered armour, and shields painted with the boar of Dalriada, she shuddered to see. 'You travel in strange company, girl,' the leader muttered, eyeing the long moustaches and braids of the Dalriadan warriors.

Minna waved a hand. 'An escort from the westlands, where my uncle lives. At heart they are all still savages, but useful enough, my father says.' Her voice was faint, but it won her a thin smile. 'They *are* rough ...' She let her nose wrinkle a little, her mouth turn down, as she had seen well-born ladies do in Eboracum, 'but good in boats, you see.'

The commander snorted, but just then was interrupted by a shout from the opposite side of the river. A soldier was galloping towards them on a black pony which foamed at the mouth. Hooves clattered over the wooden bridge, before the man reined in. 'Sir!' the rider cried. 'There's been another attack on the south side of Luguvalium. The barbarians are advancing again, and all units have been recalled to the defences.'

The leader cursed and turned to Minna. 'Then we had better get you inside the town walls, and quickly. And make sure you stay with your family, then, and keep that pretty head down!'

She was staring wide-eyed at a baffled Donal. If Luguvalium was no longer under Cahir's control, it was the last place she wanted to go. 'I ... can't,' she blurted.

The soldier's head swung around.

'I must get home, and I live ... that way.' She pointed towards the east, not the south.

His eyes grew suspicious. 'We've been roaming these lands for weeks, and I can tell you there are no steadings left untouched. Everyone is either dead, fled, or tucked up behind the walls of Luguvalium. We'll escort you there, and that's my final word.' She closed her mouth, unwilling to provoke more questioning.

As the Romans formed up, Donal held Minna's eyes, unable to understand their speech and so confused at the change in her. 'Hurry, then,' she stammered in Latin, tossing her cloak over her shoulder and pointing for his benefit. Nodding grimly, Donal followed as she trailed behind the Roman guard.

As Minna walked in silence amid the muttering pack of soldiers, her mind skittered over many things. But one thought haunted her.

How would she ever warn Cahir now?

Luguvalium had seen better days, and was now an ageing matron of a town squatting between the two arms of the river. The walls encircling its bluff were mottled rock, and inside rose the bulky outlines of an old stone fort and houses. On the other side of the river loomed the shell of an abandoned fort on the Wall itself, which marched in from the east and passed over the water on an arched bridge before continuing to the coast.

In the lowering sun the town was hazed by smoke, its sandstone walls covered with moss. Campfires were scattered about temporary defences of thorn brakes, ditches and sharpened stakes. They negotiated all these obstacles – and many hard-eyed soldiers – until at last they were prodded through an enormous double gateway into the town.

Inside, wooden houses leaned against the old Roman walls, sprouting in abandoned courtyards and among the ruins of once-fine townhouses. Mules and goats crowded yards that had once been tiled rooms.

'Here.' The soldier nearest Minna lowered his sword. 'You're on your own now. Your guards' weapons will be held by the garrison at the gate. They can have them back when all this is over.'

She spun around with dismay, then forcibly softened her eyes and voice. 'But sir, with matters so unsettled I need protection. My uncle is wealthy and paid much to have these men accompany me home.'

The soldier's lip curled. 'No weapons are allowed inside the gates. And it was barbarian lovers like your uncle that got us into trouble in the first place.'

Helplessly, Minna watched the soldiers march back out of the gates, which creaked and thudded closed, with soldiers racing to draw heavy cross-bars. Then she turned and surveyed their prison.

In the central market, an enormous yard surrounded by shops and crumbling arcades, people had set up camp beneath anything they could scavenge: branches, sawn planks, sodden blankets. Geese honked in cages, and chickens flapped with tied feet. Mothers nursed dirty babies beneath dripping shelters. Some of the timber shops were open, trading in boiled mutton, cheese and bread, their smells overpowered by the stench of open waste pits.

'Now what?' Minna muttered to Donal. 'They said the Dalriadans had attacked again, advancing from the south. They've all gone out to defend the town.'

People were breaking off their squabbling and crying to stare at them, and Donal drew their men away somewhere quieter. 'If the Romans lose, we wait here for our lads to rescue us. If they win, we need to come up with some reason why you must leave. Perhaps your family isn't here and you have had word they *are* holed up on your farm.'

Minna nodded, and Donal squeezed her arm.

Soon they needed to eat. A search among the warriors turned up three bronze armbands to trade. As Minna began to draw her beads over her head, Donal stopped her. 'Nay, lass.' He had an odd look on his face. 'It is bad luck to give away the king's gifts, since it's him we're trying to get to, see?' He closed her fingers around the beads with his fist.

She went light with relief. 'Then let me get you all some food now, at least.'

The armbands were scrutinized by a weasel-faced baker in a stall beside the square. 'Barbarian make, are they? Very nice, very nice.' The bands disappeared into the cavernous pocket of his apron, and he proffered five buns in return.

'I have ten hungry men,' Minna responded, remembering her days in Eboracum. 'If the armbands are so nice, could you be a bit more generous?'

'Oh, no, no.' The man shrugged. 'With all the fighting, who knows when I'll be able to offload them – or to whom!' He smiled ingratiatingly at someone waiting behind her. 'Take it or leave it,' he muttered to her, sucking his tongue through missing front teeth. 'Only fresh bread here today.'

With a dark look, Minna took the buns and split them among the men, who wolfed them down in one bite. Her land legs hadn't returned yet, and she was nauseous rather than hungry. Instead, eyes cast down, she lined up at the fountain in the square's centre. It was marble, but the bowl was cracked and the leaping water nymphs that graced it were headless. When her turn came she cupped her hands under the trickle of water.

'Here.' A young woman behind proffered a wooden cup, one babe on her hip and another clinging to her muddy skirts. Her pale face was pinched. 'Had to leave everything, did you?' she asked, as Minna filled the cup and drank, then nodded.

The woman sighed and jiggled the baby. Her eyes were haunted, and there were bruises along her jawline. 'So did we. They killed my da, and my man's been wounded.' Her blistered lips drew back, and she said with vehemence. 'I *hate* them, the heathens. God will curse them, though, in time.'

She handed the cup back, avoiding the woman's eyes. 'Thank you,' was all she could get out, before she made her way back to the men. They had removed themselves from public view, crouching on the remains of an old stairway that led halfway up a stone building. Minna, worn out by seasickness and worry, curled up in her cloak and was instantly asleep.

She was woken by a disturbance at the gate. The sun had faded now into the long twilight of a northern summer. Rubbing her face, Minna roused herself. Whispers were hissing through the crowd, becoming mutters and then chatter. She rose and caught the arm of a boy running past, his face puce with excitement.

'What is it?' she asked him. 'What has happened?'

The boy's eyes darted swiftly over Minna's fine dress and beads. 'The soldiers are coming back, *domina*,' he said, hopping from foot to foot. 'A whole regiment of them, marching over the hills.'

'And do we know who had the victory?'

'Not yet!' the boy cried, scampering off. 'But it looks like us!'

Slowly, Minna sank to the bottom step beside Donal and told him what was said. 'Do you think ...?'

Donal's face was grimmer. 'I think if our lot had won they'd be chasing those soldiers back here, screeching like *banshees*.' He sighed heavily, then got to his feet and helped her up. 'Come. When they open the gates there might be a good deal of confusion, with cheering and crying, and perhaps we can slip out. You never know.'

He dispersed their men among the crowd, then drew Minna along with him. Together they pushed their way out of the square and down the narrow roads to the rabble gathering around the gates. Voices clamoured for news, people yelling to the stony-faced guards. 'What has happened?'

'Have we won? Are they dead?'

'Are the savages coming?'

At this last, delivered in a wail, people cried out and began to jostle each other, panic-stricken. Donal and Minna were shouldered aside, dragging her hood from her hair.

'Keep it down!' one of the soldiers on the gate snapped. His helmet cast his face into shadow. 'We don't know any more than you.'

For a short time the agitation of the crowd became more subdued, until some time later it was stirred by a new disturbance. On the far side, the throng was being split in two by people making their way through on horseback. Minna was jostled even more forcefully by a man who cursed her, though she ignored him, craning to see.

A soldier in polished armour came first, growling at people to get out of the way. Behind him, the plump woman on a grey horse was splendidly dressed in a pristine white robe and scarlet cloak, her hair piled in oiled yellow curls.

The air was sucked from Minna's lungs.

'You!' Maeve called up to the gate-guard. 'My father must have news at once of the outcome of battle! *At once, I tell you!*' Her face was puffier than before, pressing her eyes into angry slits.

Donal swallowed a grunt of dismay.

The soldier glared. 'And I tell you, *my lady*, that everything has changed now, if you had not noticed, and you'll find out along with everybody else.'

Maeve's cheeks wobbled indignantly, as nervous titters went around the crowd.

Minna was hunching into her cloak, hemmed in by people. 'Move slowly,' Donal muttered. 'Turn around, keep your eyes fixed on the gate, face that way.'

She tried to do as he said, but just then Maeve angrily nudged her horse forward into the pressing crowd, and someone cried out in pain. Hands shoved the rump of Maeve's mare, and she dragged the reins furiously around, unbalancing the heaving crowd. Minna was almost knocked from her feet, saved only by Donal's hand. Breathlessly, she looked up. The yard sloped higher away from the river, and out of all those hundreds of people it was her Maeve saw. The rumbling chatter and angry cries faded from her ears as the old queen's eyes flared with shock, then instant malice. The terrible moments unravelled one by one, while the air escaped Minna's teeth in a hiss.

At last Maeve's face turned from waxy to mottled red. As if in a dream, Minna watched her plump hand floating upwards, her rings flashing on white fingers as she pointed at her.

Then Maeve found her voice.

Chapter 52

Behind a locked wooden door, Minna crouched alone in the tiny cell, once a bedroom in a large townhouse. There was a narrow pallet on the floor, a waste pot and a thin blanket on which she sat, hands crushed over her ears to shut out the memory of Maeve's taunts.

After the queen identified her, she was bodily dragged by the soldiers from Donal's side. They separated her from Maeve before the older woman could do anything more than inflict one scratch down Minna's cheek, and ignored her calls for Minna's immediate execution. Now they knew who she was, the commander of the town's forces wanted to question her.

She leaned back against the wall, the cold stone burning her skin, distracting her from her last sight of Donal and the others being marched away, when she saw in his mild eyes his fear for her rather than for himself.

And Cahir. She spread her trembling hands out as if she could touch him. *It was my idea to come. My choice, bold and foolish, like a tale, and now Donal ... Donal ...* She pressed Maeve's scratch on her cheek and stared at the blood on her thumb. This is what impulsiveness had brought her. The men would die. She would die. Cahir would ... A noise came from her throat, stopping that.

The cell was lit by a small window, and she dragged herself up and pressed her nose to it. The bubbled glass admitted only light, no detail, and at length she sank back and watched the twilight fail. She dug her nails into her palms and the tender skin of her wrists. She wrapped arms around her thighs and rocked; anything to keep herself from weeping.

When it was night, she curled up and sang little songs of Mamo's, and when she couldn't sing any more, she listened to the distant shouts and snatches of cheering and music. They were celebrating a victory over the barbarians. The Dalriadans had failed to retake the town.

Minna covered her ears and sang again.

By morning she was suffering from a raging hunger, having retched up her food for days at sea. She was almost relieved when the door opened. It was a young soldier carrying something that steamed. 'Here,' he muttered, placing the platter warily down and giving it a push with his foot, then closing the door.

The food was a dollop of stew, full of gristle from an unknown beast. Nevertheless, at the sight Minna's mouth salivated. She pulled the plate towards her and sniffed. Closing her eyes, she took the steam in and rolled it around her mouth. Yes, it was safe. She would never forget Maeve's eyes, fanatic with hatred.

She began to eat, her eyes glazed, focusing only on the taste of salt and the heat on her tongue. The commander here wanted to question her. She must have some strength in her bones to face him, if it mattered at all.

When sunlight was falling through the window to the bare floor, the door opened once more. Minna struggled to sit up, stiff and cold, blinking in the sudden glare.

Into the cell came a soldier wearing a well-oiled mailshirt and helmet with cheekpieces that framed a pair of pale grey eyes. A sword was looped over his back. He carried a stool which he set down, then occupied.

He braced his hands on both knees, his neck roped with tendons, forearms thick and scarred. 'I am the *optio* reporting to our commander. We have been informed that you are closely attached to the household of the Dalriadan king.'

Minna kept a still face, though her heart had broken into a gallop.

The man folded his arms, reciting a well-worn formula. 'I want to know exactly how many men he has, what his plans are, and his aims. You will tell me.'

She pulled herself straight. Her thoughts darted to Broc, and a wild pang came to name him, to beg this man for her brother's aid, to pretend. But then she knew she could not. She would dishonour Donal and herself. She would dishonour Cahir's love. She had made her choices. 'I don't know anything,' she said clearly, though she quailed inside. 'I feel I am unable to help you.'

The *optio*'s eyes flickered at her perfect Latin. Then he smirked. 'By the blood of the Christos, I've lived my whole life among you heathens. I know when you lie, how you lie, and how long it takes to get the answers I need.' From a belt at his waist he withdrew a dagger and turned it over in his hands.

Minna's eyes followed it. The soldier smiled and sat forward again, placing the dagger across one knee.

Chapter 53

'The Romans have run before us, like women!' Gede scorned. He and Cahir were alone in the Pictish king's tent, the two armies having met up once more at the appointed time south of the hills. Now, the wide and fertile vale of Eboracum lay flat and open before them, leading on into Britannia.

Gede snorted as he poured two cups of mead. 'They are cowardly, mindless beasts. We should have faced them like this long ago.'

Cahir took the proffered cup, then nursed it on his lap, wondering how to reply. For him, winning was all that mattered – the thrill of that still burned his heart. He glanced at the vessel of mead Gede was propping on a side-table, and saw it was a silver ewer of Roman make, the table a carved one of shale. Above them, an ornate Roman oil lamp hung from the roof pole, dainty and incongruous in this tent of rough furs and bloody weapons.

He wondered for a brief moment where the plundered goods came from – how many villas and towns burned, how many women killed. Minna had begged him to take his men's oaths that no civilians were to be harmed by the Dalriadan army. He had gladly given her that promise, but there was no way to control the Picts. He hoped that most of the populace had fled before the might of their advance.

'What news have you of the Saxons?' he said, briskly changing tack.

'I have had word from King Cerdic that they intend to land at Petuaria on the estuary, and take the town and river crossings. They can hide their fleet there and come down upon the Roman flank from the north.' The two kings had decided to move rapidly down the main Roman military roads and take a stand above the *colonia* of Lindum to await the southern forces which no doubt were already being gathered. If Nectaridus took the bait, enraged at this invasion of the rich midlands, then he would find not only an Alban army waiting for him, but the bloodthirsty Saxons bearing down on him from an unexpected direction.

Cahir nodded, staring into the pool of amber mead. Neither had drunk yet, for the air between them was, as ever, prickly rather than companionable. He glanced up and saw Gede's piercing eyes fixed on his hands around the cup, which robbed him of any desire to stay and trade war stories.

He swiftly decided his presence was better served elsewhere. With the Pict and Dalriadan armies camped beside each other, the atmosphere was tense with brittle talk and sneering laughter. Fistfights broke out every day between the two tribes, and there were squabbles as the men scoured the land for food. Some groups had even drawn swords trying to scrounge from the same abandoned farmsteads.

'I thank you for the offer of a drink,' Cahir said politely, rising, 'and yet I remember I have called a meeting of my own men, and will be late.'

Gede shrugged, the tattoos on his face stark in the overhead pool of lamplight. Those painted falcon eyes stared right through Cahir's flesh. Unhurried, Gede sipped his mead. 'Then we will leave tomorrow to give us time to scout out our flanks and rear. Some petty commander might yet be regrouping the remnants of their northern forces behind us.'

'Tomorrow.' Cahir picked up his helmet. 'And it might be better to separate our men slightly as well. Their tempers will fray if the Romans take too long.'

'Not too separate.' Gede smiled coldly. 'After all, we need each other.'

'How can I know any more than you do?' Minna repeated hoarsely. 'They planned to land a large force and destroy the northern army – hasn't this already happened?'

The *optio*'s face hardened at her faintly taunting tone. 'I want to know their ultimate plan.'

Minna stared at the sunlight flaring off the dagger, then bared her teeth in a smile. 'Why, to march south and attack Roman soldiers where they find them. But you already know this, too.'

Quick as an adder, the *optio* was on his feet. He grabbed her tangled braid and dragged her head back, and she bit her lip not to cry out. His eyes were pale orbs that showed no mercy, no vulnerability. 'Enough insolence, my pretty whore. I want to know exactly *where* he is going and *why*.'

A stink of unwashed skin and sour sweat wafted over her, and *garum*, the fish sauce that laced all Roman food. Fish guts fermented in the sun – how Minna had loved the taste once. A whimper squeezed past her teeth.

'You will answer me,' the *optio* said with a brutish smile, 'or I will hurt you.'

And without warning his dagger nicked the hollow of her throat. Minna cried out, the lurch of terror breaking something open inside her. And the *sight* came flooding in like a sunrise over hills, so strong and bright the truth was outlined for her to see in vivid colour.

There was a baby in her belly. Cahir's child, a nub of a thing, its spirit no more than a faint echo of life.

She clapped her hand to her throat as the soldier released her. Blood seeped through her fingers ... *There was a baby, and it would die, too.* She could not fill her lungs because of the vice that tightened around her.

Satisfaction flared in the *optio's* eyes. His voice dropped, and he stroked the blade around the curve of her ear. 'I need you to speak,' he murmured, like a man would to his lover, 'but that does not mean I need your body unmarked.' And he took her arm and dragged the blade across her white wrist.

She moaned as another line of red appeared, the blood beading on her skin. The *optio* smiled and stepped back, and suddenly Minna was dizzily remembering Cahir drawing a dagger across his soft flesh, the same warm skin she had kissed. A fist seemed to squeeze her chest and it all started to go dark. Dark, and cold.

At the final moment, a warm light arrested her descent into blackness. She was supposed to listen. Rhiann's voice came back to her, something she had forgotten from the *saor* dream. *At the times of greatest travail we will be with you.* Her Sisters, the priestesses. Minna clawed at the stone floor. *Help ... help me.*

As she wavered on the edge of the precipice, there came a brush of butterfly wings on her shoulders and throat, a touch alighting on her temples and eyelids. But there was no one else in the room. She caught a sob in her throat. The *optio's* smile blurred before her. A rustling began, like wind blowing through a forest. Her eyes sank closed. *I've fainted, then. Cahir will think me so weak.*

But the rustling became whispers echoing on the walls, layers of voices murmuring. Minna straightened, struggling back from the dark place. Each voice began whispering different things, snatches of thought and idea which wove into a kind of song, drawing her with them. The butterflies became invisible fingers, soothing her, calming her panic to give her clear sight. Breathing hard, she blinked and raised her chin, listening.

'Speak or I bring this blade to your veins!' the soldier growled. 'And worse, witch, will come when I give you to my men. Have you thought of that?'

She shuddered awake, stretched her chin high, no longer slipping into darkness. Her back was absolutely straight, the grace of the Sisters holding her. 'Witch, you say?' She smiled, her heartbeat striking loud and slow in her breast. 'You have heard, then, Caecilius Rufus, of my island of witches in the Western Sea.'

There was a shocked silence. *She knew his name. The whispers told her.*

'On a day of sunshine, the holy witches died on Roman swords. And have you heard, Caecilius Rufus, how for ever after those soldiers could seed no woman's womb, their manhoods weakened and poxed?'

A pause. 'What vileness is this?' the *optio* demanded. 'What madness do you utter?'

There were lights behind Minna's eyes. She felt the blood drying on her skin. She heard the baby, a tiny, gasping cry, and held it close. 'No madness, Roman. You *have* heard of this slaughter – for all these years later you still fear to violate the wise-women of Alba.' She leaned forward. 'Know then that *I* am of these witches, and I too can put a pox on you, and all that you are will wither away.'

Enraged, the *optio* stepped close and struck her across the face. 'You lie ... it is all lies!'

Her head snapped back, the lights dancing. She hardly felt the pain in her jaw and lip – she only saw the fear far back in his eyes. She smiled again, tasting blood. The voices flew about her head more urgently, the ghostly fingers stroking away her hurts. 'Caecilius Rufus.' The sing-song voice that now came from Minna did not seem to be hers, and she listened to it with a distant dreaminess. 'You stole three *solidii* from your father when you were nine, and he beat you until the skin came off your thighs. You killed a kitten once, by stringing it up in a noose of twine and watching it die. No one knows that. The first woman you bedded laughed at you ...'

The *optio* grunted, his hand rising again.

'On the Wall you collected taxes, and made money behind your commander's back.'

The soldier's fist wavered in the air, and he fell back one step and then another, the whites of his eyes standing out in his pale face.

She got up on her knees. 'You raped a blueskin child once, and you've never banished her eyes from your mind. They haunt your dreams still.'

'No.' His voice was strangled.

Slowly, she pointed at him, the blood oozing from the cut on her arm. 'You loved a man,' she said softly. 'It surprised you. He fought alongside you, and you loved him, and when nights were cold you shared warmth and showed nothing of what you felt in your face. He died, so near to you that in every dream you see the blade pierce his flesh again, and wonder why your own flesh was not there to take the blow.'

The soldier's body was quaking now, and her finger with it. 'Violate me,' she said very softly, 'and I will bring down upon you the wrath of every witch who died that day on the Sacred Isle. Your manhood will shrink and rot, until you scream for release from pain. Your shade will be followed even unto the halls of death, and never left in peace.' Then she opened her throat, and what came were the first lines of Davin's song, which spoke of the love of Rhiann and Eremon.

The barbarian words reverberated off the plaster walls, doubling back on themselves. They were words of great love, hope and belonging, but this soldier thought them curses, marking his flesh.

With a gagging sound he backed against the door. 'You are ours now, no matter what you say,' he gasped. 'We can use you as hostage to capture your lover, to force him to surrender. He is a man, and can die by the blade.' Halfway out the door he forced himself to speak again. 'Know that your men hang from the walls for the ravens to feed on. We toasted their deaths with ale.'

He slammed the door behind him, and Minna fell to all fours, panting. Gradually the butterfly touches faded and it became colder. The whispers in the room grew fainter, until there was nothing but the banging of a loose shutter outside in the breeze.

All the energy went from her and she curled up, arms about her belly, staring at the shadows on the wall. The soldier's last words beat on her heart, one by one, until abruptly she began to weep for Donal, her tears dripping on the scratches and cuts that marked her. The light moved across the floor and dimmed as she cried, her grief and her guilt like the seizure of poison.

For the first time she tasted the full bitterness of being a *seer*, and how those bindings could strangle, tight about her neck as any slave-ring.

Two days later, she was taken away in the dead of night. Whether this was to avoid Maeve's wrath, Minna never knew. The *optio* was not among the soldiers who guarded her.

In those first hours on the dark road, stumbling on the end of a rope, she discovered the reason for her swift removal. Her escort of ten muttered among themselves, their voices carrying in the cold. The northern army was scattered, with no central command. It wasn't safe to keep the prize of the barbarian king's whore in Luguvalium, where insurgents might take the town again. They needed to put her directly in the hands of someone who could decide how to use her best. This was to be Nectaridus, the Count of the Saxon Shore. They were taking her south, far from Alba.

Minna had little time to absorb this. No man was willing to lay hands on her after the *optio*'s interview, but that didn't stop the small torments, the nips of pain that blended into one wound on her soul. The men prodded her with spear-butts, striking her in the ribs and legs with glancing blows until she was a mass of bruises, trying desperately to protect her belly. When they wanted her to move faster they used the barbed points.

She soon learned that if she raised her eyes she would receive a blow from a fist, and once, the crack of a lance across her skull. Warding signs came, too, of course: the crossed fingers and spit in her face. They tripped her to kneel at the end of every day, and poked her awake with spears.

So the desolated landscape through which they moved became no more than a blur of suffering.

The air was rancid with smoke, and all around were blackened shells of abandoned buildings, and the bodies of warriors of both sides choking streams and piled behind breached walls. The stink of rotting corpses and taint of smoke, the bleating of wandering sheep and cawing of ravens soon merged into one dark nightmare pierced with jabbing pains.

She stumbled along with her head down. Donal was dead. She repeated that litany to keep her feet going. This punishment was for Donal and the others, hung by their necks from the town walls. So Minna would endure and not fall. She would not die of exhaustion, or sorrow, or guilt, or the sting of cut flesh.

It would take more than that, for the sake of her baby.

In daylight, the land was almost deserted of life. The soldiers moved stealthily by hidden paths, avoiding the barbarians picking over burned farmsteads around them. Gradually, as Minna's pain became constant, her mind broke free and drifted above her. And she realized that, as her body was bruised by her own people, cursed and spat at, cut and shoved, something in her was inexorably draining away. It gathered in from every part of her body, then flowed out of her feet to the earth.

Out went the old life and loyalties. The kinship with Broc, her unknown father, her dead mother. The heartbeat of Rome, of Eboracum, of Master and Mistress and the Villa Aurelius. Being Roman. Being Minna-the-nurse. Being someone else's. All of it went, bleeding away in that tormented journey across a blasted land. Only the echo of Mamo remained, for she was wound into Minna's soul.

So, step by step, Minna was stripped of her previous lodestones – blood, identity, birth – and what was left was a different being. She became only Minna of Dalriada, beloved and *seer* of the king. She found the mother in her, strong and fearless for the baby.

She would be these things alone, for the short span of time left to her.

Six weeks after the barbarian armies landed in the north, the Count of the Saxon Shore, Nectaridus, hastened to confront them at Lindum with only the five thousand men he had left, and another thousand who had escaped the northern slaughter.

The Albans had chosen their battleground, using all those fine, straight Roman roads to march down in time to pick the raised ground above an expanse of boggier earth. The irony was not lost on Cahir, that their passage was made so much easier because of Roman engineering.

Behind them they left a land stained with smoke, and scoured of the people who had fled in terror before their armies. Food was there for the taking – the crops in the grain-stores, the meat on the hoof – and the Picts and Dalriadans were well-fed and rampant with eager bloodlust.

The Romans, however, were stunned by the Dux's defeat, and had been driven north by their Count at a forced march. According to the Alban scouts, they were exhausted, disorganized and terrified.

Cahir smiled to himself. It could not have been better.

Chapter 54

Two days later Cahir raced down the high ground above Lindum towards the sea, his legs pumping, his sword held high beneath his streaming boar banner. His men bellowed as they ran. Around him, the advance of the Alban warriors was a great ocean swell breaking on a shore – a roar from thousands of throats, the flow of bodies a turbulent rush.

On his right flank Gede and his Picts were a screaming turmoil of hatred, with gaping mouths and rolling eyes. On Cahir's left came Fergus of Erin's men, red hair flying like the manes of their wild horses, their shields a battering wall; and the little, dark Attacotti, their arrows a rain of iron. And somewhere behind the embattled Roman army, another five thousand Saxons had just poured in from the shores of the estuary.

The Romans were caught between Saxons, sea and Albans like soft metal between hammer and anvil.

Screaming as he charged up and down on a white horse, the helmeted Nectaridus had put his army's back to the coast. Now they were turning in horror at the sudden and unexpected appearance of the blond-haired savages from over the Northern Sea.

Racing across trampled fields of barley, Cahir's keen senses picked up the shock that dawned over his opponents as Saxon horns droned over the battlefield, their raven banners darkening the sun. The Romans turned and saw them, and a wail went up that was swallowed by the barbarian war cries all around.

Cahir grinned triumphantly. In his heart, this made up for Eremon's shock and despair that day at the Hill of a Thousand Spears when he turned to see another Roman charge from the east. He touched his sword-hilt to his chest as he ran, in honour of his ancestor.

The Roman shield wall and disciplined lines of men again disinte-grated at the sheer force of the Alban charge, and Cahir found himself fighting hand to hand with men who struck out desperately, not skil-fully, sobbing as they went down. And he carried the fire of a whole people in his heart, the fury of centuries, and so the embattled Romans around him fled from the light in his eyes.

His days of being a measured fighter were over, as all his pain flowed out, and with a wild yell he drove the point of his sword between the collar-bones of the shouting man before him. As the man died, Cahir saw himself reflected in his eyes, the culmination of every Roman nightmare – a towering barbarian with a blood-spattered face.

He whirled again. Another man fell as flesh met his blade. Then he was hock-deep in blood, mired in writhing men, with rents opened in flesh by swords, and bellies skewered by spears. In the recesses of Cahir's mind it reminded him of maggots in a battle-wound, a wrig-gling mass of legs and arms.

A knot of men cleared around him, and he paused to wipe blood from his eyes, leaning on his sword. Gede had found a slight rise of ground and stuck his hawk banner in it. Seemingly oblivious to the danger of javelins or arrows, he was standing there challenging any comers on the exposed slope. Cahir was immediately arrested by his first sight of the Pictish king fighting, for in the other battle Gede had been on the far flank.

In contrast to his men, Gede surrendered to no wild plunges or screaming. He had taken a cut on his temple that washed his tattoos in gore, but his expression remained set. Though Gede was slight, Cahir had never seen any man move so swiftly, darting under the guard of his opponents again and again. He employed a unique tactic where he spun just *before* he reached the end of a sword lunge, suddenly reversing his momentum, taking the other fighter by surprise. Gede would twist at the waist halfway, driving the blade home in an unexpected flash of speed and force.

Over and over again Cahir watched Gede do this, as bodies piled up around his feet. And all without offering one sound or even a grimace, with an intense focus and lithe grace that made Cahir's belly lurch. It was a dance of death.

Then the space around Cahir collapsed into chaos again, and he had to put all thoughts from his mind and deal with the increasingly desperate Romans – outnumbered, surrounded and hopeless.

It didn't take long, two or three hours, for the Roman army to flee into retreat. The final blow was when Fergus of Erin and his men fought through to Nectaridus himself, and the Erin king drove a broken spear-shaft into the Count's throat.

After that the panicked Roman soldiers turned and, like a tide on the ebb, began streaming away south, leaving their wounded and dead. The Picts and the Saxons raged after them, pursuing them into the forests where the marsh and fields rose to low hills. From the woods soared the sounds of screams and the clash of iron.

Rallying Ruarc and Mellan, Fergal and Gobán, Cahir went racing after his own men to pull them back from that sickening pursuit of the helpless wounded. Their path took them dashing through patches of trees and splashing over streams, shouting for their warriors.

At last Cahir paused by the remains of a farmstead as Ruarc and his other commanders forged on, bellowing out the orders for the Dalriadan bands to return to camp. Suddenly, he was alone in the ruins.

Catching his breath, he tugged off his helmet and stretched his jaw, which had taken a blow from a Roman fist. As the battle-fury drained away, his body complained from a dozen different injuries. The muscles in his flank cramped where they had torn, he had wrenched his neck, and his knee throbbed where he had twisted it on muddy ground. There were shallow wounds on his forearms, a deeper cut on the mound below his thumb, and a graze across his brow that trickled blood into his eye and stung more than all the others. And only now did all the little irritations rise up: the itch of sweat, the insect bites rubbed raw by his mail-shirt, the dryness in his throat.

In that moment after great danger, when the mind is still dazed, Cahir thought, *I would have done better not to wait until I was an old man to fulfil this prophecy.* And that made him laugh bleakly and rub his face. Minna's cloth was tied around his wrist; now he touched it gently with his finger, the linen so dirty with blood and mud it was unrecognizable to anyone but him.

He looked over the ruins of the farm. The pale walls were smeared with soot, the red roof-tiles scattered and crushed on burned floors. He went looking for a well, and found one on the other side of a row of apple trees. Shouts and screams still drifted from the woods to the south, and moans and bellowed commands from the battleground to the north.

He tested the rope on the well, but the bucket in its depths didn't move. Tormented by thirst, he leaned over the shallow drop, peering down. Against the circle of water he saw something tangled up in the bucket, and, as it turned slowly, he realized he was looking into the dead eyes of a naked child, staring up from a bloated face. She must have been about Finola's age.

His hand fell from the knotted rope. Her skin was the texture of fish, spongy and pale, and her long, dark hair trailed like seaweed. Cahir saw she had not died by drowning, for a gaping slit marked her throat, which was white and drained of blood. The Picts had already raided these lands days ago, as the kings laid battle plans in Gede's tent.

Cahir found himself striding blindly away, but at the edge of the yard he turned back. 'May the Mother take you to her breast, little one,' he muttered.

For that is what Minna would have wanted.

Night had fallen across the battlefield, and from the slopes of a dark hill Cahir watched the plain.

Below him, the encampment of the great army was a blanket of stars, with fires stretching out for leagues, and from their massed glow came snatches of drunken song and choruses of war chants.

Drawing a breath, he turned to his left. There, around the shoulder of the hill, burned the immense pyres of the Alban dead, larger and more brooding than these sparks of the living. Druids tended them, watching over the departing spirits. He swung to his right. Over a vast area to the south flared other fires. Gede's men and the Saxons had been let loose over the land, and those fires were farms and woods set alight, and fields and crops put to the torch. These were more scattered, burning in wavering sheets or incendiary bursts of flame.

Cahir turned slowly to each direction one by one again, scenting the ash and cinders, the burnt flesh and roasting meat, and the gods knew what else that was being destroyed. And he thought of the glassy eyes of the Roman child, the way she swung on the well's bucket.

At last, walking purposefully, he went down to his warriors. He wended his way between the thousands of raucous campfires of Dalriadans on the north side of the army, and the Attacotti warriors mixed in with them, small and dark, singing at the top of their voices. But as he neared his own campfire, he was surprised to see his close comrades quiet for once.

Some of his men had their heads down, resting against their packs. And then, between a great yell from one fire and a burst of singing at another, Cahir caught a snatch of Davin chanting a lay.

He paused in the shadows of a hawthorn brake, listening. The song was entirely new – he could tell by the way Davin stumbled over the strings, stopping and starting, changing his mind. At first Cahir thought it was a song about the warriors of legend. He took a step towards the fire and then stopped, his feet sinking into the damp ground. The lay was about him.

> *Mac Greine! Son of the sun.*
> *And sun he was in his mail of bronze*
> *His eyes ablaze*
> *His helm a torch against the dark of Rome.*

> *Three wheels of five score years*
> *Since the god walked the battlefield of blood.*
> *And now Dalriada comes in swinging*
> *Their swords singing*
> *And among them he is a towering tree*
> *Crowned with sun-gold*
> *Cahir son of Conor.*
> *So the red-crests fall back from his gaze*
> *And he strides among them*
> *His sword a tongue of light in his hands ...*

The song died away, leaving Cahir's chest tight as a drum. They sang for Eremon, and now they sang for him.

He emerged from the shadows, and Davin saw him and fell silent with a last chord. Heads turned, and space was made for the king on the logs and rocks. He sat down among his commanders and looked at Davin. 'Sing me the Hill of a Thousand Spears.' Davin looked perplexed, for it was a long composition. 'Just the end,' Cahir added. 'Tell me again what happened when they charged, what Eremon did.'

Give me Eremon, was what he longed to say, only no one would understand what he meant. Eremon and Conaire were gloried and sung because they fought like gods, despite defeat – and now Cahir could stand proudly by their side because he had *won*. So why, now the battle fury had faded, did he no longer feel as if a great bird lifted his heart in its wings? Instead he only tasted ash on his tongue from the death pyres.

He knew what his Erin ancestor would say. The burden of leadership falls more heavily than the exultation of triumph because, no matter what happened, men had died this day by his order. There were gaps at the campfires, and hard sorrow on many blood-stained faces.

Davin was straightening, readying himself, when Ruarc broke in. 'I must get you an ale, my lord, to toast our great victory!'

'Aye!' Mellan crowed. 'Twice we've smashed them now. Let the Emperor stick *that* up his purple arse!'

There was a smatter of jubilant assent, and Cahir mustered a smile. 'Afterwards,' he said softly. They had fought like princes, and deserved their pride.

Davin began to sing, and Cahir stared into the flames, picturing that ancient battle day. The last thing Eremon said to Calgacus was a blessing from Hawen, and Calgacus replied by saluting Eremon with his sword. 'To Alba!' he cried in the song. 'She thanks you for her deliverance.' And as Eremon galloped down the hill, the war chants surged like a storm sea, swords beating on shields, crying, *Alba! Alba! Alba!*

Cahir's eyes glazed, his heart wandering far from his thoughts.

Suddenly he saw in the rippling flames not Eremon but the face of the slaughtered child, her hair black tendrils on her white cheeks. So like Minna's hair. Abruptly, he stood up.

After one look at his king's face, Davin's voice trailed away. 'I thank you,' Cahir said gruffly to his bard. 'All of you. But the moon is rising, and a council has been called. Mellan, Ruarc and Ardal, come with me – and bring your swords.'

Chapter 55

In the centre of the army was the command tent, a dome of goat-skins, roof raised with hazel saplings. When Cahir entered the other kings were already there drinking ale, a few camp-whores lounging with them. Gede sat on his Roman camp stool, setting himself above the others who sprawled on cushions. His facial cut had been crudely sewn, and there was blood on his tunic. Next to him squatted his second-in-command Garnat and the young druid Taran.

In the middle the bare earth was piled with stones and a fire set there, the spitted bones of a hare sticking out of the flames. The plundered Roman lamps swung in the draught as Cahir entered, Ruarc, Mellan and Ardal joining the other guards behind their lords.

'You're late, brother!' Fergus's nose was already as red as his wild hair. And why would he not be drunk? He had dealt the Count's killing blow, and been crowing about it ever since. He waved a bannock at Cahir, the gold brooches and rings that festooned his checked clothes flashing in the lamplight. 'Where've you been? Working that battle gorge out between some tasty, white thighs, eh?' He leered at the fair girl beside him, her hands in his lap.

Cahir smiled politely. 'No, brother. I had business with my own men, that is all.'

The stocky Saxon king, heavy cheeks trailing a blond moustache, was still clad in his jerkin of studded leather and bird-winged helmet. Now he barked something to a salt-stained little trader who acted as his interpreter. The man said to Cahir in awkward Dalriadan, 'My lord Cerdic say he happy at battle victory. He honour all kings.'

Cerdic bared his teeth in a smile, and raised his drinking horn. Cahir took the proffered cup from Fergus and nodded back. 'Tell your lord that the battle was won by his arrival. We salute his men's bravery.'

Through all this Gede stared at Cahir, unblinking. Now Taran rose. 'King Gede requests that I act as interpreter,' he said. 'I can speak on behalf of the Picts as well as the Dalriada, Erin and Attacotti kings.' He bowed to Cahir, Fergus and Kinet, who sat cross-legged and contained, feathers wound in his black hair. 'That only leaves my lord Cerdic, and his man speaks Pictish better than the western tongues of Dalriada. Is that acceptable?'

They all nodded. Taran began. 'My king says that this second victory has, thanks to the gods, struck a final blow for the Roman army in Britannia.'

Cahir leaned his cup on his knee. 'Our armies were courageous, and fought brilliantly, there is no denying. The results have exceeded our expectations. However, it has been six weeks since the northern battle. Even now, the Roman Emperor will be gathering greater forces to repel us from over the sea.'

There was a moment of muttered translation. 'That is no doubt true,' Taran said. 'Which makes the next part of my lord's plan that more urgent.'

'Plan?' Fergus dragged his attention back from his whore's breasts. 'What plan? We've driven the Romans to their knees, and I've taken enough plate and coin to sink my ships. I've got what I wanted and lost a good many men doing it. It's time for me to return home.'

Gede rapped something out, and Taran turned to Fergus. 'My lord says that is a ... somewhat limited view. We have been given this opportunity by the gods, who have provided two stunning victories, with little loss of life. He says it would be foolish to turn our backs and let the gifts of the gods slip through our fingers when we have come so far.'

'What opportunity is he talking about?' Fergus said testily to Cahir, his hand dropping away from the girl's rump.

Kinet broke in smoothly, his eyes jet beads. 'We talked only of crippling the Romans to free Alba,' he reminded Taran.

'And make ourselves richer along the way,' Fergus added.

Taran paused. Priests, Cahir mused with a swig of ale, might go weak-bellied at the stench of armies, but they understood a good pause.

'My lord Gede feels that we must push on to the uttermost end of Britannia, take all the lands from sea to sea, and banish or slaughter every man, woman and child of Roman blood.'

Fergus gasped, and Cahir set down his ale.

'The Roman army has crumbled,' Taran went on, 'and the roads are open now to the south coast. In our path lie villas and towns beyond counting.'

Fergus blinked and sat back. 'And what if Cahir is right? What if we get trapped down there in the south when the Emperor's army arrives from over sea?'

'We won't,' Gede said through the druid, his gaze hooded. 'There are too many of us. The Romans will flee when they see us coming. We take the plunder, plant our seed in the women, man the Roman forts on the shore and repel any army that comes from Gaul.'

'I admire your courage,' Cahir interrupted, 'but that is a foolish idea.' He ignored Gede's piercing glare and spoke to Fergus, Cerdic and Kinet. 'We have enjoyed our successes because of surprise and weight of numbers. The first battle knocked out control in the north; the second was won by the Saxons landing. But by the time we march south, the Romans will have had time to regroup and defend their walled towns. They will also be more desperate. Do you honestly believe you can hold all those towns with the Emperor's army coming on your rear? And to plunder such an area you'll have to split your men, and that will weaken you.'

As Taran finished Cahir's words, Garnat's face suffused with blood. He leaped to his feet. 'You call my king foolish? I call you coward!' Taran winced at this, but duly translated. 'This opportunity will never come again, never, gael! We will take Britannia back for its tribes – my king has already sworn this to us, in the blood he shed this day!'

Cahir gazed up at him, reining in his temper. 'The tribes you speak of have been Roman for generations: their blood has mixed. Do you think they want us rampaging over their farms, killing and raping their women, their children? Do you think they will welcome us as saviours? I tell you – you cannot hold the entire island. The Romans have an empire-sized army and they will send it here to get their Province back. However, we *have* struck the blow that will keep them behind their Wall, and leave Alba alone for ever. That is all I ever wanted. That is all we agreed.'

All of them fell silent, except for the muttering of the translators, and the nervous coughs of the guards against the walls.

Suddenly, Cerdic the Saxon king buried the blade of his *saex* in the ground at his feet. 'I not come all this way with ships and men to turn back now!' he growled, the little trader scrambling to translate. 'Romans weak, there is plunder, and for honour of gods I roll over them until I no longer lift this *saex*! I be no man, no king in eyes of warriors if I run.'

'That is your choice,' Cahir said to the red-faced Saxon king. 'But we are all sovereign leaders, are we not? Our choices are our own.'

'And what is yours, then?' Gede interrupted softly. 'Brother.'

Trying not to wince at his sore back, Cahir got to his feet. 'I forged this alliance to free Alba, just as Calgacus and Eremon fought for that day. This we have done. The outpost forts north of the Wall are destroyed and their men disbanded. Their Alban allies have been cut off from their Roman masters. The Wall forts are burning, the northern Dux executed. Their spies and scouts, their treaties, tithes and taxes are all in ruins. Is this not what our goal was? Have we not reached it? I say we have.'

Fergus gazed up, still undecided. 'But other opportunities have come to us, brother. Should we not take them?'

Cahir looked down at him. 'I have come to see that true kingship lies in gleaning what is real from the shades that lead us astray.'

'Kingship!' Garnat spat. 'Your people have always been the Roman lovers, the hounds at their table snarling and snapping for scraps. Only *we* have the blood honour, only we have remained true and free!'

Seeing the contempt in Gede's eyes, the calm abruptly deserted Cahir. Without thinking, he whipped out his dagger from its sheath and held his arm high, anger drumming in his breast. 'Out of respect for my brother kings I will not spit you like the pig you are,' he said to Garnat, 'but in answer to your lies I hereby give you *my* blood honour!' Holding Gede's eyes, he drew the blade up his wrist and forearm. Though the cut was shallow, when he lowered his arm and clenched his fist, blood dripped to the rug. 'I hereby swear on my own life-blood that I have fulfilled my oath to free Alba of the Romans. I have discharged my vow with honour. Now I pull myself back from the abyss, for I know who I am.'

A flame lit in Gede's face before he masked it. 'You weaken us by this act,' he said softly. 'Yet I will not stop you.'

'Nor do you have the right.' Cahir sheathed his dagger. 'I and my men will leave at first light.'

He nodded stiffly at the other kings, as Kinet uncurled and stood up. 'I will take my leave and return home with my men also.'

Fergus looked between them, spluttering, 'But I need to think on this; I need to take this in, what you say—'

'Then do that.' Cahir already felt lighter, as the blood dripped down his wrist. 'I have thought enough.'

As he strode out of the tent, he paused only to clasp wrists with Kinet, then continued on. Ruarc, Mellan and Ardal fell into step behind, silent as they retraced their path across camp, Cahir pressing his arm to his side to stem the blood. Though he moved slowly, his heart raced.

Warriors caroused at their fires, fought and wrestled, gamed, diced and drank. The heaving crowds were growing bigger, as drunken men threw piles of Roman shields and spear-shafts on the flames, as well as abandoned carts and boots taken from the corpses.

Cahir was surprised when, in the shadows between two fires, Ruarc's hand fastened on his shoulder. He turned to see the young man's face contorted with a mix of anger and fear at his own boldness. Cahir spoke to the other two men. 'Go back and tell our warriors all that has happened. We must be ready to march at dawn.'

Mellan and Ardal melted away. 'Come then,' Cahir said to Ruarc. 'Out with it.'

Ruarc's mouth worked, his gaze accusing. '*How can you leave this army now?*'

Cahir compressed the throbbing wound on his arm. 'Because it is the right thing to do.'

'You stood on that mound at Beltaine and told us that we must fight for Alba's honour! You drew us in with fine words about glory, about striking a blow against the invaders who had bled our land dry!'

'And this is what we have done. I have given you this glory, have I not?'

'But ... we've died for you, bled for you, and now we have the chance to go where no Alban has ever gone. We have the chance to take Britannia for our own, to make the whole island Dalriada! How can you tell us to abandon the fire *you* lit in us? *You make cowards of us all.*'

Cahir raised a hand to stem that impetuous fury. 'You forget yourself – in many ways. You heard what I said. Our gods walk in Alba, but there are other gods in this land. I advocated defence, not conquest.' He took a step closer to Ruarc. 'As for cowardice: how cowardly is it to rape and kill children, as this army has done, leaving stinking death in its wake? Is that glory? Is that honour?'

'Of course not. And we never did any such thing.'

'Because I did not allow it. Just as I know that we reached our goal while luck was with us, and now it is time to draw back. For I tell you, Ruarc, that if we give in to greed, we will be trapped on the coast when the Emperor's army comes.'

'Then we must continue to fight them,' Ruarc argued. 'They are weakened – now is the time!'

Cahir seized Ruarc's wrist, pulling him close. 'When Minna was given the visions that woke me she said only that we would free *Alba*. That was the destiny of my line, my destiny, do you hear, *and we have done it*. But if we go on now, the whole land will be scoured of life – and I will not give my name to that destruction.'

Ruarc broke away and turned to the darkness, running an unsteady hand through his hair.

'You and your sword-mates can join the Picts if you must.' Cahir's voice was icy. 'I won't hold you. But mark me, you won't return to Dunadd.'

Ruarc's shoulders tensed, then fell. 'I swore to follow you, and I will keep to that as you kept faith with us. And I don't want that blood on my hands, of course. Only ...' He glanced back with a bitter smile, 'I wanted to make a mark, somehow. I wanted glory, to make a name so they might sing about me like Davin just sang about you.'

'And haven't you earned that already?' Cahir reminded him wearily. 'Two great battles, and you by my side in each one.'

'I mean some glory for me alone, to be remembered like the prince Eremon was.'

'Then perhaps you should listen to your bard songs more carefully. The greatest warriors are not only the bravest fighters. They know when to be merciful, when to be wise, when to subsume their own needs for the greater good.'

Ruarc's eyebrows rose. 'You sound just like that Christian priest of Maeve's.'

Cahir cuffed him away with a smile. 'You are young, brother – you have plenty of time to gain a name. And if it makes you feel any better, I have an inkling that after this is settled, the Picts will be turning up on our doorstep anyway. I've only made a worse enemy of Gede now, and if he can't take Britannia he'll want Alba.'

Ruarc brightened at that, as they moved towards their fire. 'You know,' he said in a low voice, 'we could take the mountains while they are away ...'

Cahir found himself laughing, relieved. 'We'll talk about it when we get home.'

'But—'

'When we get home.'

Two nights later, Minna's guards had discovered that the ruined farmstead in a valley up ahead was held by Roman soldiers, a motley crew gathered from some of the remnants of the destroyed army.

Smoke from the burned timbers stung her nostrils as she stumbled past hastily dug pits filled with sharpened stakes, and was bodily pushed through the tangled brakes of thorn fence.

As they passed beneath a gatepost, Minna glanced up at a small statue of the goddess Minerva's owl, its wings broken off. Maimed and helpless, as Donal and his men had been helpless. Her throat aching, Minna staggered on, then suddenly stumbled to the broken edge of the wall. Leaning over, she retched up the scant remains of dried meat into the nettles. The sickness was coming every day now, and she was terrified for the baby, curling around it at night, seeking for its feeble light. One of the soldiers growled at her and dug her in the side with his spear-butt, forcing her on as she shakily wiped her mouth.

They stopped in a large yard lit by bonfires, scattered with knots of men and whinnying horses. The leader of Minna's band headed for the only roofed house, where a guard leaned against the wall. 'Is your officer in here?' Minna's captor demanded. 'We've come from the garrison at Luguvalium.'

The man's head was bandaged around one ear. 'Officer?' He spat on the ground. 'All our officers got it in the guts along with the Dux, didn't they? Savage blue bastards.'

Minna stared at her feet. Her boots had worn through, and one toe was sticking out the end, bloody and black with dirt. A shudder ran over her shoulders. She was one of those savages now. How would they name her? *Witch*.

A witch, to be hacked and burned.

Later, in the darkness, she lay fitfully beneath a makeshift shelter of branches against a crumbled wall.

During the course of the day there had been much tramping of soldiers' feet back and forth, accompanied by shouting and cursing. Horses had been led out of the gates by men with bows. Others squatted behind the thorn fences, peering out across the fields that surrounded the farmstead, the stands of barley flattened to stubble.

All day her belly had groaned with hunger, but she had ignored it, hanging on the rope that bound her wrists to the shelter, head down. When the sun was high someone had approached from the campfires, a pair of muddy boots stopping beside her. Then, to her surprise, the person proffered a hunk of charred deer-meat on a scrap of burned timber.

Unable to raise her head, she whispered, '*Grates*,' and reached for the meat with her bound hands. The man had silently walked away, hunched into rusty mail, his helmet streaked with mud.

Now, as night fell, Minna was grateful to leave the pain of the day-light for her dreams. In those dreams she was with Cahir, holding his face between her hands. And he rested one palm on her belly, his warmth radiating into her skin.

Chapter 56

Once he turned his face towards his own lands, Cahir began to breathe more freely, and the Dalriadan and Attacotti army swiftly retraced fifty miles of road.

His scouts reported no significant Roman movements ahead, so Cahir and Kinet ordered their men to spread across a wider front to scavenge for food before regrouping north-west of Eboracum. The town itself had escaped Pictish wrath, being too large and well-defended to attempt, and Cahir would certainly not be tackling it now.

The next day Kinet went his own way, and as his own Dalriadans had dispersed Cahir retained only one hundred men and his guard, as well as a dozen horses taken from dead Roman officers.

On the second night, threading his way through the campfires, Cahir listened to the murmured conversations and was satisfied that there was no disgruntlement at his decision to turn back, only relief. The exhausted warriors sat talking, mending their boots or sharpening their swords, the wounded lying pale in the firelight. It was calm now the Picts were gone.

He stopped by a copse of alders and sniffed. The damp made him think of the marshes at home. Closing his eyes, he saw Minna's face before him, her cheeks brushed by the dark waves of her hair. She was waiting for him at Dunadd, and soon he could sink into her arms, warm and replete again.

At his own tent, his warriors were laughing, Mellan and Ardal winding the bloody flesh of stolen chickens around green-sticks, then propping them over the fire.

Cahir sat down on his bed-roll, as one of the men swallowed his ale and grinned. 'Well, leaf-fall is coming, and I'm looking forward to being back at my own hearth ...' he leered around, '*and* back inside my wife's sweet thighs, eh?'

Cahir stretched to loosen his tight muscles. 'You mean back under the lash of her tongue, too, Eber?' The chuckles swelled into guffaws.

Then he heard the horses nicker. By the stream, one stallion raised its nose and neighed, tossing its head.

The horses whinnied again and Cahir peered into the darkness, frowning. Ruarc had volunteered first watch with the other guards posted in a ring at the edge of the fields. The wind was up now, blowing from the north, dragging on the upper branches of the great oak and ash trees so they groaned.

Then the starlight caught someone's sword. Satisfied, he turned his attention back to Eber telling the story of an old raid on the Picts, with some fanciful embellishments. Cahir smiled at the disbelieving snorts of the younger warriors.

A shout echoed across the darkened fields.

Instantly everyone was on their feet, as the cry came again, faint and distressed. Cahir was already reaching for his sword and bellowing orders when a horn blasted out. It was Ruarc, blowing desperately, again and again, before finally being silenced. Another sound came, an unearthly rumbling.

Cursing, Cahir fumbled with his sword-belt. There were no Romans for miles ... How could anyone approach so fast? He ran to the edge of the firelight just as a blurred throng of stallions exploded into view from the darkened fields, long-legged Roman stock like his own captives. He desperately tried to visually disentangle riders from mounts. Wild hair, mottled furs, curling tattoos – perhaps seventy or eighty.

Picts.

He must be dreaming ... but as his sword came up, his back to his men, he heard the howl of fury emerge from his own throat. The Picts were close enough for Cahir's hastily-assembled bowmen to shoot now, so, with wild screeches, the easterners threw themselves from horseback instead, and drew their swords.

The Dalriadans around him leaped forward, and both sides merged in a clash and plunge of arms. After the shock, Cahir's blood resumed pumping and he ran in, enraged beyond all reason. Many of his men, caught half-asleep, had been cut down in the first rush. But the sides were evenly matched now, as they whirred swords about their heads in the way of the tribes, double-handed.

Coals and burning branches were scattered from the fires, and in moments the black figures all struggled against a backdrop of flaming tents and bushes. The faces of the men before Cahir were twisted masks of tattoos and bloody firelight, cut across by shadows. The self-inflicted wound on his arm had opened, and blood from it slickened his sword-hilt. He felt exposed without his mailshirt, his skin itching as if a thousand spears were poised to skewer his flanks.

Now he was backed up against the fire-pit, swinging his sword slowly around, waiting for the next man to come at him. Ardal and Mellan were fighting furiously with three of the enemy beneath an ash tree. At Cahir's feet, piled in with a mound of Picts, Eber's glassy eyes gazed up. He would not reach his wife's thighs after all.

With a roar, Cahir lunged at the nearest Pict, but the man glanced at him and backed away, shouting. He tried again, pouncing at another warrior who also leaped far from his blade, looking fearfully over his shoulder to something behind him.

He whirled. A man was striding onwards towards him through the heaving knots of fighters with no glance to left or right, a long dagger in one hand and a naked sword in the other. He ploughed on through the mass of men, pausing only to cut down the Dalriadans who managed to throw themselves under the guard of Picts around him.

Gede.

Now Cahir understood that the real battle was here. Suddenly, Gede began running towards him, driving in hard and fast, and Cahir leaped to the side and lunged to block the blow. Their swords clashed, and across the blades he looked into Gede's face and saw unveiled at last his true self. Hunger. Hatred.

They blocked, jabbed and staggered back, parrying between the fire and the flaming trees. In moments Cahir's face was running with sweat: he had never fought anyone so swift and lithe. He renewed the attack, slashing and ducking, unwilling to be put on the defence. Chillingly, through it all, Gede's expression never wavered, and he kept his sharp gaze on a place below Cahir's chin, and went after it with unflinching determination. The hawk-eyes tattooed on those cheeks pierced him, the red beard a stabbing beak … Cahir tossed sweat from his eyes. *A man … he's just a man.*

Sparks flew as one of the Dalriadans flung a Pict into a pile of flaming logs, and Cahir took the moment of inattention to target not Gede's body but his hand. With a grunt, he caught Gede's sword out of his fingers, and it fell amid the tree roots. For the first time, Gede's eyes flickered.

Cahir circled him with teeth bared, but the Pict king made no move for other weapons beyond his dagger, though swords lay in tumbled piles at his feet. Then, out of nowhere, the brute Garnat came in for the attack. As Cahir swung to face him, from the corner of his eye he saw Gede dart in and grab his own blade at the base of the tree. As soon as it was in his hand, Garnat melted away, leaving the two kings alone once more amid the morass of heaving fighters. Gede lunged for him.

Parrying desperately, Cahir was forced to retreat again and again, until at last he tripped over a discarded helmet and stumbled. In that moment, frozen in time, Cahir saw how Gede fractionally shifted his grip lower, and in a flash realized what was coming – the same sword slash he'd seen Gede use on the Romans so many times.

So many times.

The memory poured into his mind: Gede on the battlefield dispatching the Roman soldier with that unexpected blow. *And here it comes,* Cahir's mind thought from afar, with perfect clarity. *The impossible twist, mid-lunge, catching me off guard, then the plunge of the blade.*

He remembered it all, but, as Gede's torso twisted on itself, Cahir could only stretch back like a bow string. He didn't have time to move his feet, he couldn't shift his body out of the way. All he could do was concave his chest, round his back and pull in his belly. Gede's blade, which should have sunk deep into flesh, instead only parted cloth and sliced skin. Cahir felt the burning trail and cried out as he over-balanced, falling backwards to his haunches, stunned. Instantly, Gede recovered his surprise from the aborted swing, and turned to deliver a more triumphant blow.

He never got the chance.

'The Boar! The Boar!' came the cracked roar, and Ruarc came stumbling into the firelight from the shadows at the side, drenched in blood from a head wound, limping from a cut across the thigh. He threw himself at Gede a moment before the second lunge. The Pict king was knocked sideways to one knee, and Ruarc snarled as he unsteadily gripped both hands around his blade, going for his head. Wildly, Gede blocked the descending sword with his own, and as Ruarc poised there, bearing down like some gory, avenging god, Gede slashed up with the weapon hidden in his other hand. The long, wicked dagger ploughed straight into Ruarc's unprotected belly to the hilt.

With a bellow of rage and grief, Cahir hurled himself from his knees while Gede's dagger was still stuck inside Ruarc's ribs. He stabbed under the Pict king's arm beneath the mailshirt, Gede's sword slipping from nerveless fingers while Cahir scrabbled furiously for Ruarc's fallen blade. As Cahir's head swooned queerly, he threw himself on top of Gede, the Pict king still stuck in the tangle of his own weapons, and drove the point into the hollow of his throat.

With all his weight, Cahir, King of Dalriada staked the king of the Picts to the ground.

As a wail went up from all the Pict warriors, Cahir found his legs going out from under him and he slumped to his buttocks with a distant, dizzy sense of surprise. Next to him Gede's bloody face was already frozen in a rictus of shock and fury.

Everywhere the Picts were stumbling back from the fight now their king was dead, Garnat alone trying to reach Gede's body. But he was dragged away by the surviving enemy, their war cries echoing from the hillslopes.

Strength was draining away from Cahir. He collapsed onto his side and watched the remaining Picts racing for the darkness.

Chapter 57

Minna thought she was still dreaming.

But the whisper was repeated with feverish impatience, like a drum struck sharply beside her, dragging her back from Cahir's smile. *Minna. Minna.*

'Minna!'

She opened one swollen eye a slit to the glow of the bonfires against the night sky and the black shapes of her captors dicing and drinking.

'By the gods, wake up!'

She went rigid – she was being tricked; she must be.

An expulsion of breath sounded on the other side of the shelter, against the crumbling wall. 'Tiger, I can see your eyes so I know you are awake. But don't say anything; just stay still.'

She could not move anyway. She tried to moisten her dry throat to say his name, but her tongue stuck to the roof of her mouth. *Cian.* She said it inside, to make him real.

Hands reached through the screen of branches and a blade sawed at the rope. 'I presume you want to get out of here,' Cian murmured. 'So no throwing your arms around me, no noise.' He paused. 'Please tell me you are better at escapes than last time.'

Minna nodded, so light-headed the flames danced before her eyes. Blood rushed to her unbound wrists, tingling painfully.

'Then listen.' Cian's voice cracked. ' We're going to slide around the wall into the shadows, past the waste pit, and push through the fence over there. Follow me closely, though, because there is a horse in the woods and we need to be off quickly. Understand?'

She groped through the gap in the shelter and found his warm, callused palm. Cian gripped her hand for the briefest moment before withdrawing his. 'No time, Minna.'

After peering over his shoulder, he helped her through a hole he tore in the brush shelter. On hands and knees they crept around the corner of the wall. It was late, and the disorganized rabble by the fires were either arguing drunkenly or had already passed out. No one looked back.

Cian went ahead, pulling back a section of the thorn fence and sliding down the slope towards a dark bank of woods. At the edge of the thorn-brake, halfway down, he paused and dragged her into a crouch. Two soldiers on watch approached from opposite ends of the farmyard. As they met, one grunted, 'Bloody idiots will bring the barbarian army down on us with a blaze that big.'

Cian waited until their footfalls faded, then, half-carrying Minna, he stumbled across the cleared ground into the woods. As soon as they reached the horse and Cian caught the reins, she sank to her knees in the soaking undergrowth and brought up the remains of the charred meat. It was brought on by terrible relief, swamping her.

He made no move to touch her, gazing down impassively as she shuddered. When she finished, he shoved a water flask at her and, after she drank, heaved her, shivering, onto the horse. He levered himself up before her and nudged the stallion into a walk.

At first Minna was dizzied by the rush of shadows and moonlight, the scents of leaf-mould and streams, the scratch of branches on her cheeks and huddled shoulders. But then her hand crept to her belly and was absorbed there.

Tentatively, she sent fingers of awareness inside, and was rewarded by the tiniest glimmer of soul-light, enough to draw her on from despair.

They rode through the hours of night, stopping every now and then to listen, peering cautiously ahead into the shadows and starlit clearings. Minna never asked him how he came to be there. All that mattered was that he was.

He was silent ... she could sense no feeling in him ... and so at last she simply pressed her cheek into his back, clinging on. Dully, she realized he was broader across the shoulders now, and the muscles under her cheek were taut and hard as iron. He was different. That was all her mind could cope with, before she closed her eyes with no thought except that she was safe.

At dawn Cian stopped in a clearing and lifted her down. She hobbled a little way, the bruises from the jab of lances still sore, her back aching. There was a hint of grey light in the sky through the trees, enough to see the mist wreathing the ground.

Enough to turn and absorb Cian's face.

Weak though Minna was, she forgot all her own pain the moment she set eyes on his face, her gaze roaming over the dreadful hollows and protruding cheekbones. It was a gaunt skull sculpted by bruised eyes and grey skin. Cuts webbed his flesh, and his black hair was hacked brutally short. Slowly, her hand rose towards him, her fingers brushing his cheek. 'Cian?' she whispered.

He flinched at her touch but did not step back, his entire body quivering. But it was when she met his eyes that she saw the true loss of him, for they were haunted and glassy, as if he looked through her because he could not face her.

'I heard of the Dalriadan witch when I came back to camp,' he said hoarsely. 'I did not believe it could be ... but then I brought you the meat to find out.' He dazedly touched her hair, fingering a matted tendril as if he had never seen the colour before. 'They hurt you. You are bruised.'

She touched a long scar on his jaw. 'You have your own wounds.' It was as her palm held his cheek that she felt the storm raging in him, and suddenly her own pain and weariness simply faded. The eyes she turned up to him held sorrow, for what was marked in his face.

He gasped as he met them. 'I have fought for so long ... killed so many. I've tried ...' He stopped. 'I wanted ...' It was terrible watching him, as if he were gagging on the words, unable to make any sense, or to think beyond pain.

Minna's other hand closed the circle to cup his face, pierced by the horror in his eyes. 'It doesn't matter,' she whispered, for that is what came to her. 'It doesn't matter any more.'

And the Source was there in her, a warmth pouring through her hands and heart, taking all her own hurts and grief and guilt with it. *It does not matter.* The light spoke with its own power, streaming through Minna as her soul simply stood aside, bowing to the Lady in surrender. *All can come before the Goddess, their Mother, and lay down their hurts and be healed. Lay them down now, my child, and be free.*

Minna knew Cian could not hear the words, but this was an ancient love that came through her, an old power from the time before speech, and so it flowed directly into his soul.

He gulped back a cry, as if he were being strangled, and suddenly he sank on his knees before Minna in the wet grass and flung his arms about her waist. His sobs were dry and hoarse, pulled up from his bowels.

Shaken by his grief, Minna clasped arms about his head and held it to her belly and chest. She turned her cheek on his crown, staring into the heart of the red sun as it rose now through the trees, and her tears for him ran into his hair.

Then the sun blurred into flame, and in its heart Minna saw visions.

It wasn't like with the soldier, when the voices of the Sisters whispered what to say. Now, she simply knew, as if she had always known, that love and surrender to the greater good, the sharing of burdens for others, opens the spirit-eye. And a heart who has so given, and so surrenders, can flower into grace and thereby see the greater vision.

Something poor Brónach had not understood.

So Minna saw a small boy, and by his side a graceful mother holding his hand, as a father and three brothers rode off to war, their spears held proudly. And the hills behind were Alban. At the head of the army rode a Dalriadan king, and a young prince beside him with dark hair. *Cahir,* Minna cried. War-horns pealed over the warriors' heads, for the father and brothers were being called to battle on the old king's behalf.

Then the picture fractured and there were only vague snatches: a warband of Picts clashing with Dalriadans in a valley, a terrible slaughter, more lurid for having been imagined by the boy, where the loch waters ran red. Then the cold light of actual memory as the father and brothers were burned on one pyre together, their shields placed over the rents in their flesh, as the old king watched with no emotion on his face but regret. And in the heart of the boy, rage was kindled, stoked by grief.

Minna saw the mother and the small boy walking away from their home, then, its burning roof dwindling behind them, swallowed by the hills. A confused sense came of time passing, and finally she glimpsed the mother, the life leached out of her body by pain until her face was only a skull covered with skin. So the cold winter took her. *Mamaí,* the boy whispered over her, brokenly. *Mamaí.*

'You are Dalriadan.' Minna spoke into Cian's thick hair.

He stiffened, his heart struggling as his thoughts darted about inside her like sparks. *He tried to hate them all, Dalriada and Picts … his father died for the wealth of one, at the hand of the other. But no matter how many he kills it does not get better, only worse … and now he can't … he can't do it any more … He had run out of killing.*

She closed her eyes, and pressed her lips to his brow. 'Peace,' she whispered. 'You don't have to.'

He went entirely still. 'No?' His voice was muffled in her clothes.

'No. But speak of those you have slain, and there you will find absolution.' She rested her chin on his head, as if bracing them both for what would come.

And so in that new dawn, with the sun shafting golden through the mist, Cian surrendered up to Minna every black deed and every blow, and every man maimed and killed. Though it had only lasted a few moons, it still amounted to a tangled hill of bodies.

It was daylight by the time he finished, and then there were no more tears to shed.

Chapter 58

Breath rattling. Fever streaming. Pain lancing across his chest.

Cahir felt the litter of branches beneath him, his hand curled into claws among the hacked leaves. Voices floated about him.

'We should stay here and care for him as best we can.'

'But the Picts could come back.'

'Yes, yes, they might. We must get him north, *now*. The druids are not far away.'

'But I don't think he can be moved. Look at him!'

'I don't care … we have to. Hurry!'

The burning came again, and the ceaseless heaving of Cahir's belly so that nothing but bile leaked weakly from the side of his mouth. And how fast his heart pounded, like the hooves of a wild horse, a mad stallion. He gulped at the air, his breathing shallow and swift.

The black night wheeled around him and torches flamed above his head, as the litter lurched along a rough track. A tracery of tree branches was lifted against the lightening sky.

'… get him north …' the murmurs came.

North. Home. Alba.

In silence Cian took Minna over a high plateau and then down defiles so narrow she could put a hand on each side; then through hidden groves of ash and birch, dappled with sunlight.

Though Cian did not speak, her own pains had faded now to dull aches, the scratches, bruises and cuts soothed by the light that had filled her body. Her skin felt as if it glowed, and she looked down at her hands in the shadows of the trees and wondered.

They stopped at the edge of a spur of forest that flowed from the moorland plateau, reaching up a long vale to the Wall. At the head of the vale, Minna could see a faint blur of smoke over the dark line of stone. He hadn't even asked her if she wanted to return to Alba. He seemed to know.

When Cian slid from the horse, he lifted a face that was not ashamed of his weeping, as she had feared. 'We do not have long. They might come after us in the daylight, but you are close enough here to reach the Wall safely, and the Albans hold that still.'

There were depths in his gaze that had not been there before; now tears had come, and release, she saw a wisdom being forged by pain. Always finely modelled, his features were no longer fey and insubstantial, but settled, harder somehow. The lines by his mouth and brow and sorrowed eyes showed his beauty as she had never seen it before. He was a man now, not a boy.

'Minna, I must know why. Why you were here. Why ... this ...' His hand sketched helplessly in the air. He had felt the change in himself, the light of grace, and must be wondering what had wrought it.

Slowly, she slipped to the ground and sat down on a fallen log in a shaft of sun. Yes, she owed him that telling and, most of all, why she would not escape from Dunadd with him.

By the time she finished, Cian was squatting in the bracken at her feet, his hands cupped around his nose, his eyes closed. 'Gods.' He shook his head, as if trying to decide what question to ask first. 'You are telling me you were born in Alba before.'

'Yes.'

He looked out over the woods, spangled with dew. 'The manyborn,' he said under his breath. 'So you are Dalriadan.'

'As are you,' she returned softly.

He acknowledged that with only a bleak smile, gesturing out towards the Wall, where the air still smelled of smoke. 'But *you* brought all this about? You?'

A fleeting guilt came, but the Mother's grace still filled her and she was able to touch it and let it go. 'Not only me, not really. Cahir felt the pressure to heed his ancestors, but he'd lost his way. And then I was sent the visions to bring him back ... to make him remember ...' She heard the passion creeping into her voice and trailed away, her face burning.

He turned to stare at her, and her chin went up a little, unconsciously. She hadn't told him all of her story with Cahir, because ... well, she wasn't sure why it was so hard. 'You see, Cahir and I had to do this together. To be one; to help Alba break free of Rome.'

Cian's brows rose. 'You may well have accomplished that, at least,' he said, with a spark of grim humour. 'The northern forces are in disarray, the Dux dead, the Wall taken. The fine Roman army is left scurrying about the hills like starving rabbits.' He dropped his chin, and when he spoke again his voice was low. 'So ... do you love him, then?'

'Yes,' she said simply, her gaze resting on the top of his black head. 'He asked me to be his *lennan*.'

Cian blew out his breath, then glanced up, his blue eyes very bright. 'Well, well. When first I saw you in Eboracum, who would have thought that one day you'd be a Dalriadan queen, and me a poor sod in the Roman army?'

'Queen?' She shook her head. 'I don't think so.'

'Near enough.' Unexpectedly, he reached out and hesitantly touched her cheek. Then she knew he had changed for ever. 'And does he love you in return?' he asked softly.

'Yes,' she breathed.

He absorbed that. 'Then I'm glad you found what you wanted, Tiger.'

'As can you.' She grasped his hand. 'Come home with me.'

He pulled back. 'No.'

'They are your people – they are good people. They will understand; Cahir will, if I explain.'

Slowly Cian uncurled to his full height. 'That boy is dead, Tiger: I turned my back on Dalriada long ago. There's no going back for me, not after what I've done ... the Alban blood I've shed.' He rubbed his palms unconsciously on his thighs. 'Once you've given up anything soft inside you to kill a man, you can't find it again.'

'That's not true!' She leaped up. 'Cahir isn't like that – he is a warrior, but he is gentle, and he can love.'

He regarded her bleakly. 'Then that's why he deserves you.'

Speechless, Minna could only turn when he took her arm and pulled her around, pointing. 'Hurry now. If you take Brand with you you'll get to the Wall swiftly enough.'

'Take your horse? But you need him.'

He shrugged. 'I will have to go south now, perhaps to one of the walled towns, or over to Gaul.' He patted the horse intently. 'Some bastard will only spear him, like they did Ruarc's black, or kill me to get him. He'll be safer with you.' He left a last stroke on the pony's neck.

'I can't do that. I can't leave you all alone.'

'Gods, you're stubborn!' He pulled her to him in frustration, and now it was him holding her head, his hands buried in her hair. 'Take the damned horse – let him get fat on good Alban grass.'

Tears sprang to Minna's eyes, as an unexpected emptiness opened inside her. 'I cannot bear never to see you again, to think you might be dead.'

He freed a hand and tilted her chin. 'You have a life to lead, Tiger.

I don't have any part in that, I can't.'

'Why not?' she cried angrily. There had been too much loss. 'Why not start again and come home?'

Cian silenced all her questions by bowing his head and taking her mouth in a brutal kiss, hard with need and frustration. She was so dumbfounded she did not pull away, until he straightened, his eyes a brilliant blue. 'That's why,' he said huskily, and gave her a little push. 'Now go.' There was a plea in his gaze. 'And let me go, too.'

She was rooted to the spot, her face aflame. 'I can only go if you accept you always have a home with us; that you have a place to lay your hurts down if you need it. If I thought you had no one ... if I thought of your loneliness ...' Her voice cracked.

He stared into her, then shook his head. 'Through many cold nights, I wondered why I couldn't forget your eyes. Now I know it's because you see right inside, and you accept people, as no one did you.'

'Then why did you not confide in me?' she whispered.

His brow creased in pain. 'My blindness lost me that chance.' Suddenly, he bent for her foot to lever her to the horse's back. 'Hurry now.'

She gazed down, torn by her need to get to Cahir, and her grief for Cian. Still she could not make her legs move until in the end Cian lifted her up at the waist, touched her lips with his fingers and gave the pony a slap on the rump.

Desperately clinging to the saddle as the little horse jogged down the slope, Minna was spared the pain of another look back.

After four terrible days, Cahir's mysterious sickness was finally abating.

He could barely sit up now to hold his side and croak out orders, but though it burned like fire, he had to. He had an army to lead. The gods needed him yet.

His stricken men had brought him to a deserted fort just south of the Wall. There the scattered Dalriadan army soon reformed in strength, its campfires starring the meadows outside.

For the first two nights a druid had dosed him with foul-tasting things and bathed his skin. Cahir had looked at death through agonized eyes, watched it coming as his body ran with sweat. The wound – so slight, so glancing – burned even as he shivered.

But death did not release its dark blade on that final arc towards him.

The druid shuffled about, muttering it must have been a strong poison indeed on Gede's blade, perhaps something from the spine or tendril of a foul sea-creature, or the wolf's-bane he had heard tell of from Gaul and Germania, though the Pict king would have had to source it from over sea ...

Blinking in the musty smoke of burning herbs, Cahir had no difficulty accepting that. When he remembered Gede's cold eyes, the bastard could easily have planned that little duel weeks ago. He had been lucky.

As he lay there he thought of those who had not been lucky, and he grieved terribly for Ruarc through the dark hours, mourning the loss of his bright valour. But he had saved his king's life, Cahir comforted himself: he would be feasting at the gods' table in the Otherworld this night, fêted as a hero.

A fifth dawn came, and Cahir was still clinging to the pallet of smoky furs, aching and cold, every muscle spasming. He tried to rise, as Mellan and Fergal endeavoured to keep him back in bed.

'No,' Cahir barked, ordering them aside with every shred of power he had left. 'It is not safe yet. I must be on my feet.' He could not slip away into exhausted sleep, the delirium of weariness and recovery – he had to force his mind back into awareness.

As Mellan and Fergal watched grimly, Cahir gritted his teeth and levered himself upright unaided, then donned his sword and tunic, holding his arm to his side when he eventually slumped in a chair in the command quarters.

He had to show his men he was alive, for reports had just come in from the scouts that in the army's absence Luguvalium had been retaken by the Romans behind his back – and his son was with them.

Chapter 59

The battered Roman garrison holding Luguvalium simply fled as the entire Dalriadan army flooded back north, covering the land once more. The sea routes were blocked by the warriors left in charge of the Alban ships, and so townspeople struggled on foot across the marshes to the south-west instead.

The royal family were tracked down at the shore. Cahir did not bother setting eyes on Maeve or Eldon, simply ordering that they be marched onto an Attacotti-manned ship to be unceremoniously dumped with their kin in Kernow. He did not want a blood feud with Eldon's kin, for such feuds never ended. He wanted peace, and freedom from fear, for that is what Ruarc had died for, what it had all been for.

His son was held in Eldon's hall, awaiting his father.

Garvan's plumpness had been stripped away by his cross-country dash to his mother's side, an escapade which Cahir could not help but admire, even though it hurt and infuriated him. The boy's face was harder, too, his eyes colder, as he raised his chin and stared unflinchingly at his father.

Ah, the arrogance, Cahir thought. The Romans bred it in, and he only realized then, with a sinking heart, that this son was lost to Rome on the day he was born.

'I understand why you did this.' Cahir suppressed a cough, the remains of his fever. 'These matters are confusing. But though you disobeyed me, we will deal with this at Dunadd, in private.'

Garvan's green eyes flashed. 'I want to go with Mother. Send me after her at once!'

The rest of that interview drained the dregs of Cahir's meagre strength, and soon he understood that Garvan would escape again, and he could not keep his heir, the future king, locked up under guard.

But any hopes were finally dashed when Garvan looked at his father with contempt. 'I would rather be a Roman exile than any mud-grubbing, *barbarian* king,' he hissed, and that blow took Cahir in the breast, as sharp as any blade.

And so he let Garvan board the ship with Maeve, to be a Roman prince with all its trappings. He watched the sails fade away over the grey horizon, and felt utterly bereft. He had done this – all of this – to leave Dunadd free in the hands of his blood, who would stay loyal and true to his ancestors, and protect Alba for ever.

That night, Cahir's fever returned with a vengeance, and he slumped at the table with his men, ignoring the sweat on his brow and his quaking limbs.

Warriors were constantly clattering in and out of the cobbled courtyard of Eldon's old royal hall – Cahir's new command quarters.

Messengers rode in from the forts further east, and scouts reported from the north, where the outpost garrisons so hated by the Albans had been destroyed and the *areani* routed. Confirmation came from his rearguard that no Pict army was advancing on them, for it had indeed continued on south, despite Gede's death. Fergus had decided to return to Erin after all. And a constant stream of news was passed on from the warbands scouring the land for fugitive Roman soldiers.

Cahir gave orders and received reports from Eldon's old chair beneath a circle of hanging oil lamps, his feet on a floor of fine mosaics. And all the while the Roman hall swam around him, and he dug his nails into the chair to keep himself alert.

Every evening, he shut the door to Eldon's bedroom – which he had stripped of Roman fripperies – and sat on the bed, grimly staying upright until he must go down again and make some pretence of eating.

The druids tutted and bade he rest, a charge he refused until, after driving himself into the ground, from grey morning to torchlit night, his strength gave, and one day he did not rise.

Instead, he lay on the bed among his familiar sleeping hides, and stared at the window of fine Roman glass, contemplating his true wounds: Gede's betrayal; Ruarc's death; his son's defection. Together, they seemed to have snatched the triumph from his soul; they were scars of the heart that made him sicker than any fever.

When a horn blew up on the walls, and a rush of horseman spilled into the courtyard late that afternoon, he gave it no thought. When the door downstairs was thrown back, and heavy feet thundered into the hall below, he continued staring grimly out the window to the grey, weeping sky.

But when all the shouting and thudding went quiet, and he distinctly heard a faint, light tread coming up the stairs, he raised his head, suddenly alert. That footstep was no warrior. He sensed the air change even before she was there ... for he knew.

It was *Minna* filling the doorway – but she was so thin and seemed so small when he'd been surrounded by ruddy, noisy men for weeks. Her white face was pinched, her eyes bruised. She hovered in the doorway as if she could not push her legs forward, and Cahir was already up, his trembling hands gripping the posts of the bed.

'Are you a ghost?' were the first, terrible words out of his mouth, for his eyes could not take her in.

'No.' She was gazing at him with the same dazed disbelief, when the mind cannot drink in what it has longed to see for many hard, dark days.

But she was so changed! His eyes roamed over her hungrily, past the matted hair that hung in lank skeins over her shoulders, and the stained, torn dress and cloak. Instead he absorbed that more solemn face, and a straightness and stillness in her body, as if she had come far in it and knew it well now. Then all light was drawn to her eyes, and he could not look away.

In one stride he crossed the space between them, and the force of his embrace lifted her off her feet so their faces were level. At last he found his voice, croaking, 'By Manannán's breath, what are you doing here?'

'I came to find you,' Minna gasped.

'Ah, gods.' And he set her down only to crush her to him, kissing her fiercely as if he could drink in her essence and wash away all pain. He buried his face in her neck to smell her, his fingers shaping the ridge of her back to remember how he cradled her hips once in his hands. But when his thumbs moved over her cheeks she winced, and he drew back and saw now what he had missed: the fading bruises and scratches on her face and neck; the scab in the hollow of her throat.

Frowning, he took her hands and stared down at the broken nails and swollen joints, and the long, thin cut along one forearm. When he slowly raised his head, she drew back her hands. 'Who did this?' he demanded, with quiet fury.

She shook her head, searching his face instead as if her hurts meant nothing. 'It does not matter, it is you I feared for. I feared that Gede would betray you ... that he would ...' She could not continue, clutched his tunic, her hands running over the flesh beneath as if making sure of him. 'And Nessa was wrong – *you are here.*'

Cahir shifted his eyes to the shadows of Eldon's room, trying not to flinch as she embraced him. She must not know how ill he had been, for he could not bear to burden her with it yet.

But she went still in his arms. 'What?' She pulled free, her fists curling over her heart. 'What has happened? Ah!' Her fingers traced his hollowed cheeks. 'You are so pale, and your skin is clammy. Something did happen.' Her face fell. 'I wasn't wrong, was I? Gede hurt you.'

He broke away, his breathing shallow. 'It's just a scratch, *a stór*.' As if to make a lie of this, the wound cramped and a small cry escaped him. The overwork compounded with his shock of seeing her now brought a tide of dizziness that infuriated him, even as it closed about his sight.

But *she* was there, strong despite her thinness, catching his weight and guiding him to the bed, throwing the door open and calling for water and wood for the braziers.

When she came back and gazed down at him with darkened eyes, he murmured, 'You are a gift of the gods, my Minna.'

It was not herbs of healing that Minna had to give to Cahir as night and day blurred into one – for the druids had done that work.

It was light.

As if he allowed himself the weakness now she was here, his dizziness swiftly descended into a swoon of delirium. And when she was able to lay quiet hands on him, she at last perceived that the wound was in his soul.

He murmured, tossing feverishly, and from this she gleaned the hopelessness that had invaded him, leaching away his success and triumph. He cried out, wondering what he had truly fought for, fretting if he had made his people safe, now that no king of his blood would sit at Dunadd.

Minna gave him draughts for sleep, bathed his face, and closed the door on all others. Then she sat and, with her eyes closed, summoned the presence of the Sisters as they had been there for her before. Gradually, their shimmering warmth filled the room, and she moved to place her hands in the air just above Cahir's burning skin.

Despite her own exhaustion, the flow came through her so easily. She understood, as it whispered to her, that Cian's blessing and the Source at Beltaine had only been a prelude to *this* – the healing with a love so great it broke the bounds of her body with no need for *saor*.

As Cahir murmured and tossed in sleep, she stared wide-eyed into the lamp-flame and beheld a marvel. As if floating far above the earth, she saw the Source being summoned to aid him, to heal him, drawn by her hands and her singing; the cascade of unknown yet familiar words under her breath. But the Source surprised her, for it was not one light, but many.

It flowed in from Cahir's men as they held vigil for him in their thousands on the plain. It spiralled in an iridescent thread from the druids downstairs, who chanted words of pride in Cahir's ancestors, and the songs already being composed of his deeds. And it poured down from the hills and in from the sea, the waves glowing as they rolled over the marshes. For he was born of this land, and his essence drew Alba's power towards him because it still needed him whole for his people.

Most of all, it was summoned by Minna's love. For the role of the Goddess did not end at Beltaine. She might have been the Maiden then, but now she was the Mother, and the Mother brought forth life.

As she held her vigil, breathing love into him, she watched in wonder as the Source was gathered like streams pouring into a bowl in the mountains, forming a lake of fire. As the life flowed into Cahir from her hands and the glow strengthened around his head, she passed some of her own life-force to him, her own Source, and was renewed by the lake around her.

It grew in force, in grandeur, until it felt as if her skin were stretched over an immense, pulsing light that might burst out of her because a human body could not contain it all. Its pressure was almost uncomfortable in its power, its otherworldliness; pushing her to open, and then open again until she was a bridge between heaven and earth.

She surrendered to it gladly. He was a king, and had the care of many – she would care only for their child.

As if hearing her, the tiny glimmer of the baby pulsed amid the greater light, like a heartbeat, and in his sleep Cahir smiled.

Chapter 60

The next morning the glow was only sunlight. It fell through the Roman window on the flagstone floor, creeping across a carved wooden chest and then the hem of the faded wool coverlet on the bed.

It gleamed along the edge of Cahir's battered shield, propped against the cupboard, and touched the gold in his sword hilt, the stained leather scabbard lying on the chest.

Minna watched its advance through weary eyes, then snuffed out the lamp and shifted on her stool to look at Cahir, rubbing her aching back. She had gone for two nights with only snatches of sleep, but she was exultant rather than drained.

Hands braced on the mattress, she leaned over and drew in his scent, watching closely the rise and fall of his broad chest under the sheet. His lashes lay long and dark across cheeks in which the colour had bloomed again, and his skin was warm and dry to touch. The wound was slight and knitting well now. Minna could not understand why it had caused him any fever at all, but when she pressed him that first night, he would only mutter, 'On the war-trail men march and sleep close together, and the food and water are bad. We pick up camp fevers too easily, that is all.'

She had added that he drove himself too hard, and didn't let the cut heal well at the start. Well ... it did not matter now. She allowed herself a small, tired smile, and sat still, content to hold his hand and watch him breathe.

Some time later, when the sun reached Cahir's face, his eyes flickered. She held still, as, after a struggle, his lids opened and he blinked at the window like a little boy waking. '*A stór,*' he said faintly.

When she leaned over him his eyes opened properly, gradually

371

clearing of sleep. And though there was love there she also glimpsed a shimmer of something else, something unearthly. She sat back, knowing he had journeyed into the Otherworld with her, and they had returned together.

To her surprise, he reached out a trembling hand and placed it on her belly. 'I saw the child,' he whispered in awe, and his smile broke over his tired face and lit up the room. 'And it is a son. You have given me my heart back.'

She nestled into his side, and they murmured together as the sun bathed them. They shared words of love and soft touches that soothed the hurts of the body and heart. Most of all they spoke of the baby, patting Minna's still-flat belly and arguing over whether they could see a swell at all; catching the awe and wonder in each other's eyes and sharing secret smiles.

Minna gave Cahir stern orders to rest for a few days longer, but when she crept back into the room the next afternoon, her fists full of yarrow stalks, he was up and looking out of the window.

Her hands slowly fell to her sides. His posture was not that of a sick man, but a king – head proud, shoulders braced, one hand resting gracefully on the sill as if he were at peace. Could he have thrown the weakness off so soon? How …? She took a step forward, he turned, and she was left speechless.

For she could see all the god-light she had drawn into him, shining now in his face, blazing from his eyes. The same fire flickered about his head and shoulders, like the luminosity she had heard lit the night sky of the far north.

'I can rest no longer,' he said swiftly, mistaking her expression. Even his voice was different, richer and more powerful. 'My people need me. My men need me.' He smiled at her confused frown, then laughed. 'I swear my limbs are strong, *a stór*, and alive – they force me from bed when I would have waited there for you a little longer!'

Awe warred with Minna's concern, for that glow was like gazing into a star, a sun. And though she had drawn it, she almost felt afraid of this power. Unsteadily, she set the yarrow down and took his outstretched hands. She could hardly see the lines wrought by illness and the healed bruises, for his skin seemed almost translucent, the radiance obscuring his strain and weakness.

'And now I am up,' he declared, 'I must address the army, for something came to me in my sleep, my—' he broke off, wondering, 'yes, my vision. When I was sleeping I saw Eremon, I know I did, and he told me what I must do.'

Minna tried to speak but his passionate kiss took her breath, and the faint glimpse of a shadow around him simply faded as his mouth drank her in. 'As to what we should do,' she eventually murmured, 'I would rather it was home so you can heal properly, and gain your strength.'

His eyes dancing, he released her to gaze out at the riverbanks, where the thousands of cookfires smoked. There, his men waited for their king, their weapons flashing in the sun over the water. 'I cannot. The news may have travelled of the attack on me, and that is not good when there has been so much upheaval, when the people know of the destruction and disruption on the Wall, when they will be afraid of what might happen now. I have to show my face to them, so they will know they are safe.'

His dark hair flowed over his shoulders, glossy now Minna had brushed it, and she longed to lift it and kiss the nape of his strong neck, never letting him stray from her side again.

But as she opened her mouth to protest that surely they must return directly to Dunadd, she took a step back instead, her words dying on her tongue. One could do nothing in that moment but surrender to what surrounded him, what had filled him.

As she had given her life-force, her essence to him, he must do the same for his people. The light was not him, Cahir; it was the God coming through him. Suddenly humbled, she knew she could not hold that power for herself.

Minna wandered far downstream on the riverbank, scattering flowers on the dark green water for Donal and his men, singing the death-song she had been unable to sing before. She squatted on the muddy bank among the bullrushes, letting the sun play over her eyelids. The warmth could not touch the cold place inside that held her guilt, and the weight of responsibility.

Perhaps she would carry it always, another thread wound into the fabric of her soul.

Her reverie was broken by all the war-trumpets calling from the walls of Luguvalium at once. She turned her head. Three short blasts and a long one came again: a royal summons.

She bowed to the water and finished her prayer, for it would take some time for all those men to down whatever they were doing and gather in to the town. By the time she got back to the gates, warriors were crowding the market-place, climbing the walls and ramparts, and eventually, pressed by space, being forced back out along the riversides, straining to hear and see their king.

Minna squeezed inside the fort and wove her way between the men. They turned, towering above her, smelly and noisy with their clanking armour, their dirty, bearded faces alight. Then the whisper went before her, 'The king's *lennan*,' and they shuffled back further for her, nodding respectfully. Eventually, she came to the fountain at the centre of the square that she had drunk from before being seen by Maeve. Holding the headless marble nymphs, she leaned up on the fountain's plinth to see.

The Attacotti had already sailed for home, and many Dalriadans were on duty at other forts or further afield, but still there were five or six thousand warriors crowding the town.

The trumpets clamoured again, rousingly, and the men pressed closer to the street that led to the royal hall, their voices a restless rustle and murmur. Cahir's guard then came out into the square, Mellan on horseback holding aloft the boar banner, which was proudly stained by blood and the smoke of many fires.

But when Cahir himself appeared on a long-legged Roman horse, all the buzzing and chatter was lost in an enormous cheer that shook the walls and towers. Spears and swords were waved wildly and danger-ously over heads, and in the midst of the frenzy Minna, propped on her fountain, looked over the throng and simply drank Cahir in.

The sun flamed on his boar helmet and mail-clad shoulders, and the fire of his eyes was framed by his dark brows and hair, intensifying its heat. As the warriors went wild, Minna realized her spirit-eye was only revealing to her sight what the men instinctively felt. Their god-king had been returned to them from death.

'Hail, my bright warriors, my brave brothers!' Cahir boomed, and the volume of acclaim rose to fever pitch. Minna closed her eyes as his voice penetrated her chest. 'We have secured a great victory over the Romans, and, as foretold, they have been banished from our lands. They will bleed us dry no more.' An enormous cry of pride beat on her ears. 'But this is only the start of a story, not the end. Now we must hold what we have fought for: Alba without Romans, without forts and ports, taxes and tithes, scouts and burning duns. Some of you will be left to garrison the Wall forts, and some to hold Luguvalium as long as you are able. The outpost forts – those to the north of this Wall, in Alban land – have already been burned, their soldiers slain. *No Roman now walks our land, and we will keep it that way!*'

Minna opened her eyes as swords were thrust towards the sun and spears danced against the blue sky. Cahir raised a hand. 'Those warriors not guarding the Wall will set out for home today. I, however, will not be going straight to Dunadd.' Cahir's hand shifted to his sword as he laid it across the saddle and told them how many in Dalriada would not know of the victory, and could be mired in fear and uncertainty. Trouble could arise with no strong guiding hand, which is why they had to see him and know his will.

The noise grew at this announcement, and Cahir smiled into the sun and shouted above the crowd. 'So I will see you at my hearth when I come home, and together we will make a song to last a thousand years, a song of your bravery, a song of your courage. *To the Boar!*'

Cahir's men took up the chant, bellowing the war-cry as they lifted their swords in unison with Mellan's dipping banner. The cry spread through the crowd of warriors, clashing shouts resolving into one song at last, rising up and down. *The Boar! The Boar!*

The king sat on his horse with an exultant smile, and Minna's heart took up its rhythm again, banishing any remains of the shadow. She was pulled into that conflagration that encompassed all the warriors, the triumphant army, and if it burned her to ashes it would still be glorious.

And one day soon, when this was over, she would be able to rest her head on Cahir's shoulder and be strong no more.

Chapter 61

Cahir sent his army ahead with orders for messengers to summon all the northern and island chiefs and the Attacotti leaders to Dunadd.

And then, in the glory days of that long, golden summer, he wove his way home in a royal procession that passed through every dun in the south and west, and every cluster of steadings in the major valleys. As news went ahead, people poured down from the mountains and remote glens, waiting for a glimpse of him and his dazzling retinue of warriors.

Travelling at his side, clinging to the mane of Cian's sturdy pony, Minna slipped into a parallel existence where her body walked on Alba's soil but she looked upon Cahir and the land with eyes of the Otherworld, seeing what lay beneath the surface. Standing at his shoulder, she witnessed the Source being drawn to him at each place he stopped, gathering where he spoke words of love and strength to his people. She saw the heart-fires flare in those who hearkened to him, and how they joined with his and made Dalriada stronger, the roots of light going deeper into the land. As they left, she looked back on people who had a new hope to lift their weary bodies, relief in their lined, fearful faces.

At night, in rude huts and grand halls, Cahir spoke long by the fires with the chieftains and warriors, and when he came to bed, he curled about Minna, resting his large palm over the baby in a silent communion.

Only once did she argue with him to return home. She saw a flicker through the god-light, glimpsed a drawn face and heard harsh breathing. 'Surely you've done enough now?' she said. 'Surely we should go home?'

But he only gazed at her with those luminous eyes and said softly, 'You helped me find my kingship, Minna, and so now I must be king.'

She did bow to that in the end, but because she loved him, fear lodged in her breast like a tiny sliver of bone and pained her dreams.

He saw how quiet she became, however, and one day, after he had spoken and feasted all afternoon, he took her hand in the dusk and, with a smile, led her to his horse. Everyone stood still in the courtyard to watch them go.

Far up in the mountains he rode, where the heather was in full bloom in whorls of purple, and the bracken beginning to turn copper. The valleys below were rivers of gold, thick with nodding heads of barley, the falling sun hazed by whirring insect wings and the damp heat coming up from the ground.

'See,' Cahir murmured, as Minna clung to his waist in the saddle. 'The chiefs say no one has seen such a summer harvest, such growth. The cattle are in twins again already.' He gazed at her over his shoulder. 'Our love did this at Beltaine, just as you said. *You* did this.'

She reached out a finger and softly outlined his nose, chin and jaw just as the sun did, and he twisted around far enough to kiss her, until the horse nickered and shifted restlessly under them, and they laughed. Up on the slopes where the bracken ran out to heather, he stopped the horse and helped her down.

They stood looking far out to the west across the peaks, marching in ever fainter bastions to the islands in the sea. The sunset was a bonfire raging across the clouded sky, turning the ocean to molten copper and the lakes to bronze.

Cahir looked out across this beauty and his face was grave, the gold reflected in his irises, the copper in his hair. She thought of Lugh now, not Apollo, the god of the Alban sun. He caught her staring at him and his eyes grew hazy with a most human desire, and he tilted her chin to kiss the pulse in the hollow of her throat. His palms were warm on the back of her thighs, bare under her long dress.

He paused and drew back to look down at her. 'Will it hurt the baby?' he said softly.

She smiled, then laughed at the concerned frown on his brow. 'Not that I've ever heard.'

'And you *are* the healer,' he murmured, cupping a palm around her breast, which already sat more rounded and heavy in his hand. He went to the horse and untied the saddle hide, rolling it out in the heather. Then, resting her down as reverently as an offering to the gods, he loved her.

With her fingers spread across his flowing back, Minna felt as if she held a living flame in her arms, consumed by the power running

377

through him so she hardly felt her body at all. The ecstasy surged but did not crash, soaring free as if it had no end. It was not sharp and earthy this time but an incandescence – spirits merging, heart, soul, body consumed by the same fire. Their soul-flames overflowed and spilled across the land until they ran together as one Source. And taken by that wildfire, Cahir loved Minna again and again until the light was exhausted.

Still he would not leave her body, rocking them slowly as a chill crept across the darkening hill, and tears were drawn from them both. She held him to her, raised her eyes to the purple sky and gave herself up to the lift and dip of that softer sea.

As she drifted slowly back to the earth around her – the scent of damp soil, the sharp tang of smoke on the air, the cold creeping under the hide – the final words came to her lips from the Goddess.

It was a blessing from the stars that littered the heavens, brought down for him alone. *Your ancestors smile upon you, Cahir son of Conor. You have done what you were born to do.*

Chapter 62

Three weeks after leaving the Wall, they returned to Dunadd. The warmth of the sunseason afternoon was gathered in the bowl of purple hills, perfumed with heather and thyme.

The army had gathered on the marsh and river meadow, with the chiefs who had not gone to war from the far islands and most remote duns, as well as Kinet the Attacotti king and his chieftains. All had come as Cahir asked, to renew their oaths now to him alone and to a free Alba, ridding their sacred bond of the taint of Rome.

Cahir paused before the walls of his dun as the crowd that lined them cheered and struck the timbers, their feet thundering along the walkway as they ran to see him. Minna, riding by his side, saw the slight compression of his mouth, whether with emotion or pain, she could not tell. But he was sitting slightly lower in his saddle. She *knew* he was exhausted and now it had hit. But at least he was back home, and could put aside his war helmet.

Then she glanced up at the screaming crowd, chanting their praise, their thanks to the gods, their joy like a wild storm in spring. No, he would not lay it aside yet. There would be no rest for the king until all was done.

Banners draped the walls and were waved over the gates. swords and spears raised; horns pealed in a discordant song as drums were beaten in no pattern at all but to make a joyous noise. At last Cahir smiled, with a proud lift of his chin. 'I have done what I was born to do,' he repeated softly, and only she heard him, as the men close by laughed and waved up at the people.

She longed to touch his hand on the rein, but before she could lean over he had moved off to enter the gates alone, and the other horses surged after him with Minna in the midst.

Once inside, she immediately lost him to the chaos, and instead was jubilantly greeted by Orla and Finola, with a long-legged Lía yapping at her ankles. To Minna's surprise, Clíona took one look at her and the king and buried sudden tears in her skirt, flapping away Keeva's amused consternation.

Later, Minna stood with Orla and Finola by their father's chair in his hall, as, one by one, every chief and headman in Dalriada and the Attacotti islands came before him and knelt with their swords across their hands. There they were blessed, taking the oath on their own iron, and raised up by their king.

His voice rang out with an almost feverish energy that caught everyone in its excitement. Councils had already been held, with plans settled for a stronger cordon of defences to be thrown around Dalriada by land and sea. More men from all the duns had been pledged to the borders to hold them against any Pictish or Roman reprisals.

The toasts and oaths were concluded when Davin came out into the centre of the hall, and sang a new lay of the great battles of the Wall, in which Ruarc featured prominently as saviour of the king.

Orla gabbled at Minna's side, excited by the din of the music and the ceaseless cheering outside, but Finola was quiet. Minna went down on one knee and gently turned her around, and only then saw that the child's small face was transfigured with awe and joy. 'He is bright!' she whispered, trembling as she gazed up at her father. 'Like a light, like a fire.'

Minna smiled at her, and touched her face. 'He is, my little dreamer.'

Finola's blue eyes gradually focused on her. 'And is it the Otherworld, Minna, like the druids say? Is it the Otherworld light?'

Though she knew this, the answer died on her tongue and she found herself looking at Cahir again. Yes, it was the Otherworld light, only she had not put it into such words in her own heart. Now she could not see his features at all, for, as Finola saw, there was only the fire of the king.

'Minna.' It was Keeva, who had squeezed through the crowd to pluck at her elbow. 'Someone has found me to give a message to you. The Lady Riona has been brought to her birthing bed.'

She turned with an exclamation of pleasure, for she had not yet seen her friend in the crowd. But Keeva was frowning, shaking her head. 'No, Minna, she is a moon early, and was visiting some kin at the Dun of the Cliffs when she was suddenly taken with the pangs. It has been hours already, and they think she is in trouble. When she found out you were back, she asked for you.'

Minna glanced at Cahir, and the throngs of warriors spilling over the dun outside the doors. She would not be missed, and a difficult birth could be dangerous. She kissed Finola's head. 'Clíona, would you take the girls, and Keeva, will you come with me?' Both maids nodded.

'Then get us horses while I gather what I need from Brónach's house,' she said to Keeva. 'I will meet you at the stables.'

Three days that birth lasted, and Riona was in great travail and pain. Minna tried everything she could think of, and many more things that came to her like soft touches on her brow amid the screams and the bloodied towels, the rocking and chanting of the old women, and Riona's clawing of her hand.

The baby was turned, its shoulder jammed into the wrong angle of the womb, and it took much gentle encouragement and long hours to turn it again. Riona's pain could not be eased too much for fear she would swoon and not be able to push, so she bit down on sticks, and sweated, and crushed the bones of Keeva's hands in her own, and cried out to the goddesses when she could not hold it in.

There were herbs to ease the gripes of the womb, though, so Minna could turn the child in stages, and others to start them up again in the exhausted mother when he was head down at last. After three nights with no sleep, existing in a kind of focused dream, she pulled from Riona's womb a tiny, squalling man-child whose lusty strength was the only thing that kept him alive.

Minna stitched up Riona and dosed her with healing brews, and, after assuring herself for another two days that both mother and child were well, she took leave of her tearful, exhausted friend with promises that she would return every day until Riona was recovered.

Utterly exhausted, nevertheless Minna wanted to hurry back. For when she left the smoky confines of the birthing hut, she saw that all the chieftains' ships were leaving the bay and heading north and west, their banners flying.

Cahir had received his oaths, and now could be hers again.

When Minna and Keeva rode back under Dunadd's gate, Clíona was waiting for them like a pale wraith on the ramparts.

Instinctively, Minna's heart swooped in a great plunge before she even slipped from the horse. Clíona came down the stairs, her face as white as bone in the shadows of the gate. 'What?' Minna whispered, but a terrible knowing was already descending on her in a dark storm.

Clíona took one step forward, clutching at the folds of her dress. 'We all saw how ill the king was when he came back, but you seemed unafraid ... and so I thought he was recovering from his wound, but now ...'

Minna watched her lips move in patterns that made no sense, as all sound seemed to die, and the light around her.

The maid was holding her arms now, nails digging into her flesh to bring her back. '... but since the chiefs left he has fallen back into a fever, and would not let us call you, for Ríona's sake ...'

Then Clíona's words faded behind her because she was already running up the path, with only her grating breath filling her ears, caught by a moan that might be rising inside.

When she stumbled up the stairs to the gallery, both Finbar and Fergal were by Cahir's bed, leaning over him as they spoke in low, urgent tones. With one look at Minna's face they melted away down the stairs, but she did not even notice them go. Step by step she moved closer to the fur-strewn bed, and the man lit there by a single lamp. Despite the warm light, she was engulfed by darkness.

How could he be so changed in five days? The godly light was entirely quenched, and his face was not blooming but deeply lined at brow and mouth, with hollowed cheeks and sallow skin. There was a blue tinge now about the lips she had kissed, and under the furs he seemed diminished, his chest fluttering with shallow breaths. The eyes he raised to her were glazed. '*A stór*,' he whispered hoarsely.

She could only stifle a moan, as horror dawned over her.

She had been named a priestess by Rhiann, and ever since had been walking half in the Otherworld, drifting between the veils. And so all this time she had been looking at Cahir with *her sight*, not her eyes. The flame that so dazzled her at Luguvalium was not his returning strength at all but his soul, flaring so bright it spilled over and through his body, and that was all she had seen and felt – an Otherworld light that erased all human frailty.

Finola had spoken a child's truth, where Minna's love had made her blind.

A shudder took her, and she fell on her knees by the bed. She groped for Cahir's hand, clammy and cold, and cried furiously, 'Tell me the truth of the wound!'

His pained eyes flickered, almost dark now in his white face. 'It seems ... that Gede's blade was poisoned ... after all.' His breathing was laboured. 'If it had gone in as he wanted ... I would not be here ...' Another rattling breath. 'So when the bout of illness faded I thought ...I was lucky ...' His words ended in a hacking cough.

If before he was on fire, now he was grey. All that radiated now from him was pain. Minna forced out an agonized whisper. 'You are suffering?'

Slowly, he nodded. 'Ever since the wound my heart has pounded ... and it's getting ... harder to breathe.' His trembling hand covered his chest, then dropped away. 'But it was only when the chiefs left and I could stop ... I felt something go from me in a rush ... the bright strength ... and then a great pain felled me, gripping me like teeth ...' He sank into the bed. 'And now ... so tired.'

Minna grabbed wildly for something to feel, and found the easiest thing, clinging to it as she drowned. Anger. 'You should have let me take you home! I could have done something ... *given you something* ...' She staggered to her feet.

Cahir drew a broken breath. 'No ... it was done then, *a stór* ... no going back. I had to hold the people as one ... or they might splinter ... fall prey to Rome ...' His head rocked back and forth on the pillow. 'And all that we strained for ... all that Ruarc and the others died for, would be lost.' His fervour took the dregs of his strength, and he sank back on the pillow.

Minna felt the blood drain from her face. 'No.' She clenched her fists. '*No.*'

His eyes were grave. 'I had to be a king ... Minna.'

Suddenly she was stumbling down the stairs, unable to see the steps or the fire, the white faces of all the silent people in the hall a blur.

At Brónach's house, she flung herself at the shelves, taking down jars, bottles and bowls and piling them on the table if they made sense to her. *His blood races ... heart pain ...* Then her breath caught on panicked sobs, and she began raking at containers instead, pulling them down around her ears. Pots rolled on the floor, baskets spilled out their powders. She tore at the bunches of herbs on the rafters, shredding them, until she sank on her knees in a cloud of dust and musty, crushed leaves. Then she grabbed at the first things that came to hand, staggered up and lurched back to him.

'See?' Minna cried, holding out a pot to Cahir. 'This, I could have given you for your heart!' She threw it to the floor where it rolled under a chair, spilling liquid over the boards. 'And this, for your blood ...' Holding his hollowed eyes, she flung a tall bottle down so it shattered into shards of green glass around her feet. 'And this ... and this!' Containers of all sizes broke against the bed-screen and the floor, until her shins were cut and bleeding, and she turned to tearing leaves and twigs from her clothing and hair.

And all the while Cahir flinched but said nothing, merely watching her with feverish eyes. Only when she snatched up a shard of glass and it sliced her fingers did he break, with a grunt of pain pushing himself to grab her flailing hand. She struggled and then sank against him, crying, 'You have betrayed me!'

'Ah ...' He clutched her weakly to his chest. 'I did not know I would give it all away ... that it would burn out. It felt so right ... so strong.' His breath rasped inwards. 'Forgive me, *a stór. Forgive me.*'

Now she heard the irregular thundering of his heart, when it did not matter any more; now she felt the heat of his fever. Abruptly she grew still, burying her head in his shoulder, the blood from her finger smearing his tunic.

His shaking hand cupped her head. 'You raised me up ... for the people ...'

'No!' The bitterness of her part in this choked her. '*Our child*—'

'Has life ... and he will hold my lands as I cannot myself ...' He cradled her as best he could while she wept, endlessly. 'Look at me,' the whisper came. 'Look at me with your sight.'

'Never again!'

He coughed, clasped her tighter. 'You must see ... what I feel.'

Unwillingly, Minna's gaze travelled over his brows and high cheekbones, hollowed beneath, and at last met his eyes. Despite the sickness they still held a glimmer of the light, and it was not fire now but a peace beyond grief. 'In the night the gods spoke ...' he wheezed. 'I have fulfilled my fate ... and few men can say that.' He stroked wet hair from her face. 'Try to feel it ... *try*.'

But Minna felt only as if she had died.

Chapter 63

The days blurred into one as the life gradually leached from Cahir's body, leaving darkness in Minna's heart. So much was spoken between them, whispers and murmurs exchanged in the lamplit bed as she sat against the wall with him cradled between her legs. But eventually even that faded to silence.

After a long, deep night where no moon rose, Cahir struggled awake. On a stool by the bed, Minna had fallen into a stupor over his hand, and when she raised her head at his movement his skin was wet, for she would only weep in sleep.

'A stór,' he coughed, and his eyes were luminous, reflecting the starlight in that Other place. 'The pain is worse now.' He had not let her dose him with anything, for he wanted his wits, to speak to her and his daughters and his men. 'Take me ... to the place we lay at Beltaine.' Her hand contracted in instinctive denial, but he clung to it, his gaze unwavering. 'I want to be in the woods, on the earth ... not here in shadow and smoke.'

She sat, feeling the heartbeats of her own life counting down until they would surely stop. But the sweetness in his ashen face pierced her. 'I saw our love ...' He smiled dreamily. 'Such a fire ... swift and bright ... burns quickly, too. It is the way.'

She stared down, the dried tears stiffening her cheeks. And despite her vow to remain open to him, her ravaged soul took refuge in coldness; an emptiness where she did not have to feel.

The litter, carried by Cahir's trusted warriors, moved along the rocky path out of the dun through an utterly silent crowd. People had come from every house and field, and Fintan and Lonán emerged from the smithy with Keeva, her black eyes on Minna's face.

As the litter passed, every man, woman and child knelt to give homage to their fallen king.

Walking at the head of the bier with a weeping Finola and Orla behind her, Minna thought distantly that never in her time in Alba had she heard silence like this. Noise was the mark of these exuberant people, but on this crowd lay the silence of the mountains. It echoed through her hollow heart.

They reached the Beltaine glade when morning sun was slanting between the white birch trees and pooling in the hollow where she first gave herself to him. The men followed a little stream through high stands of bracken, and rested the litter down. The flowers had gone, and berries were showing on the elder trees. As he sank into the ground, the dell grew hushed, with no breath of wind or birdsong.

Cahir spoke to Finola and Orla alone, holding them as they threw themselves across him, his face spasming at their storm of tears. Then it was the turn of his men. Cahir grasped Finbar wrist to wrist. 'The lady's child will be a boy,' he wheezed. 'And I name him my heir. You and Góban are to share his regency between you, and hold Dunadd safe for him.'

Grizzled Finbar, his face ashen, said something Minna could not hear and fervently kissed his king's hand. With haunted expressions the other men – Góbán, Fergal, Mellan and Ardal – came one by one and did the same. Then all retreated back up to the border of the birch trees that circled the dell, the girls following, Orla trying to be brave, holding her sister.

All strength gone, Minna sank to her knees at Cahir's head and cradled her hands around his temples. There it struck her with force, as the priestess in her spoke, though she didn't want to hear. *The three faces of the Goddess.*

In this same hollow she had been the Maiden of flowers, and here the Mother, swelling with Cahir's child. But on this day she would also be the Crone, the herald of winter. She had taken Cahir through the cycle of the Goddess, from birth to fertility to death – and it was because of this that she knew she was facing nothing less than the right order of the world. But that didn't help the girl in her, and her desperate love for him.

When Cahir's eyes at last flickered open again, they were shimmering forest pools, holding the secrets of the earth and the joy of the sky. His breath rattled. '*A stór.*' His gaze focused with terrible intensity on her. 'You have to do something for me. The … last thing.' Minna bit her lip so hard she tasted blood. His eyes closed briefly in pain. 'I need to know … all will be well with my people.'

A stone dropped into her breast.

'I need you to see for me.'

'No. I ... I cannot—'

'I need you to see for me so I can let go.'

'Think what you ask!' she cried, and turned her cheek away. How could she look at a future without him? A keening rose, clawing its way out of her, and she wondered wildly if she could go in his stead, or simply lie down and slip away with him between the worlds.

In that moment, she became aware of the hand on her shoulder, and someone standing behind her.

Her eyes sprang open, and she could see in the two worlds at once again, just as on the rowan-tree mountain. Now the light that touched every living thing – leaves, tree-trunks, grasses – did not come from the sun alone. The veils had become so thin here that the Otherworld glow was surrounding them.

Rhiann said, *You must see for him; open your heart and feel your grief, honour it. I will be here with you.*

'No,' she moaned, her soul writhing, trying to escape pain.

Cahir was breathing more shallowly now. 'Tell me,' he said again.
You must see for him.

'I am dying inside ...' Minna gasped. 'I cannot think ...'

Daughter. We are all here with you. Open your heart, for if you do not feel you will lose it all.

The warmth from Rhiann's hand penetrated her chilled flesh, and she hovered on the threshold for an endless moment. *Surrender,* her own inner voice whispered. He needed her, trusted her.

Finally she sank forward and rested her lips against Cahir's mouth, closing her eyes. And she saw for him, as the world held its breath.

'The ... the boy I carry will be king at Dunadd, a great King of Dalriada after you, and the regents will hold us safe until he comes of age,' she whispered. Beneath her, Cahir stirred with a sigh. Silence fell again, as the images flitted past Minna's spirit-eye. 'Your alliance has struck a blow that will weaken the pillars of the Empire. The Romans are already banished from Alba – but *your son* will see them leave all Britannia.'

His chest fluttered. 'The ... Picts ...?'

Minna gathered the visions into understanding. 'Through Nessa's son there will be peace between Pictland and Dalriada for many years, and then as many years of bitter war. But after this bloody birthing, the two peoples will join under a single king who will be crowned here at Dunadd, as heir of both Pictland and Dalriada. That king will be descended from you, Cahir. And because of that, for every wave of invasion that comes ever after, the Source of Alba will live on, and what makes this land its own is a flame that will never be quenched.'

Cahir's body sank deeper into the earth, his chest rising and falling more quietly as he rested in those moments between speaking. Minna smoothed his still-warm skin with quivering fingers, knowing the life in him was fading. And something in her cracked and her heart cried out denial like a child, as the light around her fractured.

Daughter, Rhiann said. *This is the greatest lesson of the priestess. Feel it.*

Then she understood. A healer can pour light into an ailing body, but each person has a fate that is their own. A seer bows in humility not only to the gods, but to that soul's choice.

But how bitter a lesson! She fought with it, tears choking her, until Rhiann rested a gentle hand on her nape.

Minna dipped her face over Cahir's and opened her eyes. Framed by his dark lashes, his irises were golden lamps now, glowing with the peace that flowed into her from Rhiann's hand. Flanked by them both, her mother and her husband, she was held and she could breathe.

'Can you see it?' Cahir whispered.

'Yes,' she said shakily. 'And you?'

In answer, he gave her a smile of great tenderness. 'Make him a good man ... and give him my sword.'

And Minna felt the Source in him gathering, readying itself to overflow into the life of the dell, the trees, the hills. In answer, she sensed the ancient death-song for a king rising from within her.

The first notes poured from her mouth, achingly sweet, with a keen of sorrow like a curlew's cry. It was a chant about strength and sacrifice, and love for the people, and it was beautiful. But Minna's grief sharpened, and when she saw how intently Cahir listened even as his face grew bloodless, she suddenly faltered. Her voice cracked into nothing, and the song died.

There was only the briefest of pauses before Rhiann took up the song in a spirit voice low and rich, and a moment later other voices joined her.

Through tears, Minna gazed around at the women now circling the edge of the clearing behind the warriors. Their indistinct figures stood as straight as the birches, blurred with light. The hollow rang with their song, sending it back from the slopes so it entered Minna's flesh, and she felt strength coursing through her for the first time in days. It rose from the soil, the bones of the earth, the roots of the mountains. Her whole body vibrated and she opened her mouth once more and the song came again, more powerful this time. It wove a cradle of light about Cahir. It came to carry her through unbearable sorrow.

Cahir could see the spirit women now, for his eyes roamed around with wonder as one by one the singers fell silent, until there was only Minna and Rhiann. And then, only Minna's sweet voice, rising and falling.

The light in Cahir grew brighter now, surging like a fountain, and then, in a great rush, it burst free and filled the entire clearing like a cup running over. Minna cried out as she felt him pass right through her soul.

Up flowed his living flame, out through the crown of the trees to join with the sky, and she was held in his joy as he had held her body in pleasure. *There is only love*, she heard him say, all the strength returned to his voice. *And you will always know me, mo chridhe.*

My heart.

Cahir's presence faded, as slowly the cool shadows of Thisworld gathered in again. Minna's cheeks were wet when at last she stirred and looked down.

On the dewy grass lay Cahir son of Conor. He looked at rest, the lines of sickness gone, the pain of life erased. He was beautiful, with his dark hair all about his face, his lashes soft fringes on his clear skin.

She felt Rhiann touch her cheek, and looked up at last into her luminous, violet eyes, shining with sorrow and joy. *I lost loved ones, and though I knew they still lived it did not soften the grief. For grief is only an honouring for the love you bore them. Do not hinder it.*

So at last Minna abandoned all need to be a healer or seer, and, giving no thought to the warriors watching, she left her solemn place at Cahir's head. She lay by his side and curled around him like a baby, the dell cradling them both.

The bonds of time were broken, and past and future became one.

Minna felt a heart beating around her and through her, frantic and fast with pain. Tight swaddling was wrapped around her tiny, baby body, and the light of a mountain sky was filtering through her transparent eyelids. The mountain on which she had once died.

She was at one and the same time Minna curled on the ground by Cahir's body, and Rhiann's girl-child, born too early, dying within days after the briefest of lives.

Her baby-self was crushed by the weight on her chest, her unformed lungs unable to take in the mountain air. She struggled in vain to open her eyes, move her limbs, but what little strength she had been born with days earlier was fast disappearing.

Crooning came in her ear, speaking words of love in a broken, grief-filled voice. Rhiann. *Mother.* Minna smelled her honey scent mingled with the sweat of hard travel and fear. But she was held tenderly, rocked to a warm breast, as stumbling, exhausted steps took Rhiann up the mountain path.

Amid the searing pain, Minna felt the baby's strength of will; the instinctive struggle for life, the grasping for one more breath, to taste a few more moments of sensory experience. But each life has its own season.

Now she was in Rhiann's lap, at the peak of the hill under a wide sky. And she was lifting, growing brighter as the small body could struggle no longer. With a sweet rush of regret her soul slipped its bonds and broke free, filling the mountains with a surge of luminescence. With her soul-eyes opened Minna hovered then in that other time, and watched as Rhiann collapsed to her knees, clutching the child's body. She heard her anguished plea to the Goddess: *Why?*

Broken by grief, Rhiann's own spirit wrenched free of its shell as if yearning to follow the child, give up on life, only a vulnerable silver thread anchoring her to the mountain. But Minna-in-soul reached out to her mother in that moment, wrapping her in love, her spirit-light dancing around Rhiann so she could see; so she could know it was not the end.

Yes, Rhiann said now, in the hollow. *When I faltered, you were there. You held me, as I had held you; you gave me the strength to endure, to find meaning in what would otherwise have been unbearable.*

Then, and now, the love radiated one to the other, Minna and Rhiann, growing thus stronger, and in that glow Minna was able to feel their ancient bond reaching far back into time, through many lives they had shared. It soared beyond the mountain dell, beyond Alba, beyond Thisworld itself and out into the space between, illuminated by flame and light. Other souls joined them, too, the stars that were the Sisters, filling the limitless ether with song. The song that was the universe itself.

And now, daughter, there is one answer you have long sought, but you have never asked the right question.

There was only one, and many others had asked it except for Minna herself. The words floated up from inside her, one by one.

Who. Am. I.

The words were taken in like precious jewels by the lights, and, as they shimmered and danced, the knowing flowed through Minna's soul: what was revealed to Rhiann on that mountain long ago to heal her heart from the loss of the child. There was meaning in so brief a life, a reason for her to come into this world, to make Rhiann love her only to lose her.

She was the vessel of the Sisters.

Not a song, a treasure, or a pool. Minna was the vessel that had survived the ages.

So the missing parts of Darine's story were revealed. Knowing they would die, the two eldest Sisters placed the knowledge of the Source – the songs, stories, healings and herb-lore – into Rhiann's body in a secret rite before they were slaughtered by Rome. Unknowingly, she carried that eternal light, that energy, long enough for that infinite pattern to be imprinted on the vessel: a baby she bore inside her.

In the time Rhiann held her within, the lore wove its way into the tiny threads of Minna's memory and knowing, the meshed pieces that make up a soul and which, when it is born, are remembered by the body. Minna held this through ages in the Otherworld until Rome's strength was weakened and it was safe enough to bring the Source alive again in Alba; until it was time for her to be born again.

The cloth unfurled, the colours bright, all the threads alive. She saw the truth.

She must birth the Sisterhood once more.

Only it was all different now. Long before, in the Otherworld, she had chosen to be a living bridge. Where once the lore was passed on by voice and deed, each generation re-learning, she had taken it into her very essence. Now she would do the same: pass it on to other women through soul and blood, so the life of Alba would endure.

Through her there would be priestesses again, and they would hold the Source strong for wheeling years, sharing it with many others, man and woman, bedding it into the very bones of the land – into the very bodies and souls of the people. And though at times in the cycle of ages women might forget how they once gathered together to summon the Source, the cloth woven by Rhiann and Minna meant they would pass the sleeping lore on to their babes, even unknowing.

So what was wrought by bravery and honour, grief and pain, valour and hardship would never be lost. It would be there, waiting to be discovered by any soul willing to surrender, to open – and, in risking all, to remember.

Rhiann's voice joined Minna's thoughts, as they had in that eternal moment on the mountain. *So hold the memory of this knowing inside you, my daughter, my sister, my friend. There is no death, and love has no limits of time and place.*

Next time, you will have longer with him.

Remember the endless spiral.

Chapter 64
SUNSEASON, AD 368

'He'll get cold!' Nessa smiled, cross-legged on a hide in the sunshine, at the place of the spiral rocks above Dunadd.

Minna nuzzled the folds of skin on her baby's thigh, blowing. The little boy gurgled at the noise, kicking his legs. 'No, he won't.' She crooked her chin on one hand and tickled her son's foot. His tiny sole curled up. 'He loves being naked, and it was such a long winter.'

Rórdán graced his mother with a gummy grin, rolling over and pushing up on his arms. The summer sun lit him from within, his skin translucent, his few tufts of hair a shining copper. As she smiled at him, Minna felt the weight of Nessa's worried gaze on her.

The moons of the dark time had passed in a blur of grief; she had felt imprisoned in permanent winter, as if the sun would never come again. She retreated from all human feeling, curling around her swelling belly, floating in wordless silence with her child as the freezing winds roared about Cahir's hall. When at last she gave him birth, the pain brought her some release in tears and fury along with blood, and love. It would have been harder to face death if the land had been greening. Minna had needed the world to grieve for Cahir as she did.

So the moons slipped by, until one day in leaf-bud the clawing pain eased enough for her to take a true breath. Now, in sunseason, it sometimes receded long enough for her to draw in lungfuls of scented air and smile, at least when Rórdán was awake.

'Minna!' She glanced up, squinting in the sunshine as Orla and Finola tore up the path from the greenwoods, Keeva trailing in their wake. The cluster of warriors standing guard at a respectful distance parted to let them by. Behind, a fully-grown Lia bounded out of the underbrush, scattering leaves and snuffling.

Finola bounced up to Minna, arms full of honeysuckle blossoms, while Orla followed more slowly. She had shot up in height in the last year, and was all awkward, gangly limbs.

'Wherever have you been?' Minna plucked a twig from Finola's hair as the little girl squatted beside Rórdán.

Intently, Finola placed the flowers on the mound of his belly. 'All over!' she whispered, so as not to startle her brother. Rórdán's dark blue eyes shifted from Minna's face to Finola's, and the girl caught his fist and kissed it passionately.

Keeva threw Minna a wry look, cupping her own swelling belly as she awkwardly sank down. Minna cocked her head at Orla. The girl's frown sharpened the intensity of her slanting eyes in just the way of her father, and her heart caught, before Orla shrugged. 'We took the path past the old man birch, and over the stream. We saw a vixen with her cubs, and *yes*,' she raised her chin, 'we ran away when she barked.'

'All well and good.' Minna hid a smile as Rórdán began fussing, and she scooped up his plump body. 'Tell Queen Nessa what you got for your birthday, then.'

Orla's stern little face transformed, glowing with pride. '*A harp*! And Davin is going to teach me every day now I'm old enough.'

Nessa was suitably impressed.

Minna cupped her son's buttocks. 'I think you'd better put another breech-clout on your brother, and something warm. Lay him down here; can you do that?'

Orla immediately darted over and knelt down, and Minna placed the baby in her arms. 'I will watch them,' Keeva volunteered. 'Though they won't let me get anywhere near him!'

Minna rose slowly, feeling old and leached of life by her grief. A few yards away, the great hump of rock curved from the ground, and she stood before it, gazing down at the new spiral carved near the top of the hill.

Cahir's soul symbol.

She knelt and placed her palm over the carving, closing her eyes. Since leaf-bud, she had been drawn almost unwillingly from her cocoon of grief to find she had taken on a new form, like a butterfly. Just as she saw on the mountain, all she had to do was breathe and surrender, and the knowing of the Source was there, flowing through her like an underground stream. All she had to do was focus her will, and it came.

She would not draw up a vision of Cahir now, though, for that was the own knowing of her heart, her love, and not ancient lore. Her finger traced another much more ancient cluster of circles instead, half-afraid, half-wondering. And drifting up through her soul came a glimpse of what it was carved for: chanting druids with their arms held to a rising sun.

Nessa lingered behind her, wanting to help and not knowing how. 'They are slowly coming right again,' she said, shading her eyes from the sun to watch the girls. 'You have done so well.'

'I think that is Rórdán's gift, not mine.' Minna turned to sink back against Cahir's carving, the rock warm against her skin. She felt his energy here, and came up often when dusk was falling. 'And it is you who have done well.' She forced a smile. 'You have all my gratitude.'

Nessa blushed, but she was no longer stooped. Her body was strong again, her eyes clear. 'I'm not sure I did anything, Minna!' she laughed, picking the leaves off a stalk of bracken. 'It was my father and cousin's doing.' As Cahir had feared, the Roman Emperor had sent another army from Gaul in the spring, and Garnat and his warriors were caught too far from home on the coast and decimated. When the straggling remnants of the Pict army returned, it was to a dun now ruled by Nessa's kin – her cousin as king and Drustan as heir. This new rule would safeguard Minna's task, and that is why Nessa had come here; to give Minna her kin's oath of protection for the chosen home of the new Sisterhood, in the mountains between Pictland and Dalriada. So the spiral turns.

'Goddess!' Nessa suddenly exclaimed, throwing down the bracken. 'I have a message for you, and in the chaos of the last few days I keep forgetting to give it. Just before I left, Darine came striding into the dun.'

'Inside your *hall?*'

Nessa smiled. 'She said she saw something in the fire; a royal baby. And she gave me a message: tell the *gael* lass to look for me when the heather blooms.' Nessa's face sobered. 'She said she would come to you wherever you were, that she wasn't going to die alone but with her Sisters.'

Minna's eyes blurred in the sun, for the relief of having Darine by her side when she undertook this task, and for the loneliness that there was no one to hold her when she felt weak. She pulled up her knees, brushing that away. She must be strong for all of them.

Orla carried Rórdán over to her on outstretched arms, like an offering. He was dressed now in a tunic and wool wrap, grizzling with hunger, but fell silent as he and his mother fell into that fathomless gaze they always shared.

Rórdán, Minna crooned in her mind, her love so fierce it choked. *Little bard-king.* She'd thought Cahir would like the name: the bard, the dreamer, for her; the king for him. Part of them both.

Finola jolted her out of her reverie. 'Who is that man?'

Chapter 65

Minna handed Rórdán to Nessa and slowly got to her feet, shading her eyes to see the figure who had appeared at the edge of the trees. The guards were brandishing their spears, demanding his name.

His hands were up away from his sword, but then he looked past them directly at Minna, and she couldn't breathe. His tunic was stained, his riding boots caked with mud, long hair caught in a black horse-tail that left a ragged fringe framing each cheekbone. New muscles squared his jaw and widened his shoulders, and at first her frozen mind refused to recognize him. But he was balanced gracefully on the balls of his feet despite his weariness, and she knew that stance too well.

She had to brace herself to meet his eyes, their vivid blue leaping to catch hold of her, dragging her forward so she stumbled. Distantly, she gestured at the guards to let him through. The men lowered their spears and suddenly she and he were facing each other alone.

'I know,' was all he said, and there in his face was the sorrow of a man.

Her voice cracked. 'I thought I would die; I wanted to.'

'And yet you are here, Minna. Alive.'

A pause, as her hands rose and dropped at her side, helpless to express. 'I gave him all of me,' she whispered.

'I know, Tiger.' His voice broke on the name, but his gaze was tender, implacable. 'He is gone, though, and you are alone.'

She flinched at that. 'I have my son, and something great to accomplish, something I must do.'

He took another step forward, holding her with that brilliant gaze. 'And what about the end of each day, when you are wearied and heartsick? What will fill those hours by the fire?' That clever face, that knowing mouth were touched now by sadness and wisdom, and his eyes were entirely open. He let her see in, and the understanding came through her like a ray of sun. He had travelled far and hard for many long months; he had been through the fire and annealed. Just like her.

Protests tangled in her throat, but then she heard Cahir's whisper. *Don't dishonour me by dying, too.* Did he say it before he faded? Did he say it now?

Suddenly Cian was turning away ...*Was he leaving?* Minna staggered forward, her hand at her mouth. But he was only digging in his pack, dropping it back on the ground. 'I brought something for you,' he said unsteadily. 'I brought it a long way.' His long fingers were holding it on his palms.

'Not ... a fig,' she gasped.

Cian released a breathless laugh. 'I couldn't find a fig, Tiger. It's only a plum, and a very dried-up, wrung-out plum it is, too.'

Guilt turned in Minna, but life crested over it all – life demanding she heed it, and a love that would hold fast over long years, a steady glow to warm her. There was more than one fate.

'Do you want it?' Cian asked. The plum came flying through the air, brown and withered but gleaming, and suddenly Minna was back in the bright sun of the Eboracum marketplace.

She didn't even bother trying to catch it, her feet taking her onwards without her mind's say, and with every step her heart beat a lifetime of moments to come. She stopped, hovering a hand's breath from him. 'I am not ready.'

'I will wait,' he said.

EPILOGUE

AD 410

On a windy ridge above the great Roman Wall, two men sat silently on their horses.

Behind them in the hollow of the hills milled the rest of their company, shining with polished iron and bronze in the cold leaf-fall sun. One held aloft a standard that streamed out in the wind above their heads. A scarlet boar on a white background.

'So it is true then, brother,' one rider said. His horse danced forward a few steps, as restless and high-blooded as its master.

The other man did not move. He was just past forty, but tall and well-muscled with no sign of bowing in his broad shoulders. On his flowing auburn hair sat a gilded helm, boasting a magnificent crest in the shape of a boar. He thrust his chin into the wind, staring down at the dark line of the Wall snaking across the bare moors. 'We have been watching them for a long time. They were drifting away gradually, some here and there, but now it seems some call has come, and ... well, you can see for yourself.'

'I would have to, otherwise I would not believe it.' The first man was younger than his brother, his lithe build and quick hands on the reins belying the threads of grey in his black hair.

Ahead, on the other side of the low moor, smoke streamed above the little Roman fort, drifting away to join the greater haze above the windy plateau. To the east, fading spires marked out other forts. At each there was a burning, but it wasn't cooksmoke.

For months, ragged Roman soldiers had been heading away from the Wall south and east on foot, but now the nearby fort was clustered with carts, and the small figures of men and women holding babes were gathered about, loading in their belongings.

Watching from the hills, the armoured men of Alba had seen the same thing repeated all along the Wall: buildings being dismantled, vital parts salvaged and the rest piled on bonfires and burned. There was no panic. There was no fighting. There was just abandonment.

An exodus that those in Alba had yearned for, hoped for, dreamed of for so many hundreds of years.

Rórdán, King of Dalriada, narrowed his green eyes, his calm exterior hiding the excitement beating in his heart. He knew the tales of his ancestors as well as the calluses on his palm, rubbed there by his sword.

And it had been his fate to see this: the ending of Rome's authority not just over Alba, but over the whole isle of Britannia.

For his scouts told him the army, the laws and taxes were all disappearing from its shores, as the Emperor deserted the Province. The people who were left would have to live beside his own, and make what they would of this land. A land unto itself, at last.

Rórdán could not speak. In his usual way, it was when things burned his soul that he was most silent, most still. His brother was of a different cast, however. 'By Manannán's balls and breath!' Lassar jerked the horse around again, his vivid blue eyes alight. He wore no helmet, preferring the freedom of the wind in his long, black hair. 'If this is true, then I must fly home to the mountains as fast as I can! Mother has to know about this immediately.' With one kick, he was by Rórdán's side. 'It has all come to pass,' he cried, his voice betraying the passion his brother held inside. 'Just as she said; just as she told us!'

Rórdán looked away from the smoke, meeting the flame of his brother's gaze. Every night of their boyhood the stories had flowed, the telling growing greater as the numbers of their mother's people grew. There, in the clear mountain air, the pools became mirrors, Mother said; mirrors of the world outside. And in them she had seen this.

'Go then, but get ready to turn around and come right back,' Rórdán remarked drily. 'She's going to demand to see this for herself.'

Lassar grinned, white teeth flashing. 'It's breeding season, and end of harvest. She'll have a fine time dragging Father away from his fields and his cattle.'

'And he'll have a fine time refusing her.'

Lassar cocked a dark brow at his brother. 'Can I take some of your guards with me? You know all our sisters will plead to come, too – I'll never hear the end of it.'

Rórdán was staring intently into the smoke, then suddenly he laughed and shook his shoulders free of the weight of years. 'Since there is nothing more to watch for, brother, it looks as if I can indeed spare warriors to send with you.'

Heads close, they spoke together as they trotted their horses down into the hollow, but there Lassar's lathered mount would not stand, picking up the tension in his master's legs. 'Sa! I must fly right now, or

I'll never bear it!' Lassar and Rórdán clasped wrists and kissed on both cheeks.

'And after Mother and Father see the Wall, come to Dunadd on your way home.' Rórdán's eyes were now sparkling like his brother's. 'We must celebrate, and there are feasts, songs and dances to be had before the snows close in.'

With a smile and a yip, Lassar let the stallion have his head, and raced away northwards to the higher hills. Rórdán trotted up to gaze out at the clearing smoke one more time before gathering his men under his boar standard, and striking out west at a more thoughtful pace.

Behind them, as the weeks and then months passed, the sun crept its way across the Wall, as it always had.

But now it gilded expanses of mossy, tumbled stone and rotting wood, broken gates and fallen roof timbers. It darkened the gaping doorways of the barrack blocks, throwing long shadows of the towers across the hills.

And then a day came when there was no longer even a hint of smoke, and the high plateau of rippling grass bore witness to nothing more than a lonely wind and kestrel cries.

Historical Note

Dalriada and Picts

Mythical and ancient sources say that warriors and kings from the Dalriada kingdom in Ireland settled in the west of Scotland, in Argyll, around AD 500. This brought them into conflict with the native inhabitants, known to the Romans as Picts. Though the tradition is therefore strong that a Dalriadan kingdom was established in western Scotland from Ireland, historians and archaeologists are divided over whether this actually included a movement of people, or merely ideas and language, and whether these spread from Ireland to Scotland or vice versa.

Regardless, Dark Age Christian sources then report that the Dalriadan kings, with their seat at Dunadd in Argyll, warred with the Pictish kings in the east of Scotland for many years, through the sixth, seventh and eighth centuries. In AD 843, the two peoples were joined by the accession of the Dalriadan king Kenneth MacAlpin to the Pictish throne, a man who was possibly descended from the Pictish royal line through his mother (some sources hint that the native peoples of Scotland passed their royal blood through women). After this, the Picts seem to disappear as a separate people from history, and Irish Gaelic became the language of Scotland, and Gaelic kings its rulers.

In this trilogy, I proposed that the 'Irish invasion' began centuries earlier, around AD 80, involving the arrival of a few nobles who intermarried with the original tribe in the area (the partnerships of Rhiann and Eremon, and Conaire and Caitlin, in *The White Mare* and *The Dawn Stag*). By the time this last novel opens, the Dalriadan Irish in the west and the Picts in the east are entrenched as opposing forces in Scotland, the former tracing their royal lineage through males, the latter through females.